Dear Readers,

Many years ago, when I was a kid, my father said to me, "Bill, it doesn't really matter what you do in life. What's important is to be the *best* William Johnstone you can be."

I've never forgotten those words. And now, many years and almost 200 books later, I like to think that I am still trying to be the best William Johnstone I can be. Whether it's Ben Raines in the Ashes series, or Frank Morgan, the Last Gunfighter, or Smoke Jensen, our intrepid Mountain Man, or John Barrone and his hardworking crew keeping America safe from terrorist lowlifes in the Code Name series, I want to make each new book better than the last and deliver powerful storytelling.

Equally important, I try to create the kinds of believable characters that wc can all identify with, real people who face tough challenges. When one of my creations blasts an enemy into the middle of next week, you can be damn sure he had a good reason.

As a storyteller, my job is to entertain you, my readers, and to make sure that you get plenty of enjoyment from my books for your hard-earned money. This is not a job I take lightly. And I greatly appreciate your feedback—you are my gold, and your opinions *do* count. So please keep the letters and e-mails coming.

Respectfully yours,

William W. Johnstone

WILLIAM W. JOHNSTONE

THE LAST GUNFIGHTER:
VIOLENT SUNDAY

PINNACLE BOOKS
Kensington Publishing Corp.
http://www.kensingtonbooks.com

PINNACLE BOOKS are published by

Kensington Publishing Corp.
850 Third Avenue
New York, NY 10022

All Kensington Titles, Imprints, and Distributed Lines are
available at special quantity discounts for bulk purchases for
sales promotions, premiums, fund-raising, or educational or
institutional use. Special book excerpts or customized print-
ings can also be created to fit specific needs. For details,
write or phone the office of the Kensington special sales
manager: Kensington Publishing Corp., 850 Third Avenue,
New York, NY 10022, attn: Special Sales Department.
Phone: 1-800-221-2647.

Pinnacle and the P logo Reg. U.S. Pat. & TM Off.

First Printing: March 2005

10 9 8 7 6 5 4 3 2 1

Printed in the United States of America

AUTHOR'S NOTE

Although this novel and the characters in it are fictional, they are loosely based on a series of clashes in Brown County, Texas, during the 1880s that became known as the Fence-Cutting War. Several cowboys lost their lives in the fighting, though the violence never reached the level described in this book.

Some of the fences that started all the trouble can still be found in Brown County and are still being used to mark boundary lines. The barbed wire sags in places, and the cedar posts are gnarled and weathered. But still they stand, a tangible reminder that those wild times were really not that long ago, a reminder that once men fought and died for what they believed in, and paid the price with courage and blood.

Still they stand.

Barbarism is the natural state of mankind.
—Robert E. Howard

1

Frank Morgan liked Waco. As he rode into the Texas town, following the gentle curves of the Brazos River, he hoped nobody tried to kill him while he was here.

That was always a nagging worry when a fella was one of the dying breed known as gunfighters.

The hooves of the big Appaloosa called Stormy clopped on the planks of the suspension bridge that spanned the Brazos. The river was wide and deep here, at least compared to the way it looked a hundred miles or so upstream in Parker and Palo Pinto Counties, Frank's old stomping grounds when he had been a boy.

Seemed like a hundred years ago, he thought, instead of only thirty-five or forty. He had spent some time in Parker County a few months earlier, and everything had changed since he was a young man. At least it appeared that way to him, although he knew that the biggest change during those years had been within himself. The relatively carefree young man he had been was long gone, replaced by the wary loner that some people called the Drifter.

For a while there, he hadn't been alone. He had married a woman, a good, beautiful woman. But Dixie was gone, murdered by a son of a bitch who ultimately had met justice at Frank Morgan's hand.

Unfortunately, meting out justice hadn't brought Dixie back.

Frank had made a friend during his crusade of vengeance, though, a young Texas Ranger named Tyler Beaumont. Beaumont was still up in Weatherford, doing his Rangering from there these days while he courted Victoria Monfore.

Frank thought about Victoria as he rode along a wide street paved with cobblestones. He still didn't know if Victoria was really his daughter. Mercy Monfore, her mother, had refused to say, and Frank wasn't going to push the question. All that really mattered, he supposed, was that Victoria was a beautiful, intelligent young woman, and she seemed to be as fond of Tyler Beaumont as he was of her. Frank was glad for his friend, and glad for Victoria, too.

"We'll find a stable and a place to stay in a few minutes," he said to Dog, the big cur that padded along beside Stormy. A man never had two more faithful companions than those two. Frank, Dog, and Stormy had been together for quite some time.

Frank moved his left shoulder around and went on. "I want to find a drugstore and get some liniment for this shoulder, first."

A couple of mornings earlier, he had gotten up with some sore, stiff muscles that twinged every time he moved his left arm too much. He figured he had slept on it wrong. The age he was getting to be, it didn't take much to make his muscles ache. He didn't have any sort of medication for it in his saddlebags, and Waco was the first real town he had come to in his wanderings since then. He had followed the Brazos from Parker County and thought he might drift with it all the way on down to the Gulf Coast.

Waco had grown a lot from the little settlement that had centered around a river ferry when it was founded.

Some of the streets were paved, gaslights sat on top of poles on nearly every block of downtown, and there were quite a few businesses housed in brick buildings that rose three or four stories above the street. Frank wouldn't have been surprised if some of the places even had those new-fangled telephones installed.

He reined to a halt in front of a building with a sign on it that read MORRISON'S OLD CORNER DRUG STORE. He ought to be able to get something for his shoulder there, he thought as he swung down from the saddle. He looped Stormy's reins over a hitch rail and told Dog to stay put. The big cur sat down on the board-walk in front of the drugstore. The people who walked along there gave him a wide berth, but Dog ignored them as being beneath his dignity.

Frank put his left hand on the small of his back and stretched before he went into the store. He was a tall man, with the broad shoulders and lean hips of a natural-born horseman. A while back he had been severely wounded and had lost a lot of weight, but his frame had just about filled back out to its normal, muscular proportions. He wore jeans and a faded blue work shirt. Thick, graying dark hair hung out from under his brown Stetson. It would have been easy to take him for a roaming cowboy.

Except for the well-worn walnut grips of the Colt Peacemaker that rode in a black holster on his right hip, and the way his big right hand never strayed far from the butt of that gun . . .

He went into the drugstore, which was the usual narrow, crowded frontier apothecary shop with a counter in the back where all sorts of nostrums and tonics and other patent medicines were sold. A counter on the right-hand wall served as a soda foun-tain, and as Frank saw that, a thirst gripped him. It was mid-afternoon, and the sun outside was hot. A cool soda would go down good right about now, he thought.

First, though, he walked back to the rear counter and said to the druggist, "Got anything for a sore shoulder?"

"Sure do, mister," the man replied. "Some of my own concoction. I call it Dr. Alderton's Muscle Cream. It'll loosen you right up."

"You're a doctor, are you?"

The young man grinned. "Well, not really, but some people call me Doc. That's close enough, isn't it?"

"Close enough for me, as long as that medicine of yours works. I'll take a jar."

The druggist got the medication down from a shelf behind him. "Anything else I can do for you?"

Frank looked around at the soda fountain. "I could use a nice cool drink."

"Coming right up," Doc Alderton said as he walked around behind the soda fountain. "You know, most fellas who come in from the trail head straight to one of the saloons. They'd rather have beer or whiskey than a phosphate."

"I don't have anything against beer and whiskey," Frank said as he faced Alderton across the polished hardwood counter and let his left hand rest on top of it. "Sometimes, though, especially when it's hot, a man needs something else to cut the dust."

"You'll like this," the druggist said as he took down a clean glass from a shelf, pulled a lever to squirt some dark syrup in it, and then filled the glass the rest of the way with carbonated water from another spout. He handed it to Frank. "Try that."

Frank took a sip of the cool beverage and nodded appreciatively. It tasted like fruit, but he couldn't put his finger on just what kind of fruit. A blend of several different ones, he thought.

"Mighty tasty. Another of your concoctions?"

"As a matter of fact, it is," Alderton responded with a proud smile.

"What do you call it?"

"Well, it doesn't really have a name yet. Folks have started calling it a Waco, after the town, but my boss Mr. Morrison says it needs a better name than that."

Frank took a longer swallow and then licked his lips. "Whatever you call it, it's good."

Alderton looked pleased as punch at the praise, but the smile suddenly vanished from his face as the little bell over the door jingled and he glanced in that direction. A worried frown appeared on his features as well.

Up until now, Frank had been the only customer in the drugstore. He supposed the middle of the afternoon like this was a slack time for business. But since Alderton didn't look pleased by the arrival of another potential customer, Frank thought it might be wise to see who had just come in.

He didn't like what he saw.

He supposed that in the back of his mind, he had been expecting something like this. No matter where he rode, his reputation followed him. And to a certain type of man, that reputation was a siren song, an irresistible challenge that must be answered.

The newcomer was young, not much more than twenty. Dark hair curled out from under his battered hat. He wore patched and faded range clothes, but the gun belt around his hips was new and well cared for. So was the Colt that rode in the tied-down holster. The handle of the gun had pearl grips that seemed to sparkle and shine even in the relatively dim light of the drugstore.

"Frank Morgan," the young man said. His voice had a hushed, almost reverent tone to it. "I thought it was you, but I couldn't hardly believe it. Folks were sayin' you was dead until you turned up in Weatherford a while back."

"I'm not dead," Frank said calmly.

"Jonah, we don't want any trouble in here," Alderton put in. "Why don't you go on about your business?"

The youngster called Jonah gestured toward Frank with his left hand. "Morgan here is my business. I been waitin' for a chance like this. Beginnin' to think it'd never come to me."

Frank looked back at Alderton and inclined his head toward the young man. "I reckon he's a bit of a troublemaker?"

"He fancies himself a fast gun," Alderton said grimly.

"Fancies himself?" Jonah repeated in a loud, indignant voice. "Listen, you snake-oil peddler, I *am* a fast gun! Faster than anybody in Waco, that's for damned sure, and that includes this old man here."

Again Jonah waved his left hand toward Frank, but the gesture was loaded with contempt this time.

Frank sighed. "I reckon you want to pull iron and kill me, don't you?"

"It's the only way," Jonah said solemnly. The contempt he had summoned up a moment earlier vanished, and for a second he sounded almost respectful again as he added, "I'm sorry it's got to be this way, Morgan."

"It doesn't. You can let me finish my drink and let me go on my way. That way you get to live, and I don't have to kill you."

"You're mighty confident, Morgan. Some'd say arrogant."

That just showed how young and inexperienced Jonah really was. A gunfighter had to have supreme confidence in his abilities. Any man who lived by the gun, by the speed of his draw and the accuracy of his eye, knew that someday he would meet a better man and his light would be snuffed out. Acknowledging that was just being reasonable.

But not today. Never today. And if a gunfighter didn't believe that with all his heart, he was doomed. The day he lost his confidence was the day he died. Plain and simple.

Frank suddenly felt more tired than ever. He said to Jonah, "If you're bound and determined to go through with this, I'll oblige you. I'd appreciate it, though, if you'd give me a minute to finish my drink."

Jonah shrugged. "Sure. I don't see that it matters."

"Thanks," Frank said, and meant it. He turned back to the soda fountain counter and lifted the glass. Taking his time, he drained the rest of the cool, dark liquid from it. When he set the empty glass on the counter, he nodded to Alderton. "Mighty refreshing."

Then he swung around to face Jonah again and said, "You've got it to do, son. Hook and draw."

The young man's hand stabbed toward the butt of his gun.

Frank waited a tick of time, and still Jonah's iron was only half out of leather by the time Frank's Colt was leveled. Flame lanced from the barrel of the Peacemaker as it roared. The bullet took Jonah in the chest and smashed him back against the door behind him. The glass in the door didn't break, which surprised Frank a little.

Jonah tried to finish his draw, but the gun slipped from his fingers and thudded to the floor. He grabbed the doorknob to hold himself up as he pressed his other hand to his chest. Blood seeped between his splayed fingers. "My God," he croaked. "My God."

"I hope you're making your peace with Him and not just cussing," Frank said.

Jonah swayed. His grip on the doorknob slipped, and a second later he crashed face-first to the floor.

Frank walked over to him. A kick sent the fallen gun sliding across the planks until it was well out of reach. Frank reached down, checked for a pulse in Jonah's neck. Finding none, he straightened.

Then and only then did he holster his own Colt.

"You're really Frank Morgan?" Alderton asked from behind the soda fountain.

Without looking at the druggist, Frank nodded.

"I've heard of you. There are books about you. We even have some of them here in the store."

Frank didn't look around for them. He had seen plenty of the yellow-backed dime novels featuring a gunfighter named Frank Morgan. That was about the only connection they had with reality. Everything else in them was dreamed up by a pack of anonymous scribblers who had nothing better to do than tell whoppers for money.

"I suppose Waco is civilized enough now so that that shot will bring the law on the run," he commented.

"Yes, I imagine the law will be here shortly."

Frank gave a little shake of his head. He remembered when Waco had been such a wild place it was known as Six-Shooter Junction, and nobody would have paid much attention to a single gunshot.

The youngster called Jonah had tried to recapture a little of that wildness, and all it had gotten him was dead. Bad luck had followed him.

Just as death seemed to follow the man called the Drifter.

2

Tyler Beaumont's heart pounded heavily in his chest. He had never been so scared in all his borned days. And he had faced the notorious slaver and killer Ephraim Swan up in No Man's Land.

Victoria Monfore tilted her beautiful face up to his and said, "What was it you wanted to ask me, Tyler?"

Beaumont tried not to gulp. He felt like the swing on the front porch of the Monfore home had suddenly turned into a bucking bronco and was threatening to pitch him into the air. His stomach was all tied up in knots, too, just like he was on the back of a sunfishing horse. He uttered a silent prayer that he could get through this before he threw up all over Victoria's shiny-buttoned shoes.

Texas Rangers were supposed to be fearless, he reminded himself. Charge hell with a bucket of water and all that. The badge on his chest, a star in a circle carved out of a Mexican five-peso piece, *meant* something, dad-gum it!

That proud Ranger heritage wasn't helping him a whole heap at the moment, however.

"Well?" Victoria said. "Cat got your tongue, Tyler?"

She was playing with him, he told himself. She knew good and well what all his hemming and hawing had been leading up to. But she had a mischievous streak in her, and she was enjoying his discomfort.

It was a beautiful Texas summer night, warm without being too oppressively humid. A honeysuckle bush grew at the end of the porch, and its sweet fragrance filled the air. A couple of night birds sang in the oak trees in the yard. You could look for a year and not find a more perfect evening for what Beaumont had in mind.

So why couldn't he just go ahead and spit it out before the damned ring burned a hole in his pocket?

"Really, Tyler," Victoria said as the smile disappeared from her face and was replaced by a solemn expression, "if you have something to say to me, you should just go ahead and say it. It's all right, really."

Beaumont took a deep breath and blurted out, "Victoria, will you marry me?" Then, before she could reply, he went on. "Oh, Lord, I'm sorry. I did it all wrong, didn't I? I'm so blamed stupid—" He slipped off the swing and went to one knee in front of her. As he caught hold of her hands, he hurried on. "Victoria, will you do me the honor—I'd be the luckiest man in the world if you said—I mean—" He gulped. He couldn't help it. Trying again, he said, "Victoria, will you make me the happiest man in the world by doing me the honor of becoming my wife?" The words all came out of him in a rush.

She smiled down at him, squeezed his hands, and said softly, "Tyler, I would have said yes if you'd stopped after asking me the first time."

His eyes widened and he started to let out a whoop of joy, but then he stopped suddenly as something occurred to him. "You said you *would* have said yes. Does that mean you won't say yes now?"

She shook her head. "No."

"By that, do you mean—"

She slipped her hands out of his and laid them gently on either side of his face as she leaned down toward him. "I mean yes, I'll marry you," she whispered, and then she kissed him.

It was a good thing his mouth was occupied right then and for a while afterward, or else he probably would have whooped and disturbed some of the neighbors. Some folks hereabouts still went to bed with the chickens.

Later, after he had put the ring on her finger and they had admired it for a while as they sat on the swing, Victoria said, "Have you asked my father's permission yet?"

Beaumont scratched his head. "Well, no, now that you mention it, I haven't. I reckon I probably should have done that first."

"Yes, he's rather an old-fashioned man. Go talk to him now, and he won't have to know you've already asked me."

"Lordy, what if he says no?" Beaumont asked, his eyes widening in horror at the thought.

Victoria laughed softly. "He won't. I can practically guarantee it."

"Practically?"

She gave him a little shove on the arm. "Go on. You can do it. He won't bite you."

Beaumont wasn't so sure about that. Judge Isaiah Monfore had a pretty fearsome reputation. That reputation had grown even more when he had survived being kidnapped and tortured by some of his political enemies.

Still, there was no point in postponing the confrontation. Beaumont put his hands on his knees and heaved himself off the swing.

He was short, no denying that. Some might even call him sawed-off, because he barely reached five and a half feet in stature. But his shoulders were broad and muscular, and he knew how to handle himself in times of trouble. It was said of the Texas Rangers that they could ride like Comanches, shoot like Tennesseans, and fight like the very devil. Tyler Beaumont met all three of those qualifications.

He paused at the front door and looked back at Victoria. She nodded encouragement to him. Beaumont drew another deep breath, opened the door, and went inside.

In life, he supposed, the challenges just kept on a-comin'.

He found Victoria's parents in the parlor. Both Judge Monfore and Mercy were reading as they sat in wing chairs. Mercy looked up at Beaumont and smiled. She had the same jet-black hair as her daughter, although it had a white streak in it, and she was nearly as beautiful as Victoria.

"Hello, Tyler," she greeted him warmly.

Beaumont stood there awkwardly turning his hat in his hands. "Miz Monfore," he said with a nod. "Judge."

The white-bearded jurist gravely returned the young Texas Ranger's nod. "Beaumont," he said. "How are you this evening?"

"I'm fine, sir." *Better than fine*, he thought, *but only if you say it's all right for me to marry your daughter.*

For a second, the thought that Victoria wasn't really the judge's daughter flitted through Beaumont's mind. He knew there was a possibility Frank Morgan had fathered Victoria. But Isaiah Monfore had raised her, and while blood mattered, so did that.

Beaumont pushed those musings away. They had nothing to do with what was going on here and now.

"Is Victoria still on the porch?" Mercy asked.

"Yes, ma'am. I, uh, I wanted to talk to the judge."

Mercy laid her book aside and stood up gracefully. "I believe I'll step out for a breath of air. It's a perfectly lovely evening, isn't it?"

"Yes'm. Perfectly."

She smiled at Beaumont and left the room. She was a sharp lady and had to know what was going on, Beaumont thought. And judging by her attitude, she approved.

Judge Monfore laid a ribbon marker in the thick, leather-bound volume he was reading and closed the book. "What is it you wish to speak to me about, young man?"

"Well, sir . . . I reckon you know how I feel about your daughter—"

"No," Monfore broke in. "You tell me."

Beaumont wasn't expecting that, but he didn't know what to do except tell the truth and plunge right ahead. "I love her to pieces, sir," he said. "I want to marry her and love her and take care of her for the rest of our lives." He paused as the judge regarded him intently. "I'm asking for your permission, sir, and for your blessing."

For a long moment, Monfore didn't say anything. When he finally spoke, there was a sharp edge to his voice. "You don't expect me to approve of this union because of what you and Frank Morgan did for me and my family, do you?"

"No, sir," Beaumont said forthrightly. "I want you to approve of it because I love Victoria, and she loves me."

The stern expression on Monfore's bearded face softened slightly. "She does, does she?"

"Yes, sir. There's no doubt of that in my mind."

"Nor in my wife's mind. We've discussed the matter, and she has spoken to Victoria. We know your feelings are genuine."

Beaumont sensed there was a "but" coming. "That's all that matters, isn't it, sir?"

"No, it's not," Monfore snapped. "You're a lawman. You have a dangerous profession. If my daughter marries you, she runs the risk of becoming a widow."

"Beggin' your pardon, Your Honor, but it seems to me that every woman who gets married runs that risk sooner or later."

"Don't call me Your Honor. We're not in court." Monfore sat forward in his chair. "You know precisely what I mean, Beaumont. Don't bandy words. What if I say to you that if you want to marry Victoria, you'll have to give up being a Ranger?"

Beaumont's hands tightened on his hat, crumpling the brim. He hadn't expected that from the judge at all. Give up being a Ranger? His pa had been a Ranger, and the proudest day in Beaumont's life had been the day he first pinned on that star-in-a-circle. The only thing that could possibly make him prouder was marrying Victoria. And yet, could he trade one for the other? Could he just walk away from the life he had chosen for himself?

"Well, sir, I'd just say that was mighty damned unfair of you."

He didn't know where he got the courage for that blunt statement, but there it was. The words were out. He couldn't call them back.

The judge's voice lashed at him. "You won't turn in your badge?"

"No, sir. Hell, no."

Their eyes dueled fiercely for a moment, and then Monfore grunted. "Good," he said as he sat back again. "I won't have my little girl marrying a man who doesn't know how to stick by his guns."

Beaumont blinked, not quite sure he understood. "Sir? Are you saying—"

"I'm saying that while I might wish Victoria had chosen

a young man in a less hazardous line of work . . . she didn't." Monfore shook his head and smiled for the first time since Beaumont had come into the room. "I won't stand in your way, son. You have my permission, and my blessing."

Beaumont tried not to babble. "Thank you, sir. And Mrs. Monfore—"

The judge waved a hand. "You don't have to worry about Mercy. She and Victoria are probably out there on the porch planning the wedding right now. You'd better get back out there if you want to have any say in what's going to happen." Monfore chuckled. "Not that you will, anyway. Might as well learn that right now if you're going to get married."

"Yes, sir, thank you, sir." Beaumont backed toward the door.

"Go on, get to it!"

Beaumont practically ran out of the room.

He found Victoria and her mother sitting on the swing. Mercy stood up and said, "I believe you must have something to ask my daughter, Tyler."

"Yes'm."

"I'll leave you two alone, then." As she passed Beaumont, she whispered, "And I won't say anything to the judge about what went on out here earlier."

Beaumont's face was hot from blushing as he sat down beside Victoria. "You told her I already asked you?" he said to her.

"I didn't have to. All she did was take one look at me, and she knew. But she's not upset. You set everything right, Tyler." She snuggled against him and laid her head on his shoulder so that the maddeningly sweet scent of her hair filled his senses. "Everything."

Beaumont put his arm around her shoulders and held her and wondered how a man could ever be more content than he was right now.

But as so often happened, even in moments of pure happiness, a worry reared its head. Beaumont frowned and said, "I reckon we'll invite a lot of people to the wedding, won't we?"

"Of course. I'm so happy I want to share it with all my friends and family."

"What about Frank?"

He felt her stiffen at the question. She hesitated and then said, "We all owe Mr. Morgan a great deal. It . . . it wouldn't be right not to invite him."

"You don't think it would make you . . . uncomfortable . . . for him to be there?"

"He's your best friend." The conviction in her voice grew stronger. "Of course you have to invite him. Do you know how to get in touch with him?"

"He was going to wire me and let me know where he was, but he never did. Reckon he's been drifting so much he never got around to it. Maybe he just hasn't lit anywhere yet. I can put out the word, though. I know the general direction he was headed when he left here. It shouldn't take long for a message to catch up to him. A couple of weeks, maybe less. I hope."

"Then you see, you don't have to worry. It'll take at least a month to plan the wedding. There'll be plenty of time to find Mr. Morgan and for him to get here."

"And you don't think it'll bother your folks—"

"You let me worry about them. But I don't believe it will be a problem, Tyler. I really don't."

He drew her tighter against him and sighed in relief. "Good."

And yet, the possibility of the judge or Mrs. Monfore being uncomfortable about having Morgan at the wedding wasn't the only worry, Beaumont thought. Like it or not, Frank Morgan had a certain reputation. Sometimes that notoriety caused trouble. Beaumont had witnessed it himself on numerous occasions.

But not this one, he told himself. Fate meant for him and Victoria to be together, and their union would be a joyous occasion. Nothing would interfere with it.

He intended to keep on telling himself that very thing until maybe sooner or later he believed it.

3

The settlement was just a wide place in the road, and if it had a name, Chas Ferguson had never heard it. He didn't care. All that mattered to him was that there was a saloon here, and he could get a drink.

There wasn't much more than the saloon, which also doubled as a general store. A blacksmith shop was the only other business. Across the road were two churches, a Baptist and a Methodist, dunkers and sprinklers. A handful of houses completed the community.

At the moment, Ferguson was the only customer in the bar. He sat at a table, idly turning over cards in a solitaire hand. From time to time he emptied the whiskey glass at his elbow and then refilled it.

He was young, somewhere in his twenties, and had long fair hair that curled from under his hat and fell almost to his shoulders. He wore a black shirt with silver snaps and gray trousers tucked into high-topped black boots. His hat was white, almost snowy. No matter what his surroundings, Ferguson came off as something of a dandy. He looked even more like one in the rather squalid little saloon.

A pearl-handled Colt rode in a low-slung holster on his right hip. Chas Ferguson could hook and draw that Colt with blinding speed, and his accuracy was good, too. But he had learned, much to his shame, that speed and accuracy weren't all there was to being a gunfighter. It took not just eye and hand, but also heart. It took courage to stand up to a man knowing that he was also fast on the draw and would be doing his damnedest to kill you, just like you were trying to kill him.

It had been Frank Morgan who taught that hard lesson to Ferguson . . . and Ferguson hated him for it.

But the days when Ferguson might have backed down were now in the past. He was ready to face Frank Morgan, and he had been ready for a while. Problem was that Morgan had up and ridden out of Weatherford, and Ferguson didn't know where the hell he was. Texas was a big place; Ferguson couldn't just ride around hoping to run into Morgan.

That was why he had hit upon another plan instead. Morgan was friends with that young Ranger, Tyler Beaumont, and Beaumont was still in these parts. Ferguson figured that if he kept an eye on Beaumont, sooner or later the Ranger would lead him to Morgan. Either that, or Morgan would come back for a visit. Ferguson didn't care how it came about; all that mattered to him was that he get another chance to face up to Frank Morgan and put a bullet in the son of a bitch.

Ferguson didn't want to spend all his time hanging around Weatherford, though. That was why he had engaged the services of a young fella to watch Beaumont for him. The youngster, who seemed to idolize Ferguson, called himself Cherokee Bob. He didn't look Indian to Ferguson, but the gunfighter didn't really care one way or the other whether Bob was really part Cherokee, as long as the pipsqueak did his job. That allowed Ferguson to retreat to this tiny settlement northwest of Weatherford.

Frowning down at the cards, Ferguson realized that the hand was blocked. He couldn't win at it. With a grimace, he swept the cards together into an untidy pile. He picked up the glass and tossed off the whiskey in it. When he tried to refill it from the bottle, only a few drops trickled out.

"I'm empty here, damn it!" he shouted at the bartender, who was the only other person in the place.

"Hold your horses," the apron said. He was a chunky, freckled man in late middle age with a short, rusty beard. He got another bottle from a shelf behind the bar and started to waddle around to bring it to Ferguson.

Bored, the Coltman slipped his revolver from its holster. "I can hurry you up a mite if you'd like," he drawled. The barrel of the gun pointed toward the bartender's feet.

The man moved a little faster. "Sorry," he grunted as he thumped the full bottle down on the table in front of Ferguson and picked up the empty one. "You want to keep runnin' a tab?"

"Sure."

The bartender nodded and turned to start back to the bar. Ferguson let him get halfway there before the boredom got to be too much. Holding the Colt loosely on his thigh, he shifted the barrel a little and fired.

The bullet shattered the empty bottle dangling from the bartender's hand. He yelped more in surprise than pain and jumped higher than a fat man ought to have been able to jump. When he came down he still had the busted neck of the bottle clutched in his hand.

He swung around toward the table, breathing heavily as he did so. His eyes were still wide with fear. But something else lurked there, too.

Anger.

He was furious, and his normally florid face flushed even more as rage spread through him. "Think that was funny, do you?" he demanded of Ferguson.

The gunfighter chuckled. "As a matter of fact, I do.

You hopped like a toad. Bet you never moved like that before in your life."

"I thought for a second you'd killed me!"

"Well, I didn't," Ferguson snapped, tiring of this game as quickly as he tired of everything else. "You ain't hurt, so leave me alone and let me get back to my drinkin'."

"Not here."

Ferguson had already looked down at the cards again, dismissing the man from his mind. The flat, angry words made him glance up.

"What did you say?"

"I said you ain't drinkin' here. What did you think, that you could just waltz into a man's place of business and humiliate him and that he wouldn't care? Well, by God, you can't. Not here."

"You're bootin' me out of this flea-ridden pus hole of a saloon?" Ferguson said in disbelief that anyone would so blatantly challenge him.

"Damn right I am. This place may not be much, but it's mine, damn it. I won't be humiliated in it."

Ferguson's mocking laughter filled the room and visibly stung the bartender. "You were humiliated just by bein' born, mister. And think how your ma must've felt when an ugly lump like you popped out of her."

"That's it," the bartender growled. He started to stalk toward the table, shifting his grip on the jaggedly broken bottle as he did so in order to use it as a weapon.

Ferguson drew and fired without getting up. He didn't have to make a fast draw, but he did anyway, palming the Colt from leather with seemingly just a flick of his hand. The gun roared, and the bartender stopped short, his mouth opening in a soundless O of pain. He looked down at his belly and saw the spreading circle of red that stained his once-white apron. The fabric had a black-rimmed hole in it, and so did his belly.

The bartender dropped the open bottle and pressed both hands to the wound. "You've killed me!" he gasped.

"More than likely," Ferguson agreed with a nod as he came easily to his feet. With his free hand he grasped the edge of the table and flipped it over, scattering cards, glass, and full bottle of whiskey. The cork came out when the bottle hit the floor, and the whiskey began to gurgle out onto the planks, filling the room with its sharp smell.

The wounded bartender tried to sit down at another table but missed the chair and crashed into the floor. He sat there leaning against the table leg and clutched his belly. His shoulders hunched over and he began to cry.

"Probably take you an hour or so to die," Ferguson said over his shoulder as he walked toward the door. "While you're doin' that, you can think about how you never should have come at me with that bottle."

"They . . . they'll hang you. . . ." the bartender croaked.

"I don't think so. It was self-defense, pure and simple."

With that, Ferguson pushed through the batwings and stepped out into the dusty street. His horse stood tied at a hitch rail nearby. He sauntered toward the animal.

He had just untied the reins when the bartender yelled, "You bastard!"

Ferguson turned smoothly toward the saloon and saw that somehow the mortally wounded man had found the strength to pull himself to his feet and reach the bar. Now the bartender had a sawed-off shotgun in his blood-smeared hands, and he was trying to bring it to bear on Ferguson.

The gunfighter drew again, with a little more urgency this time. He knew that at this range Greener was capable of blowing a mighty big hole in him.

The bartender never had a chance to line up his shot. Ferguson put four more slugs into him in a couple of seconds. Two of the bullets smacked into the bartender's chest, the third one tore out his throat, and the fourth and final one hit him just above the right eye, bored on through his brain, and burst out the back of his head in a grisly shower of blood, gray matter, and bone fragments. He sat down hard in the dirt in front of the saloon door and then slewed over onto his side.

"Well, I was wrong," Ferguson said as he opened his Colt and dropped the empties into his palm. He began thumbing fresh cartridges into the cylinder as he went on. "It didn't take him an hour to die after all."

When the gun was reloaded, he holstered it, caught up his horse's reins again, and swung up into the saddle. He was aware that people were watching him from the blacksmith shop and from some of the houses, maybe even from the churches. But nobody stepped out to try to stop him.

He wasn't sure if he was in Parker, Jack, or Palo Pinto County. If the sheriff of whatever county it was came looking for him, his claim of self-defense would be stronger than ever. After all, the bartender had come rushing out after him, waving a scattergun. What else could he have done, Ferguson asked himself, except hook and draw?

He started to ride slowly out of town, heading down the road toward Weatherford, and as he did, he spotted a rider coming toward him. The other horsebacker was moving along at a pretty good clip, and as he came closer, Ferguson recognized him as Cherokee Bob.

Ferguson reined in and waited for Bob to come to him. The young man, who was probably no more than sixteen and fancied himself a budding shootist, galloped up and brought his horse to a skidding stop that kicked up a cloud of dust in the road. Ferguson waved a hand in front of his face and glared at the youngster.

"Damn it, Bob, you're getting dust all over everything," Ferguson complained.

Bob snatched off his floppy-brimmed hat and looked apologetic. "Sorry, Mr. Ferguson," he said, "but I got some news I thought you'd want to hear as soon as possible, so I rode right out here lookin' for you."

"You found me. What's this news? Something about Ranger Beaumont?"

"Yes, sir, and about Miss Monfore, too."

Ferguson knew that Beaumont had been courting Victoria Monfore. The whole blasted county probably knew that.

"If all you want to tell me is that those two have been sparkin'—"

"No, sir," Bob said, daring to interrupt his mentor because he was so excited. "It's more than that. They're gettin' hitched!"

Ferguson frowned again. "Married, you mean?"

"That's right. I heard about it while I was hangin' around, down at the courthouse. The wedding is two weeks from this comin' Sunday."

Ferguson took out the makin's and began to build a quirly. "Well, what do you know," he mused as he rolled the cigarette. Voices drifted to him, but he didn't look around as he finished licking the edges of the paper and twirled the ends. Only when he had the cigarette in his mouth did he glance back and see that a couple of hundred yards away, several people were standing around the bloody, huddled shape of the dead bartender. They looked at Ferguson and then looked hurriedly away.

He didn't have to worry about them working up enough courage to come after him and try to stop him. It would take a long time for that to happen, and by then he would be gone.

"Did I do the right thing, Chas?" Cherokee Bob asked, daring to call his idol by his first name.

"You sure did," Ferguson said. "That is mighty

interestin' news." He heeled his horse into a walk. "You know what it means, don't you?"

Bob's mount fell in alongside. The youngster said, "It means Frank Morgan is liable to show up in town again, don't it?"

Ferguson snapped a lucifer into life with his thumbnail and held the flame to the end of the cigarette in his mouth. He puffed until the tobacco was burning good, then shook out the match and dropped it on the ground.

"That's right," he said around the quirly. "I don't reckon anything would stop Morgan from attending the wedding of his best friend, do you?"

"No, sir. The Drifter will be there. And then you can kill him."

Ferguson smiled. "That's right. I might wait until after the ceremony's over, though. Let the sight of Beaumont getting married be the last thing Frank Morgan ever sees . . . before I send him straight to Hell."

4

The shooting in Morrison's Old Corner Drug Store hadn't brought any serious repercussions for Frank Morgan. A blue-uniformed policeman had shown up a few minutes later to find out what had happened, but Doc Alderton's unhesitating confirmation of Frank's story made the lawman decide against arresting Frank. He had ordered Frank to make himself available for the inquest into the killing, though.

The coroner's jury hadn't taken long to return with a verdict of self-defense once they had heard testimony from Frank and Alderton. Frank being cleared officially of wrongdoing hadn't stopped both the Waco chief of police and the McClennan County sheriff from paying him a visit at his hotel. Both officials warned him that they didn't want any trouble in their bailiwick. Frank assured them that neither did he.

He hadn't planned to stay all that long in Waco, but a certain contrary streak made him delay longer than he had intended. He spent a couple of weeks in town, drinking and playing cards and sitting on the verandah of the hotel overlooking the Brazos River. Several times a day he strolled down to the livery stable to check on Stormy and Dog.

It was a peaceful interlude. Nobody tried to kill him.

He knew it couldn't last, of course.

One evening when he was sitting on the verandah, his attention was drawn to a man riding down the street toward the hotel. Instantly Frank sat up straighter in the cane-bottomed chair where he had been lounging. One booted foot was propped on the railing around the verandah. He brought it down. His hand moved closer to the butt of the gun at his hip.

The man on horseback sat tall and straight in the saddle as he approached. An indefinable air about him said that he was both alert and dangerous. He wore a high-crowned black hat and a cowhide vest. His shirt had leather cuffs. As he came closer, Frank saw that his bearded face was craggy and weather-beaten. It was almost like gazing in a mirror, because he knew that other than being clean-shaven, his own features had the same well-worn look. The stranger brought his horse to a stop in front of the hotel and gave Frank a nod.

Frank returned it and glanced along the verandah. Several men in suits were gathered about ten yards away, talking among themselves. Traveling salesmen, more than likely. Beyond them, several ladies sat enjoying the cooling air after the heat of the day. Frank would have preferred it if there hadn't been so many people around. He didn't care much for dusk, either; it was bad light for shooting.

"Howdy," the stranger said in a gravelly voice.

"Evening," Frank responded pleasantly enough. Just because you might be shooting at a fella a few minutes later was no reason to be impolite before the ball even started.

"I reckon you'd be Frank Morgan."

"That's right," Frank said, bracing himself for the inevitable challenge.

Only it might not be inevitable after all. Instead of insulting him or trying to goad him into a fight, the other man continued on in friendly tones. "I got a message for you from a friend of yours."

"Who might that be?"

"Tyler Beaumont."

The answer took Frank by surprise. He hadn't heard from Beaumont since leaving Weatherford. Of course, he hadn't gotten around to sending Beaumont that wire he had promised, either. He hoped the young Ranger wasn't in any trouble.

Frank came smoothly to his feet. "What's the message?"

"Got it written down here." The man grinned as he reached slowly and carefully under his vest and took a paper from his shirt pocket. "Didn't want to spook you."

The gesture moved the man's vest aside enough so that Frank suddenly saw the badge pinned to the shirt underneath it. It was the five-peso star-in-a-circle, the unmistakable emblem of the Texas Rangers.

"You're a Ranger?" Frank asked quietly.

"That's right. Name's Cobb. I was passin' through, stopped at the Ranger post over at Fort Fisher."

Frank knew the post Cobb mentioned was also on the banks of the Brazos, a couple of miles farther east.

"Seems that Beaumont sent out messages to all the Ranger posts in this neck of the woods, looking to get word to you," Cobb went on. "It just got here today. The boys in Company F knew you were in town and staying here, so they asked me to stop by and give you the message, since I was riding this way anyway."

He held out the folded paper, leaning down from the saddle to give it to Frank. Frank took it, unfolded it, and held it so that the light coming through the windows from the hotel lobby fell on it. His eyes scanned the words printed there, and as their meaning soaked in, a grin spread across his face.

"Good news?" Cobb asked.

Frank looked up at the rugged Ranger. "Mighty good news. You know Beaumont?"

Cobb shook his head. "Nope. I used to work out of the post at Veal Station, not far from Weatherford, but that was a while back. I never crossed trails with the young'un."

"He's getting married."

Cobb raised bushy eyebrows and said, "I thought you said it was *good* news."

Frank bristled a little. "He's marrying a mighty fine young woman." *Who just might be my daughter*, he added to himself.

"I don't doubt it. But Rangerin' ain't what you'd call a safe, steady profession. You're old enough to recall what Russell, Majors, and Waddell advertised for when they were lookin' for fellas to join the Pony Express."

"Orphans preferred," Frank said quietly, remembering the advertisements quite well because he had given some thought himself to joining the Pony Express.

"That's right," Cobb said. "Wouldn't be a bad idea for the Rangers to do likewise. Orphans and single men preferred." He pulled his horse's head around. "They don't listen to me, though." Ticking a finger against the brim of his hat, he added, "Be seein' you, Morgan."

Frank nodded and said, "So long, Cobb. Thanks for bringing the message."

The Ranger waved without looking around as he rode off slowly along the Brazos.

Frank watched him go for a moment and then looked down again at the paper in his hand. He read the message a second time, taking particular note of the date. The wedding was going to be on a Sunday. This was Saturday, Frank thought. Two weeks

from tomorrow, Tyler Beaumont and Victoria Monfore would be man and wife.

That meant there was a chance Beaumont would be
his son-in-law, although Frank knew good and well
neither Victoria nor her mother would ever confirm or
deny that. They had made it clear he was just going to
have to remain in the dark on that subject.

It didn't matter, Frank told himself. Either way,
Beaumont was his best friend, and Frank wanted to be
there when the young man got hitched.

No way in hell was he going to miss this wedding.

Frank rode out of Waco early the next morning,
taking the river trail that followed the Brazos north-
westward. After being cooped up in a stable for much
of the past few weeks, Stormy enjoyed being on the
move again. The big Appaloosa kicked up his heels in
a frisky fashion and stretched out into a ground-eating
lope. Dog ranged alongside, keeping up easily—when
he wasn't too busy chasing rabbits and birds.

Frank felt good about the trip, too. Sitting around
and doing nothing had been a nice change from his
usual eventful life, but only for a while. He had been
getting stale in Waco, and he knew it.

He was going to miss that drink the young druggist,
Doc Alderton, had come up with, though. The last
time Frank had been in the drugstore, Alderton's boss
had been talking about naming the stuff after a friend
of his, a sawbones named Pepper.

The terrain gradually grew more rugged as Frank
rode northwest. The river narrowed, and the banks rose
higher above its surface, turning into limestone bluffs
covered with cedar and oak trees. Frank had plenty of
supplies, so he didn't bother stopping at any of the
small settlements he came to. He slept under the stars

at night and felt just fine about it. The memories of Dixie, while still with him, were less painful now.

A week passed as he rode toward Parker County. He could have made better time, but he didn't see any need to push Stormy. As it was, he was going to reach Weatherford several days before the wedding.

He was a two days' ride away from his destination when the Appaloosa threw a shoe. Frank could have fixed the problem himself, but as it happened, he was passing through a little settlement called Nemo, and there was a blacksmith shop just a few yards farther on. Frank turned in there and called, "Anybody home?" The forge seemed to be cool, and he didn't hear the ringing sound of hammer on anvil.

No one answered his hail. Frank was about to get down and tend to the lost horseshoe himself, when he heard a couple of soggy thuds from out back of the blacksmith shop. He frowned as he recognized the sound of fists hitting flesh.

Somebody was taking a licking back there.

It was no business of his, of course, but even though he reminded himself of that fact, he found himself swinging down from the saddle and moseying through the shadowy, empty shop toward the back door. "Stay," he told Dog. The big cur could keep an eye on things up here.

The back door was a few inches ajar. Frank pushed it open the rest of the way and stepped through it as he heard more blows being struck. A man grunted in pain.

None of the five men in the little yard behind the blacksmith shop noticed him at first. That gave him the chance to study the situation. It was pretty simple, really.

Four men had ganged up on another man and were beating the hell out of him.

The victim wore a thick canvas apron that identified him as the blacksmith. So did the heavy muscles in his bare arms and shoulders. Under normal circumstances he probably could have thrashed the men attacking him. But one of the men was standing back a little, holding a revolver that he pointed at the blacksmith's head. If the smith had put up a fight, he might have gotten his brains blown out.

So he stood there unresisting with two of the men holding his brawny arms while the fourth and final attacker slammed brutal punches into his face and midsection, alternating back and forth. Blood dripped from the blacksmith's broken nose into his tangled black beard. A fist crashed into his jaw, jerking his head to the side. As the man who had thrown the punch stepped back to admire his handiwork, the blacksmith's head sagged. He was only half-conscious.

But he refused to give in, and after a moment he forced his head back up and shook it emphatically from side to side, slinging drops of crimson blood on the man who had been beating him. The man cursed and reached down to pick up a piece of wood from a stack near his feet. He brandished the makeshift club and said, "I'll kill you for that!"

"I don't think so," Frank said.

That stopped the club-wielder short. He and his companions looked around and saw Frank standing there, slim but muscular, calm and cool-eyed, obviously ready for trouble if it came.

"Who the hell are you?"

The angry question came from the man pointing the gun at the blacksmith. He didn't try to turn around and switch his aim to Frank.

"Somebody who doesn't like what he's seeing," Frank said. "It's four against one. Doesn't hardly seem fair."

"It's also none of your damn business," the gunman said. "Get out of here while you still can."

Frank shook his head and nodded toward the blacksmith. "Not without my friend here."

"Friend?" the gunman echoed. "You're a stranger hereabouts, mister. You don't even know this man."

"Is that right?" Frank looked at the blacksmith. "You and me are friends, aren't we?"

An improbable grin split the blood-smeared visage of the man. "I never saw you before, but right now there's no doubt you're the best friend I've got in this world, mister."

Frank turned his attention back to the other men and shrugged. "There. You see?"

"I don't see nothin' except some dumb son of a bitch stickin' his nose in where it ain't wanted. Are you blind? I've got a gun here."

"So do I," Frank said.

"There's four of us and only one of you."

"Those are pretty bad odds, all right, but I reckon if you don't mind being outnumbered, that's your choice."

It took a second for them to understand what he was saying, but the blacksmith got it right away. He gave a hearty laugh and said, "That's a good one."

The gunman's face flushed a deep red with anger. He growled at his men, "Forget about Craddock. I'll cover him. Just teach this bastard a lesson he'll never forget."

The two men holding the blacksmith's arms let go of him and stepped toward Frank. The one who had been handing out the beating moved toward him, too.

If Frank had been expecting any help from the blacksmith, it looked like he was going to be disappointed. The burly, bearded man tried to stay on his feet, but he had taken too much punishment. He slipped to his knees and then crumpled the rest of the way to the ground, breathing harshly through his flattened nose.

"You never did tell us your name, mister," said the man who had been hitting the blacksmith. He flexed knobby-knuckled hands and then closed them into big fists. "I like to know whose bones I'm breakin'."

"My name is Frank Morgan," the Drifter said.

And while they were digesting that, he stepped in and busted the first man square in the face.

5

Frank wasn't muscle-bound. In fact, he was fairly slender. But his punch packed plenty of power and exploded in the man's face like the kick of a Missouri mule. The man went backward in a hurry and crashed into the two men behind him. All three of them went down in a tangle of arms and legs.

That drew the attention of the man with the gun, and before his eyes could flick back toward Frank, the Peacemaker was in Frank's hand and was lined up on a spot right between the man's eyes.

"I wouldn't pull that trigger if I was you," Frank advised.

The man's eyes were wide with surprise and anger and a little fear. "How did you . . . My gun's already drawn, damn it!"

A faint smile touched Frank's lips. "First isn't always best. Just usually."

"I could still kill you."

"Maybe. Just maybe. But you'd never know one way or the other, because you'd be dead first."

The gunman's chest rose and fell raggedly as he struggled with his emotions. On the ground a few feet away, the other three toughs sorted themselves out and scrambled up, but they hung back since Frank had drawn his iron. They were handy at beating up a man they had the drop on, but clearly they had no interest in going up against an enemy with a gun in his hand.

Frank was getting tired of standing there. He prodded, "Well? What's it going to be?"

The blacksmith groaned, pushed himself onto hands and knees, and reached over to grasp the length of wood that his attacker had dropped a few minutes earlier. "Let me have 'em, mister," he rumbled. "You just keep Grady covered, and I'll handle the other three."

"Are you in any shape to do that, friend?" Frank asked.

"Not really," the blacksmith replied with a bloody grin. "But I'm going to anyway."

Frank smiled without taking his eyes off the man with the gun. "Have at it, then," he said by way of invitation.

Seeing that they were going to have no choice but to fight, the three men tried to jump the blacksmith first, before he had a chance to get set. One of them went in low, tackling him around the knees. The other two swung punches aimed at his head and body.

The blacksmith used the club to block the blow coming at his head and shrugged off the other punch which thudded into his barrel chest. He whipped the club around backhanded. It crashed into the shoulder of one of the men, who cried out in pain and lurched back, that arm dangling limply. He'd been hit so hard his whole side was probably numb.

With a heave, the man who had tackled the blacksmith threw him off his feet. The smith landed heavily but held on to the club. He rolled aside as his enemies tried to kick him. An arm like the trunk of a small tree swept out and knocked the feet out from under one of the men. At the same time, the blacksmith brought his club up between the legs of the other man and slammed it into his groin before he could get out of the way. The man shrieked in agony, doubled over, and fell to the ground clutching at himself.

That left only one man uninjured. The one who'd been hit on the shoulder was leaning against a wagon parked behind the blacksmith shop, holding his shoulder, and whimpering from the pain of broken bones. He might not ever be able to use that arm properly again.

The uninjured man was on the ground. He scuttled backward, scooting his butt in the dust, as the blacksmith stood up and turned toward him. "That's enough!" the man cried, holding out a palm toward the blacksmith. "Enough, Craddock!"

Frank noticed that the man was the one who had been doing the beating while the other two held the blacksmith, so he wasn't surprised when Craddock's pulped lips curved in a grisly smile. Craddock said, "Enough? Not hardly." He stalked after the retreating man.

"Stop him," the man with the gun said to Frank. "He'll kill Grant! He's insane!"

"No, he's probably just mad as hell," Frank said. "And I don't reckon I blame him."

The gunman finally lowered his pistol and slid it into his holster, ending the standoff. "Look, that's it," he declared. "You win, Morgan. Just call off that brute before he kills somebody!"

"Hey, Craddock," Frank said, not holstering his Colt yet. "Are you going to kill that son of a bitch?"

The blacksmith hesitated and then finally shrugged. "No, I don't suppose I will." He tossed the club aside. "I want to make sure he remembers me, though."

He reached down with both huge hands and grabbed Grant by the front of his shirt. Jerking the man up, Craddock began to shake him. "Thought it would be fun to gang up on me, didn't you?" Craddock growled as Grant's head flopped violently back and forth. Grant didn't put up a fight.

Like a dog with a rat, the big blacksmith shook the bully for a long moment, until Frank began to think Grant's neck might break. Before that could happen, Craddock tossed the man aside. Grant flew limply through the air like a toy carelessly discarded by a child and crashed to the ground, rolling over several times when he landed. When he came to a stop, he lay there motionless, out cold.

Frank looked around the little yard. Three of the men were either unconscious or incapacitated. The fourth man was pale with anger and more than a little fear. Frank said to him, "You'd better figure out a way to get your pards out of here. Then hit the trail, all of you."

Grady swallowed. "I'm just one man. I can't handle all of them."

"Where are your horses?"

"Out front," Grady answered sullenly.

"Bring 'em around here and load the men one at a time. Tie them in the saddle if you have to. Just get out, and be quick about it."

"Or what? You'll murder all of us?" The man couldn't stop a brief sneer from appearing on his face. "I've heard about you. You're a gunfighter, the one they call the Drifter. Nothing but a low-down killer."

Frank's lips curved in a humorless smile. "If I was as bad as I'm painted sometimes, you'd be dead by now, mister. You'd best remember that. Now get moving."

Muttering curses, Grady fetched the horses and struggled to lift his friends, one by one, into their saddles. Finally, all the men were mounted, although a couple of them were only half-conscious and had their hands full just staying on their horses. The other man, the one with the busted shoulder, couldn't handle the reins. Grady gathered up all the reins and led the other horses as he rode out, casting a final venomous stare over his shoulder at Frank.

"You made some bad enemies today," the blacksmith said as the bullies rode out of sight.

Frank slid his iron back into leather. "If men like that weren't my enemies, I'd know I was doing something wrong. I hate to think about what sort of world it'll be if folks ever stop standing up to varmints."

"Yeah." The blacksmith thrust out a hand. "I'm Reuben Craddock, and I'm much obliged to you, Mr. Morgan."

"Make it Frank." Smiling, Frank shook Craddock's hand. He could feel the awesome power in the blacksmith's grip, but Craddock restrained it. Clearly, Craddock didn't feel the need to prove anything, and that was the sort of man Frank liked.

"Did you come here looking for someone to do some blacksmith work, Frank?"

"Yeah, my horse threw a shoe," Frank replied with a nod. "He's out front with my dog."

Reuben nodded. "Let me get cleaned up a bit, and I'll tend to it right away. No charge."

"That's not necessary," Frank objected.

"Believe me," Reuben said with a grin, "you've more than paid in full."

After Reuben had put the new shoe on Stormy, he asked Frank to stay for supper, and Frank took him up on the offer. The blacksmith's quarters were in a small house next to the shop. "I can't promise you anything fancy," Reuben said as he led Frank into the house, "but I'm a pretty fair cook when it comes to simple things."

"Simple is fine with me," Frank assured him. He had left Stormy in a shed behind the house along with Reuben's mule. Dog was out there, too, gnawing on a bone that Reuben had given him.

"I've got beans soaking. I'll get them started cooking."

The furnishings in the house were strictly utilitarian, except for a bookcase full of leather-bound volumes. Frank had thought that Reuben sounded like an educated man, and the sight of the books confirmed it. He went over to look at the titles. Reuben noticed and asked, "Are you a reading man?"

"I always have a book or two in my saddlebags," Frank replied. "I've found they make for mighty good company on the trail."

"Or anywhere else," Reuben agreed. "Have you read Mark Twain's new one about Huckleberry Finn? It's there on the shelf."

Frank found the book, took it down, and flipped through the first few pages. "Tom's friend from *The Adventures of Tom Sawyer*?"

"That's right. Or Howells' new one, *The Rise of Silas Lapham,* is there, too. You can take them with you if you want. I've read both already. I have books sent down from a store in Fort Worth on a regular basis."

Frank found the Howells novel and added it to the Twain. "You're sure?"

Reuben waved a hand. "Of course. Once read, a book should be passed on."

"Well, I'm obliged."

"Not as much as I am. Those bastards were having so much fun they might have killed me."

Frank set the two books on a small table and turned to look at the blacksmith. There was a serious expression on his face as he asked, "What was that all about, anyway?"

Reuben frowned as he stirred the beans simmering in a pot on the black cast-iron stove. "They came in to have one of their horses shod. But before I could even get started on the job, they started making comments about dumb blacksmiths. I told them that if they felt that way, they could take their business somewhere else." Reuben shook his head. "They didn't care for that. Grady pulled a gun and covered me while Chadwick, Thomas, and Grant jumped me."

"You know them?"

Reuben's broad, powerful shoulders rose and fell in a shrug. "They've worked on various ranches around here. Mostly, though, they just hang around in the saloons in Granbury and Glen Rose and cause trouble."

"They're liable to come back and try to even the score."

"I'm not afraid of them," the blacksmith said. "Next time I see them coming, I'll grab my Greener and be ready for them."

Frank nodded slowly. "Just keep an eye out for them," he advised. "Maybe they'll decide that coming after you again is too much trouble."

"Trouble's what they'll get if they bother me again, that's for sure."

Reuben cooked some cornbread and fried up a mess of bacon to go with the beans. It was a good supper. Frank ate hungrily, relishing the simple but tasty fare.

Reuben sat across from him, and as the blacksmith breathed, Frank could hear the air whistling in the man's swollen, broken nose. He said, "Shouldn't you have a doctor look at that nose?"

"No, that's not necessary," Reuben said. "It's been broken before. I pushed the cartilage back into place already. It'll just have to heal."

Frank smiled. "Not many men could tend to their own broken nose like that. Doesn't it hurt?"

"Sure. But pain is a part of life, isn't it?"

Frank thought about Dixie and the way her loss would always be a dull ache inside him. He had never completely gotten over the death of his first wife, and he knew that losing Dixie would stay with him, too.

"Yes," he agreed quietly, "pain is a part of life, right enough."

The two men ate in silence for a while, and when Frank spoke again, he changed the subject. "I appreciate those books you said I could take with me. I've only got one in my saddlebags at the moment, but I'll trade it for the other two. You ever read anything by Henry James?"

Reuben frowned in thought and then shook his head. "I can't say that I have. Is his work any good?"

Frank grinned. "Well, you might say he chews more than he bites off, but some of what he writes is pretty interesting. He's no Ned Buntline or Colonel Prentiss Ingraham, though," he added, naming a couple of prolific, popular dime novelists. Frank had actually met Edward Judson, the man behind the Buntline pseudonym.

When they had finished eating, Reuben asked, "You'll stay the night, won't you? I can sleep out in the shed and you can have my bunk—"

"That's not necessary," Frank told him. "I'll spread my bedroll in the shed and be obliged for it."

"You're sure?"

Frank nodded. "Certain. You can feed me breakfast in the morning, though," he added with a smile. "And brew up a pot of coffee."

"I can sure do that."

They turned in a short time later, Frank pitching his bedroll in the shed as he had told Reuben he would. He never minded the company of Stormy and Dog, and the blacksmith's mule seemed all right, too. He had a final smoke, then stretched out on his blankets and went to sleep with an animal-like speed and ease.

He wasn't sure how much time had passed when his eyes suddenly snapped open and he was instantly awake. But he was certain of one thing because all his instincts told him it was true.

Trouble was afoot in the darkness.

6

The first thing that Frank noticed was the smoke. Not tobacco smoke from a quirly or a pipe, but wood smoke. He pushed himself up on an elbow and took a deeper sniff. Definitely wood smoke. Something nearby was burning, and on a warm summer night like this, no one would have lit a fire in a fireplace.

Dog growled deep in his throat, and Stormy shifted around in the stall. Knowing that his animal friends were bothered by something was the last bit of confirmation Frank needed. His gun belt was coiled close at hand, and as he came smoothly to his feet, his fingers closed around the wooden grips of the Peacemaker. He pulled the iron from leather.

A crackling sound reached his ears and the smell of smoke was stronger as Frank stepped out of the shed and looked around. The back door of the blacksmith shop was open, and a red glare came from inside.

"Damn it," Frank grated. He knew the smoke and the glare weren't coming from the forge.

He started toward the door, but he had taken only a couple of steps when something hit him from behind, slamming across his shoulders and knocking him forward. He sprawled on the ground as pain shot through him, but somehow he managed to hang on to the Colt. As he rolled over, he saw the stars above him blotted out suddenly by a looming shape. In a heartbeat, he recognized the shape as a man standing over him with some sort of bludgeon lifted over his head, ready to bring it down in a crushing blow.

Frank fired. Even with the pain of being struck down from behind, his aim was accurate. The bullet hit whatever it was his attacker was using as a club and knocked it out of his hands. At the same time, Frank's leg snapped out in a kick. His heel caught the man in the kneecap and sent him down with a cry of pain.

Frank kept rolling and used the momentum to help him come up on his feet. As he turned toward the rear of the blacksmith shop, another man came running out the door. Frank shouted, "Hold it!" but the man kept moving. Colt flame bloomed in the darkness as he snapped a shot at the Drifter.

That made it clear what the rules were in this fight, as if that wasn't the case already. Frank heard the wind-rip of a slug past his ear and then returned the fire, the Peacemaker bucking in his hand as it roared. The man who had just emerged from the blacksmith shop spun crazily, lurched to the side, and then fell back against the wall of the building. He slumped to the ground and didn't move.

The man whose leg Frank had kicked out from under him scrambled back to his feet and tried to limp away. Frank caught up to him easily and swung the Colt in a short, chopping blow. The barrel thudded against the man's skull. He folded up, stunned.

Frank ran to the door of the blacksmith shop and peered inside. He wasn't surprised to see flames licking up on all four walls. The man who had been inside must have spread kerosene all around the place and then set it on fire. The other man had been left outside to stand watch.

The fire was too far advanced for anything to be

done about it. But with any luck, Frank thought, he and Reuben could stop the flames from spreading to the house next door.

Where *was* Reuben? He should have heard the shots and come to see what was wrong.

Unless, for some reason, he couldn't do that, and the only reasons Frank could think of were bad ones.

He turned away from the doorway, glad to be away from the furnacelike heat that rolled out of the blacksmith shop. As he hurried toward Reuben's living quarters, he saw a spurt of reddish flame through a window. For a second he thought it was a muzzle flash, but then he realized he could still see it. The glare was growing brighter, too.

The house was on fire as well as the shop, Frank thought grimly.

He ran to the back door and kicked it open, then jerked to the side just in case anyone inside fired at him. No one did, so after a moment he called in a loud voice, "Reuben! Reuben, are you in there?"

His only answer was a groan. Frank darted through the doorway, looking around the flame-lit room.

The house was a small one, with a single room that served as kitchen, bedroom, and living area. Reuben's bunk was against the far wall, and that was where the fire was the worst. As the flames leaped higher, Frank spotted a dark, bulky shape lying on the bunk. He knew it had to be Reuben.

With no time to spare, Frank lunged across the room, ignoring the heat of the blaze that pounded at him like a giant fiery fist. He wore socks but no boots, and he felt the searing touch of flame through them. When he reached the bunk, he tucked the revolver behind his belt and bent to grab Reuben.

Even over the crackling roar of the flames he heard the blast of a gun and the whine of a slug over his head.

Still bending, Frank whirled and snatched out the Peacemaker. Through eyes watering from the smoke, he saw the figure of a gunman just as the man fired at him again. The bullet ripped through the fabric of Frank's jeans on the outside of his left thigh, burning a brand on the flesh underneath. Frank staggered but kept his feet. He triggered twice. The lead smashed into the gunman, making him jerk back in a jittering dance before he collapsed.

Frank turned to Reuben again and grabbed hold of him, lifting him. The muscles in Frank's neck stood out and he gave a deep groan of effort as he struggled to lift the massive blacksmith. Barely able to stay on his feet, Frank headed for the rear door.

He burst out into the clearer, cooler night air, and it seemed to give him the strength he needed to stagger away from the burning buildings. When he judged that he had gone far enough, he stopped, and his muscles chose that moment to give way. He fell, dropping Reuben's limp form. The two men sprawled side by side on the grass.

Frank drew several deep breaths, trying to clear the smoke from his lungs. He coughed a few times and then was able to push himself up onto his hands and knees. He reached out and felt under Reuben's beard for a pulse in the blacksmith's neck. Relief went through him as he found one and realized that it was fairly strong and regular. Reuben had been either knocked out or overcome by the smoke—or both—but he ought to be all right.

Frank pushed himself to his feet as he heard shouting. Nemo was a very small community, not much more than the blacksmith shop, a church, and a few scattered houses. But the citizens were aware of the fire now, and Frank saw them running toward the burning buildings. Some of the men carried buckets, but it was too late for a bucket brigade. Neither the shop nor the house could be saved.

A pang of regret went through Frank as he thought about all of Reuben's books burning up. But books could be replaced, at least most of them, and a human life definitely couldn't be.

Neither could the lives of a horse and a mule. Frank hurried over to the shed and led Stormy and Reuben's mule out into the open. Dog ran around barking. Frank tied the Appaloosa and the mule to a tree and went back into the shed to get his gear. By this time several men were throwing buckets of water from the nearby river onto the shed, trying to save it, at least. Frank wanted his saddle and the rest of his things, just in case they failed in the effort.

One of the men paused long enough to say to him, "Who the hell are you, mister? Where's Reuben?"

"He's over there, either knocked out or passed out," Frank explained, pointing to where Reuben lay on the ground. "I think he's going to be all right, though."

"That don't tell me who you are."

"Frank Morgan. I'm a friend of Reuben's."

He figured that was true enough. Even though they had known each other only a few hours, Frank considered them friends.

He hadn't forgotten about the men who had started these fires. He dropped his saddle on the ground near the tree where he had tied up Stormy and the mule, then went over to the fellow he had knocked out. Putting a toe under his shoulder, Frank rolled him over. In the light from the fire, he recognized one of the men who had been giving Reuben so much trouble that afternoon.

That came as no surprise to Frank. He had expected the men might come back for revenge. One man was knocked out here at his feet, one was inside the burning house, and another lay motionless against the rear wall of the blacksmith shop.

That made three. There had been *four* bullies. . . .

The bucket brigade had wet down the shed and then drawn back to see what was going to happen. Frank's gaze fell on one of the men standing there, and anger coursed through him as he recognized Grady, the one who had held the gun on Reuben while the other three attacked him.

Frank strode toward him, grasped his shoulder, jerked him around. Grady gave an indignant yell. "Hey! What do you think you're doin'?"

Pointing at the burning buildings with his left hand, Frank said, "You reckon burning down a man's home and business evens things up?"

"I don't know what you're talking about. Back off, Morgan."

"The hell you don't know," Frank said. With an effort, he controlled his rage, rather than letting it control him. "One of your partners is lying over there knocked out, another one is shot there by the shop, and I'll wager the third one is inside the house with my lead in him!"

Grady sneered. "Are you confessin' to murder, Morgan? Because that's sure what it sounds like to me."

"The only ones who had murder on their minds tonight were you and your friends," Frank shot back. "Two of you set the blacksmith shop on fire while the other two snuck into Reuben's house, knocked him out, and started a fire there, too."

"You're crazy!" Grady insisted. He looked around at the circle of people that had gathered to listen intently to Frank's accusations. "I never tried to hurt nobody. Hell, I came up and helped try to save that shed, didn't I?"

"Yeah," one of the men said, suspicion in his voice. "You came up, just like you said, Grady. Both fires were already burning pretty strong before you got here."

"Like maybe you were hiding somewhere in the shadows," Frank suggested, "just waiting for a good moment so you could help out and pretend to be innocent."

Grady sneered again. "You can't prove that. It's just a story."

"No, it's not," a deep, rumbling voice said. Frank glanced around to see that Reuben had regained consciousness and pushed himself into a sitting position. The blacksmith shook his shaggy head from side to side, evidently trying to clear out some of the cobwebs from his brain. "It's not just a story," Reuben went on. "I can prove Frank's telling the truth. I woke up just in time to see Grady standing over my bunk with a gun in his hand." Reuben gingerly fingered a lump on his head. "I reckon he pistol-whipped me then and knocked me out before he set fire to everything I have."

"You bastard," Grady said thickly. "You ignorant, numbskulled bastard."

"I reckon he's a heap smarter than you ever will be," Frank pointed out. "At least Reuben's not going to be headed for prison to do a stretch for attempted murder."

"Neither am I!" Grady yelled. His hand flashed toward the gun on his hip.

Frank let him get his fingers wrapped around the butt of the revolver and draw the gun halfway from the holster before he fired. The bullet smashed into Grady's chest and knocked him back a step. Grady struggled to finish his draw, but he lacked the strength now. It had all ebbed out of him, along with the blood that stained the front of his shirt. He dropped the gun and coughed once, blood spilling from his mouth over his chin as he did so. In the light from the fire, it looked black instead of crimson.

Then Grady's knees folded up and he fell. He sprawled on the ground, his face pressed against the dirt.

Only one of the quartet of bullies was still alive, and he had been caught red-handed at his dirty work. He would confess and probably go to jail. Reuben wouldn't have to worry about any more attempts on his life.

He would have enough worries, though, trying to replace his business and his home.

Frank could help with that. His first wife had been a wealthy woman, and she had made sure before she died that when she was gone, Frank Morgan would be a wealthy man. He had sizable accounts in several banks in both Denver and San Francisco, and for someone who often looked like a down-at-heels cowboy riding the grub line, he was a rich, rich man. Reuben might not want to accept the help—Frank knew he was proud—but Frank would see to it anyway that both the shop and the house were rebuilt.

He would see to it that that bookcase was filled up again, too.

"Frank," Reuben called. "Frank, are you all right?"

Suddenly dizzy, Frank turned to face Reuben, who was climbing hurriedly to his feet. To his surprise, Frank realized that his left side was wet. He put his hand on his shirt, felt the warm stickiness there.

"Well, I'll swan," he said. "Must've got nicked and didn't even know it."

Then he slid into a hot, smoky blackness tinged with the red of flames. . . .

7

Tyler Beaumont swallowed hard and fought the urge to rip the tie from around his neck and yank his collar open. He had never liked having anything tight around his neck.

He told himself it wasn't really that bad. He was just nervous, and what man wouldn't be on his wedding day?

He decided that if he thought about Victoria, that would calm him down. But that was a mistake, because whenever he thought about Victoria, his mind inevitably wandered to how sweet and hot her mouth was when he kissed her and the soft warmth of her body when he held her in his arms and how tonight they would be man and wife at last and finally able to come together in the way that a married couple should. . . .

Beaumont jumped a little and gasped as a hand came down on his shoulder. "Boy, you pert near jumped outta your skin," Luke Perkins said in a booming voice. "Calm down, son. You're just gettin' married. It ain't like you got to go fight a horde o' screamin' Comanch'."

Beaumont turned to face the bald-headed rancher. Perkins had a drooping soup-strainer of a mustache and wore his only town suit for this occasion, a sober black outfit that had been brushed clean of dust.

"Were you that relaxed on *your* wedding day?"

Beaumont asked as he ran a finger around the inside of his collar.

Luke laughed. "Well, not really, I reckon. Gettin' hitched was a mighty big step for an old bachelor like me."

"It's a big step for a young bachelor like me, too. What if . . ." Beaumont hardly dared to put the thought into words. "What if I'm doing the wrong thing?"

"Do you love Victoria?" Luke asked bluntly.

"Of course I do."

"Then you ain't doin' the wrong thing. Best decision I ever made was to pull in double harness with Carolyn. You'll see; it'll all work out."

Beaumont sighed. "I hope so. I sure hope so."

He looked around at the crowd gathered outside the Clear Fork Baptist Church. It was a small country church, not in the town of Weatherford itself but a few miles northeast, not far from the Clear Fork of the Trinity River. The church was surrounded by tall oak trees, and a heavily wooded ridge overlooked the scene. It was a beautiful place to get married, Beaumont had to admit. A big crowd had turned out, probably because the Judge and Mrs. Monfore were so well-known and well-liked. The whitewashed frame church building would be packed.

Off to the side, under the trees, ladies were putting tablecloths on long tables that had been set up. Dozens of buggies were parked nearby, and in each buggy were pies and cakes and covered dishes of food that would be set out on the tables for the celebration that was scheduled to follow the ceremony. Nobody knew how to put on a shindig quite like Texans, Beaumont thought. Weddings, funerals, baptisms, what have you . . . any kind of ceremony made a perfect excuse to bring out enough food for a small army. Not to mention jugs of tea and lemonade and pots of coffee. One fella was even setting up an ice cream freezer with its wooden handle, which would have to be cranked for several hours in order to make ice cream. It would be worth the time and trouble, though, once the sweet, cold, creamy stuff was ready.

Yes, everything was just about perfect, Tyler Beaumont thought. . . .

Except Frank Morgan wasn't here.

Beaumont had written to Ranger posts all around the state, and he knew that his message had caught up to Morgan in Waco. He had heard from Company F that his note had been delivered to Morgan, and that Frank had started for Weatherford a little over two weeks earlier. That had given him plenty of time to get here.

And yet he hadn't shown up, and Beaumont had no idea where he was.

He had planned to ask Frank to be his best man, but since Morgan wasn't there and hadn't let Beaumont know one way or the other if he was coming, the young Ranger had asked Luke Perkins instead. Luke and Morgan were old friends and had grown up together. The rancher had also been a good friend to Beaumont while he was in Weatherford. But while Beaumont certainly didn't mind having Luke as his best man, it wasn't quite the same thing. Beaumont and Frank Morgan had fought side by side on numerous occasions, protecting each other's back, and that created a bond that could not be broken, in Beaumont's opinion.

He tugged at his tie—he couldn't help himself—and said, "Any word from Frank?"

"Don't you reckon I would have told you if I'd heard anything?" Luke replied. "I'm sorry, Tyler. I reckon he got delayed somewhere."

Or he was dead, Beaumont thought. No matter how fast a man was with his gun, his luck had to run out sooner or later. No man was invincible, not even

Frank Morgan. And Beaumont knew all too well how often Frank was braced by men wanting to make a reputation for themselves. Not only that, but Frank seemed to have a positive genius for walking into trouble. That was probably because of the habit he had of sticking up for the underdog and trying to see to it that justice was done. . . .

Yet if he had been any other way, he wouldn't have been Frank Morgan. Might as well rage at the wind for blowing or the sun for shining.

People began filing into the church now, summoned by the ushers. The minister came over to Beaumont and Luke. Pastor Ford Fargo was a tall, burly, white-haired man who had been a cattleman and an Indian fighter in his time, as well as a preacher of the Gospel. He clapped a hand on Beaumont's shoulder and said in his booming voice, "Well, come on, son. Time to get you hitched proper."

"Yes, sir," Beaumont said. He swallowed hard again. "I reckon I'm ready."

But that was a lie. He cast one last desperate look around, thinking that he might spot Frank Morgan riding up. If Frank were here, Beaumont knew he could find the courage to go through with this.

Frank wasn't here, though. Beaumont had to go it alone. Well, alone except for Luke Perkins. The rancher put a hand on Beaumont's other shoulder, and the young Ranger knew that if they had to, Luke and Pastor Fargo would manhandle him right into the church and up to the altar.

"I'm all right," he said as a strange calmness came over him. At that moment, his doubts vanished, and he knew he was doing the right thing. "I'm all right. Let's go."

***

On the ridge overlooking the church, Chas Ferguson lowered a pair of field glasses from his eyes and bit back a curse. Beside him, Cherokee Bob said anxiously, "Morgan ain't there yet?"

"No sign of him," Ferguson said. "And it looks like the wedding's about to start. Everybody's going inside the church."

"I thought you said Morgan was bound to show up."

Ferguson turned sharply toward Bob, and the look on his face made the youngster draw back in alarm. But then Ferguson controlled his anger and grated, "I thought he'd be here. I would have sworn that he would be. But it looks like he ain't."

"Maybe he's dead," Bob suggested.

Ferguson frowned. "What the hell do you mean?"

"You told me how folks are always challengin' Morgan, wantin' to prove they're faster than he is. What if he came up against somebody who really is faster and got himself kilt?"

Ferguson thought about it for a second and then shook his head emphatically. "The only man in these parts who's faster than Morgan is me. If there was anybody else around who's that good, I would have heard about him."

"Well, maybe something else happened. An accident, maybe. He might've got run over by a wagon. Or maybe a beer barrel fell on his head."

Ferguson stared at the youngster. "Are you addle-pated?" he demanded. "How could a beer barrel fall on Morgan's head?"

Bob shrugged. "I dunno. But if it did, it might've kilt him."

Ferguson took a deep breath and gritted his teeth. Shooting the dim-witted youngster wouldn't accomplish anything. Well, it might make him feel a little better for a few minutes, Ferguson allowed, but other than that . . .

"Rider over yonder," Bob said suddenly, pointing to the south.

Ferguson stiffened and swung around to look where Cherokee Bob was pointing. Even at this distance, several hundred yards away, Ferguson could see that the horse had a dappled pattern to its hide. He jerked the field glasses to his eyes.

The hated face of Frank Morgan sprang into sharp relief, as if Morgan were only a few feet away. Quickly, Ferguson lowered the glasses. He didn't want Morgan to see the sun reflecting off them. Morgan was the sort of man who would notice something like that. Luckily, though, he had been looking the other direction for the second or so that Ferguson had had the glasses on him.

"It's him," Ferguson said in a hushed voice. "It's him, all right. He was almost too late, but he got here in time."

"In time for the wedding, you mean?" Bob asked.

Ferguson shook his head. "In time to die."

You couldn't ask for a prettier Sunday afternoon, Frank Morgan thought as he guided Stormy down the trail from the ridge. It was a little hot, but not bad for Texas in the summer. Under the shade of those oak trees around the church, it would be very pleasant.

He drew in a deep breath, feeling a slight twinge in the newly formed scar on his left side. The bullet had ripped a furrow in the flesh without really penetrating. The wound had bled freely but hadn't been life-threatening. It was an annoyance more than anything else, an annoyance and a delay. The doctor in Granbury had insisted that Frank rest and recuperate for a few days before riding on to Weatherford.

Frank had considered ignoring the doctor's orders, but after Reuben had put him in a wagon and driven him all the way to town, Frank figured he owed it to the big blacksmith to cooperate with the sawbones. Reuben had been scared to death that Frank was mortally wounded. That seemed to worry him more than the destruction of his home and business.

"You're the first hombre I've run into in quite a while who reads as much as I do," Reuben had said. "I'd hate to see you die, Frank."

"I wouldn't much care for it, either," Frank had agreed with a grin.

During the time Frank had spent in Granbury, he had sent wires to his bankers and lawyers, instructing them on what to do in regard to helping Reuben recover financially from the catastrophe that had befallen him. When Reuben found out about it, he had stubbornly insisted that he didn't need Frank's help, just as Frank had expected. It had taken pretty much a whole day to argue him around to seeing things Frank's way. That had been another good reason for the delay.

So that Beaumont wouldn't worry, Frank had sent word to Weatherford, explaining what had happened and promising that he would be there in time for the wedding. He almost hadn't made it, though. He had cut things a little too close. As he rode down the ridge toward the church, he fished out his pocket watch and opened it. Two o'clock, he saw with a frown. He had expected the ceremony to take place in one of the churches in town. When he discovered that it was happening out here in the country, he had ridden on hurriedly without even taking the time to change into his suit.

Dog spooked a jackrabbit out of a clump of brush

and went bounding down the hill after it, barking and carrying on. Frank smiled at his canine friend's antics. He knew better than to think that all was right with the world—that was a sure-fire recipe for disaster—but things were looking up. If he could just get to the church before they said the vows . . .

A few minutes later, he drew rein and swung down from the saddle in front of the church. He looped the reins around a buggy wheel and told Dog to stay put. The door of the church was open a few inches. Piano music came through the gap. Frank hoped that was a sign that the actual marrying hadn't gotten under way yet.

He slipped inside, taking off his hat as he did so. The little church was crowded. Folks were packed shoulder to shoulder in every pew, and quite a few were standing up at the rear of the sanctuary. Most of them were dressed in their Sunday best, and Frank felt a little awkward in his range clothes coated with trail dust. Still, he knew Tyler Beaumont wanted him to be here, dressed up or not.

Beaumont stood at the front of the church next to a vision in white silk and lace. Frank's breath caught in his throat as he looked at Victoria. That was his daughter up there, he thought. Maybe not legally, but in his heart, he knew it, the same way he could look at his boy Conrad and recognize the bond between them. Of course, he didn't get along all that well with Conrad—the boy didn't really want to have anything to do with him—but blood was still blood, and Frank felt the same thing toward Victoria.

Luke Perkins stood at Beaumont's right. Frank guessed that Luke was the young Ranger's best man. That was good. Frank felt a little disappointed that it wasn't him up there, but under the circumstances, Beaumont had done good by picking Luke for the job.

As if feeling Frank's gaze on him, Luke glanced toward the rear of the church. His eyes widened as he saw the tall, slim figure of the Drifter standing there, hat in hand. Luke made a move like he was going to nudge Beaumont in the ribs, but Frank shook his head. He didn't want to interrupt the ceremony, and Beaumont didn't need to be distracted right now.

The minister, a big white-haired fella, had his Bible open in his hands and was just getting some steam up as he talked about what a sacred and holy institution matrimony was. Frank listened with a smile, but his eyes and his attention wandered. He picked out Mercy and Judge Monfore sitting in the front row. Mercy dabbed at her eyes with a lace handkerchief, and even the stern old judge looked a mite misty-eyed. The rest of the audience watched the ceremony raptly.

Frank had attended quite a few weddings, including two of his own. Some of them went by quickly and some didn't. This one didn't. The minister had a lot to say in his stentorian voice. Finally, he got to the part about how if anybody had any objections to this union, let him speak now or forever hold his peace. Folks glanced around sort of nervously, including the would-be bride and groom. Nobody ever objected, at least not that Frank had ever heard of, but the possibility was still there, and it was just enough to make people a mite skittish.

In this case, when Beaumont glanced over his shoulder, he saw Frank Morgan standing there at the rear of the church by the door. A huge smile appeared on his face. That was enough to make Victoria look in the same direction, and she smiled, too, when she saw Frank. That made a warm feeling spread through the gunfighter's chest. He nodded solemnly to the young couple, indicating not only his blessing, but a desire that they get on with the ceremony.

"Well, then, if nobody has any objections," the

preacher started up again, "we'll get to it. Do you, Victoria, take this man, to have and to hold? . . ."

The vows went smoothly, and this part of the ceremony was over almost before Frank knew it. Then the preacher said to Beaumont, "You can kiss your bride, son," and Beaumont did, a long, healthy buss that prompted one of the men in the audience to say a loud "Amen!" Everybody laughed.

Beaumont and Victoria turned and came down the aisle arm in arm toward Frank. There were hugs for Victoria and slaps on the back for Beaumont along the way. The piano player pounded the ivories. An air of pure jubilation filled the church.

Frank had never seen Victoria looking lovelier. He stepped up to kiss her on the cheek and then shook Beaumont's hand. "I didn't think you were going to get here, Frank," the young Ranger said.

"Sorry I was a mite late," Frank said. "Didn't you get my message?"

Beaumont frowned and shook his head. "No, we never heard a word from you."

Frank muttered a curse under his breath. Something had happened to the note he had sent from Granbury. Obviously, it had gone astray somehow. But that didn't matter now. He was here, and he had arrived in time to see these two fine young people get hitched. That was all that was important.

Beaumont felt the same way, because his frown disappeared and was replaced with a grin. "Come on," he said. "Wait'll you see all the food. There's even going to be ice cream!"

Victoria laughed and held on to his arm. "I think you're more excited about that than about marrying me," she teased him.

"Not hardly!" Beaumont said without hesitation.

Then he added, "But I *do* like ice cream, especially when it's made with fresh peaches."

Frank stepped aside to let the happy couple step out of the church first. People streamed after them and spread out around the heavily laden tables. Now that the church part of the afternoon was over, men took off ties and opened collars. The festivities didn't take long to get under way.

Mercy and Judge Monfore came up to Frank. Mercy caught hold of both of his hands and came up on her toes to kiss his cheek. "Frank, I'm so glad you're here," she said. "I know Victoria is, too."

"I wouldn't have missed it," he assured her. "I got delayed a little, or I would have been here a few days ago."

"You got here for the important part, Morgan," Judge Monfore said. He thrust out his hand, and Frank took it. The men shook, a look of understanding passing between them as they did so. They would never be good friends, but they respected each other, and Frank felt a debt of gratitude toward Monfore for the way the judge had given Mercy such a good home and a good life. She deserved all the happiness in the world.

They all did, Frank thought. The West was settling down a little at last, so that life out here wasn't the constant struggle for survival that it had once been. Sure, there were still dangers, as all of them knew all too well, but there were moments like this, too, moments of peace and joy and a promise for the future. . . .

"Morgan! Morgan, it's time, you bastard! Turn and face me!"

8

Frank had lived through blizzards in Wyoming and Montana, but never in his life had he been any colder inside than he was at that moment. The loud, angry voice came from behind him. He recognized it, knew who it belonged to. Frank had hoped never to see him again.

"Damn it, Morgan, I'm talkin' to you!"

Slowly, Frank turned. He saw Chas Ferguson standing there twenty feet away, blond hair curling out from under his creamy Stetson, looking as dandified as ever. And as dangerous as ever, too. His right hand hovered over the butt of the Colt on his hip, ready to hook and draw.

A moment earlier, people had been talking and laughing, but now a hush hung over the gathering. Ferguson's loud, profane challenge had shocked everyone into silence. They stared at him, sensing the violence that was about to erupt.

But not if Frank Morgan could help it. He managed to put a friendly smile on his face as he said, "Hello, Chas. It's been a long time."

"Bet you wish it had been longer," Ferguson said. "Bet you wish you never had to face me."

Frank shook his head. "I don't want to have to kill you, but other than that, I'm glad to see you." That was stretching the truth. In a way, Ferguson was right:

Frank could have lived the rest of his life without running into the younger gunfighter again, and it would have been just fine with him.

From a few feet away, Tyler Beaumont said quietly, "Frank, I'm not armed. Not today."

"That's fine," Frank assured him. "This isn't any of your business."

"Well, it's some o' mine," Luke Perkins put in, "and I *am* armed." He swept back his coat to reveal the butt of a revolver and confirm his statement.

Judge Monfore stepped forward and glowered at Ferguson. "See here, young man," he said. "You're disrupting my daughter's wedding, and you're not welcome here. If you know what's good for you, you'll turn around and leave right now."

"The wedding's over, ain't it?" Ferguson asked without taking his eyes off Frank.

"Well, yes, but—"

"Then it shouldn't bother any of you folks when I gun down Morgan."

Beaumont said, "Blast it, Ferguson, I'm a Texas Ranger, and I'm about to put you under arrest if you don't get out of here."

"Can't arrest a man for havin' a fair fight with another man."

"Yes, he can," Judge Monfore said. "I'll issue a warrant right here and now, on a charge of disturbing the peace."

"Nobody's arresting me," Ferguson snapped. "Bob!"

Another voice called, "I hear you, Chas! And I got 'em all covered!"

Frank glanced toward the sound and saw an eager-faced young man standing behind one of the buggies, covering the crowd with a rifle. A few women cried out in fear, and a couple of men cursed and started forward, stopping short when the rifle barrel swung toward them.

"Bob!" Judge Monfore said. "Bob Milton, is that you?"

"It's Cherokee Bob," the youngster called back. "Cherokee Bob the outlaw! I'm gonna be famous!"

"What you're going to be is in jail unless you put down that gun and stop acting like an idiot," the judge warned him.

"No, sir. Chas and me are partners now, and it's my job to see that nobody interferes while he has his finish fight with Morgan there. It's time somebody taught that old-timer he ain't the fastest man with a gun no more!"

Still looking intently at Ferguson, Frank said, "This all goes back to that shooting contest up in the Panhandle, doesn't it? You just can't stand the idea that somebody might be better with a gun than you."

"You're not better!" Ferguson said in a strained voice. "You were just lucky that day. I'm faster, and I'm a better shot, and I'm goin' to kill you. You just wait and see!"

Frank sighed. "You go to shooting with all these folks around, somebody's liable to get hurt."

"Only one who'll get hurt is you, Morgan. And you'll get dead."

Luke Perkins said, "Frank, all my hands are here. If we rush him, he can't get all of us. . . ."

"No," Frank said emphatically. "I don't want anyone else to get hurt." To Ferguson, he asked, "Will you give everyone time to get back in the church, so they'll be safe?"

Ferguson sneered. "Hell, no! I want everybody to be watching when I kill you."

In a way that simplified things, Frank thought.

He just had to kill Ferguson before the younger man could get off even a single shot.

"You've got it to do, then," he said. "Get it over with."

Ferguson's face contorted in a fierce grimace of hate and exultation, and his hand stabbed toward the butt of his gun. He really was fast. In truth, he was one of the fastest Frank Morgan had ever seen.

But his iron was only halfway out of its holster when Frank's Peacemaker roared and sent a slug driving into Ferguson's chest.

Ferguson took a step back and looked down at his shirtfront in disbelief. A spot of crimson appeared against the black as blood welled from the bullet hole. He swallowed hard and the muscles in his neck stood out with effort as he struggled to pull his gun. To him, though, the weapon must have suddenly seemed to weigh a ton. It slipped from his fingers and slid back down into the holster.

"No," Ferguson said quietly. "No, it can't . . ."

Then his eyes rolled up in his head and his knees buckled. He went down onto his face, the immaculate Stetson coming off his head and rolling in the dirt.

"No!" the young man called Cherokee Bob screamed. "You killed him!" He jerked the trigger of the Winchester in his hands, slamming a bullet toward Frank Morgan.

Frank was already pivoting toward the new threat. He triggered twice, but Cherokee Bob ducked behind the buggy he was using for cover and Frank's bullets just knocked splinters from the seat. The horse hitched to the buggy was spooked by the gunfire and tried to rear. Unable to, it suddenly bolted forward, exposing the young man. Bob dashed toward a nearby tree, levering and firing the rifle from the hip as he ran. People screamed and yelled and tried to dive out of the way of the wildly flying lead.

Bob made it only a few steps before he ran into a hailstorm of bullets from the guns of Luke Perkins and his tough crew of cowboys. The young man was jolted back and forth by the impact of the slugs so that it seemed like he was performing a grisly dance. He dropped the rifle and staggered another step before his bullet-riddled body dropped lifeless to the ground. He had been almost literally shot to pieces.

Frank had fired only three shots. Instinct and habit made him dump the empties and thumb fresh cartridges into those chambers of the Peacemaker's cylinder. The uproar from the crowd washed around him as women cried and men cursed and shouted questions. Frank swung around to see if anyone had been hit by Cherokee Bob's wild shots. He intended as well to apologize to Beaumont and Victoria for the trouble that his presence had inadvertently brought to what should have been the happiest day of their young lives.

That was when he froze, petrified by horror, the gun in his hand forgotten. Beaumont, Mercy, and the judge were all kneeling around a figure lying motionless on the ground. A figure dressed in a gown that had been beautifully, purely white only moments earlier, a gown that was now blotched with ugly red stains, stains of blood . . .

Victoria.

"I don't know," the doctor said, shaking his head. "I think she'll pull through, Judge, but I can't promise that."

Judge Monfore's face was ashen as he stood next to his wife, his arm around Mercy's shoulders. She held a crumpled handkerchief to her face and sobbed quietly into it. Next to them stood Tyler Beaumont, and his features might have been carved out of stone for all the emotion they displayed. But his hands, which hung loosely at his sides, trembled slightly, giving evidence of the struggle that was going on inside him.

They were in the vestibule of the church. One of the tables had been cleared off hurriedly and carried inside. Victoria had been lifted carefully and placed on the table, and the doctor, who was one of the guests at the wedding, had gone to work on her, cutting away the bloodstained gown and examining her to find out the extent of her injury.

"The bullet passed through her body at an angle," the medico went on with his report to Victoria's worried husband and parents. "I can't be sure, but I don't think it hit any vital organs. That's almost miraculous." He gave a humorless laugh. "Hell, it *is* miraculous."

"Then she should live," Beaumont said tightly.

"She lost a lot of blood, and I can't be absolutely certain about any internal damage the bullet might have done," the doctor cautioned. "That's why I said I think she'll pull through. I've cleaned the wound and stopped the bleeding as best I can out here. We'll need to get her back to town and into the hospital as soon as possible, though."

Mercy took the handkerchief away from her red, moist eyes and asked, "When . . . when will you know for sure?"

The doctor thought it over for a moment and then said, "If she makes it through the next couple of days, I'll feel a lot better about her chances."

"A couple of days," Beaumont repeated, and from the sound of his voice it might as well have been a lifetime.

Frank Morgan stood just outside the open door of the church, smoking a cigarette and listening to the conversation. He didn't want to intrude on Beaumont and the Monfores, even though a part of him wanted to rush in and go to Victoria.

But there was nothing he could do for her, and he knew it. He took lives, he thought bitterly. He didn't save them. It seemed to him that Death was his constant companion, every bit as much so as Dog or Stormy.

Luke Perkins stood with him. With a doleful shake of his head, the mustachioed rancher said, "It wasn't your fault, Frank. You tried to get Ferguson to hold off until everybody was clear, and then when he wouldn't, you downed him before he could even get a shot off." A note of awe entered Luke's voice. "I thought I'd seen you hook and draw fast before now, but man alive! I don't know that anybody ever made a faster draw than you did today, Frank. Not Wes Hardin, not Ben Thompson, not even Smoke Jensen."

"And it didn't do a damned bit of good," Frank said hollowly.

"Don't say that. Nobody can blame you because that young idiot went crazy and started blazin' away like that."

Frank dropped the quirly and ground it out in the dirt with the toe of his boot. Then he looked at Luke and said, "He wouldn't have even been here if it wasn't for Ferguson, and Ferguson wouldn't have been here if it wasn't for me."

"That's right," Beaumont said from behind Frank. The young Ranger's voice was cold as ice, hard as flint.

Frank turned to look at him. Beaumont's expression was still carefully controlled, but his eyes glittered with anger. "I'm sorry, Tyler—" Frank began.

"Don't," Beaumont interrupted. "Don't say any more, Frank. There's nothing you can say that will change things. Nothing that will make Victoria get up and be whole and unhurt again."

"Listen here, son," Luke said. "You saw what

happened. Frank did his damnedest to stop the whole thing."

Beaumont nodded. "I know. That's the only thing that keeps me from hating him right now."

"What about all the times you two fought side by side? Hell, you owe him your own life—"

"I don't *have* a life without Victoria," Beaumont said, cutting in. "If I lose her . . ." He couldn't go on. He broke off and drew a deep, shuddery breath. After a moment, he looked at Frank and continued. "I heard what you said about you being the only reason Ferguson was here. That's the truth."

Frank nodded. "I know it."

"Death follows you around, Frank."

"I had the same thought."

"That's why—" For a second, the carefully constructed façade that Beaumont had put up so that he wouldn't go completely to pieces slipped, and the depth of his anger and suffering was visible on his face. With an effort, he regained control of himself and went on. "That's why I don't want to have anything more to do with you. I appreciate everything you've done for me in the past, but from here on out, you and me are done, Frank."

"Damn it, boy!" Luke burst out. "You can't just—"

"He can do whatever he feels like he has to do," Frank said. "Are you sure that's what you want, Tyler?"

"I'm certain. The doctor says there's a good chance Victoria will recover, but even if she does, I won't let you put her life at risk ever again. Stay away from her, and stay away from me." He started to go back inside, but he paused long enough to add, "I'm sorry."

"So am I," Frank Morgan whispered. But Beaumont had already shut the door of the church.

9

No one else had been hurt in the shooting, not even so much as a nick. They had that to be thankful for, Frank Morgan thought as he sat in a saloon in Weatherford that night and drank coffee. Luke Perkins sat with him. The rancher had a bottle and a glass and would have shared, but Frank had refused the whiskey. He wanted to keep a clear head.

"What'll you do now?" Luke asked. "You goin' to stay around here?"

Frank shook his head. "You heard what Beaumont said. He doesn't want me anywhere near him or his wife."

Who is probably my daughter, Frank thought for maybe the thousandth time. Beaumont's anger—which was totally justified in Frank's opinion—had cut Frank off not only from his friendship with the Ranger, but also from any sort of relationship with the young woman who was quite likely his own flesh and blood.

Some men might bitch and moan about that not being fair. Complaining wasn't Frank Morgan's way. He might not like the decision Beaumont had made, but he wasn't going to argue with Beaumont's right to make it.

"So you're just gonna ride on?" Luke said.

Frank took another sip of coffee. "I don't know what else I can do."

"You could take a singletree and wallop that fool youngster on the head a few times," Luke suggested. "Might knock some sense into that thick skull o' his."

"You can't blame a man for being worried about his wife."

"Hell, I reckon pert near everybody in Parker County is worried about Miss Victoria tonight. Most of 'em are probably prayin' for her, too."

"I hope so. She could use a hand from El Señor Dios."

"How about you?"

A grim smile touched Frank's lips. "I'm not sure the Lord and I are on good speaking terms anymore. He might've given up on me a few dozen dead men ago."

"You just hush up that sort o' talk!" Luke admonished him. "You act like you're the sinner in all this, instead o' the sinned against."

Frank looked down at his right hand. "Maybe that's right," he said softly. "Maybe there's some inherent evil in a fast gun hand, no matter how it's used."

Luke snorted and said, "What a load o' horse apples *that* is! You ain't got an evil bone in your body, Frank Morgan! Oh, I ain't sayin' you're perfect—nobody is—but I've seen evil, and you ain't it."

"I appreciate that, and I'd like to think you're right, Luke. Maybe someday Beaumont will feel differently about everything. Until then, I guess I'll be riding on. He doesn't want me around here, and I don't feel much like being here, either."

Luke sighed. "Well, I reckon I've known you too long to think there's any use arguin' with you once your mind's made up. Just remember, you've always got friends here, and you're always welcome on my ranch. Anything I can do for you, just let me know."

"Actually, there is one thing," Frank said. "I'll write to you once I get where I'm going and let you know how to get hold of me. That way, if there's anything that comes up you think I ought to know, you can write to me."

"Like how Beaumont and Miss Victoria are doin', you mean?"

"Anything," Frank said again, but he was glad that his old friend had sensed what he really meant.

"I'll do that," Luke promised. He frowned. "But ain't you even goin' to stick around for a few days, just to make sure the gal's goin' to be all right?"

Frank drained the last of the coffee from his cup and stood up. "She'll be all right," he said firmly. "She's strong, and she has good blood flowing in her veins."

"Yeah," Luke agreed, his tone meaningful. "That's the truth."

Then he sat there, his face solemn, and watched his friend walk out of the saloon and vanish into the night.

Frank picked up Stormy and Dog at the livery stable, saddled the Appaloosa, and rode southeast out of Weatherford. He camped just a few miles out of town that night and then the next day continued riding toward Granbury. He could see the huge, flat-topped bluff known as Comanche Peak ahead of him. It was the most distinctive landmark in this part of the country; the town of Granbury lay just this side of it.

Frank reached the settlement that evening and stopped at a hotel on the downtown square, across from the ornate Hood County courthouse. The county was named for Confederate General John Bell Hood, and the towns of Granbury and nearby Cleburne were named for generals who had served under Hood's command, Hiram Granbury and Patrick Cleburne. Both men had been killed in battle while serving under Hood, in fact.

Frank had lived through that war, and didn't see much cause to commemorate it, but he couldn't blame people for wanting to honor the dead. And the gallantry exhibited by the outmatched Southerners who had tried to defend their homeland from the aggression of the North was certainly enough to stir the blood. But Hood, to put it bluntly, had been a terrible strategist and had led his troops into disaster on more than one occasion. Frank didn't think much of generals, and thought even less of those who wasted the lives of their men needlessly.

He mused on that during the supper he ate in the hotel dining room. Then he walked across the square to a saloon and had a drink, but only one. When he returned to the hotel and turned in, he had succeeded in pushing all the unpleasant thoughts out of his brain. It wouldn't last, he knew, but it was a welcome respite.

The next day he followed the Brazos River south toward Nemo, and he came to the tiny community late that afternoon. He heard hammering before he got there, and as he came in sight of the place where Reuben Craddock's house and blacksmith shop had stood, he saw that the rubble of the burned-down buildings had been cleared away. The framework for a new blacksmith shop was going up. Reuben hammered nails into the heavy boards as the frame took shape.

Frank reined in and rested both hands on the saddle horn as he watched Reuben work for a moment. Then he called, "You need a good carpenter's assistant?"

Reuben turned around in surprise. He had been so engrossed in the work that he hadn't heard Frank ride up. "Frank!" he exclaimed. "I didn't expect to see you again so soon. How are you?"

Frank swung down from the saddle and gripped the hand that Reuben thrust out. "I'm fine," he said.

"You must not have stayed in Weatherford for very long after your friend got married." Reuben frowned at the shadow that passed over Frank's face. "What is it? What's wrong?"

"I'll tell you about it later," Frank said. "You got another hammer?"

"Yeah, but are you sure you're up to doing that sort of work? It's only been a little over a week since you got shot, remember?"

"I'm fine," Frank assured him. "Nothing helps a man heal up like some good hard work in the fresh air. Anyway, that was just a scratch."

"If you say so."

For another couple of hours, until the light began to fade, the two men worked side by side, putting up wall studs. "I'm glad you're here," Reuben said at one point. "I'll be ready to start putting up the rafters in a day or so, and that's a two-man job, at least."

"I'm glad to help," Frank said.

"You've already done so much . . . the money and all . . . There's no way I could have afforded to do this without your help. I'll pay it all back, you know, every cent."

"There's no hurry," Frank assured him. "I figure I'll be around here for a while. . . ."

Reuben was staying with the pastor of the local church. The man didn't have another spare room, but there was plenty of space in his barn. In pleasant weather like this, Frank didn't mind staying in the barn. If it was good enough for Stormy, it was good enough for him.

Late summer turned into early fall and then into Indian summer. The blacksmith shop was finished, and Reuben began working as a smith again, rebuilding the house between jobs of horseshoeing and repairing wagon wheels.

Every week a letter arrived for Frank from Luke Perkins. Frank had written to the rancher early on, letting him know where he was staying. Luke's letters were a mixture of good news and bad. Victoria pulled through, just as the doctor had expected. It had been touch and go for a while, but her strength and her will to live, not to mention her love for Tyler Beaumont, had prevailed in the end. Her recovery had been long and hard, but she was out of danger now.

The bad news was that she couldn't walk.

The way the doctor explained it, as Luke passed it on to Frank, the bullet that had struck Victoria had nicked her backbone on its way through her body. That had damaged something the sawbones called the spinal cord, and as a result Victoria could no longer use or even feel her legs.

When Frank read that, his fingers clenched the paper involuntarily until it crumpled in his grip. He had to take several deep breaths before he calmed down enough to smooth out the letter and read the rest of what Luke had written there in a laborious scrawl. The doctor didn't know if the damage to Victoria's backbone was permanent or not. It might heal by itself, but that was the only hope. There was nothing medicine could do for her.

So what it came down to, Frank thought grimly, was that while Chas Ferguson's desire to prove that he was a faster gun hadn't resulted in Victoria's death, it had condemned her to likely spending the rest of her life in bed or in a wheelchair. That vital, energetic young woman, who had once fought off several hard cases who had been doing their best to kidnap her, was now pretty much helpless. The thought brought up a bitter, sour taste under Frank's tongue.

He had gotten over blaming himself for what had happened. Not the sort to wallow in self-pity, he saw clearly that everyone bore responsibility for his or her own actions. He hadn't forced Ferguson to hate and envy him. It had been Ferguson's decision and Ferguson's own hand that had reached for that gun. Likewise, the young man who called himself Cherokee Bob had let his own desire for notoriety cause him to throw in with Ferguson. An impulse given in to, a moment's dangerous recklessness, and lives had been ended or altered almost beyond recognition. It was a terrible thing, and Frank still didn't blame Beaumont for not wanting to have anything more to do with him, but he wasn't going to torture himself with thoughts of what he might have done to change things, either.

A stagecoach came through Nemo a couple of times a week. One day in October, the coach stopped in front of the blacksmith shop and the new house and the driver unloaded a couple of crates. Reuben looked at them, curious as to what they might hold. Frank grinned and said, "Why don't you get a hammer and open them up and have a look?"

"All right." Reuben frowned over at his friend. "What have you done now, Frank?"

"Just open the crates," Frank said with a chuckle.

Reuben got a hammer and pried the top off one of the crates. Inside, wrapped in brown paper, were books . . . dozens and dozens of books. Novels, biographies, histories, a fair selection of the classics, including the complete works of Shakespeare. Reuben took them out one by one, unwrapping them, running his fingers over the bindings, opening them to flip almost reverently through the pages. He even lifted some of them to his nose and smelled them.

"Lord, there's nothing like a book," he breathed. "Frank, I . . . I don't know what to say."

"You don't have to say anything," Frank told him. "You've done a lot for me, Reuben—"

"No more than you've done for me," the big blacksmith said.

Frank shrugged. "You're my friend, and I know what losing all those books meant to you. This is a start on replacing them."

"Thank you." Reuben laughed. "I'll have to get started building some shelves now!"

By the end of October, the shelves were up and the books were arranged on them. Only part of the shelves were filled; Reuben had plenty of room to add to his collection. Frank had kept a couple of the books for himself, to slip in his saddlebags when he rode on.

And he knew that the day was coming soon when he would be doing just that. The weeks he had spent with Reuben had been good ones and had erased some of the bleakness that had come over him following the tragedy at that country church outside Weatherford. But his restless nature was beginning to assert itself again. He hadn't been born fiddlefooted; circumstances had forced him into a life of wandering. But by now drifting was a habit, too ingrained to be ignored.

He rode over to Nemo's tiny post office to check the mail and found a letter waiting there for him from Luke Perkins. As Frank came out of the little frame building, he paused by the hitch rail where Stormy was tied and broke the seal on the letter. He unfolded the paper and began to read.

He had read only a few words when the sound of hoofbeats made him glance toward the road. He saw a rider coming toward him at a walk. To Frank's surprise, the man suddenly reached under his coat and pulled a gun. As he kicked his horse into a gallop, he shouted, "I've got you now, Morgan!"

He opened fire, spraying bullets toward Frank.

10

Instinct took over, sending Frank in a dive toward a water trough that stood to one side of the post office door. At the same time, he dropped the letter from Luke Perkins and drew his gun. As he landed, he heard a sharp whinny of pain from Stormy and knew the Appaloosa had been hit by one of the bullets flying around.

White-hot rage coursed through Frank at the thought of his horse being hurt. He lunged up from behind the trough as slugs thudded into it and triggered twice at the onrushing gunman. The first shot missed, but the second clipped the man on the left shoulder and slewed him halfway around in the saddle. He had to grab the horn to keep from falling off. His other hand, the one with the gun in it, went straight up in the air as he struggled to balance himself.

That gave Frank time to shoot him again.

This bullet struck the man squarely in the chest and knocked him backward over his horse's rump. He tumbled to the ground, but his left foot caught in the stirrup on that side. As the horse continued to bolt along the road, the man's body was dragged along with it.

Frank leaped up and stepped out into the road to

grab the reins as the horse went past. He was jerked around and almost pulled off his feet, but the horse slowed as Frank dragged down hard on the reins. After a few seconds, the animal came to a stop, its sides heaving with a mixture of fear and exertion. All the shooting had spooked it.

"It's all right now," Frank said quietly. "Just take it easy, horse. The ruckus is all over."

It was all over for the man who had attacked Frank, that was for sure. He lay on his back, his shirtfront wet with blood. He stared sightlessly up at the sky from a face that had been battered against the ground a couple of times as the horse dragged him. His features were smeared with dirt and blood, but Frank could still tell that he had never seen the man before in his life.

The man had known him, though. There was no doubt about that. He had shouted the name "Morgan" as he started firing.

The shots had drawn the postmaster out of the little building that housed his office. He walked toward Frank carrying a shotgun. "What happened, Morgan?" he asked.

Since the gunman was dead, Frank reloaded the spent shells in his Peacemaker and then pouched the revolver. "I'm not quite sure," he admitted. "This fella was gunning for me, but I don't know why or even who he is."

The postmaster scratched his jaw and frowned in thought. "Looks a mite familiar," he said after a moment. "I can't place him, though."

He wasn't the only one who had heard the shots. Down at the blacksmith shop, a quarter of a mile away, Reuben had, too. He came riding up on his mule, also carrying a scattergun like the postmaster. "Frank!" he called as he caught sight of his friend. "Are you all right?"

Frank nodded. "I wasn't hit." That reminded him of

Stormy. He swung around quickly to check on the Appaloosa.

The big horse appeared to be fine at first glance. Then Frank found a bloody streak on his flank where a bullet had burned him. That had been enough to provoke a reaction from Stormy without doing any real damage. Some ointment would fix up the bullet burn. Luck had been with both Frank and Stormy today.

Reuben swung down from the mule and studied the face of the dead man. "He looks familiar," he said, echoing the postmaster's comment. "But I can't quite . . . I know! He looks a lot like Tom Grady."

Frank remembered that name for some reason, but it took him a few seconds to pin it down. Then he recalled that Tom Grady had been the man who held the gun on Reuben while his friends beat up the blacksmith several months earlier. Later, the men had come back to take their revenge on both Frank and Reuben, but while they had succeeded in burning down the blacksmith shop and Reuben's house, three of the four had died that night. Grady had been one of them.

The postmaster went through the dead man's pockets and found a letter addressed to Al Grady. "I reckon that's him," the man said, straightening. "Brother to Tom, from the looks of it. The address on this letter is Del Rio; it's from the foreman of the spread where Grady worked last. Got the news of his death in it."

Frank nodded as he figured out what had happened. "It took this long for the letter to catch up to this man and let him know that his brother was dead and that I killed him. He rode all the way up here from Del Rio to settle the score."

The postmaster snorted. "Hell, from what I've heard, Tom Grady needed killin'."

"Maybe so," Reuben said, "but a blood bond is mighty strong. It probably didn't matter to Al Grady that his brother got what was coming to him. He just wanted to avenge his death."

"All that got him was a couple of slugs and a hole in the ground." The postmaster shook his head. "Damned fool."

Something white caught Morgan's eye as it blew along the ground not far away, and he remembered the letter he had dropped when the shooting started. He hurried after the paper and snatched it up. He didn't want to lose even one of Luke's letters, not when they contained news about Beaumont and Victoria. And in the brief glimpse he had gotten before all hell broke loose, Luke had mentioned Beaumont.

Frank stood there now and read the letter. After the usual *"Dear Frank, Hope this finds you well"* opening, Luke got down to business in a hurry.

Tyler Beaumont had left Weatherford. And he hadn't taken Victoria with him.

That came as something of a shock to Frank. He never would have pegged Beaumont as the type to leave a woman once he had married her. Beaumont was an honorable man; the words "for better or worse" would hold great meaning for him. But as he read on, Frank saw that it wasn't a case of Beaumont abandoning Victoria.

The Rangers had sent him away on a job, instead.

"There's some sorta trouble down in Brown County," Luke wrote. *"Judge Monfore told me about it, but he didn't know what it was exactly. Said it probably has something to do with a squabble they're having down there over barbed wire. But the Rangers wanted a man who wasn't knowed in those parts to look into it, and Tyler got picked. Miss Victoria is staying with her folks whilst he's gone. Don't worry about her, Frank, the judge and Miz Mercy will see to it that she's took care of."*

Frank knew that. Mercy and the judge were devoted to Victoria; anything she needed, they would see to it that she had it. They had been helping Beaumont look after her ever since the tragic accident on the day of the wedding. Frank knew from previous letters that Victoria had insisted she and Beaumont have their own place, just like any other married couple, so they had rented a house not far from the Monfore place. That way Mercy and the judge could help out when Beaumont's Rangering took him away from home.

From the sound of this letter, though, Beaumont was going to be away for quite some time, or else Victoria wouldn't have moved back in with her parents. And if there was trouble brewing in Brown County over barbed wire, then Beaumont was definitely riding into danger.

Barbed wire had been around for more than a dozen years, having been developed in the Midwest by a man named Glidden. Its use had been spreading slowly westward ever since, and its introduction had caused trouble in nearly every area where it showed up. Cattlemen hated the stuff for two reasons: The cruel metal barbs sometimes injured the cows who rubbed against it, and the very notion of fencing off land rubbed men who had always lived with the concept of open range the wrong way. A man didn't have to *own* land when there were millions and millions of acres free for the grazing. He didn't have to worry about water when he could drive his cattle to any number of creeks or rivers and let them drink their fill. It was a simple system—a man had the right to use whatever he could hold—and the ranchers didn't want to change it, saw no need to change it. It was the farmers, the damn sodbusters and homesteaders, who wanted to come in and ruin everything, the cattlemen thought.

There had been shooting wars over barbed wire in Montana, Wyoming, and other places, and now it looked like there might be one in Texas, too. Beaumont was going to be right in the middle of it, from the sound of things.

And while Beaumont was a good Ranger, Frank thought, he didn't know if the young man was good enough to tame a whole county.

Frank had already begun to feel the urge to move on. Now he had a reason to do so, and a destination.

The Drifter would be drifting to Brown County. . . .

Reuben didn't try to convince Frank not to go. "I've enjoyed your company, and I really appreciate everything you've done to help me get back on my feet, Frank," the blacksmith told him that night over supper. "But I know you're ready to ride and you want to help out your friend Tyler." Reuben paused and then said, "The question is, will he want your help?"

As they had become better friends, Frank had shared the story of what had happened at the wedding. He was, by nature, a reticent man most of the time, but after working side by side with Reuben for weeks, he had come to trust the blacksmith. Now Frank just shrugged and shook his head.

"I don't know. He was pretty angry the last time he spoke to me, but some time has gone by since then. Maybe he doesn't blame me quite as much now for what happened to Victoria."

"He shouldn't have blamed you at all," Reuben rumbled. "It wasn't your fault Ferguson and his friend were kill-crazy young lunatics."

"I'm the one Ferguson was gunning for, though."

Reuben put down his fork and looked steadily across the table at Frank. "If a man dies trying to climb a mountain, is it the mountain's fault? The man is the one who decided to try it."

"It's not quite the same thing."

Reuben grunted. "Seems like exactly the same thing to me."

What Reuben said made sense, Frank thought. But he still didn't know whether or not Tyler Beaumont would see it that way.

The only way to find out would be to ride to Brown County and offer his help to the young Ranger. And if Beaumont turned it down . . . well, there was no law against hanging around a place and being close by just in case a friend needed some assistance.

Once he made up his mind to do something, Frank Morgan didn't waste any time. He was up early the next morning, packing a few supplies that Reuben could spare. He would provision up in Tolar, the next settlement on the trail that led southwest toward Brown County. Brownwood, the county seat, was about a three-day ride, Frank estimated.

Reuben tried to talk him into taking even more than he did. When Frank refused the food, the blacksmith tried to press more books on him as they stood in front of the shop.

"I've got plenty to read," Frank said with a smile and a shake of his head. "One of the books I put in the saddlebags is *Moby-Dick*. I've been trying to get through it, off and on, for years."

"Ah, Ishmael," Reuben said. "The wanderer. An apt book for you, Frank." He put out a hand. "Good luck to you."

Frank shook with him. "And to you, Reuben. If you ever need help, get in touch with my lawyers. They'll know where to find me."

"And if you need help, here I am. Don't forget that."

Frank swung up into the saddle. Stormy frisked a little back and forth, knowing they were leaving and eager to be on the trail again. Dog was the same way, running around and around the horse and letting out an occasional excited yip.

Frank heeled the Appaloosa into a trot and turned in the saddle to lift his hand in a wave. Then he turned his attention to the trail in front of him.

The countryside was rolling hills, heavily wooded in places and open and lushly grassed in others. Fall was far enough along so that many of the leaves on the trees had changed color, painting a tapestry of red and gold and orange across the slopes. The air was cool but not cold, crisp and clear and invigorating as Frank drew in deep breaths. As much as he had enjoyed the time he'd spent with Reuben, it felt mighty good to have a purpose again.

The miles fell behind him. He spent the nights under the stars, snug in his bedroll against the autumn chill, and during the days crossed small rivers such as the Paluxy, the Bosque, and the Leon. He stopped briefly in Stephenville and Dublin, the latter so called because the rolling green countryside around the settlement had reminded one of its founders of his native Ireland. Beyond Dublin the terrain grew a little more flat, and the soil was sandier. This was cotton, peanut, and sorghum country.

Around noon on the third day after leaving Reuben's place, Frank rode into the town of Comanche, with its famous hanging tree on the square next to the courthouse. One of the first settlers in the area had used that big oak for cover as he fought off an attack by a band of warriors from the tribe that had given the town its name. The settler, Uncle Mart Fleming, had objected so strenuously when the townspeople wanted to cut down the oak that they had left it there to appease the old pioneer. Since then, more than one badman had danced at the end of a rope thrown over one of the wide-spreading branches.

One famous badman who hadn't been strung up on that oak was John Wesley Hardin. Some years earlier, Wes Hardin had shot and killed Brown County Deputy Sheriff Charley Webb in a saloon right here in Comanche. Webb was out of his bailiwick— Comanche was the seat of Comanche County—and not only that, he had treacherously drawn and fired first at Hardin after convincing the gunslinger that he was his friend. Hardin had repaid that betrayal with a fatal bullet, and even though he might have made a case for self-defense, he ran instead, taking off for the tall and uncut. Later a mob, incensed over Hardin's escape, had lynched a couple of his relatives from that very tree on the corner of the courthouse square.

Frank thought about those things as he rode past the oak and reined Stormy to a halt in front of one of the saloons facing the courthouse. Texas had a long and bloody history, all right, and he was afraid it was due to get bloodier before it got better.

He went into the saloon, and when the bartender came over, Frank asked him for a pot of coffee. "Sure thing, mister," the man replied. "You don't want a beer or some whiskey, though?"

"Nope, just the coffee," Frank said.

When the bartender brought the cup of the strong black brew, Frank sipped it appreciatively and then, as if he were just making idle conversation, he said, "I hear there's been some sort of ruckus going on next door in Brown County."

The bartender snorted. "Ruckus is puttin' it mildly, mister. There's been several shootin' scrapes, and if it keeps up, somebody's goin' to wind up dead. It's a wonder nobody's been killed already over there."

"Fighting over barbed wire or something, aren't they? I heard a little about it."

"Yeah. I tell you, that stuff is the Devil's invention, sure enough. Every time it comes into the country, there's blood spilled. Seems like that, anyway."

Frank drank some more coffee and nodded. "Yeah, from what I've heard, the big ranchers really don't like it."

"Well . . ." The bartender scratched his jaw. "That ain't quite the way it is down here. This fight is a mite different."

"How's that?" Frank asked with a frown, still sounding just curious.

"It's the big ranchers who brought in the wire. The way they see it, there are too many small spreads startin' up, as well as too many farmers movin' in. So a year or two back, they just bought up all the land they could get their hands on and started fencin' it in. Trouble is, a lot of the little fellas are free-rangers, and they don't want to be fenced *out*. So they started cuttin' the fences."

"That's different, all right," Frank agreed. In the other range wars that had been fought over barbed wire, the conflict had come about because the smaller ranchers and farmers used the wire to protect their smaller holdings from the cattle barons. Frank was glad he had run into this talkative bartender, who obviously kept up to date on what was going on in the neighboring county. What Frank had learned here in this saloon could turn out to be important information.

Luke's letter had said that Tyler Beaumont had been sent to Brown County because he wasn't known in this part of the state. That could mean only one thing: Beaumont was working undercover. Frank wondered which side he had allied himself with.

There was only one way to find out. He finished his coffee, dropped a coin on the bar to pay for it, and went back outside. Dog sat on the boardwalk in front of the saloon, keeping an eye on things. He bounded up and wagged his tail when Frank came out of the building. The big cur was ready to be on the move again.

So was Frank. He pulled the reins loose from the hitch rail and swung up into the saddle. He turned Stormy toward the southwest, figuring that he could make Brownwood by nightfall.

But he had ridden only a short distance down the street before a harsh voice called sternly, "Morgan! Hold it right there, mister!"

11

Frank brought Stormy to a halt and looked over to see that he was in front of a large, two-story building made of tan sandstone blocks. The iron bars in the windows on the second floor told him the building was Comanche's jail. A man had just stepped out the front door of the place and was now striding toward Frank, a grim expression on his face. He wore a dusty black suit, a black Stetson, a white shirt, and a string tie. His face was lined and weathered, and a gray mustache drooped over his mouth.

The tin star pinned to the lapel of his coat made it clear that he was a lawman, mostly likely the sheriff of Comanche County.

"Don't try anything, Morgan," he said as he walked up.

"I wasn't planning to," Frank responded calmly. "I was just riding by, Sheriff. I assume you *are* the sheriff?"

"Damn right I am. I was at my desk inside when I saw you through the window and recognized you. What are you doing in Comanche County?"

"Passing through," Frank said with a shrug. "I stopped for a cup of coffee. No law against that, is there?"

"There's a law against gunfighters coming in and shooting up the town," the lawman snapped.

Frank's eyes narrowed. He controlled the anger he felt welling up inside him and kept his voice steady and quiet as he said, "Look at my gun, Sheriff."

The man's eyes dropped to the walnut grips of the Colt. "Yeah? What about it?"

"It's in the holster. That's where it's been ever since I rode into town, and that's where I intend for it to stay . . . unless somebody forces me to do otherwise."

It was the sheriff's turn to squint angrily. "Is that a threat, mister?"

Frank shook his head. "Nope. Just a simple statement of the facts."

The two men traded intent looks for a moment, and then the sheriff said, "What's your business in Comanche?"

"I told you, I don't have any." Frank kept a tight rein on the impatience he felt. "I'm just riding through on my way somewhere else."

"Where?" The question came quick and sharp.

"Brownwood, not that it's any of your business."

The lawman nodded. "I figured as much. Going over to Brown County to hire out your gun, aren't you? I know all about you, Morgan."

"Evidently you don't. I've done a lot of things, Sheriff, but selling my services as a gunman isn't one of them."

"Oh, no? Then how come you seem to wind up in every shooting scrape that comes along, wherever you go?"

Frank's lips curved slightly in a thin smile. "Sometimes I just can't help taking cards in the game, especially if there's some cheating going on."

"But you don't plan on starting any trouble here in Comanche?"

Frank sighed in frustration. He said, "No, Sheriff, I don't. But I can if you've got your heart set on it."

The lawman's face tightened. "There's no call for that. Just ride on, Morgan. I don't want to see your face in these parts again."

Frank didn't say anything, just turned Stormy and hitched him into a walk again. He didn't like the sheriff's attitude, but it would be more trouble than it was worth to keep arguing with the man.

"Go see Duggan, gunslinger!" the sheriff called after him. "He'll pay you your blood money!"

Frank didn't turn around, didn't give the sheriff the satisfaction of seeing him respond to the taunt. But he filed the name away in his brain. Somebody called Duggan was hiring gunmen.

That might be a good place to start looking for Tyler Beaumont.

West of Comanche was a long line of rugged, rocky bluffs running north and south. The trail meandered through a shallow pass. Frank left the farmland around Comanche behind and entered country that was more suitable for ranching. There was only one settlement between Comanche and Brownwood, a little place called Blanket. Frank skirted it and pushed on, eager to reach Brownwood before nightfall.

The sun was sinking behind a big hill just west of the settlement when Frank rode into Brownwood. He stopped at the first saloon he came to, dismounted, tied the Appaloosa's reins to a hitch rail, and told Dog to stay. He stepped up onto the boardwalk. Since the afternoon had been fairly warm, the saloon's doors were open, with only the batwings barring entrance. Frank pushed them aside and stepped into the room.

It was the sort of place he had seen hundreds of times in hundreds of other towns and settlements, a big, high-ceilinged room lit by oil lamps that gave off a smoky haze. That haze mixed with tobacco smoke from a dozen quirlies to turn the air a permanent grayish-blue. Sawdust littered the floor to soak up any spilled beer or whiskey, but it couldn't soak up the raw tang of alcohol. Underlying that were the smells of manure and sweat that followed men who worked with cattle. To the right was a long, polished hardwood bar with mirrors and paintings of nude, extremely voluptuous women on the walls behind it. Tables where men sat and drank or played cards were scattered over the floor to the left. At the back of the room, also to the left, was a staircase that led up to the second floor, where rooms opened onto a balcony that overlooked the main room. To the right of the stairs was a small stage with a piano tucked into a corner of it. The sign outside had proclaimed this to be MCKELVEY'S PALACE. It was nice enough, as frontier saloons went, but it didn't really look all that palatial to Frank Morgan.

Since it was early, the place wasn't very busy. Half-a-dozen men stood at the bar drinking while four more played a lazy game of poker at one of the tables. Only one bartender was on duty, a tall man with a rust-colored beard, and he wasn't having any trouble keeping up with the demand. He sauntered along the bar, refilling shot glasses and drawing mugs of beer whenever one of the cowboys standing at the hardwood asked for a drink.

There were two women in the saloon as well, one of them standing at the end of the bar, the other watching the poker game, her right hand resting on the shoulder of one of the players. Both wore spangled dresses with the necklines low in the front and the skirts high enough to reveal stockings rolled just below the knees. The one at the table was older, probably in her thirties, with a doughy face and short, tightly curled brown hair that was starting to go gray.

The woman at the bar was no more than twenty, slender and blond and still relatively pretty, although the ravages of her life were starting to show in her face, especially at the corners of her mouth and eyes. She gave Frank a smile and started toward him as soon as he came into the room.

"Hello, handsome," she greeted him. "Just ride in?"

He saw her reaching to take his arm and turned slightly so that she grasped the left one instead of the right. Her eyes narrowed a little, and he knew she had noticed the move. She had enough experience to recognize a Coltman when she saw one, and he had just confirmed her judgment.

"That's right," he answered.

"You must be thirsty, then. You come right on over here with me and have a drink. First one's on the house, you know. That's Mr. McKelvey's policy."

"No, I didn't know that," Frank said. "It's been a long time since I've been to Brownwood."

"Oh, you're not a complete stranger in these parts, then?"

He shook his head and allowed her to steer him over to the bar. Bartenders and saloon girls always knew a lot about what was going on in a town, probably because people tended to talk around them and sort of forgot they were there. In a way it was an insult that they went so easily unnoticed, but Frank knew that was the way a lot of them wanted it. More than one apron and calico cat had supplemented their income with a little discreet blackmail.

"My name's Annie," the blonde said. "Annie Milam. What's yours?"

"Frank." He didn't offer a last name.

"Rusty, bring Frank here a drink," Annie said to the bartender, who obviously got his nickname from his beard.

"Sure. What'll you have, Frank?" the barman asked.

"Beer will be fine."

"Comin' right up." Rusty drew the beer, filling a mug and sliding it across the bar. "There you go. No charge. I guess Annie explained the house policy."

Frank nodded. "She did." He picked up the mug and took a sip. The beer was cool and not too bitter. He nodded his approval.

Rusty picked up a rag and began polishing a glass. "Just passing through Brownwood?"

Beside Frank, Annie still had hold of his left arm, and she looked up at him expectantly, waiting for his answer to Rusty's question. They were pumping him for information, Frank knew, and they weren't even being very subtle about it. Well, turnabout was supposed to be fair play, he thought. He had come in here intending to find someone and get as much information out of them as he could.

"Actually, I'm looking for a job," he said.

"Cowboying?" Rusty sounded a little doubtful, probably because Frank was a little old to be doing such work . . . even though he was still perfectly capable of it.

"I can make a hand if I have to," Frank said, "but I was really thinking about something a little more lucrative and less boring than following a bunch of cows around."

Rusty scratched at his beard. "What did you have in mind?"

Frank took the plunge and said, "I was told that a man named Duggan might be hiring."

That made both Annie and Rusty stare at him, and he said it loudly enough so that the men along the bar and at the table heard him, too. One of the men at the bar set his half-empty beer mug down with a thump and turned toward Frank, his eyes narrowing. "What did you say?" he demanded.

"That I heard a man named Duggan might be hiring," Frank replied.

"Yeah—hirin' killers!"

"Shut up that kind of talk," one of the men at the table said.

The first man swung sharply toward him. "Don't tell me what to do!"

Suddenly there was a lot more tension in the saloon than there had been when Frank first walked in. Well, he had intended to stir the pot a little, he thought, and from the looks of things he had succeeded.

"Boys, boys," Rusty said, holding out his hands palms down and motioning softly toward the bar. "We don't want any trouble in here. You know Mr. McKelvey doesn't allow any fighting."

The man who had spoken to Frank gave a disgusted snort. "You mean McKelvey wants to straddle the fence and not make anybody mad." He picked up his beer and downed the rest of it. Again he thumped the mug on the hardwood. He wiped the back of his hand across his mouth and said, "But you know what happens when somebody tries to straddle a barbed-wire fence?"

Rusty just shook his head.

"He's liable to get his balls cut off," the cowboy said. He looked back at Frank and went on. "Duggan is a coward and a snake, and so is anybody who wants to work for him."

"I never heard of the man until today," Frank pointed out.

"That don't matter. Get this straight, mister—if Duggan starts bringin' in hired guns, the Pecan Bayou will be runnin' red with blood before long!"

"That's mighty fine talk," Frank said.

"It's more than talk. It's a promise! And if you don't

believe it—" The man stepped away from the bar, and his hand swung dangerously close to the butt of his gun.

Frank bit back a sigh. Even when folks didn't know who he was, they kept challenging him to gunfights. Did he have a damn sign on his back or something?

"Annie, you'd better move," he said quietly to the saloon girl.

Her face had gone pale under its war paint. "I was just thinking the same thing," she said. She let go of his arm and stepped back. Behind the bar, Rusty was edging away. The other men in front of the bar picked up their drinks and scattered, but as they moved across the room, Frank noticed that they steered well clear of the table where the poker game had been going on. That told him something, too. There were two factions in this saloon, and while they didn't like each other, they weren't quite ready to start shooting.

Except for the man facing him, who stood there with his hand clawed over the butt of an old Remington. It was a single-action revolver, Frank noted, and would have to be cocked before it could be fired. That would slow things down even more and assured that the man had no chance against the Drifter in a gunfight. He probably wouldn't have stood much of a chance even without that disadvantage.

"You don't want to do this," Frank said.

"The hell I don't. It's time somebody sent a message to Duggan and Wilcox and all the others like them. They can't run roughshod over the whole county anymore. It's a new day."

Actually, it was the end of an old one, as dusk was gathering outside. Frank had just enough time for that thought, and then the man grabbed for his gun.

12

Frank didn't wait, as he sometimes did, for the other man to get his gun out of its holster. He went ahead and drew right away, giving himself as much time as possible to place his shot where he wanted it.

The Peacemaker roared and the slug ripped through the man's upper right arm, to the outside of the bone. He rocked back and yelled in pain. His iron had just cleared leather. It slipped from suddenly nerveless fingers and thumped to the floor. He hadn't had a chance to ear back the hammer, so there was little danger of it going off from the impact.

The man clutched his wounded arm with his other hand and slumped against the bar. Tears sprang unbidden to his eyes and rolled down his cheeks. "You . . . you son of a bitch!" he gasped as he glared at Frank.

"Looks to me like you ought to be thanking him instead of cussing him, Rawlings," one of the men at the table said. "His gun was out fast enough he had time to put four pills in your belly if he wanted to, instead of just creasing your arm."

A tendril of smoke curled from the barrel of Frank's gun. He glanced around, saw that nobody else in the room seemed inclined to continue the fight, and then reloaded the spent chamber before he slipped the Colt back in its holster.

"See if you can move your arm, mister," he said to the man he had wounded. "I was trying not to break the humerus."

"I don't see . . . nothin' funny about this," the man grated. But when he moved his arm gingerly, it seemed to work. Frank nodded in satisfaction.

"Go find a sawbones and get that cleaned and patched up," he told the man. "It ought to heal just fine, and you shouldn't have any trouble using it in the future." He added, "Just don't use it to draw on me again. I'll kill you next time."

Muttering curses and still holding his bullet-creased arm, Rawlings stumbled out of the saloon. His friends followed him, casting baleful glares at Frank as they went past him.

When they were gone, the man who had spoken up from the table said to Frank, "Bring your drink over here and join us, stranger."

Frank hesitated only a second before he picked up his drink and walked across the room to the table. He gave a polite nod to the four men seated there. He didn't know much about which side was which in the conflict dividing Brown County, but talking to these men might give him the opportunity to learn more.

The spokesman held out a hand as Frank pulled back a chair and sat down. "Ed MacDonald," he introduced himself. He was tall and lean, with a ready grin and wiry black hair under a cuffed-back Stetson.

Frank shook hands with him and then MacDonald continued the introductions, nodding to each man around the table in turn. Like MacDonald, they wore range clothes and looked tough and capable, but there was nothing of the gunslinger about them. They were just top hands.

"Pitch Carey, Dave Osmond, and Stiles Warren. We all ride for Earl Duggan."

"Reckon you can tell me, then, if he's hiring."

"I reckon the boss is always in the market for a good man. More so lately, when a fella can handle a gun like you just did."

"Who was that I had to shoot?" Frank asked.

"Al Rawlings. Got a small spread southeast of town. Those fellas with him were the same sort. They run little greasy-sack outfits that don't amount to much." MacDonald shrugged. "They probably don't have more than a few dozen cows apiece."

The cowboy's voice was tinged with contempt. Frank didn't necessarily approve of the attitude, but he could understand it. A man like MacDonald who was used to working for a big outfit would naturally look down on men who ran smaller ranches, even though those men actually owned property and a cowboy might not own anything except a saddle and the clothes on his back.

Frank took a sip of his beer and said, "Sounds to me like there's some trouble in these parts."

"You could say that," one of the other cowboys put in. "Rawlings and the men like him are getting too damned big for their britches."

The older saloon girl still stood there by the table. She said, "Oh, they're not so bad, Pitch. They just don't want to be squeezed out. You can't blame them for that."

Pitch Carey snorted. "I can damn sure blame 'em for cuttin' fences, though, and for takin' potshots at us when we try to fix what they've torn up!"

"You don't know they're the ones doing the shooting," the woman argued.

MacDonald said, "Who else could it be, Midge?"

"Well, I don't know, but I believe in giving folks the benefit of the doubt."

"Around here that'll get you killed," Carey said.

Annie had been at the bar talking to Rusty. Now she came over to Frank and said to him, "Rusty says to tell you thanks for not shooting up the place. If you'd shot Al Rawlings in the body, though, the bullet might not have gone all the way through. Now there's a hole in the back wall Rusty has to patch."

"Rawlings was on the prod," Frank said with a shrug, "but I didn't think he deserved killing. Sorry about the bullet hole."

"Oh, don't worry about it," Annie said. "I think Rusty was halfway joking, anyway. It could have been a lot worse." She glanced at the batwinged entrance. "Speaking of which . . ."

Frank glanced in that direction. A couple of men in town suits pushed through the batwings and came into the saloon. They carried shotguns and looked around quickly, their gazes coming to rest on the table where Frank sat with the cowboys from Earl Duggan's ranch. The two newcomers started toward them.

Frank would have had no trouble recognizing them as lawmen, even without the badges they wore. He had been expecting at least one star-packer to show up to investigate the shot that had been fired.

"I got a report of a gun going off in here, Mac-Donald," one of the men said as he came up to the table. He was medium height and thick-set, with a close-cropped brown beard. "What happened? Which of you Slash D boys fired that shot?"

"Wasn't any of us, Marshal," MacDonald replied. He nodded toward Frank. "It was this fella here." He smiled. "Come to think of it, I don't believe I ever got your name, mister."

"It's Morgan," the Drifter said. "Frank Morgan."

That drew stares from everyone in the room. Obviously, all of them had heard of him. Silence stretched out for a moment and then was broken by the tall, lanky Stiles Warren exclaiming, "Lord have mercy! I've read books about this fella, but I figured he was dead by now!"

"Looks plenty alive to me," the second lawman said. He was short and bandy-legged, with bristly sand-colored hair under his hat. His eyes were pale blue and watery. Frank didn't like what he saw in them.

The bearded lawman looked at Frank and said, "I don't care for gunslingers in my town, Morgan. What were you doing, showing off?"

Before Frank could answer, Ed MacDonald said, "You could call it that, Marshal. Al Rawlings got his back up and drew on Morgan here. Morgan could've killed him without any trouble, but he just creased his arm instead. It was mighty good shooting, if you ask me, and Morgan did Rawlings a favor."

The marshal grunted. "Is that so? That the way it happened, Morgan?"

Frank nodded. "You didn't see Rawlings outside?"

"No. A citizen reported the shot."

"Go check with your local doctors," Frank suggested. "I told Rawlings he ought to get the wound cleaned and bandaged. Of course, I don't know if he took my advice or not."

The marshal regarded Frank intently for a moment and then said, "You're a mighty cool customer, aren't you?"

Frank drained the last of his beer from the mug. As he set the empty on the table, he said, "I just didn't think there was any law against defending myself."

The lawman looked around the table. "You'll all swear that Rawlings drew first?"

The Slash D cowboys nodded, and Rusty said from behind the bar, "So will I, Marshal. The girls and I saw the whole thing."

Annie and Midge nodded agreement.

The marshal looked a little disappointed, but not as much as the deputy with him. Frank thought the little sandy-haired man had been itching to arrest somebody, and if the potential prisoner had resisted, so much the better.

"Looks like we're not needed here," the marshal said grudgingly. "Come on, Skeet."

He turned and started toward the door. The deputy waited a moment longer, staring meaningfully at Frank as he stood there. Then he turned and sauntered after his boss. Both men left the saloon.

"Your local law isn't very friendly," Frank commented with a thin smile.

"Marshal Keever's not so bad," Dave Osmond said.

"Skeet Harlan's loco, though," Pitch Carey put in. "He handles most of the gun work, when there's some to be done."

"And I'd wager he enjoys it," Frank said.

Carey nodded. "He seems to."

"Which side are they on?"

"What do you mean by that?" MacDonald drawled.

"I mean, in this war that seems to be brewing between your boss and the other big ranchers and the small outfits, which side is the marshal on?"

MacDonald shook his head. "Keever says he's neutral, just like Ace McKelvey and Newton over at the hardware store and the Covert brothers and all the other businessmen in Brownwood. I reckon they think they can't afford to take sides. When push comes to shove, though, I imagine they'll back Mr. Duggan and his friends. Storekeepers always know who's got the most money to spend."

That was true, Frank thought.

He was getting a pretty good idea of the layout now. Clearly there had been violent incidents before this shooting tonight, and he could understand why the Texas Rangers would want to get a man on the scene before the conflict turned into a full-fledged range war. Hard feelings ran deep, though, especially on the side of the smaller ranchers, and Frank wondered if Tyler Beaumont—or anyone else—could head off the trouble that seemed to be on the horizon.

He was intensely curious where Beaumont was and what he was doing, but he had already decided not to ask the cowboys if any of them knew him. For one thing, Beaumont might not be using his real name, and for another, Frank had no idea how the young Ranger was conducting his investigation. He didn't want to do anything that might inadvertently ruin Beaumont's plans or put him in even more danger.

No, for the time being Frank would play his own cards close to the vest and continue learning as much as he could about the situation. To that end, he said, "Getting back to what brought me here, I reckon I ought to take a ride out to this Slash D ranch of yours and talk to Duggan himself about a job."

"That's what you'll have to do," MacDonald agreed. "I ramrod the crew, but Mr. Duggan does all the hiring and firing. We'll be riding that way in a while. You're welcome to trail along with us if you want to."

The other three cowboys nodded their agreement with that invitation.

"Much obliged," Frank said with a smile as he took out the makin's and began to build a quirly. "I reckon I'll just do that."

"Good," Pitch Carey said. "Now, let's get back to the game. The cards've probably gotten cold, just when I was startin' to win a few hands."

"Deal you in, Morgan?" Stiles Warren asked.

Frank shook his head. "I'll just watch, if you boys don't mind."

No one objected, so he snapped a lucifer to life, lit the cigarette, and sat there watching as the cards were dealt and the game continued. Annie brought him another beer from the bar and then stood behind him, resting a hand lightly on his shoulder. Frank figured she would have been amenable to going upstairs with him if he had wanted to, but even though more than a year had passed since Dixie was murdered, those fires were still banked within him.

A pleasant hour or so passed while the cowboys played cards. Their luck ebbed and flowed. Ed Mac-Donald probably won the most, Frank judged, but everybody came out close enough to even that they wcre all happy when the game finally broke up.

"Guess we'd better be getting back to the ranch," MacDonald said as he stowed away his winnings and stood up. The other men got to their feet as well, including Frank. Pitch pulled Midge into his arms for a quick kiss that made her laugh in pleasure.

A few other customers had come into the Palace while the game was going on, mostly townsmen and a couple of men who looked like freighters. Annie had drifted over to the bar to try to get somebody to buy her a drink, but as Frank started toward the door with the cowboys, she cast a wistful glance toward him, as if the evening hadn't worked out the way she had hoped it would. He noticed but pretended he didn't. He had enough to worry about right now without any romantic entanglements.

Before he could get out of the saloon, his plate got a little more crowded as the batwings were slapped aside and a woman strode in, demanding in a loud voice, "Where the hell's the bastard who shot my brother?"

13

She was an impressive specimen of womanhood, even at first glance. Even though she was tall and broad-shouldered, there was nothing mannish about her. The lush curves of her body saw to that. Fiery red hair fell around her shoulders and tumbled down her back. She wore a gray wool shirt, a brown leather vest, and a brown riding skirt. A brown flat-crowned Stetson hung on her back, held there by the chin strap around her neck. A black bandanna was also tied around her neck.

It was a pretty odd getup for a woman, but the most unusual thing of all was the gun belt strapped around her waist. The butt of a Colt jutted up from the holster attached to the belt.

Angry green eyes searched the room until the hostile gaze lit on Frank and stayed there. The woman put her fists on her hips and said, "You. You must be the one."

"Take it easy, Miz Stratton," Ed MacDonald said. "If Al told you the truth about what happened, you already know he could've been hurt a lot worse. Matter of fact, he could have been killed without too much trouble on Morgan's part."

"Morgan?" the redhead echoed, still looking at Frank.

"That's right," Pitch said. "This is Frank Morgan, the gunfighter."

The redhead didn't look impressed. If anything, she grew even angrier. "So you picked a fight with my brother, knowing that you had him outmatched," she accused.

A voice in the back of Frank's brain warned him that arguing with this redheaded Amazon would be a waste of time. But he ignored it and said, "That isn't the way it was."

"No? Then tell me how it really was, Mr. Frank Morgan."

He rubbed his jaw and then nodded. "All right, I will. I came in here not looking for any trouble, and your brother braced me and insulted me just because I mentioned Earl Duggan's name. Then he went for his gun. I didn't have any choice but to draw mine, but I tried not to hurt him too bad, just like Ed here said. And *that's* the way it was."

By the time he finished, his voice was pretty forceful, though he hadn't really raised it. The redhead still glared at him, but she didn't say anything for a moment. When she spoke, she said, "Al didn't say anything about reaching for his gun first."

"There you go," Frank said.

"Are you calling him a liar?"

"Just saying that he didn't tell you the whole story. Take that for what you will, ma'am."

"Don't ma'am me!" she snapped. "I'm no puling little Southern belle!"

"I reckon I can see that," Frank said.

He knew that was going a little too far, but the woman was starting to irritate him. He thought for a second she was going to haul off and take a punch at him, just like a man might have. Instead she pointed a finger at him and said, "Stay off our range. If I catch you out there, I'll shoot you on sight. You understand, Morgan?"

"I don't know that it's legal to shoot a man just because he rides across your place."

That bit of logic bounced right off her. "Just remember what I said," she warned him. Then she turned and stalked out of the saloon, slapping the batwings aside with greater force than necessary.

Stiles Warren let out a low whistle. "I'd say she don't like you even a little bit, Frank."

"I got that impression," Frank agreed with a wry smile. "Who was she, anyway, besides Al Rawlings' sister?"

"Callie Stratton," Ed MacDonald said. "She's older than Rawlings and a widow woman. Moved back in on his place when her husband died. He was a tinhorn gambler up in Dallas. The way I heard it, somebody didn't care for the way he dealt the cards one night— off the bottom of the deck—and ventilated him."

"She talked like the ranch was as much hers as her brother's."

MacDonald shrugged. "I reckon that's pretty much the way she feels about it. She's the sort of woman who barges in and takes over, if you know what I mean."

Frank did, although luckily he hadn't encountered too many women like that in his life.

They left the saloon and untied their horses from the hitch rails along the street. After everyone was mounted up, Ed MacDonald led the way out of town, heading south. The sun had set and the stars were out overhead, a sparkling canopy against the black sky. The air had grown cool with the setting of the sun.

"I reckon our cook'll have some grub heated up for us when we get there," MacDonald said. "You'll be welcome to join us, Frank."

"I'm obliged. I didn't get any supper back there in Brownwood."

"Mr. Duggan never turns a man away hungry."

That didn't surprise Frank. Western hospitality demanded no less.

He thought about the geography of the area as he rode, and after a few minutes he said, "I guess Rawlings' spread must lie east of the Slash D?"

"Due east," MacDonald replied. "Of course, it's pretty small, like I said. We only share a few miles of border with it. Below that is Thad Wilcox's Flying W."

"Wilcox is another of the big ranchers?"

"That's right. The Slash D is probably the biggest spread in the county, but Wilcox's place is almost as big. North of Rawlings is the Horseshoe, another good-sized ranch that belongs to a man named Calhoun. It loops around east of Rawlings, too."

A frown creased Frank's forehead as he thought about that. "Wait a minute," he said. "Rawlings has Duggan to the west, Wilcox to the south, and Calhoun to the north and east. Have all those spreads put up fences?"

"Damn right. Otherwise Rawlings would be running his cows on land that doesn't belong to him."

"But how does he get them out when it comes time to take them to market?"

"I don't rightly know. It hasn't come up so far, since Jim Calhoun just finished fencing his spread this past summer. But it's Rawlings' problem, not ours. He's got no legal right to cut the fences, and he sure as hell's got no right to shoot at punchers from the other spreads."

"Do you know he has?"

Pitch Carey said, "I've heard more than one bullet sing past my ears while I was ridin' the east line. The shots came from Rawlings' range."

"But you didn't actually see him?"

Carey shook his head. "No, whoever was burnin' powder was behind some trees on a hill, and he took off when I loosed a few rounds back at him. But it was Rawlings, all right, or one of those hard cases who work for him."

"Yet you were all in the Palace tonight, getting along all right from the looks of it," Frank pointed out.

"Well, I couldn't *prove* it was Rawlings," Carey said with a shrug. "And McKelvey's got the coldest beer in town."

In its own way, that made perfect sense to Frank. For the most part, range disputes stayed out on the range. Men who might slap leather if they ran into each other elsewhere would ignore each other in a saloon. Of course, sometimes the bad feelings boiled to the surface anyway, no matter what the surroundings, especially when folks had been drinking. Nothing fueled the flames of hatred quite like a few shots of Who-Hit-John.

Nor could he blame Al Rawlings for resenting the big ranchers and the men who rode for them. From the sound of it, Rawlings was penned in, surrounded by barbed wire so that he couldn't get his stock to market without cutting one of the fences, which was illegal, and driving the cattle across another man's land. That just wasn't right.

But until he located Tyler Beaumont and talked to the young Ranger, there wasn't anything he could do about it. He just hoped Beaumont had some sort of plan, and that he wouldn't be so stiff-necked and stubborn that he wouldn't accept a little help.

A big harvest moon rose, casting silvery light over the landscape. Frank and his four companions trotted their mounts easily along the trail. They didn't stop until MacDonald suddenly reined in and motioned for the others to halt. He sat tensely erect in the saddle as if something were wrong.

"What is it, Ed?" Dave Osmond asked in a whisper.

"I saw something down yonder in the trees," MacDonald replied, gesturing toward the left of the trail. "A light, like somebody struck a match."

"What's wrong with that?" Frank asked.

MacDonald's voice was grim as he answered, "Right over there is where the Slash D fence starts. There shouldn't be anybody poking around it."

"Unless they plan on cuttin' it!" Pitch Carey said. He reached for his gun, loosened it in its holster. "Come on! Let's ride down on 'em, whoever it is."

"Hold on," MacDonald said. "Maybe they've got a good reason for being there. If we go galloping up and start shooting, somebody'll get hurt."

"Damn right," Carey growled.

"Let's get down and take a look-see on foot, quietlike." MacDonald turned to Frank. "This isn't your fight, Frank. You don't ride for the Slash D, at least not yet. Why don't you stay here and hold the horses for us?"

Frank tried not to bristle at that suggestion. MacDonald was just trying to do the right thing. But Frank Morgan had never hung back and held the horses in his life, and he wasn't about to start now.

"I'll trail along with you boys, if that's all right," he said softly. "We can tie the horses to those little trees."

"It's your decision to make. Take off your spurs, boys. We don't want to announce that we're coming."

The men swung down from their saddles and quickly divested themselves of their jingling spurs. Frank ordered Dog to stay there and watch over the horses. Then the five men walked quietly toward a line of larger trees, live oaks and cottonwoods from the looks of them, Frank thought, although it was hard to be sure by moonlight.

"Those trees run along a creek," MacDonald

whispered to Frank. "The fence is just the other side of them."

Frank could make out the fence posts now, jutting up from the ground at fairly regular intervals on the far side of the trees. He couldn't see the barbed wire itself yet.

He hadn't seen any lights down here, either. Maybe MacDonald had been mistaken.

But then a faint whiff of tobacco smoke drifted to his nose. The Slash D ramrod had been right. Somebody had lit a quirly, and MacDonald must have seen the flare of the match.

MacDonald had smelled the smoke, too, just like Frank. He slid his gun from leather. The other three cowboys followed suit. Frank left his Peacemaker pouched for the moment. He could unlimber it quick enough if need be.

Voices came faintly on the night air. Frank and the Slash D men reached the trees and catfooted between them. The creek was narrow enough to step across, with shallow banks on each side. The bank on the far side had cottonwoods growing on it, too. The men paused in the shadows underneath them and looked out at the fence line.

A pair of dark shapes stood near one of the fence posts. Frank knew by their broad-brimmed hats that they were cowboys. A faint red glow marked the end of the cigarette one of the men was smoking. He said around the quirly, "We better get at it."

"Yeah," the other man agreed. Whatever they had planned, though, neither man made a move to carry it out.

They were stalling, Frank realized. It seemed that they were unsure if they wanted to go through with the chore that had brought them out here in the night. Once they cut that fence—and there was no other logical reason for them to be here—they would be lawbreakers, no two ways about it.

"Damn it," the man with the quirly suddenly muttered. "It ain't right what they're doin', and I ain't gonna worry about it no more. I'm cuttin' that damned bob-wire."

He pulled a pair of fence-cutters from a pocket in the leather chaps he wore and stepped up to the fence. As he put the metal jaws of the cutters against the top strand of wire, MacDonald moved out from the trees with his gun leveled and said sharply, "Hold it! You cut that fence and I'll ventilate you, mister!"

The man froze where he was. His companion turned quickly and muttered a curse as he saw the gun-toting figures emerging from the shadows under the trees. "Slash D," he grated.

"That's right," MacDonald said. "We're Slash D riders and that's Slash D fence you're fixing to cut. We'd be within our rights to burn down both of you right here and now. Instead, though, I want you to drop those fence-cutters and your guns, and we'll take you into town and turn you over to the law."

"Go to hell, MacDonald," said the man at the fence.

"Kane?" MacDonald snapped back at him. "Chris Kane, is that you?"

"That's right. And if you're goin' to shoot, you might as well get it over with, 'cause I ain't goin' anywhere with you. I'll drop these cutters, all right, but only to go for my gun."

"Don't do it, kid," MacDonald warned. "There's four of us and only two of you."

"I don't care," Kane said, his voice shaking a little from the depth of the emotions going through him. "You've pushed us too far. I ain't backin' down."

With that, he opened his hand and let the fence-cutters drop. To Frank they seemed to fall slowly, floating toward the ground as Kane twisted toward the Slash D men and reached down for the butt of the gun on his hip. . . .

That was when the trees *behind* Frank and the men with him erupted with flame and lead.

14

Gun thunder filled the night. Frank spun around, drawing as he turned. One of the men with him yelled in pain. Muzzle flashes lit up the darkness under the trees. Frank threw himself to the ground and triggered the Peacemaker as he did so. Three shots roared from the Colt in the time it took him to hit the dirt.

MacDonald and the other cowboys returned the fire, too. The racket was deafening as shot after shot blasted out. The air began to stink of burned powder.

"Get down!" MacDonald yelled over the uproar. "Slash D, everybody down!"

The problem was that there was no cover between the trees and the fence line. All Frank and the cowboys could do was hug the ground. Slugs kicked up dirt around them.

To make matters worse, they were in a perfect position to be caught in a cross fire. Those two fence-cutters were behind them.

But when Frank risked a glance over his shoulder, he didn't see the two men anymore. Had they fled when the shooting started? He didn't know, and he didn't really have time to ponder the question. He waited until a gun flashed under the trees again and then snapped a shot just above the orange spurt of flame.

A man screamed, and Frank knew his shot had found

its target. MacDonald and the others were throwing a lot of lead into the trees, too, and some of it might be hitting its mark. The gunfire from the shadows seemed to be tapering off. Maybe the bushwhackers were losing heart since their intended victims were putting up a good fight.

Frank squeezed off his fifth round and was rewarded with another yelp of pain from under the trees. His Colt was empty now, since he nearly always carried it with the hammer resting on an empty chamber. Moving with smooth, practiced efficiency, he slipped more cartridges from the loops on his belt and reloaded. As he did so, a bullet buzzed past his ear, only a few inches away. It sounded like a giant bee.

He snapped the cylinder closed and started firing again, placing his shots carefully. A moment later, during a lull in the fighting, a man yelled, "Let's get the hell out of here!"

Frank stayed where he was, stretched out flat on the ground, mindful that the shout might have been the bait for a trap. The shooting abruptly fell off to nothing, and a couple of minutes later, Frank heard the swift rataplan of retreating hoofbeats. The bushwhackers were running. They had abandoned their ambush.

At least so it appeared. When the other men started to get up, Frank barked, "Stay down. Give it another couple of minutes."

"You heard the man," Ed MacDonald said. "Stay on your bellies."

A long few minutes passed by, and then Frank said, "I reckon it's all right now." He hadn't heard a sound from the trees since the hoofbeats had dwindled off into the distance.

Still, he kept the Peacemaker trained on the shadows, just in case the bushwhackers had left a man or two there.

Nothing happened as the Slash D men climbed to their feet. Now that the echoes of the shots had died down, silence once again ruled the night. There weren't even any sounds of small animals rustling in the brush. The storm of gunfire had made all the wildlife go to ground.

As Frank looked around, he became aware that he saw only three men standing instead of four. "Who's hit?" he asked sharply.

"Sound off," Ed MacDonald ordered, his voice ragged with strain.

"I'm all right, Ed," Stiles Warren said.

"Me, too," Pitch Carey added between gritted teeth. "A bullet knocked a chunk of meat outta my leg, but I can stand on it."

"That leaves Dave," MacDonald said. "Dave, where the hell are you?"

The only answer was a low groan.

MacDonald cursed, and a couple of seconds later, a match flared into life in his hand. The flickering flame cast only a small circle of light, but as MacDonald moved around, that unsteady glow fell on a figure sprawled facedown in the grass.

Frank and Warren rushed over with Carey limping behind them. The two able-bodied men got hold of Dave Osmond and carefully turned him over. The right half of Osmond's shirt was sodden with blood. He had been hit high on that side, just under the shoulder.

Frank knelt beside Osmond and ripped the shirt back so that he could see the wound. He had barely gotten a look at it when the match went out and Ed MacDonald cursed because the flame had reached his fingers. That look was enough to tell Frank what he needed to know, however.

"I think he'll be all right," he said. "The wound's

messy and it may have busted his collarbone, but I reckon with a doctor's care he'll recover."

"We'll take him on to the ranch house," MacDonald decided quickly. "It's closer. Stiles, you head back to Brownwood right now and fetch Doc Yantis. Bring him straight to the Slash D."

"What if he doesn't want to come?" Warren asked.

"Then make him, damn it!" MacDonald drew a deep breath. "I reckon he'll come along without any trouble, though. Him and the old man are friends."

"I'll go with Stiles," Frank volunteered, "and bring the horses back down here. Pitch doesn't need to walk on that wounded leg any more than he has to."

"I'm all right, I tell you," Carey insisted. His voice was thin with pain, though.

"Stay here with me and Dave," MacDonald ordered. "Frank, I'm obliged for your help."

"I'll be back in a minute," Frank promised as he straightened to his feet. He and Warren hurried through the trees and across the open range toward the trail where they had left their horses.

Along the way, Frank worried a little that the bushwhackers might have freed their mounts and hazed them off. The gunmen hadn't taken the time to do that, though, he saw as he and Warren approached the trail. Stormy and the other horses were right where Frank and the Slash D cowboys had left them.

It took only a few minutes to untie the horses and lead them down to the creek. Warren helped Carey into the saddle, and then Pitch said, "Lift Dave up here in front of me. I'll hold him on. Nothing wrong with my arms."

That sounded like a good idea to Frank. Dave Osmond was unconscious, although he let out a low groan now and then. He wouldn't be able to stay on a horse by himself.

As carefully as possible, Frank, MacDonald, and Warren lifted Osmond to the back of the horse and positioned him in front of Carey. Carey put his arms around him and held on.

"Somebody will have to lead my horse," Carey said.

"I'll do that," MacDonald said. "Frank, you come along with us and keep an eye out for trouble. Stiles, light a shuck for town and the doc."

"I'm already gone," Warren said as he swung up into his saddle. He kicked the horse into a run that carried him back toward Brownwood.

Before the rest of them left for the Slash D, Frank took a quick look along the fence line where the two wire-cutters had been. There was no sign of them now, almost no indication that they had ever been there.

But Frank's keen eyes spotted a dark splotch in the grass, and when he bent over and touched it, he felt a sticky wetness on his fingertips. He rubbed his fingers together, recognizing the all-too-familiar texture.

"You coming, Frank?" Ed MacDonald asked.

"Yeah," Frank said. As he mounted up, he didn't mention what he had found by the barbed-wire fence.

Blood had splashed on the grass over there. One of the fence-cutters had been wounded, probably in that first volley, and from the looks of it, he had been hit pretty bad.

Frank couldn't help but wonder where those two men were now.

Chris Kane cursed repeatedly under his breath as he rode along through the darkness, leading the other horse. From time to time he looked back over his shoulder and said urgently, "Hold on, Will. Just hold on, damn it."

Will Bramlett's only response was a groan. The older

man sat hunched over in his saddle in obvious pain. He held on to the horn somehow and kept himself from falling off. There was no telling how long he would be able to make it, though. He was hit bad.

Kane rasped his tongue over dry lips. He hoped that if he could get Will to the little spread they shared on Blanket Creek, he could take care of his friend. He could make Will more comfortable, anyway, and then fetch the doctor.

What the hell had happened back there? he asked himself over and over. The Slash D men had come out of nowhere, and then all that shooting started. . . .

Kane had thought at first that all the shots came from Earl Duggan's riders and were directed at him and Will Bramlett. Will had been wounded right away, and after that Kane hadn't thought about much of anything except getting both of them out of there before they got killed.

But even though he couldn't be sure about it, he had gotten the impression that somebody else was shooting, that the Slash D cowboys were being fired upon, too. That there had been men under the trees along the creek and they had been shooting at anything that moved. That didn't make any sense, but that was the way it had looked to Kane in those brief moments filled with gun thunder and fear.

He had lifted Will to his feet, slung an arm around his waist, and half-carried, half-dragged him away from the fence and back to the spot where they had left their horses. Then the struggle to get Will in the saddle had taken several minutes. Once that was accomplished, Kane got on his own horse and spurred away, holding tightly to the reins of Will's mount.

And as he had done that, the gunfire had still continued along the creek.

Somebody had to have jumped the Slash D men. That

was the only explanation that made sense. But who? Al Rawlings and some of the other small ranchers?

The thing was, nobody knew that he and Will had planned to come down here and cut Duggan's fence tonight. They had kept it to themselves and hadn't told Rawlings or any of their other allies in the struggle against the big ranchers. So their friends hadn't been looking out for them tonight.

It was a puzzle that Kane couldn't work out, so he shoved the questions aside and concentrated on more pressing problems instead.

Like the fact that Ed MacDonald had recognized his voice. MacDonald would go to the law. Despite the coolness of the night, beads of sweat stood out on Kane's forehead. He wasn't going back to jail. They would have to kill him first. He had done a year on a rustling charge, back when he'd been riding for a spread over close to Hico. Fact of the matter was, he had stolen those cows and deserved the sentence, but he didn't care about that. He had gone straight ever since . . . until tonight.

Damn a state legislature that would make it a crime to cut a damn bob-wire fence, anyway, he thought.

Will Bramlett muttered incoherently behind him. Suddenly his voice grew stronger and he said, "Chris . . . God, Chris, it hurts! You got to do something!"

"I'm trying, Will," Kane said. "I'm going to get you back to the ranch, and then I'll go get the doc."

"Doc won't do me . . . any good," Bramlett grated. "I'm shot in . . . the belly . . . You know I'm a goner."

"The hell I do!" Kane swore. "Don't talk like that. You're gonna be fine—"

"Chris . . . don't get yourself killed . . . over this. I ain't worth it . . . The spread ain't . . . worth it . . ."

If that was true, Kane asked himself, then what was worth dying for? If avenging a friend and defending a simple piece of ground didn't justify fighting and maybe dying, then what would?

Kane couldn't answer those questions. He rode on into the night, leading the other horse.

Blanket Creek was less than ten miles away, but it seemed to take forever to get there. The hour had to be close to midnight before Kane and Bramlett rode up to the double log cabin with a dogtrot in between the two sides. The fella who had owned this spread before them had built the cabin and done a good job of it, erecting a sturdy structure. But it hadn't helped his wife and son when they fell victim to a sudden fever, and the grieving man had wanted to move on. He had been more than willing to sell his place to a couple of cowboys who had been saving up their wages for just such a spread. Old Man Duggan hadn't been happy when Kane and Bramlett told him they were quitting to start a ranch of their own.

That had been a couple of years earlier, before things had gotten so bad. Before the war had started brewing . . .

As Kane reined to a halt in front of the cabin, a voice came from the shadows inside the dogtrot. "Who's there?" a man asked, and the low, dangerous tone of his voice made it clear that the question was backed up with a gun.

Kane recognized the voice of the stocky young cowboy he and Bramlett had hired a couple of weeks earlier. He said urgently, "Give me a hand, Tye. Will's been shot."

The young man, no more than five and a half feet tall but very broad-shouldered, stepped out of the dogtrot holding a Winchester. The moonlight fell on his fair hair and open, friendly face.

Kane and Bramlett knew him only as Tye, but his real name was Tyler Beaumont.

15

Frank Morgan, Ed MacDonald, and Pitch Carey followed the same trail they had been on earlier, before they had gotten sidetracked by the shoot-out along the creek. Carey held Dave Osmond on the horse in front of him. The riders moved fast but didn't rush. They didn't want the wounded man jolted around any more than was necessary.

In less than a half hour after the brief gun battle, they came to a gate in the barbed-wire fence. Two men stood there inside the wire, holding rifles. Before they even had a chance to call out a challenge, MacDonald shouted, "Brad, Joe, it's us! Open the gate! Dave's been shot!"

The two guards sprang to obey the order. They swung the gate back so that Frank and the others could ride through. Dog loped along behind them.

"The ranch house is only a couple of miles away now," MacDonald told Frank. "Pitch, how's Dave doing?"

"He came to enough to cuss a little," Carey answered. "I think he's passed out again, though."

"All right, just hang on to him. Morgan, I'm riding ahead to warn them at the house that we've got an injured man. Just follow the trail. If you start to go wrong, Pitch can steer you back where you're supposed to go."

"Don't worry about us," Frank told the ramrod. "I can find the place."

MacDonald nodded and then heeled his horse into a gallop. The drumming hoofbeats faded into the night as he rode toward the ranch house as fast as he could.

Frank and Pitch Carey followed at a more deliberate pace. The trail curved around some shallow hills. A few minutes later, the riders came in sight of some lights up ahead. As Frank watched, more lamps were lit, and he took that as a sign that MacDonald had reached the ranch headquarters and roused everyone there.

A good-sized group of men was waiting for them when they rode up to the sprawling ranch house. Several of them held lanterns. Others hurried forward. A rawboned man with a thick shock of white hair and a rugged, weathered face said, "Careful with him, boys. Don't jostle him too much."

The note of authority in the man's voice told Frank he was probably Earl Duggan, the owner of the Slash D. The white-haired man stood by, watching intently as Dave Osmond was lifted down from the horse and carried into the house. Then a couple of the men helped Carey dismount and assisted him inside despite his protests that he was all right.

"Doc Yantis will need to take a look at that leg of yours, too, Pitch," said the man Frank had pegged as Earl Duggan. He was about to follow the others in when he stopped on the porch and turned to look at Frank, who stood there holding Stormy's reins. He asked, "You're Morgan?"

Frank nodded. "That's right."

"I'm Earl Duggan," the man said, confirming Frank's guess. "Ed told me you fought side by side with my boys during the ruckus tonight. I'm obliged to you for that, Morgan."

"Well, those bushwhackers were shooting at me, too," Frank pointed out. "Only seemed fair that I shoot back at them."

Duggan grunted, and it took Frank a second to realize that the sound had been a laugh. The rancher went on. "Ed said you had a run-in with Al Rawlings in Brownwood, too. You didn't kill him, though."

"Didn't quite seem necessary."

"You may regret that. I don't believe in leavin' a snake alive. I'd hate to think I was bit by the same rattler I could've stomped when I had the chance."

"I guess we'll see," Frank said.

"Yeah. Come on in, Morgan. I've already told the cook to rustle some grub for you and the other fellas. Told him I'd cut his pigtail off if he didn't hurry it up, damn his black Chinaman's heart."

Frank tied Stormy's reins to a hitching post and followed Duggan into the house. He found that Dave Osmond had been taken straight to one of the bedrooms. By looking around, Frank could tell that no woman lived here. The furnishings were strictly utilitarian. There were no curtains on the windows, only oilcloth shades, and no pictures hung on the walls. The floor was bare wood. The house was big, though, as if it had been built for a family. He wondered if Duggan had ever had a wife and children.

Duggan checked to make sure that Dave Osmond had been made as comfortable as possible under the circumstances. Then he returned to the parlor, where Frank waited, and asked, "Care for a drink, Morgan?"

"I wouldn't mind," Frank replied. "It's been sort of a thirsty night."

Duggan made that grunting sound again. "Nothing like nearly gettin' ventilated to make a man appreciate the pleasures of life, is there?" He paused and then added, "But I reckon you'd know that, bein' the one they call the Drifter and all."

"So you know who I am," Frank said.

"Sure. I reckon most folks west of the Mississippi know who Frank Morgan is, and plenty of 'em east of there do, too." Duggan took a bottle and a couple of glasses from a cabinet. "All I've got is whiskey."

"That'll do," Frank told him.

Duggan poured the drinks. They knocked back the whiskey. "Another?" Duggan asked.

Frank shook his head. "No, thanks."

Duggan looked like he wanted to refill his glass, but since his guest had refused a second drink, he put the bottle away instead. Turning back to Frank, he slipped his hands into the hip pockets of his jeans and said, "Ed tells me you're looking for work."

"That's right."

Duggan frowned. "You know, Morgan, I've heard a lot about you, but I don't recollect ever hearing that you sold your gun."

"I don't. You've got a good-sized spread here. I thought maybe you could use another hand. I cowboyed when I was a kid up in Parker County."

Duggan just stared at him for a moment and then said, "Am I hearin' right? Frank Morgan, the famous gunfighter, wants to hire on as a forty-a-month-and-found cowpuncher?"

"I reckon you could call it getting back to my roots," Frank said.

"I reckon I call it crazy. Nobody's going to believe you hired on as a cowhand, no matter what I tell them."

Frank shrugged. "I don't have any control over what people believe or don't believe."

"I suppose that's true." Duggan thought it over for

a moment more and then said, "You gave my boys a hand tonight. I owe you for that. If you want a riding job, Morgan, you got it. But you're smart enough to have figured out there's trouble brewin' in these parts. You could find yourself smack-dab in the middle of a shootin' war."

"I'll take my chances," Frank said easily. Smack-dab in the middle of this range war was exactly where he wanted to be . . . because that was the place where he was mostly likely to find Tyler Beaumont.

Setting the Winchester aside, Beaumont hurried forward. As he did so, Will Bramlett's waning strength finally gave out and he began to tumble from the saddle. Beaumont got there in time to catch him. He felt wetness against the palms of his hands as he grasped Bramlett's blood-soaked jacket and shirt.

Kane slid to the ground and sprang to help Beaumont, but the young Ranger said, "I've got him."

"Take it easy with him," Kane said worriedly. "He's got a bullet in his belly."

"Damn," Beaumont said, his voice soft. Like most frontiersmen, he knew what it meant when a man was gut-shot. Almost without fail, it was a death sentence. Only very rarely did anyone recover from such a wound.

Carefully, Beaumont lifted Bramlett and carried him into the right-hand side of the cabin. Kane hurried ahead and lit the lamp that Beaumont had blown out when he heard the approaching hoofbeats. With things the way they were in this part of the country, a man had to be careful whenever anybody rode up at night. There was no telling who might be coming to call, but there was a very good chance their intentions were hostile.

Once Kane had the wick burning in the lamp, he

lowered the glass chimney and a yellow glow spread through the room. It had a hard-packed dirt floor with a couple of Indian rugs thrown on it, a rocking chair, and three bunks, one each for the two owners of the place and their hired hand. On the other side of the dogtrot was the kitchen, which was also where the men ate.

Beaumont lowered the wounded man onto one of the bunks. Bramlett's face was pale as milk, probably because he had lost so much blood. His whole midsection was black with it. He moved his head a little, and a sound that was half-sigh, half-moan came from his lips. His eyes remained closed.

"What happened?" Beaumont asked as he straightened. He wore jeans over a pair of long-handled underwear and his feet were bare. He didn't seem to notice that the night had grown chilly. The upper half of the gray underwear was stained with blood from where he had carried Bramlett.

"Some Slash D men jumped us," Kane answered. He took his hat off and ran his fingers through his thick brown hair. He was fairly young, only a few years older than Beaumont, of medium height and slender build. He was a tough, experienced cowboy despite his relative youth. He wore a Colt belted around his waist and knew how to use it.

"What were you doing over by the Slash D?" Beaumont knew that as a hired hand, which was all he was to Chris Kane, he didn't have any right to be demanding answers. He posed the question anyway.

"We went down there to teach Duggan a lesson," Kane said. "It's not right what he and the others are doing to Al Rawlings."

"You tried to cut Duggan's fence?"

"That's right." Kane's chin lifted in anger. "He had it comin'."

Beaumont wasn't going to argue with that. He rode for the KB spread—or so everyone thought—so what the bosses said went. Or in this case, the boss, because Bramlett was in no shape to give orders. All the responsibility now fell on his partner, Chris Kane.

Bramlett was older, a chunky, graying man in his mid-thirties. He and Kane had known each other for several years, both of them having worked for Earl Duggan at the same time, and they got along well enough that they had decided to go in together as partners in a ranch. Beaumont had learned that and more in the two weeks he had worked for the men.

They hadn't wanted to hire him at first, even though their herd had grown large enough so that they really needed an extra hand. They didn't have enough money to pay regular wages, Kane had said when Beaumont rode in and asked if they were hiring. Beaumont had agreed to work for his keep and ten dollars a month. That was less than a third of a cowhand's usual pay. Kane and Bramlett had probably wondered why Beaumont had accepted such a proposition. But he made a good hand, and they had decided they were lucky to have him.

More importantly as far as Beaumont was concerned, he was now on the inside of the loose-knit organization of small ranches and farmers who were opposed to the way the big ranchers had fenced off huge sections of land in Brown County.

You knew things had to be really bad when cattlemen and sodbusters started working together, Beaumont had thought more than once during the time he'd spent here. The hatred and anger caused by the high-handed actions of Duggan, Wilcox, Calhoun, and the other big ranchers in the county had united men who might have been enemies under other circumstances.

It was Beaumont's job to find out just how bad things really were and keep them from getting worse.

From the looks of the bloodstained figure on the bunk, so far he had been spectacularly unsuccessful in the latter part of that chore.

"I thought you'd gone to town and Will was riding night herd," he said now to Chris Kane.

Kane hung his hat on the back of the rocking chair. "I didn't know we had to clear things with you," he said curtly. "Last time I checked, you still worked for us."

Beaumont held up his hands. "I'm sorry, Chris. You're right. I was out of line."

"Forget it," Kane said with a shake of his head. "You know anything about doctorin'?"

"I've seen plenty of bullet holes patched up. I can take a look at Will if you want."

"You do that. I'm going to get a fresh horse and light a shuck for Brownwood. Will needs Doc Yantis."

Beaumont wasn't sure a sawbones could do Bramlett any good at this point, but he didn't say that to Kane. Instead, he said, "I'll clean the wound and try to get the bleeding stopped."

Wearily, Kane scrubbed a hand across his face and then nodded. "Thanks." He started out of the cabin, snagging his hat from the back of the chair as he passed.

"Don't you want some coffee or something to eat before you go?"

"No time," Kane said over his shoulder. The door banged behind him as he went out.

Beaumont looked at the man on the bunk and sighed. He pushed the sleeves of the long underwear higher on his arms. He had his work cut out for him just keeping Will Bramlett alive until Kane got back from Brownwood with the doctor.

16

Despite the lateness of the hour, Brownwood's saloons were still open for business. Light spilled out through their windows and into the street. Ford Nairn's Double O Saloon, Pomp Arnold's place, Happy Jack Young's tavern, and Ace McKelvey's Palace all had customers.

One of them was bound to know where Doc Yantis was, Chris Kane thought as he reined his horse to a halt in front of McKelvey's. He would start there.

Actually, the first place he had stopped at in Brownwood was the physician's house, which doubled as his office. The place was dark, and no one had answered when Kane pounded on the door and called Yantis's name. The doc was gone somewhere, and Kane wanted to know where. If Yantis was in town, Kane intended to get him and take him out to the ranch, by force if necessary.

If the sawbones was out in the country somewhere on a call, Kane didn't know what he would do. Will Bramlett needed medical attention as soon as possible, and even then it might not be enough.

His partner might already be dead, Kane thought grimly as he stepped onto the shallow porch in front of McKelvey's.

He opened the door and went inside. Three townsmen

stood at the bar, drinking. The tables were all empty. Behind the hardwood, the tall, red-bearded bartender looked bored as he polished glasses. Kane had been coming in here for several years, ever since he had gone to work for Earl Duggan after being released from the penitentiary in Huntsville. He knew Rusty and knew the girls who usually worked here, too. One of them, the blonde called Annie, leaned against the bar, looking as bored as Rusty. The other one, Midge, was nowhere in sight. Either she had taken a customer upstairs or had simply called it a night and turned in alone.

Annie's face lit up as she looked over and saw Kane. He knew she liked him, probably because he made a point of always being polite to her. He might have felt the same way toward her if he'd had time for such things. He didn't hold it against her that she was a whore. After all, he was a convicted rustler, an ex-jailbird.

She smiled as she came toward him. "Hello, Chris," she said in a quiet voice. "It's been a long time since I saw you last."

"Yeah, I've been busy," he said curtly. He didn't have time to flirt with some calico cat, even one as nice as Annie. "Have you seen Doc Yantis this evening?" Kane knew that the doc sometimes liked a little nip after supper. Something to help him sleep, the sawbones claimed.

Annie shook her head. "No, I haven't seen him. Is something wrong?" She laid her hand on his forearm in a gesture that managed to be solicitous and sensual at the same time.

"I just need to find him, that's all." He sure as hell didn't want to explain that he needed help because his partner has been shot just as they were about to cut the Slash D fence.

Annie caught hold of the sleeve of his denim jacket.

"Why don't you stay and have a drink with me?" she suggested. "Then you can go look for Doc."

Kane pulled away more roughly than he intended to, but in his distraction, he didn't notice the surprise and the hurt feelings in Annie's eyes. "Sorry, I don't have time." He turned and walked out.

Inside the Palace, Annie gazed after Kane with disappointment. She didn't hear the door at the far end of the bar open, didn't know that Ace McKelvey had emerged from his office until the owner of the place came up behind her and touched her shoulder. She gave a little gasp of surprise and turned to look at him.

McKelvey was a sturdily built man with dark hair and a mustache. He said, "Was that Chris Kane who just left out of here?"

Annie nodded.

"He hasn't been to town much lately," McKelvey mused. "I reckon he got to missing you, Annie."

"No, he didn't," she said with a faint edge of bitterness in her voice. "He just came in here looking for Doc Yantis. He wanted to know if the doc had been in tonight."

"What does Kane need a doctor for?"

"He didn't say."

"Must not have been for him. He looked healthy enough."

"He didn't seem to be hurt," Annie agreed.

"Well, I suppose we'll hear about it sooner or later if it was anything important." McKelvey rubbed Annie's bare upper arm. "Why don't you come back to the office with me? I could use some help with the, ah, books, and you're the smartest girl I know."

Annie was smart enough to know that her talents didn't lie in bookkeeping. That wasn't what McKelvey wanted help with.

But he was the boss, so she had to do pretty much

whatever he said. She put a smile on her face and said, "All right, Mr. McKelvey. I'd be glad to."

"Call me Ace," he chided. "I've told you that before."

"Sure . . . Ace."

Brownwood had only four saloons, and they were all fairly close together. It didn't take long for Chris Kane to visit all of them. Unfortunately, he got the same lack of results in each place. No one had seen Doc Yantis.

He stopped just outside Pomp Arnold's saloon and rubbed his eyes as he tried to think. All the other businesses in Brownwood were closed at this hour. He didn't know who else he could ask about the doctor.

Then it occurred to him that more than likely somebody would be awake at the marshal's office. And Keever or his deputy, Skeet Harlan, might know where Doc Yantis was. Kane didn't like the idea of approaching the lawmen, but he didn't know what else to do. He remembered that Ed MacDonald had recognized him during the confrontation out at the Slash D fence line. MacDonald could have ridden to town by now and reported what had happened to the sheriff, and if the sheriff knew about it, then Marshal Keever probably did, too. Of course, that was assuming MacDonald and the other Slash D riders had lived through the gunfight, which had still been going on while Kane and Bramlett lit a shuck out of there.

It was a chance he would have to take, Kane decided. The marshal's office was only a couple of blocks away on a side street just off Fisk Avenue. His steps carried him swiftly toward it.

Kane saw a light burning in the window of the small frame building as he approached. He tried the door, found it locked, and rapped sharply on it. A moment later a man asked from inside, "Who's there?"

For a second Kane hesitated, unsure whether he

should give his name. Then he plunged ahead and said, "Chris Kane. I'm looking for Doc Yantis."

A key rattled in the lock and then the door was jerked open. Skeet Harlan, Marshal Sean Keever's deputy, peered out at him. Kane squinted against the light coming from inside the office as Harlan asked, "What do you need the doc for, Kane? You hurt?"

"No, but my partner Will Bramlett is," Kane replied. "He was cleaning his gun and it went off. Accidentally shot himself in the belly." It was a weak excuse, but the best Kane had been able to come up with. And Harlan couldn't prove that he was lying.

"Shot in the belly, eh?" Harlan sounded amused by the situation. "Might as well forget about Doc and go roust out the undertaker. By tomorrow Bramlett'll need plantin'."

Kane had never liked Skeet Harlan. The deputy got too much enjoyment out of the power he wielded. He was fast to use a gun when there was trouble, too. He liked to pistol-whip drunks, and he had shot more than one cowboy who'd gotten a mite too rambunctious while celebrating payday. Kane was already on edge tonight because of everything that had happened, and now Harlan's callous comments got under his skin, probably just the way Harlan intended. Kane couldn't help it. He snapped back, "Just tell me where the hell Doc Yantis is, Harlan."

The deputy gave him an ugly grin. "He's out at the Slash D. Stiles Warren rode in to fetch him a while ago. It seems that Dave Osmond and Pitch Carey got themselves shot earlier tonight. There was some sort o' dustup along Duggan's fence line, there by Stepps Creek."

"I hadn't heard anything about that," Kane said hollowly.

"From what Warren said, a lot of powder got burned

and a lot of lead slung. You sure you don't know anything about that, Kane?"

"I told you I didn't." Kane struggled with the anger and fear that welled up inside him. Did Harlan know for sure that he and Bramlett had been there when the shooting started? Did the deputy know they had aimed to cut Duggan's fence?

"Funny thing," Harlan drawled as he leered at Kane. "Warren heard Ed MacDonald call your name just before the shootin' started. Are you sayin' that MacDonald's a liar?"

"Maybe he was just mistaken," Kane rasped. He started to turn away, feeling empty inside. If Doc Yantis was out at the Slash D, there was no way Kane could get his help for Bramlett. The poor gut-shot son of a bitch was doomed, if he wasn't dead already.

"Hold on!" Harlan ordered.

"I don't have time—" Kane began.

"You got plenty of time. Bramlett's as good as dead, and you know it. That'll save the county the expense of hangin' him."

Kane bristled. "You've got no right to say that! Will didn't do anything."

"Fence-cuttin' is a crime, you know."

"Not a hanging offense," Kane said. "Anyway, Will never cut a fence in his life."

That was true. Kane had been the one about to cut the fence. And when you came right down to it, he hadn't actually done it, so he was still legally in the clear, too.

"How about attempted murder?"

"We didn't shoot anybody! It was somebody else—"

Kane stopped short as he realized what he had just done. Harlan gave a wicked laugh and said, "So you admit you and Bramlett was there, do you? I thought as much. Get your hands up, boy. You're under arrest."

Kane started to back away. "I haven't committed any crimes in town," he said as he held up his left hand but kept the right close to the butt of his gun. "You don't have any right to arrest me."

"I know the sheriff's lookin' for you," Harlan said as he stood there silhouetted in the doorway, his hand curved into a claw just above the Colt on his hip. "The marshal and me like to cooperate with our fellow lawmen. I'll just take your gun and march you over to the sheriff's office. He can lock you up in that nice new jail o' his."

"I'm not going to jail." Kane's voice trembled slightly, but it was from anger, not fear.

"You did time before, I hear. Served a stretch for rustlin'. You'll go away for a lot longer this time. I don't know how bad those Slash D cowboys are hurt, either. If one of 'em was to die, then you'd swing for murder, Kane."

"No! We didn't shoot anybody, I tell you!"

"You gonna drop your gun and put your hands up . . . or am I gonna have to drop you?" Harlan's voice was an evil purr as he asked the question. Kane knew the deputy wanted him to fight. Harlan was just looking for an excuse to kill him.

Harlan might do it, too. He was fast on the draw. But Kane was no slouch, and he knew it. He might beat Harlan in a fair fight.

But even though he was convinced he was in the right, if he gunned down a lawman he would be on the run for the rest of his life. It probably wouldn't be a very long life, either. Every lawman in the state would be on the lookout for him, even the Texas Rangers. Maybe if he surrendered, he would at least have a chance to tell his side of the story. . . .

"Damn it, I told you to drop that gun and elevate!"

Harlan growled. He wasn't going to wait any longer. His hand stabbed toward the gun on his hip.

Instinct kicked in and made Kane grab for his own gun. As his fingers closed around the grips, he saw that he had seriously underestimated the deputy's speed, even though he had heard stories about Harlan being a fast gun. Harlan's Colt was already out of the holster and the barrel was tipping up even as Kane began to haul his own iron out of leather. Kane's eyes widened as he saw flame bloom from the muzzle of the deputy's gun.

What felt like a huge fist smashed him in the chest. He rocked back a step under the impact. But he kept trying to complete his draw. The problem was that his Colt suddenly seemed to weigh a ton. He got it out of the holster and struggled to lift it, but as he did, Harlan's gun roared again and another bullet struck him. Kane stumbled backward again but stayed on his feet somehow. A small part of his stunned brain was still functioning, and it tried to warn him that the smart thing to do would be to drop his gun and go ahead and fall down. Otherwise, Harlan was just going to keep blazing away at him.

But a white-hot rage that refused to surrender filled Kane and gave him the strength to try one final time to get a shot off. He let out an incoherent yell as he brought the gun up.

Harlan shot him again, and this time as the lead crashed into him, Kane went down and out.

He never heard the chuckle of sheer satisfaction that came from Skeet Harlan's throat.

17

Doc Yantis was a small man with bushy gray eyebrows over deep-set brown eyes. He reminded Frank Morgan a little of a horned owl. He wasn't Brown County's only sawbones, but he was the best at his profession and the one that folks relied on. He never complained about being called out in the middle of the night, either.

When the doctor came out of the room where Dave Osmond had been taken, he had his coat off and his sleeves rolled up, and was carrying his medical bag. He looked around and asked, "Where's the other patient?"

"Sitting in the kitchen with his leg propped up," Earl Duggan replied. "How's Dave?"

"I'm reasonably confident that he'll be all right. He lost a lot of blood and the bullet nicked the collarbone, but it missed his lungs. That's the main thing I was worried about. He's going to be flat on his back for a good long spell, though, while he recovers."

"That's not a problem," Duggan said. "He can take as long as he needs. That Chinaman of mine will look after him."

Doc Yantis nodded. "Wing's a good man and quite intelligent, despite the fact that you persist in acting as if he's nothing but a coolie, Earl. I'll have a talk with him about what needs to be done for Dave."

"I'm obliged, Doc."

"Now, let me have a look at Pitch." The sawbones bustled out of the room.

Once Yantis was gone, Frank said to Duggan, "I'd better go take care of my horse and dog and then settle in at the bunkhouse. I guess there'll be at least one empty bunk, since Osmond is staying in here."

"There's more than that," Duggan told him. "I don't have a full crew right now. Fall roundup's not for a couple of weeks yet. I'll take on more hands then."

Frank nodded and started out of the parlor, but Duggan stopped him.

"Morgan . . . Don't you want to know more about what's going on around here? I'm not sure you know what you're getting yourself into."

"I know there's trouble between the big ranchers on one side and the small ranchers and farmers on the other." Frank waited to see what else Duggan would say.

"That's right. Why don't you sit down? I've got some good cigars. . . ."

Frank smiled. "That sounds fine."

When the two men were settled down in armchairs in front of the fireplace—where the fire that had been burning earlier in the night had gone down to embers—Duggan lit their cigars with a lucifer and then blew out a cloud of smoke in a tired sigh.

"Five years ago Brown County was all free range," he began. "Me and Calhoun, Wilcox, the Coggin brothers, Park, Brooks Lee, Baugh, and all the other cattlemen in the county worked together. We had a couple of roundups every year, one over on Blanket Creek in the eastern part of the county and the other along Jim Ned Creek to the west. Every outfit was repped and the reps kept track of the gather for their brand."

Frank nodded. "Sounds like common practice to me."

"It was, and it worked just fine as long as there were

only ten or a dozen ranches in the county. But then new fellas started moving in, and before you know it, everywhere you looked there was some little greasy-sack outfit calling itself a ranch. They didn't have any land and damn few cattle, but they wanted to think that they were just as good as me and the others who had been here twenty years." Duggan put his cigar in his mouth and his teeth clenched on it. Around it he said, "Us who fought the Comanch' and the fever and spilled our blood and put our loved ones in the ground . . ."

For a moment he couldn't bring himself to go on, and Frank sat quietly, waiting for the rancher to bring under control the emotions and the memories that threatened to overwhelm him. Finally, Duggan took the cigar out of his mouth and continued. "Even some of the hands who rode for me and the others quit and decided to start spreads of their own."

"You can't blame a man for being ambitious," Frank said.

"You can when he wants to latch his ambitions onto somebody else's coattails," Duggan snapped. He waved the hand holding the cigar. "Anyway, it wasn't just them. It was the farmers, too, especially in the eastern half of the county. Any piece of halfway decent ground that didn't have a so-called ranch on it had some sodbuster trailin' along behind a mule and a plow. Those of us who'd been here for a while looked around and saw that we were going to have to do something; otherwise, we'd be crowded out."

"So you got legal title to the range you'd been grazing all these years and bought some barbed wire," Frank said.

"Damn right we did," Duggan barked defiantly. "Those pissants thought the county would stay free range, so they could run their cows wherever they pleased. They found out different, let me tell you."

"And when they found out, they didn't like it," Frank guessed.

"Not even a little bit. Hell, they acted like they had a right to our grass, like it was our duty to feed their cows . . . some of which same had probably been rustled from the big outfits to start with!"

"But you don't know that."

Duggan shrugged. "I'll admit there hasn't been a lot of rustling, at least not that anybody can prove. I've lost stock and so have the other fellas, but not enough to cause a problem. What causes the problem is the way those bastards cut our fences and run their cows on our range."

"I was talking to Ed MacDonald on the way out here," Frank said. "From what he told me, an hombre like Al Rawlings is in a bad spot. He's not a free-range man, right? He owns his spread fair and square, it's just not very big?"

"That's right," Duggan admitted grudgingly. "Rawlings has got clear title to his range. Only because he beat me to it, though."

"Yes, but he bought the land. Now he can't use it, though, because he's closed in on all sides by fences."

"That's not our lookout," Duggan said stubbornly. "It's Rawlings' problem and nobody else's."

Frank puffed on the cigar for a moment as he thought about everything Duggan had said. He could tell that the cattleman was in no mood to budge in his beliefs. The way Duggan saw it, he and the other big ranchers were the ones being wronged, and they were doing what they could to protect their interests. And, Frank had to admit, it was certainly legal for a man to string fences around his own range. But it was just as legal for smaller ranchers like Rawlings to try to establish their spreads and compete with Duggan and the others. Frank could see right and wrong on both sides of the argument.

"Who's Chris Kane?" he asked, recalling the name that MacDonald had spoken just before all hell broke loose along the fence line.

Duggan snorted in disgust. "Kane's one of those ambitious cowboys I was talking about. He used to ride for Slash D. I gave him a job, even though he was a jailbird."

"What did he do time for?"

"Rustling. Two-bit stuff, over around Hico and Hamilton. He was honest enough to tell me about it when he asked me for a job, I'll give him that."

"You hired him even though he's a convicted rustler?" Frank asked.

"I believe in giving a man a second chance if I think he deserves it," Duggan declared. "Kane said he'd gone straight and just wanted some honest work. I gave it to him."

"Did he make a good hand?"

Duggan grimaced and hesitated a second before saying, "Yeah, he made a good hand. I don't have any complaints about the work he did while he was riding for me. But then he decided that he wanted a place of his own. Him and another fella who worked for me named Bramlett drew their time and went in as partners. They put down some money on a little spread up on Blanket Creek. I didn't begrudge 'em that . . . but then they had to go and throw in with Rawlings and the rest of that fence-cuttin' bunch."

"When did the fence-cutting start?"

"A couple of years ago, but only on a small scale at first. The law knew who was responsible and brought them up on charges, but the grand jury wouldn't bring in an indictment."

Frank nodded in understanding. Frontier jurisprudence was sometimes a pretty haphazard process.

"That just made them think they could get away with even more," Duggan continued. "Ever since it's been getting worse and worse. Shots have been fired on both sides. I don't reckon it's ever going to stop until—"

He halted abruptly. Frank finished the thought for him. "Until the big outfits get together and wipe out the smaller ones. Isn't that what you meant?"

Duggan clenched his left hand into a fist and thumped it on his knee. "A man's got a right to defend what's his! Cutting our fences is bad enough, but when they start bushwhacking our men, like they did tonight—"

"Those shots didn't come from the men who were fixing to cut the fence," Frank pointed out.

"You know they had to be some of the same bunch, though. It was a trap, damn it! They meant for somebody to see them and try to stop them. A bunch of the polecats were hidden in the trees along the creek just waiting for you."

A frown creased Frank's forehead. That theory seemed a little farfetched to him. If Ed MacDonald hadn't happened to be in just the right place at just the right time to see the flare of the match as one of the men lit a cigarette, the riders from the Slash D would have passed on by without ever knowing what was going on.

Of course, the gunmen in the trees could have been standing guard, just in case someone came along and interrupted the fence cutters. The only other possible explanation was that the bushwhackers had followed Frank and his companions from Brownwood . . . and for the life of him, he couldn't see how that made any sense.

Duggan leaned back in his chair. Lines of strain

creased his rugged face. "Well, now that you know the situation, do you still want to sign on, Morgan? You may say you're not hiring out your gun, but there's a mighty good chance there'll be more shooting before it's all over."

Frank smiled faintly. "You're not saying that the possibility of some shooting worries me, are you?"

"Hell, no! I know you've been in more corpse-and-cartridge sessions than I can count. But I know you're a strong-willed hombre, too. Is it going to bother you if you have to shoot at Rawlings and the rest of that bunch?"

"I've already swapped lead with Rawlings once tonight, remember?"

Duggan grunted. "Yeah, that's true."

"I've got this informal rule," Frank said. "If anybody shoots at me, I shoot back."

"But not always to kill."

"Not always," Frank admitted. "Just usually."

Duggan came to his feet and stuck out his hand. "All right then. If you want a job on the Slash D, you're hired."

Frank shook hands with the rancher. That sealed the deal. In the West, a man's word was his bond, and a handshake was more binding than any legal document back East could ever be.

"Guess I'd better get out to the bunkhouse now."

Duggan managed a grin. "Those boys are going to be mighty excited to have the famous Frank Morgan living right there in the bunkhouse with them. They're liable to pester you with a bunch of questions. I hear tell you've killed a thousand men, not counting Injuns."

"If all the stories they tell about me were true," Frank said, "there wouldn't be anybody left alive west of the Mississippi. I'd have already shot them all by now."

Duggan gave a real laugh at that, the first one Frank

had heard from the man. "Try not to disappoint 'em too much with the truth," he said. "Folks need their heroes, even cowboys."

18

Beaumont sat beside the bunk and listened to Will Bramlett's hoarse, ragged breathing. Bramlett was unconscious. He hadn't come around while Beaumont was cleaning the wound in his belly and bandaging it as best he could.

His efforts weren't going to do any good, Beaumont knew. The bullet was still inside Bramlett, and there was no telling how much damage it had done to the man's guts. Bramlett was probably bleeding inside, and there wasn't a damned thing Beaumont could do about that.

The young Ranger slid his watch from his pocket and opened it. Nearly three o'clock in the morning. Kane should have been back from Brownwood by now if he had found Doc Yantis without any trouble. The fact that he hadn't returned meant that he hadn't found the doctor . . . or else he had run into some other problem.

Like being arrested and thrown in jail for fence-cutting.

Beaumont wished that Kane and Bramlett hadn't taken it into their heads to go cut Earl Duggan's fence tonight. He had been working his way into their confidence, and he figured that before much longer he would have been fully accepted into the circle of small ranchers and farmers opposed to Duggan and the other rich cattlemen. Then he could have tried to persuade them that fence-cutting and bushwhacking weren't going to work. They needed to take their disputes to court and try to settle them there, rather than with wire-cutters and six-guns. Hell, the West was supposed to be civilized now, wasn't it?

Beaumont shook his head at that thought. Civilization had its place, but pioneers like Duggan didn't put much stock in it. There hadn't been any law and order in this part of Texas when they first came here. The only justice was what they brought with them and enforced with fist and knife and gun.

As for men like Kane and Bramlett and Al Rawlings, they were full of ambition and the hunger for something better that could be found in all men. They might keep it in check under normal conditions, but when they felt threatened, all bets were off.

Beaumont rubbed his eyes tiredly. If he couldn't convince the small ranchers and farmers not to resort to violence, at least he could find out their plans, hopefully in time to tip off the authorities and prevent any real outbreaks of bloodshed. That sort of underhandedness went against the grain for Beaumont, but his job was to stop the war in Brown County any way he could.

The problem was that in the time he had known them, he had come to like and admire Kane and Bramlett. Al Rawlings was a hothead, but deep down he wasn't too bad. That redheaded sister of his was a worse hellion than Al.

Beaumont sighed and wished Victoria was here. She wouldn't tell him what to do—she wouldn't think of interfering with his work—but she would listen to what he had to say and help him think through everything. She was mighty good at that. Just talking things out with her allowed him to see them much more clearly.

For example, she had talked him out of going after Frank Morgan and trying to kill him . . . which probably wouldn't have accomplished anything except getting his own fool self shot. Beaumont could handle a gun as well as or better than most men, but he was no match for the Drifter.

No match for the man who had been his friend . . .

"It's not his fault," Victoria had said. "He didn't make that man come after him."

"But he *did*," Beaumont had insisted. "He did it just by being Frank Morgan."

"He can't help who he is. . . ." Victoria had laid her hand on his. "Any more than you can help who you are."

"Who's that? I'm not sure I know anymore."

"You're the man who loves me, even if I have to spend the rest of my life in this chair. And bitterness and self-pity don't suit you, Tyler Beaumont. They don't suit you at all."

He looked at her then, still beautiful even though she was sitting in the wheelchair her father had had made for her. And he knelt and put his arms around her and held her, wishing that things were different, wishing that he could go back and change that one small moment in time when their world and all their plans had come crashing down around them.

Well, not all their plans, he supposed. They were still married, and there were times, like when they held each other in the dark, when he could almost forget that Victoria might never walk again. Those moments were what kept them going.

As the weeks had turned into months, they had grown more accustomed to her limitations. The pain of what she had lost was still with them, of course, but time had dulled it somewhat. With the resilience that was bred into the human animal, they had adapted.

Then Beaumont had gotten the word from Captain

McDowell himself that he was being sent to Brown County to quash the trouble simmering there. At first he had thought about refusing, even though that might well have meant that he would have to resign from the Rangers. Once Victoria got wind of that idea, she put a stop to it immediately.

"All you ever wanted to be was a Ranger, Tyler," she had told him. "You can't just walk away from it. It may sound a little foolish, but . . . that's your destiny."

"You really think there is such a thing?" he'd asked her.

"I know there is." Her smile was as brilliant as ever. "It was our destiny to be together, wasn't it?"

He couldn't argue with that.

So he had come to Brown County, and now here he sat beside a dying man, not knowing what else to do.

He wished Kane would get back.

Suddenly, Will Bramlett's eyelids flickered open. The man gasped, and for a second Beaumont thought that death had come to him at last. But Bramlett's chest continued to rise and fall, though in an erratic rhythm, and he turned his head to stare at the young Ranger.

"Chris . . . ?" Bramlett whispered.

"No, it's me," Beaumont told him. "Tye. Chris isn't here, Will. He's gone for the doctor."

"Too late . . . too late . . ."

"Don't talk like that—" Beaumont began.

The wounded man lifted his hand. It shook, but he managed to reach out and grasp Beaumont's hand. "Tye . . ." Bramlett husked, "don't let Chris get himself . . . killed . . . over me. Tell him . . . it ain't worth it . . . not me . . . not the fences . . . not the ranch . . . he can't fight . . ."

Beaumont knew he would be wasting his breath if he told Chris Kane those things. Kane just wasn't about to back down now that he had made his decision to fight Duggan and the other big ranchers.

"Just rest easy, Will," Beaumont said as he put a hand on Bramlett's shoulder. "Chris will be back soon with the doctor."

Bramlett shook his head. "No . . . you got to . . . promise . . . promise me you won't . . . let him get killed."

"I'll look after him, Will," Beaumont promised.

"Your . . . word . . ."

Beaumont bit back a curse. "You've got my word on it," he said.

The breath went out of Bramlett in a long, exhausted sigh. His chest fell . . . and didn't rise again. Beaumont stared at him intently, waiting for the sound of another breath, waiting for his chest to rise, waiting for any sign of life.

But the life was all gone. It had slipped out of Will Bramlett with that sigh. His eyes were still open, but they stared sightlessly at the roof beams and began to grow glassy. Carefully, the young Ranger closed Bramlett's eyes.

Beaumont looked at his watch again. Three-fifteen in the morning. Just in case anybody wanted to know later on.

By the time the sun came up the next morning, Beaumont already had a grave half-dug on a hill overlooking the cabin and the winding course of Blanket Creek. During the time he had been in Brown County, Beaumont had already heard several conflicting accounts of how the creek had come by its name. The one that most people seemed to accept said that some of the earliest white visitors to the area, a party of surveyors that had passed through in 1852, had come across a band of Tonkawa Indians spreading their blankets on some bushes that grew along the creek in order to dry them and air them out. The Tonkawa were peaceful—at least they had been that day—and the surveyors had carried the story away with them and given the creek its name. That explanation sounded as good as any to Beaumont.

Kane still hadn't come back from Brownwood, and Beaumont was convinced by now that something had happened to him. Later, after he had buried Will Bramlett, he would have to saddle up his horse and ride the fourteen or fifteen miles to town so he could find out why Kane hadn't returned.

The shovel rasped in the dirt as he kept digging. Despite the early morning chill, the exertion made him warm. He paused to sleeve sweat off his forehead. While he was stopped, he heard hoofbeats in the distance. As he listened, the sounds drew nearer. Several riders were coming, he judged.

His gun belt was already strapped around his waist. He drove the shovel blade into the dirt and left it standing upright as he stepped over to the tree where he had leaned his Winchester. As he picked up the rifle and started down the hill toward the cabin, he saw four horsemen ride up. Three horsemen and a horse*woman*, he corrected himself. Even at this distance he had no trouble making out the fiery red hair that tumbled from under one of the horsebackers' Stetsons. The ripe curves of her body were a further indication of her sex. Had to be Callie Stratton, Beaumont thought. Nobody else around here looked like that.

By the time he reached the cabin and walked around it to meet them, they had dismounted and were standing there holding their horses' reins. Al Rawlings was one of them, of course; Beaumont had expected that as soon as he saw Rawlings's sister. He recognized the other two as Simon Clark and Vern Gladwell, both of whom owned small spreads and were friends with Kane and Bramlett.

"Tye's your name, ain't it?" Rawlings asked harshly without any preamble.

Beaumont nodded. "That's right. What can I do for you?"

"Where's Will Bramlett?"

"In there." Beaumont inclined his head toward the right-hand side of the cabin. "I was just up on the hill back yonder, digging his grave."

"He's dead?" Callie Stratton exclaimed.

"Yes, ma'am. I did everything I could for him, but he died a little after three this morning. You know about what happened?"

"We know," Rawlings said curtly. "Vern here was in Brownwood last night and heard about it. He brought the word to my place this morning and we decided we'd better head into town. Picked up Simon along the way."

"We wanted to check on Will first, though," Callie said. Her voice had softened a little. She was normally a brash, outspoken woman, but the news of Bramlett's death appeared to have subdued her somewhat. "I'm sorry we didn't get here before he passed on."

"When we heard how bad he was shot, we knew he didn't have a chance," Rawlings said, and Beaumont thought that was a mite callous. Rawlings was haggard, as if he'd had a bad night. Probably hung over, Beaumont decided. Although the way he held his right arm so stiffly, he looked almost like he'd been hurt.

"We'll help you finish up the burying," Simon Clark offered. "Then we got to get on to town and see about Kane."

"What about Kane?" Beaumont asked sharply.

Rawlings used his left hand to rub his beard-stubbled jaw. "You ain't heard about that, have you?" Without waiting for an answer, he went on. "No, of course not. You been out here with Bramlett all night. Kane's been shot, too."

Beaumont's eyes widened in surprise. "Shot!" he repeated. "By who?"

"Skeet Harlan, Marshal Keever's deputy. Kane went into town to look for Doc Yantis—"

"I knew that."

Rawlings looked a little irritated by the interruption. "When he couldn't find Doc, he went to the marshal's office. I guess he thought maybe somebody there could tell him where Yantis was. Harlan already knew about that dustup along the Slash D fence line last night, so he tried to arrest him. Kane didn't want to give up." Rawlings shrugged and then winced. There was definitely something wrong with his right arm, Beaumont thought. "When Kane went for his gun, Harlan shot him three times."

"Is he dead?"

"Nope," Vern Gladwell replied. "Shot up pretty bad, of course, but still breathin'. When Doc got back to town from the Slash D, he took a look at Kane and said he might live. Maybe."

"What was the doctor doing at the Slash D?"

"A couple of their men got hit when they were bush-whacked along Stepps Creek." Rawlings stared hard at Beaumont. "You know all about that, do you, Tye?"

"Chris told me he and Will went down there to cut Duggan's fence. Then some of Duggan's riders jumped them and all hell broke loose. I never really got the straight of it. Chris didn't seem all that sure himself what had happened."

"You weren't there?" Rawlings asked.

Beaumont shook his head. "No, if Chris and Will had somebody with them, it sure wasn't me."

The men looked at each other, clearly puzzled by

something. Simon Clark shook his head and said, "I'll ask around, Al, but as far as I know everybody in our bunch was close to home last night. I don't know who could have bushwhacked those Slash D boys."

"Well, we'd better find out," Rawlings snapped, "because we'll damn sure get the blame for it."

"Where's Kane now?" Beaumont asked.

"Locked up in the jailhouse," Gladwell answered. "Doc said he could take care of him just as well there, and it'd be better not to move him."

"What are they going to do with him if he recovers?"

"Probably string him up from the nearest tree," Rawlings said. "That's what those high-and-mighty bastards think of as justice. But it won't happen if we've got anything to say about it. You ridin' with us to town, Tye?"

Beaumont nodded. There wouldn't be any lynching. He would see to that, even if it meant revealing his identity as a Ranger.

"Let's get Bramlett in the ground, then," Rawlings said. "Time's a-wastin'." His voice lost a few of its rough edges as he added, "I don't want to find that another friend o' mine has died before I got there."

19

The hour was early and not many people were stirring on Brownwood's streets when Ace McKelvey emerged from the Palace and strolled around the downtown square. The saloon keeper had an unlit cigar clenched in his teeth. He hadn't been to bed yet—well, not to sleep, anyway, he thought with a faint smile as he remembered the enjoyable time he'd spent with the blond whore called Annie—and he was tired. Before he turned in and slept away most of the day, though, he had to check on some important business.

He paused across the street from the marshal's office and waited for a few minutes, chewing on the cigar. The door of the office opened and Skeet Harlan stepped out and stretched. The little deputy spotted McKelvey across the street and gave him a miniscule nod. Then both men moved off, heading in different directions.

By the time a few minutes had passed, however, they had circled around a couple of blocks, and each had headed for the same destination. They met in an alley behind a hardware store that wasn't open for business yet. No one else was in sight, and all the nearby windows were tightly closed.

Harlan frowned worriedly anyway and said, "I don't like this meetin' in broad daylight."

"There's no reason to be concerned," McKelvey

assured him. "You're an officer of the law and I'm an honest businessman. There's no reason why we shouldn't exchange a few pleasantries if we happen to run into each other."

Harlan snorted. "Honest businessman. Now that's a good one."

McKelvey's face flushed with irritation. "Never mind that. Where's Kane?"

"Locked up in the county jail," Harlan answered with a jerk of his head in that direction.

"Is he going to live?"

"Doc Yantis says he might."

McKelvey rolled the cigar from one corner of his mouth to the other. "It might be better if Kane was dead," he said slowly. "That would just stir up Rawlings and the others that much more."

Harlan shook his head. "I hope he ups and dies, too, but I ain't goin' in there to make sure of it, if that's what you're gettin' at, McKelvey. You got me in your pocket and Keever's an idiot, but Sheriff Wilmott and his deputies are too damned honest to let something like that pass."

"Well, we'll hope for the best," McKelvey said with a shrug. "Or the worst, if you want to look at it from Kane's point of view."

Harlan spit in the dust of the alley and said, "I ain't lookin' at nothin' from Kane's point of view. He was a damn fool to think he could buck Duggan and the other big dogs in the first place."

McKelvey smiled thinly. "He might have been successful if not for all the hard feelings caused by the fence-cutting. That was a good idea you had, Harlan."

"It wasn't all my doin'," Harlan said. "Once Flint and his boys cut a fence or two, Kane and the other little ranchers got the idea, all right. All we had to do was prime the pump, and the trouble's been flowin' ever since."

McKelvey nodded in satisfaction. "Yes, and that ambush Flint pulled off last night on MacDonald and the rest of those Slash D riders will just throw more fuel on the fire. It'll soon be an all-out war."

"Good thing you were able to get word to him in time to set it up," Harlan commented.

McKelvey frowned a little. He had sent the swamper from the Palace with a message to Flint Coburn, who was camped with his men on Pecan Bayou north of town. Then Coburn and the other hired guns who rode for him had trailed the Slash D cowboys out of Brownwood toward the home ranch. It had been sheer luck that MacDonald and his companions had stumbled over Chris Kane and Will Bramlett trying to cut the Slash D fence. Nobody would ever believe now that it hadn't been some of the small ranchers who had opened fire on the cowboys.

Yes, everything was working out perfectly for his plans, McKelvey thought . . . so perfectly that he was getting nervous. Something was bound to go wrong.

But right now, he couldn't see what it might be. Both sides in the clash drank and gambled in his saloon, so he was able to keep track of what they were planning. Men ran off at the mouth when they had been putting away the booze, and they talked to the whores they bedded, too. McKelvey was able to get vital information from Midge and Annie and the other calico cats who worked in the saloon without them even being aware of what he was doing. And if events didn't go exactly the way he wanted them to, he was able to manipulate them subtly by dropping a word here and there to the leaders on both sides. Al Rawlings probably regarded him as a friend. That was ironic, McKelvey thought. Rawlings was nothing to him but a tool to get what he wanted.

Now that redheaded sister of Rawlings' . . . that might be a different story, McKelvey mused. He enjoyed his times with Annie, but Callie Stratton was twice as much woman. He wondered what it would be like to bend her to his will, to make her do whatever he damned well pleased. . . .

Skeet Harlan broke into that pleasant reverie by asking, "You know when the rest of the gunmen will be here?"

McKelvey shook his head. Flint Coburn had about fifteen men riding with him. Thirty or forty more were on their way down from Colorado and Wyoming, veteran Coltmen, hardened killers who had been summoned by the telegrams Coburn had sent them. Once they got here, McKelvey would have a small army at his command, and it would be time for the big dustup, the inevitable showdown.

"Sometime in the next month, that's all I know," he told Harlan.

The gunslinging little deputy chuckled. "This town won't know what hit it. Nobody around here is a match for what we'll throw at them."

McKelvey nodded his agreement. "We'd better get on about our business. If you *do* happen to get a chance to dispose of Chris Kane . . ."

"Don't worry. If I get the chance, he's a dead man." Harlan stroked his chin in thought. "It might be better, though, if he lives."

"How do you figure that?"

An ugly grin stretched across Harlan's rawboned features. "Then he could get strung up by a lynch mob. Think how Rawlings' bunch would take to that."

McKelvey nodded slowly and said, "Skeet, you

have a positive genius for coming up with these things."

They went their separate ways then. McKelvey was ready to get some sleep. It would probably be a busy night at the Palace. By evening, the whole county would know what had happened out at the Slash D fence line and would know that Chris Kane was wounded and locked up in the Brown County jail. Folks would choose up sides. Tempers would run high.

And the big blowout would be that much closer to happening.

With the ease of a true frontiersman who knew he had to take his slumber where he could get it, Frank had gotten a good night's sleep in the Slash D bunkhouse. First he'd had to spend some time talking to the cowboys, of course, as Duggan had warned him he would. They had all wanted to know what the famous Frank Morgan was doing in their neck of the woods. Frank had told them that he was just passing through the area and needed some work. They didn't know that he probably had as much money as their boss and all the other big ranchers in Brown County put together.

Like the others, he was awakened before dawn by the ringing of an iron triangle on the porch of the main house. The cowboys stumbled out of their bunks, washed up, and got dressed by lantern light, then trooped over to the house for breakfast. Duggan's Chinese cook and majordomo, Wing, had the dining room table groaning under platters piled high with flapjacks, bacon, and thick slices of ham, as well as bowls full of scrambled eggs and fried potatoes. A full pot of coffee sat at each end of the table, along with a pitcher of buttermilk.

"Wrap your gums around that, you worthless, bowlegged waddies," Wing said, sounding more like a native Texan than a Chinaman. "When you get done, there's biscuits and honey."

Frank enjoyed the meal. It had been a while since he had experienced the camaraderie of being part of a ranch crew. When he was growing up, that was the only world he had known, but life had taken him on much different trails than what he might have expected as a youth.

Wing went around the table, seeing that the men had all they wanted to eat. He paused by Frank's chair and said, "That dog of yours is out by the cookshack, Mr. Morgan. I gave him a ham bone."

"I'm much obliged for that," Frank said. "And I'm sure Dog is, too."

"That's his name—Dog?"

"That's right."

"Do you call your horse Horse?"

Frank grinned. "Sometimes. One I'm riding now, though, is named Stormy."

Wing returned the grin and started to turn away, but Frank stopped him with a question.

"How are the two boys who got shot last night doing this morning?"

Wing's expression grew more serious. "Dave is sleeping soundly. He was awake a while ago. He's in some pain, of course, but seems to be doing about as well as can be expected. Pitch is asleep, too, but I'm sure he'll wake up soon, and then he'll insist he's all right and can do a regular day's work. I told Mr. Duggan he might have to hog-tie Pitch to keep him off that wounded leg."

"I wouldn't be surprised," Frank said. He regarded the Chinese majordomo intently. "You've been up all night, haven't you?"

"There'll be time for sleep later," Wing replied.

Frank nodded in understanding. A true Westerner did what had to be done, and he suspected that Wing fit that definition, no matter what the color of his skin.

Earl Duggan came into the dining room and sat down to eat with his men. A short time later, hoofbeats rattled outside the house, making everyone look up from the table. Duggan tossed his napkin down and got to his feet, adjusting the gun belt around his waist as he did so. Clearly, he wasn't expecting any early morning visitors.

As Frank glanced around at the tough, gun-hung crew of punchers, he thought that if the rider was looking for trouble, he was liable to get more than he bargained for with this bunch. The ambush the night before had everybody on edge and ready to fight.

Duggan started toward the door, but without seeming to hurry, Frank was on his feet and there before the rancher. Frank put out a hand and said quietly, "Better wait a minute, Boss, and let me take a look first." In times of trouble, more than one man had gone to his front door and gotten a bullet for his trouble.

Duggan jerked his head from side to side and rasped, "I don't hide behind nobody, not even a fast gun like you, Morgan." With that, he jerked the door open and stepped out onto the porch.

Frank was right behind him, just in case.

The man who was swinging down from his saddle in front of the house didn't look like he was hunting trouble, though. He was tall and lean and wore a sober black suit. The light that came through the open door of the house glittered on the badge pinned to his coat lapel. He looked up at Duggan and gave the rancher a friendly nod.

"Mornin', Earl," he said.

"You're out early, Sheriff," Duggan said.

"I've got some news I thought you might like to know about."

"You could have called me on the phone. We've got a line strung out here now, you know."

The lawman shook his head. Like Duggan, he had white hair and a weathered face. If not for the fact that he was a little taller and much slimmer, they could have been two peas in a pod.

"I don't use that newfangled thingamabob unless I have to. I like to look at a man when I'm talkin' to him, especially if I've got something important to say."

"Then I reckon this must be important."

"It is. I've got Chris Kane locked up in my jail this mornin'."

Duggan's nostrils flared with anger. "That damn fence-cutter—"

The sheriff raised a hand to stop him just in case Duggan was about to launch into a rant. "I didn't lock him up on account of that, although I reckon I could have."

"Then he's behind bars because it was some of his friends who bushwhacked four of my riders last night?"

"No, I don't know who was responsible for that."

Duggan grunted. "Kane won't talk, eh?"

"Kane *can't* talk. He hasn't regained consciousness since Skeet Harlan shot him three times last night."

Frank had been lounging with his shoulder against the door jamb. He straightened at the mention of the deputy's name. Remembering the viciousness he had seen lurking in Harlan's watery eyes, he wasn't surprised to hear that the man had shot somebody.

"Kane went for his gun first," the sheriff went on. "At least, that's the way Harlan tells it, and I don't have any reason not to believe him. If he did, it was a damned fool stunt, because he never had a chance against Harlan."

"I'm surprised Kane's not dead," Duggan said.

"He may be yet. Doc Yantis didn't know whether he'd make it or not. He didn't want him moved, though, so we left Kane in jail. If he recovers, he'll go on trial for trying to kill Harlan. I can charge him with attempting to cut your fence, too, even though from what I hear, he never quite got around to it."

"Damn right I want him charged," Duggan snapped. "What about that ambush?"

The sheriff shook his head. "We'll have to wait and see if I can find out more about that. I just thought you might want to know about Kane . . . seein' as how he once rode for you and all."

Duggan waved that off with a curt gesture. "I don't care about that now. Kane up and quit me. Whatever happens to him is his own lookout."

"Fair enough." The lawman started to turn back to his horse.

"Wait a minute, J.C.," Duggan said. "You've ridden all the way out here. Why don't you come inside and have some breakfast? There's plenty of food, and Wing can put on another pot of coffee if he needs to."

The sheriff smiled and looped the reins around the hitching post. "Don't mind if I do," he said.

"And afterwards, I'll ride back into town with you. I want to have a look at Kane and maybe talk to him if he's come to. He'll tell me who was responsible for that ambush. I had two men wounded."

"I know," the sheriff said as he stepped up onto the porch. "I'm not sure it's a good idea letting you question my prisoners, though, Earl. I'm still the sheriff of Brown County, not you."

There was enough crisp irritation in the lawman's voice so that Duggan nodded and said, "Didn't mean to poke in where I'm not wanted. I just want to get to the bottom of this."

"So do I," the sheriff assured him. As they started inside, the lawman glanced at Frank and asked, "New man?"

Duggan nodded. "Yeah. Meet Frank Morgan. Frank, this is Sheriff J.C. Wilmott."

"Morgan!" Wilmott exclaimed as he came to a sudden stop. "The one they call the Drifter?"

"That's right," Frank said as he put out his hand. "I'm pleased to meet you, Sheriff."

Wilmott shook hands, but he looked suspicious. "You ain't aimin' to cause trouble around here, are you, Morgan?"

"I never aim to *cause* trouble, Sheriff."

"But you damned sure don't run away from it, neither."

"When the Good Lord made me, He didn't put a lot of backup in me."

"But from what I hear He sure stubbed His toe when he was puttin' in the gun speed and the sharp eye. You're ridin' for the Slash D now, Morgan?"

"That's right."

"Just what this county needed," the sheriff muttered as he headed for the table. "One more stick o' dynamite, with the fuse just a-sputterin'."

20

Simon Clark, who was a lay minister, said the necessary words over Will Bramlett's grave, and then Beaumont and Gladwell took turns shoveling the dirt back in. Beaumont had knocked together a crude coffin from some lumber in the barn before starting on the grave. The thudding of dirt clods on the coffin's wooden top was one of the most mournful sounds in the world, Beaumont thought.

With that grim chore attended to, he saddled his horse and joined the others for the ride into Brownwood.

Al Rawlings was impatient to get there and had chafed at the delay as they finished the job of burying Bramlett. Clark and Gladwell had insisted, though. Beaumont couldn't tell how Callie Stratton felt, other than being upset. She was still acting more restrained than usual.

The sun was well up in the morning sky by the time they rode through Early, a little settlement a few miles east of Brownwood. A couple of men were lounging in front of the town's only store. They raised their hands in a signal for the riders to halt.

"You look like you're fixin' to cloud up and rain all over somebody, Al," one of the men said to Rawlings. "Where are you headed?"

"We're going to the Brown County jail," Rawlings

replied. "Chris Kane was shot last night, and now they've got him locked up. We intend to make sure he's bein' treated right."

"Yeah, we heard something about that," the other man said. "You want some company?"

Rawlings jerked his head in a curt nod. "Sure, come along. The bigger group we have, the better. That way anybody'll think twice about trying anything funny."

By this time Beaumont had recognized the two men as Clay Harrell and Ben Mullins. They owned small spreads down toward Zephyr and were part of the informal group opposed to the big ranchers. Harrell mounted up while Mullins said, "If there's gonna be a showdown, somebody needs to ride around the county and spread the word. I can do that."

"Good idea," Rawlings agreed. "Tell everybody on our side to meet at the Palace as soon as they can get into town. We'll go there after we've been to the jail to check on Kane."

Mullins nodded and bounded into his saddle. He wheeled his horse and raced off while the others proceeded at a more deliberate pace toward Brownwood.

Beaumont didn't like what he had just heard. If all the small ranchers and farmers came into town and got together, they might decide to take Chris Kane out of the jail, even though he was wounded and probably in no shape to be moved. In their anger and resentment, they might not think about that. Beaumont couldn't allow a raid on the jail. A rescue attempt would be just as illegal as a lynching.

Maybe it wouldn't come to that, the young Ranger thought. Surely even a hothead like Rawlings had more sense.

The tall clock tower—which didn't have a clock in it—of the Brown County Courthouse came into view. A few minutes later the riders came to the wooden bridge over Pecan Bayou. The hooves of their horses clopped loudly on the planks as they crossed. The road curved up ahead and led to the downtown area. Folks at houses and businesses along the way began to notice the riders as they passed. Beaumont heard excited shouts behind them. When he glanced over his shoulder, he saw people on horseback and in wagons following them. Quite a procession was forming, in fact.

If there was going to be trouble, the townspeople wanted to be on hand to witness it. It was a human quality dating all the way back to the old Roman days and probably before that, Beaumont thought. Nobody wanted to miss the excitement, even if blood and death might be involved.

Especially if blood and death might be involved, he amended with a slight bitter quirk of his mouth.

Someone must have seen them coming and dashed ahead to the jail, because several of Sheriff Wilmott's deputies were out in front of the sandstone building by the time the group of riders reached it. A couple of the lawmen had shotguns tucked under their arms.

Beaumont didn't see the sheriff himself, and he wondered where Wilmott was. There was no sign of Marshal Keever or Skeet Harlan, either, but that came as no real surprise. Chris Kane had been turned over to the sheriff, so Wilmott had authority over him now, not the two town lawmen.

One of the deputies stepped forward as the riders reined in. His attitude seemed easy enough on the surface, but there was a definite undercurrent of tension in the air. The deputy nodded and said, "Morning, boys." He tugged the brim of his hat as he looked at Callie Stratton. "Ma'am. What can we do for y'all?"

"We want to see Chris Kane," Rawlings said. His voice was harsh with dislike.

"Kane's locked up," the deputy said.

"We know that, damn it."

"And he's been shot," the deputy went on. "He doesn't need to be disturbed. You better let him rest. You folks can come back later."

"We'd like to see him now," Clark said.

"We want to be sure he's all right," Gladwell added.

"That's right," Rawlings snapped. "There's no telling what kind of treatment he's been gettin' here."

That made the deputy bristle. "Nobody's been mistreating him, if that's what you're getting at, Rawlings. Doc Yantis patched him up last night, and the doc's been back by to check on him this morning. Nobody could do any more than that for him."

"There was no reason for Skeet Harlan to shoot him three times!"

"You'll have to take that up with Skeet," the deputy said coolly. "From what I heard, Kane went for his gun first, so he doesn't have much room to complain about what happened."

Rawlings edged his horse forward, crowding the deputy. "Are you gonna let us see Kane or not?" he demanded.

The lawman started to swing the barrels of the shotgun up toward Rawlings. "I told you, you can't go in there—"

The other deputies were bringing their Greeners to bear, too, and Rawlings, Clark, Gladwell, and Harrell were sliding their hands toward their guns. Callie had a gun belt strapped around her hips, too, and she closed her fingers around the butt of the Colt sticking up from the holster. If there was a gunfight, she planned to be part of it.

Beaumont saw all that and knew what was about to happen. He couldn't just stand by and let blood be spilled in the streets of Brownwood. He would have to speak up and tell everyone involved that he was a Texas Ranger. . . .

"Hold it!"

The shouted command came from behind the riders. They looked around to see another group of men on horseback trotting quickly toward them. The order had come from a white-haired man in a black suit who rode in the front of the bunch. A sheriff's badge glittered on his lapel.

Beaumont felt relief wash through him. He recognized Sheriff Wilmott and knew the grizzled old lawman would put a stop to the trouble that was brewing, at least for the time being. Beaumont wouldn't have to reveal his identity as a Ranger after all.

That was when Beaumont's gaze strayed to the men riding with Wilmott, and he got the shock of his life. Earl Duggan was just behind the sheriff, and riding beside Duggan was one of the last men Beaumont would have ever expected to see here.

Frank Morgan.

Following breakfast at the Slash D, Duggan had repeated his intention of riding back to Brownwood with the sheriff. Frank had saddled Stormy, and Ed MacDonald had gotten one of the horses from his string ready to ride, as well as saddling Duggan's mount. Then the four men had started along the road that led to town.

There hadn't been much conversation along the way. Wilmott evidently wasn't a talkative man by nature, and the other three tended toward the taciturn as well. The relative silence didn't bother Frank. He was nearly always comfortable with his own thoughts.

When they rode into Brownwood and approached the county jail, Frank's keen eyes were the first to spot a crowd gathering in front of the building. "Looks like some sort of trouble going on up there," he said.

"Damned if you're not right, Morgan." The sheriff spurred his horse into a trot. "Come on!"

As they hurried along the street toward the jail, Frank saw that several riders appeared to be confronting a handful of deputies in front of the lockup. One of them had long red hair under a brown Stetson. Callie Stratton, Frank decided. There might be another woman in Brown County who dressed like a man and had hair that color, but somehow Frank doubted it.

As they drew nearer, he recognized Callie's brother, Al Rawlings, too. The men with them were probably small ranchers or farmers. He wondered if they were there because of Chris Kane. That seemed to be the most likely explanation.

Seeing that gunplay was about to break out, Sheriff Wilmott yelled, "Hold it!" Everyone in front of the jail turned to look at the newcomers. . . .

Frank felt the shock of recognition almost like a physical blow. One of the men confronting the deputies was Tyler Beaumont.

The young Ranger hadn't changed in the months since Frank had seen him. Well, he might look a little older, Frank decided. Beaumont had been through a lot. It wasn't surprising that some of the strain showed on his face.

Beaumont looked even more startled to see Frank. That was understandable. Frank had known Beaumont was somewhere in the area. Finding him was why he had come to Brown County in the first place. Beaumont, on the other hand, had had no idea Frank was within a hundred miles of Brownwood.

Frank kept his face expressionless as he reined in and sat there with Wilmott, Duggan, and Ed MacDonald.

The sheriff demanded in a loud voice, "What in blazes is going on here?"

"We want to see Chris Kane," Rawlings said. He glared past Wilmott at Frank. "Nobody—not even Duggan's hired gun—is going to stop us."

"The law's going to stop you," Wilmott snapped. "I'll be damned if anybody tells me how to run my jail, and I say you and your friends ain't goin' in, Rawlings."

"You afraid of what we'd see?" Rawlings asked with a sneer.

Before Wilmott could respond to that gibe, Callie moved her horse forward, putting herself between her brother and the sheriff. "We just want to see for ourselves that Chris is being taken care of," she said.

"Now I've seen everything," MacDonald drawled in a whisper to Frank. "Callie Stratton as the voice of reason. Wonders ain't never gonna cease."

Wilmott shut him up with a frowning glance. Then the sheriff turned back to Callie and said, "You have my word, Mrs. Stratton, that everything's being done for Kane that can be done. Tell you what . . . I'll allow you to go in and see him, but the rest of your bunch has to stay out here."

Rawlings started to protest, but Simon Clark said, "That sounds all right to me."

"Me, too," Vern Gladwell put in. "As long as Callie doesn't mind."

She nodded. "Sure, I can do that." She swung down from her saddle and handed the reins to her brother. Rawlings took them grudgingly. He still looked like he wanted to fight.

Frank watched Beaumont from the corner of his eye. The youngster was making a point of it not to stare at him now. It was pretty clear to Frank that Beaumont was working undercover. He wasn't wearing his silver five-peso Ranger badge, and he was sort of hanging back in the group led by Rawlings.

Frank was anxious to talk to him and find out exactly what was going on and what his plans were, but that would have to wait. Out here in front of this crowd, they couldn't even acknowledge that they knew each other, let alone carry on a conversation. For the time being, they were going to have to pretend they were on opposite sides of the clash that threatened to split Brown County right down the middle.

As Callie and Sheriff Wilmott started into the jail, Earl Duggan said loudly, "I want to see Kane, too." He started to dismount.

"Wait just a damned minute!" Rawlings burst out. "Sheriff, if you won't let Kane's friends in to see him, I don't think you should let his enemies in, either."

"That's a good point," Wilmott admitted reluctantly. "Earl, I'll have to ask you to wait out here."

"I ain't accustomed to bein' told where I can and can't go, J.C.," Duggan growled.

"Well, you better get used to it when it comes to this jail," the sheriff snapped back. "I'm in charge here, and don't none of you forget it."

What he was going to be in charge of, Frank thought, was a whole mess of trouble if the lid ever came off the boiling cauldron that Brown County had turned into. For the moment, though, Duggan subsided with a grunt and a curt nod.

"I still want to know who was responsible for bush-whackin' my men," he said.

"So do I. When Kane wakes up, I'll ask him."

With that, Wilmott ushered Callie into the jail, and the crowd in the street waited tensely for them to return.

21

Rawlings and Duggan did their best to glare holes in each other. The men with Rawlings didn't seem quite as hostile as he was, but it was clear they didn't feel very friendly toward Duggan, either. For his part, Frank remained impassive. Beside him, Ed Mac-Donald was tense.

"It could've been some of this bunch that bush-whacked us last night, Frank," he said quietly.

But not quietly enough so that Rawlings didn't overhear him. "That's a damned lie!" he exclaimed. "We heard about what happened, but none of us were anywhere near the Slash D last night."

Now that the argument was out in the open, MacDonald edged his horse forward a little. "What about that fella with you?" he asked, gesturing toward Beaumont.

"You mean Tye?"

So that was the name he was using, Frank thought.

"I've seen him around," MacDonald said. "He works for Kane and Bramlett, doesn't he? For that matter, where's Bramlett?"

"I can speak for myself," Beaumont said tersely. "Yes, I ride for Kane and Bramlett. At least, I did. Will Bramlett is dead."

That announcement brought mutters of surprise from the crowd.

"He was shot in that ambush you're so eager to blame on us," Beaumont went on. "He died early this morning, and we buried him out on his spread. Now tell me, if any of our bunch was responsible for the ambush, why was Will shot? That just doesn't make sense."

"He could've been hit by accident when your friends were tryin' to cut down my riders," Duggan said.

"That's not the way it happened," Beaumont insisted.

Frank had known from the blood on the grass that one of the men who had been about to cut the Slash D fence had been hit. And it could have been an accident, as Duggan said.

But Frank had been in many gun battles, and it seemed to him that when the men hidden in the trees had opened up with that vicious first volley, they hadn't cared who they might hit. Surely if the bushwhackers had been friends of Kane and Bramlett, they would have been more careful.

But if they hadn't been part of the loose-knit organization of small ranchers and farmers, then who in blazes *had* they been? Frank still couldn't answer that question.

Beaumont wasn't through. "Listen to me," he said. "When Chris brought Will back to the ranch last night, he told me he didn't have any idea who had started all the shooting. He thought it was just the Slash D riders."

"It wasn't us," MacDonald said. "Some fellas threw down on us from the trees along the creek."

Beaumont nodded. "That's what I'm hearing now. But I tell you Chris and Will didn't have anything to do with it."

"And neither did any of the rest of us!" Rawlings said. "How do we know your men ain't lyin' about the whole thing, Duggan?"

"I've got two men with bullet holes in 'em, you

damned fool!" roared Duggan. "What do you think happened, they shot themselves?"

Rawlings bristled and moved his hand closer to his gun. Everyone else followed suit, and once again the street was locked in a tense tableau that might erupt into bloody violence at any second.

The door of the jail opened before that could happen, and Callie Stratton came out, accompanied by Sheriff Wilmott. All eyes swung to them, breaking the potentially deadly tension.

"I've seen Chris," Callie announced. "As far as I can tell, everything possible is being done for him."

"Is he still unconscious?" Duggan asked.

Callie nodded. "He is. And he looks terrible. I don't know if he's ever going to wake up again."

"He shouldn't have tried to draw on Skeet Harlan," Duggan said. "He got what was comin' to him."

For a second Frank thought Callie was going to flare up again, maybe even reach for the gun on her hip, but she suppressed her anger at Duggan's callous comment and said to her brother, "Let's go, Al. There's nothing we can do here."

"Yeah, I guess not," Rawlings agreed. With a hate-filled glower, he turned his horse and started away from the jail. The others followed, including Callie.

Frank, Duggan, and MacDonald sat their horses where they were, forcing the other delegation to go around them. As Beaumont rode past Frank with only a few feet between them, he turned a cold-eyed gaze on the Drifter. Anyone looking at them would have no idea that they knew each other, let alone that they had been good friends and comrades-in-arms.

Frank hoped that was just a pose. He hoped that Beaumont didn't really hate him as much as he seemed to. . . .

***

They headed for Ace McKelvey's Palace, as Rawlings had said earlier. Beaumont didn't look back as they rode away. He didn't want to give Morgan the satisfaction.

What the hell was Frank Morgan doing with Duggan? Was he really the cattle baron's hired gun? That wasn't like the Morgan that Beaumont had known. That Frank had taken pride in the fact that he'd never hired out his gun.

But times changed and so did the men who lived through them. Beaumont himself was not the same man he used to be; the tragedy that had befallen Victoria on their wedding day had seen to that. Maybe Morgan had decided that such things as honor no longer meant anything to him. Maybe he had finally become what so many people had always taken him to be: a ruthless, cold-blooded killer.

One thing was for sure, Beaumont thought. Morgan would do well to steer clear of him. No matter what Morgan was doing here in Brown County, Beaumont wanted nothing to do with him.

They dismounted in front of the Palace, tied their horses at the hitch rail, and went inside. It was only the middle of the morning, so the saloon wasn't busy. A chubby gent with slicked-down black hair and a narrow mustache was working behind the bar. A drunk was sprawled facedown on one of the tables. He was the only customer.

"Gimme a bottle and six glasses," Rawlings snarled at the bartender. The man hurried to follow the order. He brought the bottle and the glasses over to the table where the group sat down.

Rawlings grabbed the bottle by the neck and poured the drinks. Beaumont thought it was a little early in the day for whiskey, but since none of the others objected, neither did he. He threw back the fiery liquor just like everyone else, even Callie. No ladylike sips for her.

"What are we going to do, Al?" Clay Harrell asked.

"I can tell you what we're *not* going to do," Rawlings replied. "We're not going to let Duggan and the rest of those big ranchers buffalo us. We got a right to be here, and by God, we're through bein' pushed around!"

"We can't stop them from stringing barbed wire," Simon Clark pointed out. "And as long as we're fenced in like we are, there's not much we can do."

"We can cut those damned fences," Rawlings grated. "That's what we should've been doing all along. Every time we come across a fence, cut every blasted strand of it, at every post for a hundred yards or more!"

"That won't do any good," Gladwell said. "They'll just put up more. And if any of their men catch us at it, there'll be shooting, just like last night."

Rawlings glared at him. "Whose side are you on, anyway?"

"I just don't want to see anybody else get killed."

"As long as it's Duggan or one of those other bastards like him, I don't care how many of them get killed," Rawlings said with a snort.

Beaumont didn't like the way this conversation was going. It couldn't lead to anything but trouble. He said, "We've tried cutting fences. From what I've heard, fences have been cut every now and then for the past couple of years, and like Vern said, it hasn't done a bit of good. Maybe we could come to some sort of arrangement with the big ranchers instead."

Rawlings stared at him. "Arrangement? What kind of arrangement could we have with those greedy bastards?"

"They understand money," Beaumont said with a shrug. "We could pay them a fee to drive our cattle across their spreads when it's time to take them to market. Same thing for water rights where we're fenced off from the creeks and such."

"You're just a grub-line rider," Rawlings snapped. "You're mighty free and easy about spending other people's money, Tye. You don't have anything riding on this. We do."

"Al's right," Clark said. "Our profits have been cut to the bone. There's no money to pay fees to men who don't really need the cash."

"That'd bust us," Gladwell added gloomily.

"Well, I'm not sure we can fight them." Beaumont took a chance. "Did you see that stranger with Duggan? Do you know who he is? He looked like a gunfighter to me."

"He is a gunfighter," Rawlings said with a grunt of disdain. "His name's Frank Morgan. I ran into him in here last night. I told him what was what."

"And you got a bullet through your arm for your trouble," Callie said. "Morgan could have killed you just as easily."

"Frank Morgan?" Beaumont repeated with a frown. "The one they call the Drifter?"

"That's him," Callie said.

"He's supposed to be one of the fastest guns still alive. Faster than Smoke Jensen, even."

"If you're scared of him, you can pull up stakes and ride on any time you're of a mind to," Rawlings said. "I ain't afraid of him."

"Maybe you should be," his sister said. "He might kill you next time."

"I'll be ready for him next time," Rawlings vowed. "Morgan won't kill me unless he shoots me in the back like the low-down skunk he is."

It was all Beaumont could do not to bristle angrily at that comment. Frank Morgan was no backshooter, and Rawlings ought to know that.

It took a couple of seconds for Beaumont to realize that he had automatically defended Morgan's good name, at least in his mind. He wasn't sure why he'd had that reaction. He didn't even like Morgan anymore. Just a matter of habit, he supposed. After all, he and Morgan had ridden together and fought side by side for quite a while.

He didn't have to defend Morgan. Callie Stratton did it for him. She said, "Frank Morgan may be a lot of things, but he's not a skunk, Al. He wouldn't shoot anybody in the back."

Rawlings sneered. "If you think so highly of him, why the hell don't you marry him?"

Callie reached over and snagged the bottle. As she poured herself another drink, she said, "I don't plan on ever getting married again. I already buried one husband, and that was enough. Morgan's a handsome man, though, in his way."

Rawlings snorted. "Don't go soft on him, Callie. He works for Duggan, remember? We may wind up swapping lead with him."

If you do, Beaumont thought, you'll probably wind up dying, too.

The door to the saloon's office opened. Ace McKelvey came out and looked around the room. In the time since he'd been in Brown County, Beaumont hadn't heard anyone mention McKelvey's real first name. Ace just seemed to suit him so well, even though he seldom took part in the poker games that went on in the saloon. Spotting the group at the table, he came over to them.

"Good morning, Callie," he said politely. He nodded to the others. "Boys. I heard about what happened to Chris Kane. I'm mighty sorry about that. He seemed like a decent sort, if a mite hotheaded."

"He's not dead yet," Rawlings said. "Don't talk about him like he's already in the ground."

"I meant no offense. But he was shot three times. Surely it's pretty unlikely that he'll recover."

"Doc Yantis says he might pull through," Callie said.

"Well, I certainly hope so. The way I hear it, the only reason Kane came to town was to look for the doc because his partner had been shot. What happened with Bramlett, anyway?"

"Dead," Beaumont answered heavily. "We buried him before we came into town."

McKelvey shook his head. "That's a damned shame. Sounds like Duggan's bunch pretty much made a clean sweep of them."

"It was Skeet Harlan who shot Chris," Beaumont pointed out. "And nobody seems quite sure who the bushwhackers were that killed Will."

McKelvey dismissively waved a hand and said, "Everybody knows that Harlan and Marshal Keever really work for Duggan and the other big ranchers. Do any of their cowhands ever get arrested when they come into town and go on a bender? Of course not. Keever and Harlan don't want to rock the boat. They know who has the most money and power in these parts."

"I'm not sure about that," Callie said with a frown. "Marshal Keever's always seemed reasonably honest to me."

"The man's dumb as a goat," Rawlings snapped. "And Harlan's just a snake-blooded killer."

Callie shrugged. "Well, I can't argue with that part. I always shiver a little whenever Skeet Harlan looks at me."

McKelvey took out a cigar and put it in his mouth. "It's just not right, the way Duggan and the others try to run roughshod over you fellas."

Simon Clark asked, "If that's the way you feel, McKelvey, why do you let them drink in here?"

The saloon keeper spread his hands and clamped his teeth on the unlit cigar as he said, "I'm just a businessman, boys. I can't afford to play favorites, no matter what my personal feelings may be." He glanced toward the entrance and frowned. "That's why I don't want any trouble in here, understand?"

Beaumont looked at the door, too, and knew what had prompted McKelvey's words. The door opened and Earl Duggan stalked into the Palace, followed by Frank Morgan and Ed MacDonald.

22

Duggan headed straight for the bar. MacDonald did, too, so Frank followed them, even though he had spotted Tyler Beaumont sitting at a table with Al Rawlings, Callie Stratton, and three other men. Frank didn't do more than glance in their direction as he joined Duggan and MacDonald at the bar.

"Whiskey," Duggan grated at the bartender. The apron hurried to fill the order. Without asking, he put glasses in front of Frank and MacDonald, too.

The group at the table looked like they were having a council of war. A man in a suit stood beside the table. Frank didn't know him, but from the looks of him he was a businessman of some sort, maybe the owner of the saloon. He spoke briefly to Rawlings and then came over to the bar.

"Hello, Earl," he said as he paused beside Duggan. The cattleman gave him a curt nod and then swallowed the whiskey in his glass.

"McKelvey," Duggan said shortly, confirming Frank's guess about the man's identity.

"I was just telling Rawlings and his bunch that I don't want any trouble in here," the saloon keeper said. "I hope I don't have to tell you the same thing. You should already know."

"Yeah, yeah, it ain't your fight," Duggan said with

the air of a man who'd had this conversation before. "Doesn't it get a mite uncomfortable straddling that fence all the time, McKelvey?"

"I just want peace in the county, Earl. If I can't have that, I'll settle for having it in here. But by God, I *will* have it in here."

Duggan shrugged. "We ain't looking for trouble."

McKelvey glanced over at the rancher's two companions. "I know Ed, of course. Who's this new fella?"

"Frank Morgan," Duggan said. He went on. "Frank, this is Ace McKelvey."

"Morgan," McKelvey repeated as he stepped past Duggan. "I know the name. You were in here last night. Rusty told me about what happened."

McKelvey didn't offer to shake hands, and neither did Frank.

"Sorry about the hole in your back wall," Frank said. "I thought fixing it might be a little easier than mopping up a lot of blood from the floor."

McKelvey chuckled, but there wasn't much genuine humor in the sound. "And you were probably right, at that." He lowered his voice more. "But you may regret not killing Al Rawlings. He's been making quite a few threatening comments concerning you, Mr. Morgan."

Frank shrugged. "I never worry overmuch about what somebody *says*."

The implication was clear. Frank took actions a lot more seriously than he did words.

"Just thought you should know," McKelvey said as he shifted his cigar from one side of his mouth to the other. "Better keep an eye on your back."

"I always do," Frank said.

McKelvey moved on to the end of the bar and conversed in low tones with his bartender for a few minutes. Then he went through a door and closed it behind him. That left the two factions alone with only the bartender, and he looked more than a little nervous about being in the same room with them.

Frank sipped his whiskey and tried to think of some way he could get a few minutes alone with Beaumont. He hoped that a quick conversation would clear up a lot of things. From what he had seen so far of the situation in Brown County, though, there wasn't going to be any quick, easy solution to the problems here. The anger and resentment on both sides ran too deep for that to be possible.

The door opened and half-a-dozen more men entered the room, boots clomping on the floor and spurs jingling. They glared toward the bar where Duggan, Frank, and MacDonald were standing and went straight to the table where Beaumont and the others sat. That was enough to tell Frank that the newcomers belonged to the same loose alliance of small ranchers and farmers.

"We might ought to move on, Boss," MacDonald said quietly to Duggan. "There's a dozen of those boys now, and they don't look happy."

"I never ran from sodbusters and pissants, and I'll be damned if I'm going to start now," Duggan declared. The apron had left the bottle. Duggan picked it up and splashed another drink into his glass. His voice had been pitched loudly enough so that the men at the table and those gathered around it must have heard him.

A moment later one of the newcomers pulled away from his friends and stomped toward the bar. "Hey, Duggan!" he said. "Were you talkin' about me, old man?"

Frank turned, apparently casually and completely at his ease. The man who had spoken to Duggan was tall and powerfully built, with a cowhide vest stretched over his broad shoulders and a high-crowned hat perched on a thatch of blond hair.

Duggan looked around disdainfully. "That depends, Anderson," he said. "Are you a sodbuster?"

"You know I ain't!" the big man said.

"Then you must be a pissant, because I sure as hell *was* talking about you and your friends." Duggan turned back to the bar, contempt evident in every line of his body.

Anderson started forward, his broad face contorting in anger. Before he could get there, Frank took a couple of steps, smoothly interposing himself between Duggan and the furious rancher.

"That's far enough, mister," Frank said, lifting his left hand and holding it out toward Anderson. His right hung near the butt of his gun.

"Who's this, Duggan?" Anderson asked with a sneer. "Your new bodyguard?"

Before Frank could say anything else, Beaumont got to his feet and said, "Better be careful, friend. That's Frank Morgan."

"Morgan the gunfighter?" Anderson hesitated, but he was too angry and too proud to back down. "I don't care. I aim to have a talk with Duggan. He can listen to me like a man, or I'll beat some attention into him."

Duggan turned around again. "Anderson, you don't have a thing to say that would interest me the least bit. Better go back over yonder with your friends if you know what's good for you."

"That's mighty big talk for a man hidin' behind a hired gun," Anderson said.

Duggan's face flushed. "Morgan, step aside. I'll handle this."

Frank began, "Mr. Duggan, I'm not sure that's—"

"You're ridin' for me, damn it!" Duggan barked. "When I give you an order, I expect you to follow it!"

"Better do as he says, Morgan," MacDonald advised. "The boss can handle himself. You and me better keep an eye on those others, though, to make sure they don't mix in where they ain't wanted."

For a moment Frank didn't move. Then he stepped aside. Duggan was considerably older than Anderson, but he was still spry enough to fight his own fights, as long as the odds were even. Frank intended to make sure they stayed that way.

"Nelse, don't be an idiot," Callie Stratton said, but Anderson ignored her. He stepped closer to Duggan, balling his hands into fists as he did so.

"You need to take down your fences, old man," Anderson rasped. "You agree to do that, and maybe I won't beat the hell out of you."

"The fences stay up," Duggan shot back at him. "And I'll shoot the first man I see cutting one of them!"

"Like you did Will Bramlett?"

Duggan shook his head. "My men didn't have anything to do with Bramlett gettin' shot. You and your bunch are just too damned stupid to realize that, though."

"A good man is dead because of you, Duggan, and another may die. It's time somebody taught you a lesson, and I'm just the man to hand you your needin's!"

Duggan smiled grimly. "You plan to talk me to death, Anderson?"

That taunt was enough to push Anderson over the edge. With a curse, he swung a big fist at Duggan's head.

The punch was wild and looping, and Duggan flung up his left and blocked it easily. At the same time, Duggan shot out his own right fist and slammed it into Anderson's face. Anderson was bigger and heavier, but the force of the blow rocked him back anyway. Duggan went after him, trying to follow up on his momentary advantage.

Anderson caught himself, though, and threw both

arms around Duggan in a bear hug. Duggan cried out involuntarily as those arms tightened around him in a bone-crushing grip.

MacDonald took a step toward the two combatants, but Frank put out an arm to stop him. "Let them fight it out," he said. "This is what the boss wanted."

By now everyone else in the saloon was standing up, anxious expressions on their faces as they watched the struggle between the two proud, stubborn men. Frank glanced at Beaumont and saw the worry on the young Ranger's face. It must go against the grain for Beaumont to just stand by and watch like this, Frank thought. Beaumont's lawman instincts were probably telling him to step in and break up the fight before someone got seriously hurt. In the role he was playing, though, as a member of the forces arrayed against the big cattlemen in the county, he couldn't afford to do that, no matter how much he might want to.

Duggan's face was bright red. He couldn't breathe with Anderson's apelike arms around him. In desperation he brought his knee up hard into Anderson's groin. Anderson grunted in pain but hung on. Duggan kneed him again and this time Anderson's bear hug slipped. Duggan managed to jerk his arms free. He smashed his open hands against Anderson's ears, drawing a howl of agony from the bigger man. Anderson let go of him entirely then.

Stepping back, Duggan drew several deep breaths into his air-starved lungs. He set his feet and peppered a couple of punches into Anderson's face. Frank could tell that Anderson was confused now, reeling in pain from his smashed privates and the blows to his ears. The jabs that Duggan landed just staggered him that much more. Duggan threw a haymaker that should have ended the fight.

Sheer luck sent Anderson weaving out of the way of

the punch, however, and Duggan's momentum made him lose his balance and stumble forward. Anderson recovered his wits enough to bend slightly. One hand shot out and grabbed Duggan's thigh. The other clamped onto Duggan's arm. With an inarticulate shout of effort and rage, Anderson lifted Duggan into the air and slammed him down on one of the nearby tables. The legs of the table snapped and splintered, and man and table collapsed into a heap on the floor. It had happened too quickly for anyone to stop it, even Frank Morgan.

From the corner of his eye Frank saw that McKelvey had emerged from his office again, drawn by the commotion of the fight. The saloon owner looked worried by the destruction that was going on, but at the same time he didn't seem all that upset about the ruckus. For a moment while no one in the Palace was watching him except Frank, what might have been a smile of satisfaction flashed across his ruddy face. Then it was gone and might as well have never been there.

"Damn it, you've killed him!" MacDonald roared as Duggan lay there motionless amidst the wreckage of the table. The Slash D foreman started toward Anderson, and this time he didn't give Frank a chance to stop him. He launched into a flying tackle that caught Anderson around the hips.

Anderson was still a little disoriented from the damage Duggan had heaped on him, and he didn't even try to defend himself. MacDonald's charge bore him over backward. Both men crashed to the ground. MacDonald landed on top and started smashing blows to Anderson's head.

Wounded arm and all, Al Rawlings lunged forward with a curse and tackled MacDonald. They tumbled over and over, slugging at each other. When two more of the small ranchers started to jump into the fracas, Frank knew that things had gone too far. This was going to turn into an all-out brawl, and there was nothing he could do to stop it.

But he couldn't stand by and let MacDonald take a beating, either, so he sprang forward to block the path of the other two men who wanted to get in on the fight. He knew he couldn't last long against two-to-one odds, but there was nothing else he could do.

Then suddenly, with a roar, Tyler Beaumont came barreling between the two men who were about to throw punches at Frank. He shouldered them aside, his compact, muscular form knocking them out of his way like a bowling ball flattening a couple of pins.

Frank lowered his guard for a second, thinking that the odds had just gotten a little better. With Beaumont helping him out he might even be able to hold his own against the angry ranchers.

That was when Beaumont yelled, "Let me have him!" then cocked an arm back and hit him square in the face, knocking him against the bar behind him.

23

The punch took Frank completely by surprise. He hadn't even tried to block it. The edge of the bar dug into his back, making him grimace in pain.

He became aware that Beaumont was boring in on him, fists poised. "You've got it coming, mister," the young Ranger grated. He sent a left whistling toward Frank's jaw.

Instinct brought Frank's right arm up to block the blow. He wasn't sure what the hell was going on here. The only explanation that made sense was that Beaumont was attacking him in order to solidify his position with the smaller ranchers. It was part of the act, the role he was playing.

Either that or he was remembering what had happened to Victoria back there on their wedding day, and all the grief and rage that he had bottled up inside were finally boiling over, a small voice in the back of Frank's head warned him.

Either way, Frank wasn't going to just stand there and let Beaumont whale on him. As soon as he had blocked Beaumont's second punch, he snapped a stinging left jab into Beaumont's face that bloodied the Ranger's nose.

Beaumont roared in pain and anger and let fly with another punch. Frank ducked to the side and let the blow graze his ear. Even the glancing blow packed enough power to stagger him a little. He hooked a right to Beaumont's belly. At first glance the young man might appear a little soft, even fat, but Frank found that it was like punching a washboard. The blow seemed to have no effect on Beaumont.

Standing toe to toe, they began to slug it out, trading punches, absorbing all the punishment the other had to give and dishing out tremendous punishment of their own. Frank wasn't aware of anything else going on around him. All he saw was Beaumont's twisted, blood-streaked face. All he heard were their grunts of effort and the soggy thuds of fists striking flesh and bone. Beaumont's punches slammed into his midsection. They crashed into his jaw and rocked his head from side to side. Pain washed over him, filling his senses.

But he gave as good as he got, and as his arms tired until they felt like lead and he could barely lift them, he sensed that Beaumont was just as exhausted and worn down. Gasping for breath, Frank struck again and again until he just couldn't do it anymore. As overwhelming weariness engulfed him and his arms dropped, he became aware that Beaumont was sobbing and choking out, "You bastard . . . you bastard . . ." over and over. Looking as if he had the weight of the world on his shoulders, Beaumont managed to lift his right arm one final time. Clenching his swollen, bloody hand into a fist, he threw a last punch.

At the same time Frank summoned up the last of his strength and struck out a final time as well, aiming a shaky punch at Beaumont's battered face.

Both men missed by a mile.

Off balance, they sagged against each other and would have fallen except for the fact that they were inadvertently holding each other up. Frank found himself looking into Beaumont's face from a distance of only a few inches, and as their eyes met, Frank saw that the hatred that had been there moments earlier was gone now, faded away. It might come back in the future, but for now, at least, it had disappeared.

He struggled to lift his hands and got them against Beaumont's shoulders. With a shove, he pushed the man away and stumbled backward. Frank caught himself against the bar. Beaumont leaned on a table, his chest heaving. As the pounding of the pulse in Frank's skull slowed somewhat, his head cleared enough for him to be able to look around. He became aware that silence had fallen over the saloon.

That was because everyone was looking at him and Beaumont, even Earl Duggan, who had recovered from the stunning impact of being thrown down on the table and was now sitting up amidst the debris. MacDonald and Rawlings had drawn apart but were still glaring at each other. Anderson was being helped to his feet by some of his friends. Callie Stratton looked on, white-faced with concern, probably for her brother and their friends. But Frank thought he saw some sympathy on her face when she glanced at him, too.

"Well," Marshal Keever said from the doorway, where he had just entered holding a shotgun, "who's going to pay for the damages?" Deputy Skeet Harlan stood beside him, licking his lips as his hand hovered over the butt of his Colt, ready to hook and draw. More than that, Harlan was ready to kill. Frank could read that in his eyes.

And at this moment, as beaten up as Frank was, he wasn't sure he could beat Harlan to the draw if the deputy decided to start the ball.

"I'll pay for whatever's busted up," Duggan said from the floor. "And well worth it to get in a few good licks like that. Somebody help me up, damn it."

McKelvey motioned for the bartender to help

Duggan. The apron hurried out from behind the bar and gave the cattleman a hand. Duggan was a little unsteady on his feet once he was up, but he shook off the bartender's attempts to help him further.

Pulling a wallet from his hip pocket, he fumbled out some bills and slapped them on the bar. "There!" he said to McKelvey. "Does that cover it?"

The saloon keeper picked up the money and riffled through it. "Sure, Earl," he said. "In fact, it's a little too generous."

"Keep the extra," Duggan growled. "It's the last *dinero* you'll get from me. You've straddled the fence long enough."

"Yeah," Rawlings added as he wiped blood from his mouth. "Better make up your mind which side you're on, McKelvey . . . because it's damn sure a war now." He picked up his hat, jammed it on his head, and said to his friends, "Let's get out of here."

"You go ahead, Al," his sister said. "Tye needs to have the doctor look him over before he leaves."

"I'm fine—" Beaumont started to insist, but Callie stopped him with a curt gesture.

"Don't argue with me," she told him. "I'm taking you over to Doc Yantis's office, and that's that." She looked at Frank. "You're coming, too, Morgan."

Frank gave a little shake of his head, not so much arguing as he was just uncertain that he had heard her right. "I don't need a doctor," he said. "I've been in fights before."

"You're coming," Callie declared, "or you and Beaumont will both have to fight *me*. And the shape you're both in, I think I can whip you."

"Go ahead, Frank," MacDonald said. "We'll wait here for you."

Frank could see that it wasn't going to do any good to argue with Callie Stratton. Once her mind was made up, changing it would be nigh on to impossible. "All right," he said. "As long as Tye here doesn't want to fight anymore."

Beaumont shook his head. "I'm all tussled out, Morgan. I'll call a truce if you will."

Frank nodded. "Sure."

"Come on, then," Callie said. "Al, I'll see you later at the ranch."

Rawlings frowned. "You're sure about this, Callie?"

"Have you ever known me *not* to be sure? There's nothing else we can do here in town. Chris Kane is in the hands of Doc Yantis, and the Lord. We'll just have to wait and see what happens."

Grudgingly, Rawlings and the other ranchers left the saloon. Duggan said, "We'll wait for you at the livery instead of here, Morgan." He cast a surly glance toward McKelvey. "I don't want to stay here anymore."

The saloon keeper just shook his head regretfully, as if he wished it had never come to this.

Frank wasn't convinced, though. He remembered that fleeting look of satisfaction on the man's face just as the brawl broke out.

"Let's go," Callie said to Frank and Beaumont. "I hope Doc's got plenty of sticking plaster. You two just about pounded each other into raw meat."

She was between the two men as they left the saloon. The streets of Brownwood were busy now since the hour was approaching midday. Quite a few people stared at Frank and Beaumont, both of whom bore numerous marks from their battle. Frank could already tell that by tomorrow he would be covered with bruises and would ache all over. Beaumont was in the same shape.

Doc Yantis's office was upstairs over a drugstore and was reached by a set of steps that climbed the side of the building. The little owl-like medico stood on the landing at the top of the stairs, his coat off and his hands thrust in his pants pockets. He chuckled as Frank, Beaumont, and Callie started up toward him.

"When I heard there was a big ruckus in the Palace, I figured I'd be getting some business soon," he said. "What did you boys do, light into each other with two-by-fours?"

"They did it with their fists," Callie said.

"I'll be surprised if they didn't bust every bone in their hands," Doc said with a shake of his head.

Frank had already thought of that. It generally wasn't a good idea for a gunfighter to indulge in fistfights. He had already flexed his right hand enough to know that there were no broken bones in it, however. That was lucky. He wasn't sure about the left. He thought he might have cracked a knuckle in that one.

Doc stepped back and ushered them into the office. In a stern voice he cautioned them, "Just in case you two are still holding a grudge against each other, you'd better forget about carrying on your battle up here. I'll chloroform the both of you if I have to before I treat you."

"And I'll help you, Doc," Callie said as she closed the door behind her.

Frank shook his head. "Don't worry, the fight's over. Isn't that right, Tye? That's your name, isn't it?"

Before Beaumont could answer, Callie said, "Oh, stop it. There's no point in pretending you two don't know each other. What I want to know is where from."

Doc raised his bushy eyebrows in surprise while Frank and Beaumont both stared at Callie. She crossed her arms over her ample bosom and looked at them intently. After a moment she snapped, "Well? Spit it out."

In a surly voice Beaumont said, "What makes you

think I know this gunslinger? I never saw him before today."

"Now that's just a bald-faced lie," Callie insisted. "I saw the look that passed between you two when Morgan came into the Palace. And I saw the way you lit into him, Tyc. That was a personal fight. Nobody goes after a stranger that way." She paused and then said, "Actually, more than anything else, it reminded me of the way brothers sometimes fight when there's something really hurtful between them."

"We're not brothers," Frank said. He didn't see any point in continuing to deny the relationship between him and Beaumont, not as convinced as Callie was. "But we do know each other. We used to ride together."

Beaumont's eyes flicked worriedly to Frank, and Frank knew what he was concerned about. Beaumont thought Frank might say too much and ruin his undercover activities.

He didn't have to worry about that. Frank had no intention of revealing that Beaumont was really a Texas Ranger. He went on, "We haven't seen each other for a long time, though."

"What's the grudge Tye's holding against you?" Callie wanted to know.

Frank shrugged. "What do you think? It was all over a woman."

Pain flashed through Beaumont's eyes, and Frank knew there was a lot of truth in what he had just said. At least part of the reason Beaumont had jumped him like that was because of what had happened to Victoria. Callie no doubt interpreted Frank's comment differently, but that was her problem, not his.

"It was a long time ago," Beaumont said. "I thought I was over it."

"Didn't look like it to me," Callie said.

"I'm willing to put it behind me, though," Beaumont

offered as he put out his hand and looked steadily at Frank.

Frank didn't hesitate. He took Beaumont's hand. Both of them winced a little as they squeezed.

"Be careful," Doc exclaimed. "I haven't checked those hands for broken bones yet. Now, one of you climb up on my examining table and the other one sit down over there in that chair and wait your turn."

Frank motioned for Beaumont to go first. He sat down in a straight-backed chair against the wall while Beaumont climbed onto the examining table.

Doc Yantis worked quickly and efficiently, cleaning the scrapes and cuts on Beaumont's face, swabbing them with antiseptic and covering the worst of them with sticking plaster. He checked for broken bones in the hands and prodded Beaumont's ribs to make sure none of them were cracked. When he was finished, Beaumont said, "I must look like a wild Indian, the way you painted that stuff all over my face, Doc."

"Nobody's going to mistake you for a Comanch', young man," Doc said. "Now hop down from the table. Your turn, Morgan."

Frank underwent the same treatment, and when Doc was through, the sawbones said, "Both of you are very lucky. You might have been laid up for a week, the way you thrashed each other."

"I'm glad it wasn't worse than it was," Frank said. Beaumont nodded in agreement. Frank went on. "Is there a place around here we can get a drink? I'd rather not go back to the Palace right now."

"You mean you want to have a drink with me?" Beaumont said in surprise.

Frank shrugged. "Why not? We've called a truce, haven't we?"

Callie frowned and said, "I don't know if that's such

a good idea, the two of you sitting down to have a drink together."

"We'll be fine," Frank assured her. "We used to be partners, remember? There won't be any trouble, will there, Tye?"

Beaumont shook his head. "Not a bit. You've got my word on that, Callie."

"All right, then," she said reluctantly. "Don't forget, though, Morgan, your friends are waiting for you at the livery stable."

"They can wait a few minutes longer. Or they can head back to the Slash D if they want to. I know how to get there."

"Maybe I should go with you. . . ." Callie offered.

Beaumont shook his head. "We're all right, really. You can head back to your brother's ranch if you want."

She thought it over for a moment and then nodded. "All right. But I don't want to hear anything later about the two of you shooting each other."

"Don't worry about that," Beaumont told her. "I'm just not about to draw on the famous Frank Morgan."

There was a mocking, slightly bitter edge to the words. Beaumont hadn't gotten completely over the emotions that had sent him tearing into Frank earlier. But at least he had taken a step in that direction, Frank thought.

"We'll go over to Pomp Arnold's place," Beaumont went on. "It's not as big as the Palace, and it won't be very busy at this time of day."

Frank nodded. "Sounds good to me." He reached in his pocket. "How much do we owe you, Doc?"

"Let's see, four bits apiece for the office visit, plus some plaster and antiseptic . . . Call it a dollar each."

Frank took out a couple of coins and handed them over. "I've got it," he told Beaumont.

The young Ranger frowned. "I don't need you to pay my doctor bills."

"You can get 'em next time," Frank said with a grin.

"Not gonna be a next time," Beaumont muttered as they left the office.

Callie went on her way when they reached the street, but not before she gave them a stern warning to behave themselves. The two men started walking toward Pomp Arnold's saloon, which was right on the square downtown, and as they went, Beaumont said out of the corner of his mouth, "What the hell are you doing here, Frank?"

"Let's wait until we get that drink," Frank suggested. "Then if it's quiet enough in there, we've got a lot to talk about, you and I."

24

There were a few drinkers in Arnold's saloon, but Frank and Beaumont were able to get a table in a rear corner where no one was around. By keeping their voices pitched low, they could converse without being overheard. As they talked, they nursed the mugs of beer they had brought over from the bar.

"So, Frank, what are you doing here?" Beaumont began.

"Luke Perkins wrote to me and told me you'd been sent down here to do a job." Frank didn't mention the Texas Rangers by name, just in case anyone was trying to eavesdrop, even though he didn't think that was the case. "I came to see if I could help."

Beaumont frowned at him. "Let me get this straight. You rode all the way down here from wherever you were just to lend me a hand?"

"After Dixie died," Frank said, "I might have given up if it hadn't been for you, Tyler. You helped get me through those bad times. You know that as well as I do." He took a sip of his beer. "I couldn't get you through your bad times, not under the circumstances. But maybe I can do something for you now."

Beaumont stared down into his beer for a long moment before he said, "For a while there I hated you."

"I know," Frank said quietly.

"Victoria . . ." Beaumont had to stop and take a deep breath as emotion threatened to overwhelm him. "Victoria tried to tell me it wasn't your fault. She doesn't hate you."

Frank closed his eyes for a second in relief. What Beaumont had just told him meant a great deal to him.

"I figured I'd get over it in time," the young Ranger went on. "But every time I looked at her and knew she'd be stuck in that chair for the rest of her life, just like she was locked up in prison, I hated you all over again for your part in what happened. I told myself that Ferguson was really to blame, him and that crazy kid with him, but then I'd think that if you hadn't been there, none of it would have happened."

"That's a fair statement," Frank allowed.

"Victoria told me that if a man was trying to climb a mountain and fell off and died, it wasn't the mountain's fault. That made sense. I could wrap my mind around that idea. But it didn't make the feelings go away. It didn't make things any easier."

"That usually takes time."

Beaumont nodded. "I know. And I've got to admit, when I first saw you walk into McKelvey's, the first thing I thought other than being surprised was that I was glad to see you. Then I started remembering what happened to Victoria, and how mad I was at you, and it sort of all came back and just swelled up inside me until I thought I was going to bust."

Frank touched one of the bruises on his jaw and smiled. "It busted out, all right."

"Yeah. I went loco, no doubt about that. But I'm not sorry. I think I needed to get it all out like that."

"You don't need to apologize to me," Frank said. "And I won't insult you by saying we're all square now. I know that a few punches can't make up for what happened."

"But it's a start," Beaumont said. "And now that I've calmed down . . . well, damn it, I'm glad to see you, Frank. I really am."

Frank nodded. What Beaumont was saying filled him with hope that eventually everything would be all right between them again. In the meantime, he had no doubt that the truce would hold and enable them to work together to quell the war that was about to explode in Brown County.

"Maybe we better talk about what's going on around here," Frank suggested.

Beaumont leaned forward. "All hell's about to break loose, that's what's going on," he said. "And the bad part is, I'm not sure which side is in the right. Duggan and the other big ranchers have the law behind them, but what they're doing with those fences . . . well, it just doesn't seem fair."

"The same thought occurred to me," Frank said.

"But you're working for Duggan."

"That's just how things happened to work out. I came to Brown County looking for you, remember? The way it seems to me, we're in good shape because between us we're in both camps. If we pool our knowledge, we'll know what both sides are planning."

"And maybe we can keep them from killing each other."

"My thought exactly," Frank agreed.

"Rawlings and some of the others think they should be cutting more fences."

"And Duggan has threatened to kill anybody he catches doing that. I figure he'll have his men start patrolling the fence lines even more than they already are. The next dark night there could be a lot of trouble."

Beaumont sighed. "I'll try to talk some sense into Rawlings and his bunch. I already suggested they might be able to work out some sort of deal with the big ranchers."

Frank smiled faintly and said, "I don't imagine that went over too well."

"Not hardly. None of them have the money to make any kind of financial arrangement. And hotheads like Rawlings would rather fight than negotiate their way out of trouble, anyway."

"Sometimes a fella has to fight," Frank pointed out. "Sometimes if you just sit around and talk and talk, the trouble just gets worse and even more folks die than would have if you'd taken action. But some people just can't seem to understand that."

"I'm not saying I don't agree with you, Frank, but my job is to stop trouble, not start it."

Frank nodded. "I know. And I'll help you any way I can."

"Try to convince Duggan that shooting isn't the answer. That'll be hard to do with an old-timer like him, who's always had to fight just to get by, but I'm hoping that if everybody will just calm down, the worst of the trouble will blow over."

Frank had his doubts about that. Trouble hardly ever went away on its own.

He changed the subject somewhat by asking, "What do you know about McKelvey?"

Beaumont frowned in puzzlement. "Ace McKelvey? I know he owns the Palace Saloon, but that's about all."

"He's not on either side in the fight?"

"Hell, no. He goes out of his way to stay neutral. It doesn't seem to be working, though. You heard Duggan. That's one thing he and Rawlings can agree on, that McKelvey's going to have to choose sides. That'll be true of everybody in Brownwood if this goes on."

"And both sides say folks are either with them or against them," Frank murmured.

"Yeah. Why do you ask about McKelvey?"

"Because when that ruckus broke out in his place, for a second he looked pleased about it, even though some of his furniture was about to get busted up."

Beaumont shook his head. "That doesn't make any sense. Why would McKelvey want the two sides to fight when he's been trying so hard to stay out of it?"

"Has he really?" Frank asked. "Both sides drink in the Palace on a regular basis, from what I'm told. Who would be in a better position to sort of stir the pot every now and then than McKelvey? All it would take is an innocent-seeming prod here and there, and all the while he's pretending to want peace."

"That just doesn't make sense," Beaumont insisted. "You're basing your whole idea on one quick glance, Frank, and that doesn't have to mean anything. There's no reason for McKelvey to want to stir up trouble."

"You're right," Frank said with a nod. "It doesn't make sense. Guess I was just grasping at straws."

But despite what he told the young Ranger, he wasn't going to forget about Ace McKelvey. He was still convinced the saloon keeper warranted keeping an eye on. . . .

"What about Chris Kane?" Frank went on. "You worked with him. Is he just a hothead, like Rawlings?"

"Pretty much. He's really not a bad sort, though, when he doesn't lose his temper. He didn't come to town to make trouble and swap lead with Skeet Harlan. He just wanted to fetch the doc to help Will Bramlett. Of course, it was too late for that, but still, Chris had to try."

Frank's eyes narrowed. "Harlan's a snake," he declared flatly.

"Damn right," Beaumont agreed without hesitation. "I wouldn't be surprised if he's wanted somewhere under another name. I never saw anybody with eyes like that."

"I have," Frank said. "John Wesley Hardin. Always ready to kill, and he doesn't need much of an excuse."

"If Kane dies, Rawlings and his crowd are liable to go on the rampage, trying to settle the score for him."

Frank drank the last of his beer. "And if he lives, Duggan will press to have him put on trial. You ever heard the old saying about being between a rock and a hard place?"

"Sure."

"I'd say that's where Chris Kane is right now." Frank paused and then added, "In fact, I'd say that's pretty much where we all are."

They parted company after agreeing on a spot where they could rendezvous from time to time, an old cave on Blanket Creek where an Indian camp had once been located. It was on land belonging to a rancher named Binnion, who had so far stayed out of the dispute over barbed-wire fences. They would meet there every third night if possible to swap information about what the two sides were planning to do next.

Frank walked down to the livery stable to pick up Stormy. Duggan and MacDonald were already gone, and the old-timer who ran the place told Frank that they had returned to the Slash D.

"Earl was a mite unhappy with you, too, young feller," the liveryman added. "He don't like to be kept waitin'."

Frank wasn't sure how long it had been since anybody had referred to him as "young feller." He didn't feel very young, that was for sure. He thanked the old-timer, swung up into the saddle, and rode out of Brownwood.

He wasn't worried about whether or not Duggan

was mad at him. If Duggan fired him, it wouldn't be a catastrophe. On the other hand, Frank wanted to continue riding for the Slash D until he and Beaumont had come up with a plan to put an end to the violence in the county.

He followed the road southwest out of town toward Zephyr and Goldthwaite and then veered off on the trail that led to the Slash D. Most of the countryside was low rolling hills, but some shallow rocky bluffs reared up here and there. Frank was passing one of them when he saw a sudden glint of light from a patch of brush on top of the bluff.

Without him even thinking about it, instinct made him kick his feet free from the stirrups and throw himself to the left out of the saddle just as a sharp crack sounded. As he was falling, a bullet whined through the space he had occupied only a second earlier. Frank landed with practiced ease, rolling over to break the force of his fall. He let his own momentum pull himself back up on his feet. Another bullet kicked up dust only inches from his feet as he dived into a little gully beside the trail.

He bellied down as much as possible as more slugs chewed up the rim of the gully and showered him with dirt and pebbles. His Winchester was still in the saddle boot on Stormy, and the Appaloosa had taken off down the road when the shooting started. Frank could have called him back. The horse would come to his whistle. But that would just put Stormy back in the line of fire, and Frank didn't want to do that if it could be avoided.

In the meantime, however, he was armed only with his Colt, and while the Peacemaker was a fine gun, it didn't have the range needed to reach that bluff where the bushwhacker was hidden in the brush.

But as long as Frank stayed where he was, the bushwhacker couldn't get a good shot at him, either. Letting himself stay pinned down like this sort of stuck in Frank's craw, but for once, waiting out an enemy might be the best course of action, despite what he had said earlier to Beaumont.

Damn, he wanted one shot at that bushwhacking son of a bitch, though, he thought.

The gunfire gradually died away. The rifleman could be reloading, Frank told himself. He had recognized the sound of a Winchester and knew it probably held fifteen rounds. Load it on Sunday and shoot it all week, people used to say about a Winchester. But even a rifle like that ran out of bullets sooner or later when lead was being sprayed like it was from the top of that bluff.

Frank waited and listened to the silence, knowing that the rifleman could be trying to draw him out. After a few minutes, he heard hoofbeats in the distance. Either the bushwhacker was leaving or someone else was coming along the trail. When the hoofbeats receded, Frank decided that it had been the bushwhacker taking off. The man must have realized that his bullets couldn't reach Frank in the gully.

Just as a precaution, he crawled a hundred yards or so along the shallow defile before standing up. Nobody took a shot at him. The top of the bluff seemed deserted.

Frank walked back to the spot where he had flung himself out of the saddle. His hat had come off, and it was still lying there in the dust of the trail. He picked it up, slapped it against his leg a couple of times, and then settled it on his head. When he looked down the trail, he saw Stormy a couple of hundred yards away. The Appaloosa lifted his head and then galloped toward Frank in response to a whistle.

"Good boy," Frank murmured as he caught the reins and patted Stormy on the flank when the horse came up to him. "You got out of the line of fire just like you were supposed to."

That wasn't going to be so easy for him and

Beaumont, he told himself. As long as a range war loomed on the horizon in Brown County, both of them were going to find themselves smack-dab in the line of fire.

25

Ace McKelvey was in his office that night when a soft knock sounded on the door that led to the alley behind the Palace. He knew the sound of that knock, so he got up from behind the desk and shot the bolt on the door into the main room of the saloon before he answered the summons. He didn't want to be interrupted while he was talking to his visitor.

When he swung the alley door open, Skeet Harlan stepped inside quickly. The deputy had a Winchester under his arm. McKelvey closed the door behind him and said coolly, "Well? I expected to hear from you before now."

"That idiot Keever put me to work as soon as I got back to town," Harlan explained. "I didn't get a chance to get away until now."

"Morgan must not be dead, or else I would have heard about it by now."

"That bastard's got a sixth sense or something," Harlan complained. "He went diving out of the saddle just as I let fly at him. I emptied this damn Winchester but never hit him."

"You're sure?"

"Positive. I rode off a ways, then got up on top of a hill and took a look back through a pair of field glasses. I saw him ride off. Didn't seem any the worse for wear."

McKelvey cursed. "Why didn't you make another try for him?"

"I could have," Harlan allowed. "I got to thinking about it, though. I know you thought we ought to get Morgan out of the way, but I ain't sure but what it's better the way it turned out."

"How do you figure that?" McKelvey asked with a frown.

"Morgan rides for the Slash D. Who's he going to blame for trying to bushwhack him? Rawlings or some of that bunch, more than likely. If he rode on out to the ranch and told Duggan about it, that's going to make Duggan more convinced than ever that the only way to deal with the little ranchers is by squashing them."

McKelvey rubbed his heavy jaw, which was beginning to show stubble. "Yeah, maybe," he said slowly.

"Look, I don't like having a gunslinger like Morgan take a hand in the game, either. A man with speed like he's got is too much of a wild card. But if it ever comes down to the nub, he's only one man. He can't stand up to Coburn's whole bunch."

"That's true. And Flint is pretty fast with a gun. . . ."

Harlan glared at the saloon keeper. "Coburn's no match for me, and neither is Frank Morgan. I'm faster than either of them. You'd do well to remember that, McKelvey."

"Are you threatening me, Skeet?"

"Nope. Just reminding you that we're partners. Equal partners. I've let you handle most of the planning because you're in a better position to see everything. But you're not running the whole show, McKelvey."

"No, of course not," McKelvey said quickly. "And I know how fast with a gun you are. I've seen that speed demonstrated before, remember?"

"Just don't forget," Harlan said. He waited a moment

and then asked, "What do you reckon we ought to do now?"

"Every pot has to simmer a little," McKelvey said. "Tensions are high right now. Let's leave them that way for a little while. There's a good chance either Duggan or Rawlings will do something stupid and set off more trouble on their own. If they don't, we'll give them a prod. And there's the matter of Chris Kane, too. Whether he lives or dies, he could set off a nice little explosion."

Harlan nodded. "He's still alive this evening. I checked at the jail on the way over here. Doc Yantis was there, and he said Kane seems to be a mite stronger."

"Good. Let him recover, if that's what fate has in store for him. As soon as he's back on his feet, we'll push for a trial. That can't help but fan the flames."

"All right. Let me know if you come up with anything else you need me to do."

"Of course," McKelvey said. Harlan gave him a curt nod and slipped out of the office, disappearing into the shadows of the alley.

What a fool, McKelvey thought. Harlan liked to believe that he was an equal partner in this setup, but it was obvious he didn't have the mental capacity for that. He was a fast gun and a reliable killer, that was all. Even after boasting about him and McKelvey being partners, he'd had to turn right around and ask for instructions about what to do next. McKelvey shook his head in disgust.

He would keep using Skeet Harlan for now, but when this was all over . . . well, Deputy Harlan might just find himself the victim of a fatal accident.

By the time he had gotten back to the Slash D earlier in the day, Frank had decided not to tell Duggan about the attempt on his life. Frank didn't know who had been pulling the trigger of that Winchester, but the most likely suspect was either Al Rawlings or one of the other ranchers allied with Rawlings. They knew that they couldn't match gun speed with Frank, so one of them could have decided to try to get rid of him by ambushing him.

Frank wasn't completely convinced that Rawlings was a bushwhacker at heart, though, and none of the other ranchers had struck him like that, either. Sure, they were mad about the fences. Rawlings had been angry enough to try to draw on Frank the night before. But that had been a face-to-face confrontation. Rawlings hadn't been skulking around in the bushes when he took his shot.

Not for the first time, the nagging feeling that something else was going on here rustled around in the back of Frank's brain. So he decided for the time being to play his cards close to the vest and not say anything about the shooting.

As he rode up, Dog came bounding out of one of the barns to greet him happily. Frank dismounted and petted the big cur for several minutes before starting toward the house. Earl Duggan was waiting for him on the porch, a frown on his weathered face.

"Run into more trouble in town?" the cattleman asked.

Frank shook his head and told the truth. "Nope."

"When you didn't meet us at the stable, Al got worried and went to look for you." Duggan's deep-set eyes narrowed in suspicion. "Said he saw you goin' into Pomp Arnold's place with that young fella you got in a fight with."

"That's right," Frank admitted. "I didn't think it would hurt anything to have a drink with Tye."

"Thinking about switching sides in this fight already, Morgan?" The scornful words lashed at Frank. "You really think those greasy-sack outfits can pay you better than I can, gunslinger?"

Anger welled up inside Frank. He controlled it with an

effort and said, "Once he got over being so mad, Tye seemed like a reasonable young fella. I thought maybe it wouldn't hurt to feel *him* out about switching sides."

Duggan gave an emphatic shake of his head. "I don't want the likes of him working for me. He'll never ride for the Slash D."

"Maybe not, but I know from talking to him that he doesn't want an outright war here in Brown County." That much was true anyway, Frank thought, whether the rest of what he was saying was or not. "You'd like to know it if Rawlings and his bunch have anything big planned, wouldn't you?"

Duggan's eyes narrowed even more. "Are you sayin' you talked that youngster into spyin' for us?"

"Not yet. He's too stiff-necked and bullheaded for that. But with some work he might come around to our way of thinking."

Duggan rasped a hand over the white bristles on his jaw. "Well, then, maybe it's a good thing you talked to him," he admitted after a moment. "We'd better be careful, though, if he acts like he's tryin' to help us. He might slip us some bad information that would lead us into a trap."

"I don't think that'll happen," Frank said honestly. "Tye's already seen the two men he worked for gunned down. He wants an end to the violence."

"It'll end," Duggan said with a grim nod. "One way or another, before too much longer, it'll end."

For the next week, an uneasy truce held over Brown County. No more fences were cut, no line riders for the big spreads were ambushed. The whole county seemed to be holding its breath.

And in the Brown County jail, Chris Kane finally woke up.

He didn't know where he was or how much time had passed. All he remembered was falling in the street with the thunder of Skeet Harlan's gun echoing in his ears. He was aware of only two things now: that he hurt like hell and that his mouth was as dry as cotton. He tried to ask for water, but all that came out was a husky croaking sound.

Gradually, he realized that he was lying on his back and that something was wrapped tightly around his torso. Bandages, he thought. He could barely breathe, they were so tight around his chest. Again he tried to talk, and this time he was able to whisper, "H-hey . . ."

No one responded. Kane tried to force his eyes open but was too weak. He listened instead. He heard muted voices somewhere in the distance but couldn't understand what they were saying. Trembling with the effort, he tried to call out, but he couldn't do it.

He smelled wood smoke, probably from a stove somewhere in the building. The air was chilly but not too cold. His fingers moved convulsively. He felt rough wool against them. A blanket?

So he was lying on a bunk somewhere. In the cabin on Blanket Creek? "W-Will . . . ?" he whispered.

No. Will had been shot. Those memories came flooding back in on Kane's brain. He shuddered and then whimpered as even that slight movement made pain shoot through his body. Will had been shot and was almost surely dead by now. Kane didn't know how much time had passed, but he held out no hope that his partner had survived.

"Tye?" This time the whisper was a little stronger, but there was still no answer.

When Kane tried to open his eyes again, he was able to lift his eyelids enough to form tiny slits. Light struck his eyes and made him wince, and then he winced again as fresh waves of agony rolled through him. He squeezed his eyes closed, having accomplished nothing except to get a glimpse of a sandstone wall and a ceiling made of heavy beams.

Footsteps echoed somewhere nearby and came closer. Kane forced himself to breathe regularly as if he were still unconscious. As surprised as he was to find himself still alive, he was starting to get a bad feeling about the place he was in now.

That feeling was confirmed when the footsteps stopped and then metal clanged against metal. The door of a jail cell opening, he thought. He was locked up. Skeet Harlan had shot him, and then he had been locked up.

It would have been better if he had gone ahead and died.

A man's voice spoke, sounding loud and aggressive. "I don't know if this is a good idea, you comin' here like this every day, Miss Annie."

"Somebody has to look after him," a woman replied. Her voice was softer, but it still sounded unnaturally loud to Kane's ears.

"Well, I'll be right down the hall. You holler if you need anything."

The heavy footsteps went away. Lighter ones approached Kane. He heard a scraping sound. A stool being drawn up closer to the bunk where he lay, maybe? Then he smelled a sweet fragrance, like a field full of wildflowers in the spring.

Something cool and soft touched his forehead, bringing blessed relief to the pounding that filled his skull. "Poor baby," the woman murmured, as much to herself as to him. "Poor, poor baby."

Kane opened his eyes and looked up at her.

Her mouth opened in shock, and it was only with a visible effort that she stifled the scream that tried to escape from her mouth.

"Miss Annie?" the deputy called from down the hall in the cell block. "You say something?"

"N-no," she managed to reply. "I'm fine."

Kane stared up at her, recognizing the curly blond hair and the sweet face that was only beginning to show the signs of dissipation. Too many men, too much whiskey, the occasional bit of opium . . . but those things hadn't completely destroyed the innocence within her. Annie, he recalled, Annie from the Palace. And according to the deputy, she had been coming to see him every day.

"H-how . . . how long . . ." he rasped out.

She leaned closer, an anxious look on her thin face. "You mean how long have you been here?" she whispered.

He was too weak to nod, but she saw the look in his eyes.

"A week. It's been a week since Skeet shot you."

"How . . . bad?"

"You've got three bullet holes in you. Nobody thought you were going to live. Even when Doc Yantis said you might, nobody really believed him."

Her mention of Doc Yantis brought back memories of what he had been doing in Brownwood on the night he was shot. "M-my partner . . . Will Bramlett . . ."

"I'm sorry, Chris," she said. "He's dead."

Kane closed his eyes. Even though he had expected that answer, it still hurt to know that his friend was gone. They had made a lot of big plans, he and Will. But not a damned one of them had come to pass.

He opened his eyes again. It was a struggle, but he managed to turn his head enough to see the cell door. It stood open. He could get up and waltz right out of here, he thought.

Sure. And right now he was just about as likely to flap his arms and fly to the damned moon.

Annie bent even closer and pressed her lips to his forehead. "I'm so glad you're awake," she murmured. "I didn't think I'd ever get to talk to you again. You just rest now, Chris, and get better. I'll come every day and take care of you—"

"Well, now, what's this?" a new voice asked sharply. Annie gasped in surprise and jerked upright, and she was so close to Kane that the movement jostled him. He couldn't keep from groaning in pain.

"Hey, your prisoner's awake down here," the voice went on. Annie moved, and Kane could see Skeet Harlan standing in the open door of the cell. He had come up without either of them noticing him, moving as quiet as a snake.

Kane had figured out that he was in the county jail, not the little town lockup behind Marshal Sean Keever's office. That was a little better. He didn't trust Sheriff J.C. Wilmott—as far as Kane was concerned, all the law in Brown County was in the hip pockets of the big ranchers—but at least Wilmott was a relatively honest man. He couldn't say the same for Keever and especially Harlan, the town lawmen.

One of the sheriff's deputies came down the hall and looked into the cell. "Son of a gun," he said. "You're right, Skeet. I'll go tell the sheriff. He'll probably want Doc Yantis to come over and take a look at Kane." The man started to turn away but then paused. "You'd better come of there, Miss Annie. Now that Kane's awake, I got to lock this door again."

"Why?" Annie asked. "Can't you see he's in no condition to go anywhere? You can't be worried that he's going to escape!"

"Rules is rules," the deputy said stubbornly. "Step on outta there, now."

Annie looked down at Kane. "I'll be back," she promised. "I'll see to it that you're treated right, Chris."

He managed to smile his gratitude up at her, even

though he was thinking that she didn't have any power to back up a promise like that. She was just a saloon girl, a whore. She didn't have any real control over her own life, let alone what happened to anybody else.

But still he felt a certain sense of loss as she stood up and moved out of the cell. Whether she could do anything about it or not, at least she *cared,* and that was more than he could say for anybody else.

Annie and the deputy left, but Skeet Harlan lingered. He didn't work here, but as a fellow lawman he probably could come and go as he liked in the county jail. He stood there grinning through the bars at the wounded man, and in a low voice he said, "I never expected you to live, Kane. It don't really matter, though. You know what's going to happen to you now, don't you?"

Kane didn't say anything.

"You go ahead and recover from those holes I put in you," Harlan went on. "As soon as you're able, you're going to stand trial for fence-cutting and for attempting to kill an officer of the law, namely me. You're already a jailbird, Kane, and you'll go right back to prison as soon as the jury finds you guilty. And they *will* find you guilty. You know that, don't you?"

Kane didn't have any doubt of it. Any jury impaneled in Brown County was going to be on the side of Duggan and the other big ranchers.

"Yeah, right back to prison," Harlan gloated. "If you live that long. Some folks in these parts don't like the way you fence-cutters defy the law. They might just decide to make an example of you." Harlan grasped the bars and put his ugly, grinning face against them. "You might just get strung up, Kane. What do you think of that? Dancin' your life out at the end of a rope . . . It's a mighty pretty picture, ain't it?"

26

No one on the Slash D had forgotten about the trouble with the smaller ranchers. Earl Duggan had ordered his foreman, Ed MacDonald, to set up regular patrols on all the ranch's fences. Slash D punchers rode the fence lines at least twice a day, looking for any signs that the barbed wire had been tampered with.

Frank Morgan took his turn on these patrols. He had said that he signed on with Duggan in order to be a regular hand, so he couldn't refuse to do his part in the work. With the fall roundup rapidly approaching, he was sure he would do his share of hazing cattle from the brush and the draws. He might even have to do some branding, although it had been a powerful number of years since he'd held a branding iron in his hand.

In a way, he was actually looking forward to it. There was nothing like doing a good day's work to make a man feel like he had a rightful place in the world.

Since the night of violence that had claimed Will Bramlett's life and left Chris Kane shot up, Frank had met twice with Tyler Beaumont at the old Indian cave on Blanket Creek. Neither of them had had anything to report. Things were quiet. But neither Frank nor Beaumont expected them to stay that way for much longer.

Dave Osgood was still recuperating from his wound, but Pitch Carey had recovered enough so that he was back at work. It was Carey who rode in hard and fast from Brownwood one afternoon with news.

"Chris Kane woke up yesterday," he reported to Duggan, Frank, MacDonald, and the other men who had gathered around him when he came galloping into the yard between the house and the barns. The drumming hoofbeats had caught their attention. Carey went on. "Doc Yantis says he's going to live. No doubt about it now."

Frank didn't know Kane, but he was aware that Beaumont liked the man, so he was glad that Kane was expected to recover. He felt an instinctive dislike for Skeet Harlan, too, so it pleased him that Harlan wouldn't have another notch to carve on his gun. Harlan struck Frank as just the type to do that.

"From the talk I heard in Higginbotham's Hardware, the grand jury's going to indict Kane," Carey continued, "and the district attorney plans to put him on trial as soon as he's well enough."

"On what charges?" Frank asked.

"Fence-cutting for one, I hope," Duggan said.

"Well, Boss," MacDonald put in, "I don't know if you remember or not, but Kane never got around to actually cutting the fence that night. . . ."

"Doesn't matter," Duggan insisted. "He had wire-cutters on him, didn't he?"

"He did."

"That's a crime, right there. And I'm sure Kane cut other fences when he didn't get caught at it."

That was a pretty big assumption to make, Frank thought, but he didn't say anything. He knew he would be wasting his breath if he tried to change Duggan's mind.

"And Kane drew on Skeet Harlan," the cattleman went on. "That's a crime, too, as well as being a damned stupid thing to do."

Frank couldn't argue with either of those statements.

"Kane's going back to prison where he belongs," Duggan concluded. "Good riddance."

"He made a pretty good hand when he worked here," MacDonald said slowly.

Duggan snorted. "Then he should have stayed here, instead of gettin' too big for his britches and going off with Bramlett to start his own ranch."

Frank said, "A man's got a right to have some ambition, doesn't he?"

"Not when his ambition is to crowd onto my range," Duggan snapped.

Frank could have pointed out that the spread started by Kane and Bramlett had been purchased by them legally. But again, it would have been a waste of breath.

"Let's get back to work," Duggan said with a wave of his hand. "We've got a lot to do yet before the roundup's over, and when it is, we'll have cows to push over to Zephyr."

The group dispersed as men went back to their work. A few more days would see the completion of the roundup, and then the cattle that Duggan planned to ship out and sell would have to be driven over to the cattle pens in the little town of Zephyr. A railroad line was being built from Temple to Brownwood, but it hadn't gotten there yet. The railhead was at Zephyr, and construction hadn't started on the last leg of the line to Brownwood. Still, Frank thought, Zephyr was a lot closer than Fort Worth, and that was where the nearest railroad had been until the tracks were laid from Temple.

As Frank rode toward the spot where smoke rose into the autumn sky from branding fires, he wondered if Beaumont knew yet that his friend Chris Kane had regained consciousness.

***

Beaumont had returned to the ranch on Blanket Creek established by Kane and Will Bramlett. He had talked to Al Rawlings and the other small ranchers, and they had been in agreement with his offer to keep the place going until they saw whether Kane was going to live or die. Beaumont would try to look after the stock by himself, but if he wound up needing any help, Rawlings and the others would be glad to provide it. They had to stick together, Rawlings said.

Beaumont was riding the range when the bawling of a cow drew him over to the creek. He saw right away that a calf had gotten bogged down in some mud. The old mama cow stood off to the side, letting out the mournful, miserable sounds that had drawn Beaumont's attention. As he shook out a loop in his rope, the young Ranger grinned and called to the mama cow, "Don't worry, bossy, I'll get your baby out of the mud."

He edged his horse farther out on the creek bank and swung the loop over his head. His first throw dropped neatly over the calf's head. He took a dally around the horn and backed his horse away from the stream, taking up the slack in the rope. He couldn't pull the calf out by the neck, but by giving the calf something to brace itself against, he thought the critter would now be able to extricate itself from the mud. If it couldn't, he would just have to wade out there and move the loop so that it was around the calf's body. That would be muddy work, though.

It felt good to be doing things like this, Beaumont reflected as he kept the rope taut and watched the calf struggle for purchase. Just because he hadn't done much cowboying in his life didn't mean that he was no good at it. He could make a hand. It wouldn't be a bad way to live, if he hadn't been a lawman.

Being a Ranger was always going to come first and foremost in his life, though. Well, first after Victoria . . . The thought of his wife made a pang of longing go through Beaumont. Lord, but he missed her!

Between concentrating on freeing the calf from the mud and thinking about Victoria, Beaumont didn't even hear the man riding up behind him until the gent was right there on the creek bank beside him.

"Howdy," the man said. He was lean and dark, with a black leather vest over a wool shirt. A black Stetson sat on thick, glossy dark hair. He wore a Colt in a tied-down holster, but he had a friendly smile on his face and didn't appear to be looking for trouble.

Beaumont returned the stranger's nod. "Afternoon," he said.

"Looks like you've got a calf bogged down," the man said, stating the obvious.

"Yeah, but he'll get loose here in a minute."

As if to prove Beaumont right, the calf finally reached solid enough ground so that it was able to stumble up out of the mud. The mama cow rushed over and started trying to lick its offspring clean.

Beaumont rode close enough to loosen the rope around the calf's neck and then flip it free. As he began coiling the rope, he walked his horse back over to the stranger and asked, "Something I can do for you?"

"I'm looking for Al Rawlings' spread."

"It's about four miles from here," Beaumont explained. "Follow the creek for a ways and then cut west. You'll probably run into some fences, though. I'd advise you to go around them. It'll be out of your way but safer."

The stranger smiled again, but this time the expression

wasn't so friendly. "Fences, eh? Never cared for them, myself."

"Maybe not, but the ranchers who put them up don't take kindly to having them cut."

The man took out the makin's and began to roll a quirly. "I never worry overmuch about what a man will think of me, especially some fat, pompous cattle baron." He lipped the cigarette and said around it, "My name's Coburn."

"Call me Tye," Beaumont said.

Coburn grinned as he struck a lucifer. "What you're sayin' is that Tye ain't your real name?"

"That's pretty much my business," Beaumont said stiffly.

"It sure is. No offense meant."

"None taken," Beaumont allowed. "Why are you looking for Rawlings?"

"*That's* pretty much *my* business."

Beaumont shrugged. He glanced at the gun on Coburn's hip. "Al and his sister are friends of mine," he said. "I don't want to see any trouble come calling on them."

The thought had crossed his mind that Coburn might be a hired gun. He had that look about him.

"Don't worry," Coburn said. "I heard that Rawlings and the rest of the little ranchers around here have been having problems. The big ranchers are trying to stampede them."

"You could say that," Beaumont agreed cautiously.

Coburn puffed on the quirly and said, "I thought I'd offer to give them a hand. I hate to see a bunch of damn rich men trying to lord it over the little fellas."

"You mean to volunteer your services . . . or sell them?" Beaumont asked bluntly.

Coburn chuckled. "Nobody's ever called me charitable. I don't mind givin' folks a break, though, when I think they're in the right. And it's sure as hell *not* right what the big cattlemen have been doing around here."

"You've heard all about it, have you?"

"Word gets around," Coburn said, "especially in my line of work."

"I'll tell you the truth, Mr. Coburn," Beaumont said. "You can make a lot more money by hiring out to Earl Duggan and his friends." He had a reason for pointing Coburn in that direction. It was Beaumont's hope that if the gunfighter went to work for Duggan, Frank Morgan could keep an eye on him. If Coburn wound up on the side of Rawlings and the other small ranchers, the fact that they had a fast gun working for them might make them bold enough to stir up more trouble. That was what Beaumont wanted to avoid. He still held out a faint hope that the conflict might die a natural death.

"Like I said, I like to choose the side I work for in any range war," Coburn replied, his voice a little cool now. "Maybe I should start wondering which side *you're* on, my young friend."

"I'm with Rawlings and the others," Beaumont said without hesitation. He realized a little too late that his comments to Coburn might bring him under suspicion if the gun-thrower passed them on to Rawlings. He went on. "In fact, just to prove it, I'll take you to the Rawlings ranch right now."

"Well, that's mighty kind of you. I'll take you up on that offer."

Beaumont heeled his horse into motion and rode toward the cabin. Coburn fell in alongside him. As they came in sight of the cabin a few minutes later, Beaumont saw a pair of riders drawing to a halt there. More visitors, he thought, wondering who they were.

As he and Coburn came closer, he recognized Al Rawlings and Callie Stratton. "Looks like I won't have to take you to see Rawlings after all," he said to Coburn. "That's him right there, along with his sister."

Coburn grinned. "I've heard that she's a real hellion."

"Miss Callie's got red hair and the temper to go with it," Beaumont admitted. "But she's a good woman."

Rawlings and Callie had dismounted and were waiting there, holding their horses' reins, when Beaumont and Coburn rode up. Rawlings looked warily at the stranger and said, "Afternoon, Tye. Who's this?"

"Says his name's Coburn. He was looking for you, Al."

"Is that so?" Rawlings looked directly at the gunman. "I'm Al Rawlings. What can I do for you?"

Coburn leaned on his saddle horn and grinned. His gaze darted to Callie, lingered for an appreciative second. Then he said to Rawlings, "I'm hoping I can do something for you, friend. I've heard that you're having trouble with the big ranchers hereabouts. I'd like to throw in with you, if you'll have me."

Callie said, "You don't look much like a rancher."

Coburn's grin widened. "No, ma'am, I'm not. But I'm sort of a specialist in handling trouble, if you know what I mean."

Rawlings rubbed his jaw. "You're a hired gun," he said flatly.

"That's right. I never believed in sugarcoating things."

"Why do you want to throw in with us? You can make a lot more money by hiring out to Duggan."

Coburn glanced over at Beaumont. "That's what our young friend here told me. I told him I preferred to pick my own side in any fight."

"You told him that?" Rawlings snapped at Beaumont.

The young Ranger shrugged. "So did you," he pointed out. "It's pretty darned obvious, ain't it?"

Callie laughed at that. "He's got you there, Al," she said.

Rawlings ignored her and turned his attention back to Coburn. "What did you say your name was?"

"Coburn. Flint Coburn."

"I reckon I've heard of you. You were mixed up in some bad ruckuses up in Wyoming and Montana."

"It says something for me that I'm still alive, then, doesn't it?"

"I suppose so." Rawlings frowned in thought and then nodded. "I'd like to talk to you about this some more, Coburn, as well as bringing in some friends of mine. It might be we could get together and make it worth your while to stay around Brown County for a while."

"Al, I don't know if that's such a good idea," Callie began.

Again her brother ignored her. He went on. "Right now, though, I've got to talk to Beaumont here. There's news from town."

Beaumont's interest quickened. "News? About Chris?"

"That's right," Rawlings said. "He woke up yesterday, but we just heard about it today."

Beaumont couldn't help but grin. "That's good news, then. He must be going to recover."

"It looks like it, but I don't know how good the news is," Rawlings said.

"But . . . if he's going to be all right . . ."

"The law plans to put him on trial," Rawlings said, "if it gets that far. But there's already talk around town that it may not."

"May not come to trial, you mean?"

"Yeah . . . because some folks are talking about lynching him instead."

27

Skeet Harlan was at the bar in the Double O when Marshal Keever found him. Keever jerked his head peremptorily and said, "Come on back to the office, Skeet. Trouble's brewing."

Harlan didn't like being talked to that way, but he was willing to put up with it for a while longer, at least until he saw whether or not McKelvey's plan was going to come together and result in the big payoff that the saloon keeper insisted it would.

"What's up, Marshal?" Harlan asked as the two lawmen left the saloon and turned down Fisk Avenue toward their office.

Keever scowled and said, "I'm hearing rumors that some of the cattlemen plan to bust Chris Kane out of the county jail and string him up."

"That's Wilmott's lookout, ain't it?"

"He's liable to call on us for help. We need to be ready."

Keever was a damned fool, Harlan thought. He was content to settle for petty graft and corruption instead of keeping his eye on bigger things. Harlan had known that when he first drifted into town and went to work for the man, but he figured he would be able to find someone else in Brownwood who was more ambitious. It hadn't taken long for him and Ace McKelvey to recognize in each other kindred larcenous spirits. There was already trouble brewing between the big ranchers like Duggan and the greasy-sack owners like Rawlings. McKelvey's plan was to fan those flames until they blew up into a real blaze. Then, when the conflagration threatened to consume the whole town, the gunmen McKelvey had hired would sweep in and loot the place, emptying out the banks and all the businesses. It was a daring, audacious plan that would net them a fortune.

Unfortunately, even as hotheaded as Duggan and Rawlings were, the friction hadn't yet blossomed into a full-fledged range war. McKelvey was going to have to help it along even more.

That was where Chris Kane came in. There was nothing like a martyr to start a war.

"You heard anything about what Rawlings plans to do?" Harlan asked.

Keever shot him a sharp look and demanded, "What do you mean by that?"

Harlan shrugged his narrow shoulders. "Well, it seems to me that if Duggan's bunch wants to lynch Kane, then Rawlings and his friends might want to bust him out of jail before that can happen."

"Good Lord, you're right!" Keever exclaimed. "They're liable to be coming at us from both directions at once."

They went in the office and got down shotguns from the rack, then stuffed their pockets full of shells and headed for the county jail. One of Wilmott's deputies met them at the door and said, "You look like you're loaded for bear, Marshal. What's wrong?"

"What's wrong?" Keever repeated. "Haven't you heard, man? The big ranchers are going to try to lynch Kane, and Rawlings and his friends plan to break him out of jail and rescue him!"

Harlan managed to look worried and resolute, when

he really wanted to grin in satisfaction. Keever was as easy to manipulate as a little kid.

The deputy frowned. "I hadn't heard nothin' about that. Maybe you better come in, Marshal, and talk to the sheriff."

Keever gave the man a curt, satisfied nod and stalked past him into the jail as the deputy stepped aside. Harlan followed.

Sheriff Wilmott looked a bit dubious as Keever explained, but when the marshal was through, Wilmott nodded and said, "I reckon you've got your ear closer to the ground than I do, Sean. I'll call in the rest of my deputies right now. There won't be any prisoners busted out of this jail, by God."

"Skeet and I will stay here and give you a hand," Keever offered.

"I'm much obliged for that." Wilmott stood up from behind his desk and went to the telephone that hung on the wall of the office. He picked up the earpiece and turned the crank on the side of the wooden box. Quite a few homes in Brownwood had been wired for telephone service in the past year or so, and even some of the outlying ranches had it, like Earl Duggan's Slash D.

Wilmott talked to the operator and told her to ring up all his deputies who were off duty. The message to be passed along to them was a simple one: strap on their guns and get to the jail as soon as they could.

Harlan suppressed a smile and managed to maintain a solemn, concerned expression. Underneath, though, he was quite pleased with the way things were going.

Before this day was over, the two sides in the conflict would hate each other more than ever before.

Brownwood was soon buzzing with rumors, artfully spread by men who worked for Ace McKelvey. No one noticed how the rumors originated at the Palace Saloon, just as rings rippled outward from a stone tossed into a pond.

Inside the jail, Chris Kane didn't hear any of the talk. He sat up on his bunk, eating the stew that Annie carefully spooned into his mouth from a steaming bowl. She sat on a stool in front of the bunk and balanced the bowl on her knees. She wasn't wearing a short, spangled, gaudy saloon girl's getup today but rather a modest, pale blue dress that was more like something a settler's wife would wear. In that garb, with the makeup scrubbed off her face, she looked much younger and innocent. Kane was surprised at how pretty she was. He was even more surprised that he noticed, considering how badly he'd been shot up and the fact that he had been unconscious until the day before.

But he had made quite a bit of progress in the past twenty-four hours. Doc Yantis himself had said so, when the sawbones came by to check on him earlier in the day. "You'll live, son," Doc had said as he snapped his medical bag shut. "But you won't be getting up and dancing a jig any time soon."

That comment had brought back memories of what Skeet Harlan had said about dancing at the end of a rope. Kane tried to put those thoughts out of his head. He hadn't really done anything, he told himself. Sure, he had tried to cut the Slash D fence, but he had failed in that effort. And during his confrontation with Skeet Harlan, the deputy had drawn first. Kane couldn't really claim self-defense, since Harlan was a lawman and was allowed to draw his gun in carrying out his duties, but still, the fact that Harlan had slapped leather first surely would carry some weight. . . .

Unless, of course, Harlan had told the story differently. There had been no witnesses. Harlan could have claimed that Kane drew first, could have said that the young rancher was acting crazy, like a mad dog. In which case a jury would likely believe him and convict Kane of attempting to murder a lawman. It would be back to the pen for him, sure enough. But what he'd done wasn't bad enough to get him lynched.

There was one small, barred window in the cell. The glass on the inside of the bars was raised a few inches to let in some fresh air. Through that gap, some sort of commotion sounded. Kane turned his head toward the window and frowned. "What's going on out there?" he asked.

"Never you mind about that," Annie said as she spooned up another bite of the stew. "You just go ahead and eat. You heard what the doc said about keeping your strength up."

It was true that Doc Yantis had ordered him to eat and rest in order to regain his strength. Kane opened his mouth and took the bite of savory stew. He seemed to feel stronger with each passing minute, even though he knew that in reality he was still as weak as a kitten.

The noises from outside continued to grow louder, until they couldn't be ignored. Kane recognized them as the sound of men shouting angrily. He said to Annie, "You'd better look and see what that's about."

With a worried frown, she set the bowl aside and stood up. "All right," she said as she went to the window. She had to open the glass more, grasp the bars, and pull herself up on her toes in order to see out. "There's a bunch of men down the street. . . . They seem upset about something. . . . They look like they're coming this way. . . . Oh, my God! One of them's waving a noose around!"

Kane closed his eyes and felt a cold emptiness inside.

He didn't think he was the only prisoner in the Brown County jail.

But he was likely the only one anybody cared enough about to want to lynch. . . .

Beaumont had insisted on riding into town to see Kane, and not surprisingly, Rawlings and Callie wanted to come with him. Coburn rode along, too, and on the way they stopped at Vern Gladwell's place and he joined them. So there were five of them that rode through Early and on into Brownwood.

They heard the commotion before they reached the downtown area. Coburn commented, "I don't much like the sound of that. I've heard such things before. Sounds like the citizens are working themselves up for a necktie party."

"Know the sound of a lynch mob, do you?" Gladwell said.

Coburn grinned lazily, not taking offense. "The places I've been, it was a pretty common occurrence."

They rode on hurriedly, and as they approached the jail Beaumont saw the crowd in front of the big sandstone building. It reminded him of the confrontation that had taken place there a little over a week earlier, the morning after Skeet Harlan had shot Kane. It looked like this situation had the potential to get even uglier, though.

"That's a lynch mob if I've ever seen one," Coburn said.

"We'll put a stop to that," Rawlings snapped. "Nobody's lynching Kane while I'm around." He glanced over at Coburn. "Are you in?"

The gunslinger nodded. "Yeah. I'll take a hand in the game."

Several dozen angry, shouting men formed a knot in the street in front of the jail. Sheriff Wilmott, Marshal

Keever, Skeet Harlan, and several of the sheriff's deputies stood just outside the door, confronting them. Wilmott raised his hands for quiet, but the mob ignored him. They didn't fall silent until Skeet Harlan impatiently discharged one of the barrels of his shotgun into the air. The loud boom made everybody hush.

"Damn it!" Sheriff Wilmott bellowed. "What do you folks think you're doin'? Go on home!"

"We've come for Chris Kane!" one of the men in the mob shouted. "He's a murderer!"

Beaumont looked for the man who had made that accusation, but he couldn't tell exactly where it came from. The crowd was too thick.

"Kane didn't kill nobody!" Wilmott insisted.

"He shot Dave Osmond!" That cry came from somewhere else in the mob.

"Osmond ain't dead," Wilmott pointed out. "Last I heard, he was doin' fine. And Kane didn't shoot him in the first place."

"You don't know that! He's a rustler and a fence-cutter! String him up!"

Cries of "String him up! String him up!" began to come from the crowd. The men surged forward.

Rawlings jerked his Winchester from its saddle boot, worked the lever, and blasted a shot into the air. Again, the sudden report served to quiet the crowd. Most of the men jerked around to see who had fired the shot.

Beaumont muttered a curse as he swung up his own Winchester. Gladwell brought his rifle to bear, too, and Callie drew the revolver on her hip. Only Coburn didn't draw his gun, but he still radiated menace as he sat there, seemingly indolent, in the saddle.

"There's not gonna be any lynching!" Rawlings shouted.

From the front of the jail, Wilmott called angrily,

"Blast it, Rawlings, I'm in charge here! Put up those guns!"

"Like hell," Rawlings shot back. "We've got these bloodthirsty bastards in a cross fire now, Sheriff. They won't dare try anything."

That was the wrong thing to say. From somewhere in the crowd a voice yelled, "There's another one of 'em! They're all rustlers!"

"We'll string up Rawlings, too!" another voice agreed.

Beaumont wished he could pin down just who was doing all the yelling. He didn't recognize the voices.

The atmosphere was plenty tense. A gun battle could break out at any moment, and people would die here in the middle of the street. Beaumont glanced at his companions. Their faces were white and drawn, but resolute. The only one who seemed at ease was Flint Coburn.

And Beaumont knew why. At this moment Coburn reminded him a great deal of Frank Morgan. The supreme confidence that bordered on arrogance, the fatalism that gave him such a cool, calm demeanor . . . those were marks of the true professional Coltman.

Beaumont wasn't the only one who had noticed those things. From the doorway Skeet Harlan suddenly said, "Wait a minute! I recognize that hombre with them. That's Flint Coburn! He's a hired gun, a killer!"

"That's right," Rawlings grated. "And he's on our side now. Duggan and his bunch have Frank Morgan, and now we've got Coburn."

"Frank Morgan, eh?" Coburn muttered. "Didn't know he was in these parts."

Rawlings glanced sharply at him. "Morgan rides for Duggan's Slash D now. Does that make a difference, Coburn?"

The gunman shook his head. "No difference. Just makes things a mite more interesting, that's all."

Vern Gladwell spoke up. "Then things are about to get really interesting, because here comes Morgan now!"

28

The news that Chris Kane had regained consciousness intrigued Frank. He knew what had happened on Stepps Creek the night of the ambush, at least from his point of view, but he thought it might be worthwhile to talk to Kane about the incident and try to find out if the young rancher knew anything about the ambush that had wounded Dave Osmond and Pitch Carey. No one on the Slash D had objected or asked any questions when he saddled up Stormy and started into Brownwood.

The sound of angry voices reached his ears before he got to the jail. When he rounded a corner and saw the crowd in front of the building, he knew right away what was going on. The fire that had been banked for the past week was on the verge of blazing up again.

He heard someone shout his name and knew he had been spotted. He didn't slow down or turn aside, just kept riding deliberately toward the mob. His keen eyes took in the whole scene. He spotted Al Rawlings and his sister Callie Stratton on horseback at the rear of the crowd, along with one of the other ranchers and a man Frank didn't know.

And Tyler Beaumont, who once again seemed to have found himself in the thick of things.

Frank didn't rein Stormy to a halt until he was about ten feet from the other riders. Then he brought the

Appaloosa to a stop and nodded. "Afternoon," he said pleasantly to the crowd at large. "There a prayer meetin' going on?"

"Chris Kane is the one who'd better be prayin'," a man called from the crowd. "He's about to meet his Maker!"

"I heard Kane was doing better," Frank said.

Beaumont inclined his head toward the mob and said, "These fellas plan on taking him out of the jail and stringing him up."

"And we're not gonna let that happen!" Rawlings put in.

Red-faced with rage, Sheriff Wilmott roared, "Damn it, none of you are in charge here! I am, and I say there ain't gonna be no lynchin'! Now all of you scatter before I arrest the lot of you!"

No one paid any attention to him. Tempers were too high for anyone in the mob to be afraid of the law.

"Where do you stand in this, Morgan?" Rawlings demanded. "I figure your boss would like to see Kane swing."

"Mr. Duggan's not here," Frank said, "and I've never believed in lynch law."

Rawlings sneered in disbelief. "You mean you're on our side now?" he asked sarcastically.

"I still ride for the Slash D," Frank said, his voice hardening. "Make no mistake about that. But I don't want to see these folks take the law into their own hands, because I know they'll regret it later." Something was familiar about the other man with Rawlings's bunch, and Frank gave in to his curiosity by looking at him and asking, "Do I know you, friend?"

"We've never met," the man replied. "But we travel in some of the same circles, Morgan. My name's Flint Coburn."

Frank's mouth tightened just slightly. He knew that

name, all right. Coburn was a fast gun, a veteran of numerous range wars and other conflicts, and he had a reputation for ruthlessness.

"You're no rancher," Frank said. "What are you doing with Rawlings?"

"He's thrown in with us," Beaumont said before Coburn could answer. Frank sensed a warning in the young Ranger's words. Beaumont didn't want a showdown here in the middle of the street. Neither did Frank, for that matter.

It suddenly looked like he was going to get it, but from an unexpected source. Two men abruptly pushed their way out of the mob, and one of them said loudly, "Morgan! You killed some friends of ours over in Santa Fe last year. We aim to settle the score for them!"

Frank's eyes narrowed. He had never seen these two men before, and he hadn't even been in Santa Fe the previous year. "I haven't been to Santa Fe for a while," he said. "You've got me mixed up with somebody else."

"The hell we do," the second man said. "It was you, all right, and now you're gonna die for it!"

"Here now!" Sheriff Wilmott yelled. "You men back off! Break it up, damn it! Break it up!"

The crowd began to disperse a little, all right, but not because of anything the angry lawman said. They were getting out of the line of fire. Chris Kane and the hostilities between the big ranchers and small were abruptly forgotten in the face of this personal vendetta. Rawlings reined his horse to the side, out of the way, and motioned for his companions to do likewise.

Frank caught the intent look that Beaumont gave him and knew the young Ranger was about to intervene. He jerked his head in a negative, indicating that he would handle this himself. Reluctantly, Beaumont withdrew with the others.

The two gunmen took Frank's shake of his head to

mean that he wasn't going to fight them. One of them yelled, "Get down off that horse and draw, Morgan, or we'll blast you right out of the saddle!"

"Hold on," Frank said. "This is a good horse. Wouldn't want him getting hurt." He swung down from the saddle and motioned Beaumont back over. He handed the Appaloosa's reins to the young Ranger. "Appreciate it if you'd take Stormy out of the way, Tye."

"You sure?" Beaumont asked under his breath.

"I'm sure."

Beaumont led Stormy to the other side of the street. There was a large empty circle around Frank and the two men facing him. Sheriff Wilmott gave up on getting anybody to listen to him and motioned for his deputies to go back into the jail. Marshal Keever went inside, too, but Skeet Harlan stayed in the doorway so that he could watch. Anticipation shone in his watery eyes.

"All right, Morgan," one of the gunmen said. "Hook and draw any time you're ready."

"This is your fight," Frank said mildly. "It's up to you to start the ball."

Glowering at him, the two men edged farther apart. That was a good move and would make it more difficult for Frank to drop both of them before one of them had a chance to get him.

At least, that was the idea.

It didn't work out that well, because a shaved instant of time after the men grabbed iron, Frank's Peacemaker was already out of its holster and level. He took the man on his right first, firing once, bringing the revolver down from the recoil, pivoting smoothly at the hips, firing again at the man on the left. The first man never got a shot off. Frank's bullet took him in the chest and sent him stumbling backward a couple of steps. He dropped his gun and then sat down hard in the dust of the street. The second man managed to squeeze the trigger just as a slug ripped into his body. The shot went into the dirt at his feet as the impact of Frank's bullet spun him around. He wound up facing away from Frank, and when he tried to turn, his strength deserted him and he fell to his knees.

"My God," the man who was sitting down rasped. "You've killed me."

"It was your idea," Frank told him.

Blood gushed from the man's mouth and he fell over on his side. The other man, the one on his knees, pitched forward at the same moment and landed on his face. Blood began to form a dark pool underneath him.

Frank walked over, checked them both, and then reloaded the two spent shells when he was satisfied that the men were dead. He slid the Colt back into leather and turned to see Sheriff Wilmott and Marshal Keever coming toward him.

"It was a fair fight and they went for their guns first," Wilmott said heavily. "Nobody's going to arrest you, Morgan. But I wish you'd stay the hell out of town from now on."

"That goes for me, too," Keever put in. "You're not welcome in Brownwood."

"This trouble wasn't my doing," Frank pointed out.

"It found you all the same. If you hadn't been here, it wouldn't have happened."

"So you're telling me to get out of town?"

Both of the local lawmen nodded.

"I thought maybe you'd let me talk to Chris Kane."

"Not hardly," Wilmott said.

Frank saw that the crusty old sheriff wasn't going to budge. He turned away and looked for Beaumont, thinking that he would reclaim Stormy's reins and ride out.

Behind him, Wilmott told one of the bystanders to fetch the undertaker. "Tell Groner there's plenty of work for him today," the sheriff added.

If nothing else, the sudden outbreak of violence seemed to have defused the emotions that had gripped everyone earlier. The crowd had continued to split up, and now some of the men glanced at each other in something resembling embarrassment as they headed back to their businesses and homes. Maybe his words about taking the law into their own hands had gotten through to some of them, Frank thought. No matter what the reason, it looked like there wasn't going to be a lynching today after all.

Beaumont met him halfway across the street with Stormy. As the young Ranger handed over the reins, he said quietly, "I heard what the sheriff said about this being your fault because you were here, Frank. I can see now that's not fair. I reckon I understand—"

Rawlings was coming up behind Beaumont, and since Frank didn't want Rawlings to overhear what his young friend was saying, he nodded and said, "Thanks for holding my horse." Then he turned away before Beaumont could say anything else. They could talk about it more the next time they met at the cave on Blanket Creek.

"So that was Frank Morgan," Coburn commented a short time later as he stood at the bar in the Palace.

"Yeah," Rawlings said. "You got to see how fast he is for yourself. That going to make any difference?"

"You mean in whether I stand with you and the others?" Coburn shook his head. "Morgan's fast. But so am I."

"Which one of you is faster?" Rawlings asked bluntly.

Coburn tossed back his drink and smiled. "Maybe we'll find out one of these days."

Beaumont was sitting at a table with Callie Stratton and Vern Gladwell. Gladwell said, "I thought for sure there was gonna be a big fight out there today."

"So did I," Callie said. "And we were outnumbered."

Gladwell jerked his chin toward the bar where Rawlings and Coburn stood. "Nothing to worry about," he said sarcastically. "We've got a hired gun on our side now."

"Coburn's only one man," Beaumont said. "He couldn't have stood up to that whole mob."

"You don't like him, do you?" Callie asked.

"He rides up out of nowhere, admits he's a gunslinger, and says he wants to side with us in our fight with the big ranchers. Doesn't that sound the least bit suspicious to you?" Beaumont wanted to know.

Callie shrugged. "Maybe. But it could be just the way Coburn says it is."

"Yeah," Beaumont said, but he didn't sound convinced. "I'd still keep an eye on him, if it was me."

"I plan to." Callie paused, then said, "Coburn and Frank Morgan are in the same line of work, but they're not the same sort of man, are they? There's something about Morgan that's different."

Gladwell said, "I wish *he* was on our side instead of Coburn, to tell you the truth."

Callie nodded slowly, and Beaumont thought she looked like she was thinking the same thing.

The front door of the saloon opened and Skeet Harlan came in. Beaumont's instinctive dislike of the little deputy made him frown. Harlan ambled toward the bar. He stopped beside Rawlings and Coburn and gave them what was intended to be a pleasant nod. It didn't look all that pleasant, though.

"I went back to the office and looked through all the reward dodgers, Coburn," he said.

"You didn't find me on any of them, did you?" Coburn asked smugly. "I'm not wanted by the law, Deputy."

"You mean you're not wanted, period."

Coburn tensed. "I'm not looking for trouble," he said.

"Good. Stay that way." With a sneer of contempt, Harlan turned away.

For a second, Beaumont thought Coburn was going to reach for his gun. The look that passed across Coburn's face was one of sheer hatred and viciousness. But the gun-thrower controlled himself and turned back to the bar. With his left hand he thumped his empty glass on the hardwood and said to Rusty, "Another drink, damn it."

Ace McKelvey came out of his office, noticed Harlan standing there, and said, "Deputy, can I talk to you for a minute?"

"Sure," Harlan said with a shrug. "You got a problem, McKelvey?"

"Let's go in the office," the saloon keeper suggested. "Rusty, give me a bottle and a couple of glasses."

"Sure, Boss." The red-bearded apron handed over the bottle and glasses. McKelvey ushered Harlan into the office and shut the door behind them.

Beaumont watched them go and frowned slightly as the door closed. There was nothing unusual about a local businessman having a talk with a deputy marshal. They could be talking about anything.

But Frank Morgan was convinced there was more going on in Brownwood than was apparent on the surface, and Beaumont found himself wondering if there was some connection he didn't know about between McKelvey and Harlan.

One thing he knew for sure, Harlan and Flint Coburn had hated each other on sight. If they ran up against each other too often, then sooner or later blood would be spilled. There was Morgan to consider, too. Would Coburn feel compelled to test Morgan's speed?

You could draw a line from Morgan to Coburn to

Harlan and back to Morgan, Beaumont thought. It made a triangle, a deadly triangle formed of gunsmoke and hot lead. . . .

"I had the door open enough to see what was going on," McKelvey said as he sat at his desk and toyed with the drink in his hand. "You should go on the stage, Skeet. Anybody watching must have thought that you and Flint hate each other and wanted to draw. That was quite a fine job of acting."

Harlan grunted and threw back his drink. "It wasn't all acting. I could tell Coburn thinks he's faster'n me. I'd like to see him try to prove it sometime."

McKelvey leaned forward and frowned. "Don't get too carried away," he warned. "We're all on the same side, remember?"

"I don't see why we had to bring Coburn in before it was time to loot the town," Harlan complained.

"Because we needed something else to tip the balance into open war!" McKelvey thumped a fist on the desk. "We've been working behind the scenes for weeks now, trying to push the two factions into fighting. Other than a few little skirmishes, we haven't accomplished a damned thing. Now, with a famous gunman on each side, there's bound to be bigger trouble."

Harlan picked up the bottle and poured himself another drink. "Maybe you're right," he allowed. "That still doesn't mean I have to like Coburn."

"Just be patient. The fuse is short now. It won't be long until the explosion."

"I hope you're right," Harlan said. "And when it blows, it better be a damned big one."

29

The Brown County grand jury met the next day and indicted Chris Kane on charges of attempted murder—drawing his gun on Skeet Harlan—and destruction of private property—cutting the Slash D fence. The second charge would be difficult to prove, since Earl Duggan's fence still stood unmolested along Stepps Creek, but that didn't matter. The first one would be enough to send Kane back to the pen, and there was no doubt in anyone's mind that Kane would be convicted of it. Skeet Harlan would testify that Kane had been on the prod and had drawn first.

Nelse Anderson stopped at the little double cabin on Blanket Creek that evening and told Beaumont, "Al has called a meeting of all the small ranchers in this area. Some of the farmers are comin', too. I'm headin' there now. You better come along, Tye."

Beaumont had finished the day's work and was looking forward to a few hours of rest before he met Frank Morgan at the cave for their regular rendezvous. That would have to wait, though. He knew he needed to attend the meeting called by Rawlings. Rawlings might have it in his mind to do something crazy, and Beaumont would have to try to talk him out of it.

He threw a saddle on his horse and rode southwest with Anderson toward the Rawlings spread. They had to go the long way around to avoid some fences, and night had fallen before they finally rode up in front of the ranch house. Quite a few horses were tied up there. Light spilled through the open doors of the barn. The meeting was big enough so that it had to be held in the barn rather than in the house.

Several lanterns hung from nails around the inside of the barn, casting a flickering yellow glow over the two dozen or so men who were gathered there. Callie Stratton was the only woman in sight, Beaumont noted as he and Anderson entered the barn. Some of the ranchers and farmers in attendance were married, but obviously they had left their wives at home. This was man's business. Callie wouldn't see it that way, of course.

Everybody was talking at once. Rawlings climbed up on a bale of hay and raised his hands to call for quiet, and when he didn't get it right away, he bellowed, "Hey! Settle down, damn it!"

An uneasy hush fell over the crowd, broken only by a few muttered comments. Even though Rawlings had assumed a leadership role in the effort to defy the big ranchers, not everybody in this group liked him all that much, especially among the farmers. It was unusual to see homesteaders and ranchers working together in the first place, but everything in the situation in Brown County seemed to be turned topsy-turvy from the usual state of affairs on the frontier. Barbed wire had made allies of men who normally would have despised each other.

"That's better," Rawlings said. "Settle down now, because we've got to decide what to do."

"About Chris Kane, you mean?" one of the farmers asked.

"That's right."

"What *can* we do? The sheriff's got him locked up, and he's been indicted. He'll have to stand trial."

"And be sent to prison for something he didn't do?" one of the ranchers said angrily.

"Well, we can't just ride into Brownwood and take him out of the jail, now can we?"

"If there's enough of us, we can!"

"Hold on," Rawlings said, lifting his hands again. "I don't like the idea of leavin' Kane in jail, either, but if we try to break him out, there'll be a lot of shooting, and some of us will get killed."

More muttering came from the crowd, especially among the farmers who were clustered together. They weren't gunmen. They might fight for their own land, but it would be difficult to meld them into any sort of force that could take the battle to the big ranchers. Beaumont was counting on that, in fact, to help keep the lid on the situation.

"I've been thinkin' about it," Rawlings went on, "and what we have to do is give Duggan and the others something else to worry about. They're the ones who'll be pressing for Kane to stand trial, and if they've got other things on their mind, maybe they won't get around to it for a while. That would give us time to find him a lawyer and maybe get the case moved out of Brown County."

Beaumont frowned slightly. With that talk of a lawyer and a change of venue, Rawlings was actually making sense for a change. He wondered if Callie had come up with that. She seemed more the type. But Rawlings's comments about giving the big ranchers something else to worry about was what really made Beaumont frown. What was he planning now?

It didn't take Rawlings long to answer that question. He said, "I think what we have to do is spread out all over the county and cut every damned fence we can find. It's a new moon tomorrow night. It'll be mighty dark, and if we all make our move at the same time, the cattle barons won't be able to stop us."

"Won't that just make 'em mad and even more determined to put Kane on trial?" someone in the crowd asked.

"Kane can't be blamed for cutting the fences," Rawlings pointed out. "He's locked up in jail."

"But they could decide to make an example of him."

"No more so than they already have." Rawlings made a curt, sweeping gesture with his hand. "Look, anybody who wants out can leave. But don't come crying to the rest of us for help later on."

Beaumont could tell that the crowd was divided. All the ranchers and some of the farmers seemed to be in favor of a massive fence-cutting effort, but the rest of the farmers were worried about the consequences of such an act. Beaumont spoke up, saying, "Miss Callie, what do you think about this?"

Callie looked surprised that he was asking her opinion, but just as Beaumont expected, she wasn't shy about giving it. "I think it might be enough to convince the big ranchers that they can't fight us. We're going to win sooner or later. At the very least they'll be distracted from their vendetta against Chris."

"Well, I think it's a bad idea," Beaumont stated.

Several men turned to glare at him. "You don't have any stake in this, cowboy," one of them said, the same argument that had been used against him before.

"You're my friends, and I don't want to see anybody else hurt," Beaumont said. "Duggan and the others are liable to send their crews after you. They might even try to burn some of you out."

Another of the ranchers shook a fist. "I'd like to see them try it! If they want a war, we'll give them a war, by God!"

That was just the sort of talk Beaumont didn't want to hear.

An older man took up the cry. "The Yankees tried to burn us out in the Shenandoah Valley!" he shouted. "But Mosby and the rest of us fought all the way to the end! We'll do that here if we have to!"

Shouts of agreement came from the other men. Even the ones who had been reluctant a few minutes earlier seemed to be getting caught up in the spirit of the thing. Mob violence had been narrowly averted more than once in this conflict. They couldn't keep dodging that bullet, Beaumont thought.

Nor could he argue too strenuously against the idea without running the risk of arousing the ire—and the suspicion—of Rawlings and the others. He nodded and said, "All right, if that's the way all of you feel, I'll go along with it."

But already his mind was working, trying to come up with some way to stop this madness in its tracks.

Maybe Frank Morgan would have a suggestion when they met later, he thought hopefully.

"I don't know of any way to stop it," Frank said. "Not without getting a lot of people hurt or killed."

He and Beaumont stood in front of the dark mouth of the cave on Blanket Creek, holding the reins of their horses.

"What if you tell Duggan what Rawlings and the rest of them are planning to do?" Beaumont said. "They could increase the patrols along their fence lines. Maybe once Rawlings and the others see that the ranchers are ready for them, they'll back off."

Frank shook his head. "More than likely, Duggan would order his men to shoot first as soon as they saw anybody moving around. I expect the other big ranchers would do the same thing." He rubbed at his jaw as he thought. "You know, the best thing might be to let Rawlings and his friends cut those fences. Maybe Miz Stratton's right. If every fence in the county is cut, maybe the ranchers will see that they can't win this fight, not in the long run."

"You really think they can't?"

"You know there are a lot of electric streetlights in the cities back East now?" A wistful note crept into Frank's voice. "There are telephones in a lot of places, including right here in Brown County. There'll probably be electricity here before too many more years go by."

"Yeah, maybe," Beaumont said, sounding puzzled. "But what's your point, Frank?"

"The West, the way it was, is just about gone. Cattle barons like Earl Duggan are relics. I hate to say it, but so am I."

"Not hardly," Beaumont protested.

Frank chuckled. "Oh, I don't mind all that much being a relic. Better than being completely extinct, I reckon. But the days of the big cattle spreads are numbered, no matter what happens here. The small ranchers and the farmers will embrace the use of barbed wire like they have in other places, and they'll take over. It's as sure as the sun coming up in the morning."

"I'm surprised the idea doesn't bother you more."

"I never said it doesn't bother me. But I don't argue with the sun and tell it that it can't rise, either."

"That's all well and good," Beaumont said impatiently, "but what do we do about Rawlings and his plans?"

"You can't talk him out of it?"

Beaumont shook his head. "Not a chance in hell."

"Let it go, then, and we'll see what happens."

"I was afraid you'd say that," Beaumont said with a

sigh. He changed the subject by asking, "What about Chris Kane?"

"I've been thinking about that. Rawlings has got the right idea for a change. Kane needs a good lawyer who can get the case moved to another county. If that happens, I'd say he stands a good chance of beating the charges, or even getting them dismissed before the case comes to trial."

"I think it was Callie Stratton who came up with that idea."

"I wouldn't be a bit surprised," Frank agreed. He took a folded piece of paper from his shirt pocket. "I rode into town this afternoon and wired my lawyers in Denver, got the name of the best lawyer in Fort Worth. He'll be on his way down here tomorrow."

"Kane doesn't have the kind of money it takes to pay for that."

"No, but I do," Frank said. "You give the fella that paper when he gets here. It'll explain everything and give him his orders."

"You'd better hope Duggan doesn't get wind of this. He'll fire you faster than you can say Jack Robinson."

Frank grinned. "I've said it before and I'll say it again: let him."

They said their farewells and went their separate ways, Frank heading back to the Slash D. He was challenged by a couple of guards when he got there. One of them was Pitch Carey, who asked, "What are you doin' wandering around at this time of night, Frank?"

"Just taking a ride along the fences," Frank said.

"Patrolling, eh? You think something's gonna happen?"

"You can count on one thing, Pitch," Frank said. "Something's always going to happen. We just don't know what it is yet."

***

The rest of that night and the next day passed quietly. Frank didn't have an inkling that something was wrong until that evening when he noticed that Ed MacDonald and most of the other ranch hands were not in the bunkhouse. There was nothing that unusual about their absence—Duggan had men patrolling his fence lines every night now—but too many of the crew were gone for that to account for it. They had been there at supper and then slipped off afterward for some reason.

Still, Frank didn't think too much about it until he walked over to the main house and found that Duggan himself was gone.

Wing was in the kitchen, cleaning up from supper and getting ready for breakfast the next morning. "Evening," Frank said to him. "Where's everybody gone, Wing?"

The cook shook his head. "Not know what you mean, Mr. Morgan."

"Duggan, MacDonald, and just about all the other hands aren't anywhere around. Is something wrong?"

Frank knew that this was the night Al Rawlings and his friends planned to cut all the fences in the county, but there was no way for Duggan to be aware of that . . . at least not as far as Frank knew.

"Nothing wrong, Mr. Morgan," Wing said. "Everything all-ee fine."

Frank frowned. "Don't try that coolie talk on me, damn it. I know you speak English just as good as anybody around here and better than most."

Wing sighed in resignation and said, "I'm sorry, Mr. Morgan. I've been sworn to secrecy. I'm afraid Mr. Duggan no longer trusts you."

"Why the hell not?" Frank exclaimed. "I haven't done anything to give him cause not to trust me."

Wing glanced around nervously. "I shouldn't tell you this. . . . Mr. Duggan will never forgive me if he knows I betrayed his secret. . . ."

"He won't hear it from me," Frank promised.

Wing hesitated a second longer but then said, "Mr. Duggan knows you've been meeting with that young man called Tye. He's afraid that you're double-crossing him."

Frank said, "Damn it!" and smacked his right fist into his left palm. He had no idea how Duggan had found out about his clandestine meetings with Beaumont, but that didn't matter now. "What's Duggan up to tonight?"

"I shouldn't tell you—"

"Listen to me, Wing," Frank said. "I know how it must look, but I give you my word I haven't betrayed Duggan. I want to stop the trouble around here from getting worse, that's all. If you know where Duggan and the rest of the crew have gone and what they plan to do, I need you to tell me, so that I can keep folks from getting hurt."

It cost Wing quite an effort, but after a moment he nodded and said, "Mr. Duggan found out somehow that the smaller ranchers plan to try cutting his fences again tonight. He said . . . he said that when they do, they're going to be in for a really big surprise."

This time Frank couldn't help but grate out a curse. "Which way did they head?"

"I heard him say something to Ed about Stepps Creek, so I guess they're going out there again, where Chris Kane tried to cut the wire before."

Frank clapped a hand on the cook's shoulder. "Thanks, Wing. You did the right thing by telling me, but I won't let Duggan know where I found out." He turned toward the door.

"What are you going to do, Mr. Morgan?" Wing called after him.

"Put a stop to it, I hope, before a lot of people get killed."

He hurried out to the stable and swiftly saddled Stormy. No one was around to stop him as he rode out, but he saw Wing standing tensely on the porch, silhouetted by the light coming through the open door behind him, watching worriedly as Frank galloped off into the night.

Frank had ridden over every foot of the Slash D, and his natural frontiersman's instincts insured that he could find his way, even on a night like this one. Not only was there a new moon, but clouds had moved in during the late afternoon, obscuring even that feeble glow. It hadn't started to rain yet, but the air was heavy, as if it might later.

With Frank's expert touch on the reins, Stormy didn't miss a step on the trail. Dog raced along behind, eager to see where his master was going. Frank didn't slow down until he figured he had almost reached the creek. As he pulled Stormy back to a walk, he peered intently into the darkness. He was able to make out a line of thicker shadows that marked the trees along the stream. He swung down from the saddle and was about to approach on foot so that Duggan and the others wouldn't hear him coming, when something happened that made any sort of stealth utterly unnecessary.

A huge explosion roared out, tearing apart the veil of darkness with a ball of flame and shaking the very earth itself under Frank Morgan's feet.

30

Frank was shocked by the blast. Stormy let out a shrill whinny and reared up on his hind legs, pawing the air. Dog hunkered, whining. None of them had expected anything like the explosion that had just rocked the night.

While the roar was still echoing over the rolling, wooded hills, guns began to bang. As Frank hauled down on the reins and brought the Appaloosa under control, he saw spurts of muzzle flame here and there, briefly lighting the darkness like giant, deadly fireflies. Somewhere not far off a man screamed in agony.

Frank bounded into the saddle and heeled Stormy into a run that carried them toward the scene of battle. As he rode he jerked his Colt from its holster, but then he cursed as he realized he wouldn't know who to shoot at. He figured the clash was between Duggan's men and some of the members of Rawlings's bunch who had come to cut the fence, but it was too dark out here for him to tell who was who.

That wasn't stopping the other men. They blazed away at each other. Frank heard more than one man cry out in pain. He pulled the Appaloosa to a stop again and yelled, "Hold your fire! Hold your fire!" He didn't know if any of the combatants would pay attention to the order, but it was worth a try.

Unfortunately, all it accomplished was to make several of the gunmen open fire on *him*. More gun flashes stabbed out, and bullets hummed a deadly tune past his ears. Frank jerked Stormy around so that the horse faced back the other way. Then he slid out of the saddle and yanked his hat off. He slapped the Stetson against Stormy's rump and sent the Appaloosa lunging away, hopefully out of the line of fire.

Then Frank called, "Dog! To me!" and darted into some nearby trees.

He knelt there with Dog beside him, fallen leaves crackling underneath him as he watched the battle and tried to make some sense of it. From time to time a bullet whistled through the branches above them or thudded into one of the tree trunks, but for the most part none of the lead came near them.

Gradually, Frank began to make some sense out of what was going on. There were two groups of gunmen, one on each side of the fence, just as he would have expected. Slash D on one side, smaller ranchers on the other. What he still didn't know was what had caused the big explosion. Whatever it was had set some of the grass and brush on fire, and the flames began to spread and flicker higher, casting a nightmarish glare over the scene. As the blaze grew, Frank saw men darting here and there, firing on the run. The light was too uncertain for him to recognize any of them.

Footsteps crashed into the trees behind him. He swung around, knowing that anybody on this side of the fence was likely a Slash D man. "Hold it!" Frank barked as a dark shape loomed up in front of him.

"Morgan?" It was Stiles Warren's voice. "You damn traitor!"

Instinct made Frank dive to the side as the Colt in Warren's hand roared. Frank could have gunned the tall, lanky puncher, but he didn't want any more killing tonight. Instead he kicked out and swept Warren's legs out from under him.

Warren yelped in surprise as he fell and then grunted as he hit the ground. Frank aimed at that sound and swung his gun. The barrel thudded into something, and Warren stretched out on the ground with a long sigh. Frank checked him in the darkness, finding the lump on his skull. Warren was out cold.

Frank sprang to his feet as a sudden burst of barking and growling sounded nearby. Another Slash D man must have entered the trees, and Dog had jumped him. The man screamed and shouted, "Call him off! Call him off!"

"Dog!" Frank said. "Dog, hold!"

That command would make the big cur stop attacking, but if the man he had pulled down made any move to get up, Dog would stop him. Frank hurried toward the low growling and said, "Whoever you are, mister, you'd better stay put, or else he's liable to tear your throat out before I can stop him."

"Morgan!" the man gasped. Frank recognized Ed MacDonald's voice. "Morgan, have you gone crazy? Call off your dog!"

"First tell me what's going on here." The shots continued, but they came less frequently now. The fight was dying down.

"We . . . we set a trap for those damn fence-cutters!"

"What kind of trap?"

"We rigged some dynamite with a friction trigger . . . attached it to the wire . . . hid it next to the fence . . . For God's sake, Morgan, get this dog away from me!"

Frank was in no mood to call off Dog. He had gone cold inside as MacDonald explained the blast. He said, "You mean you rigged the dynamite so it would go off if the wire was cut?"

"Yeah . . . It was the boss's idea, I swear! We didn't

know the hombre would be standing almost right on top of it when it went off!"

Beaumont. Frank had advised the young Ranger to let Rawlings go through with his plan, even though it was dangerous. It was even possible that Beaumont had been the one to step up to the fence with a pair of wire-cutters in his hand. He might have slipped the cutters over the wire and pressed the handles together. . . .

One thing was certain. Whether the blast had killed Beaumont or not, it had surely killed *someone*. It had been too big, too powerful, not to.

"Back off, Dog," Frank said, and MacDonald let out a sigh of relief. He was probably rethinking that a second later as Frank hunkered beside him and pressed the barrel of his Colt under the foreman's chin, digging it in painfully.

"You said the dynamite trap was Duggan's idea?" Frank asked coldly.

"Y-yeah!"

"How did he know the fence was going to be cut tonight?"

"Somebody told him. . . . One of the farmers, I think. He said Rawlings got all his bunch together and planned to cut fences all over the county tonight. . . . That's all I know, I swear, Morgan!"

So one of the men who had been at that meeting in Rawlings's barn had sold them out, Frank thought. In a way, he wasn't really surprised. In every group there was usually at least one man who was weak, who was more interested in protecting himself and feathering his own nest rather than looking out for his friends.

"So you snuck out here and set your trap, and when the blast went out you opened fire on the men who weren't caught in the explosion. Is that it?"

"Yeah," MacDonald said, and though he was still scared, his voice sounded a bit stronger. He had enough backbone so that even the threat of Frank's gun prodding his jaw wasn't going to cow him forever. As if to prove that, he went on. "Either pull that trigger or let me up, Morgan."

"Not just yet," Frank grated. "How come I wasn't told about any of this?"

"Because the boss knows now you're a damned traitor! Stiles has been keepin' an eye on that young fella Tye. He saw the two of you getting together last night. You sold us out, Morgan!"

Frank grimaced. He had made sure that no one followed him to the rendezvous with Beaumont, but obviously the young Ranger hadn't been that careful. Frank didn't absolve himself completely from the blame, either; he should have noticed that someone was tailing Beaumont.

"I didn't sell anybody out," he said. "I was just trying to keep people from getting killed."

"Go to hell, Morgan!" MacDonald snarled.

A new voice said from behind Frank, "You move a muscle, Morgan, and I'll send you there. I've got a Winchester trained on you."

Frank recognized Earl Duggan's raspy tones. He heard leaves crunching under the cattle baron's boots as Duggan approached. He realized now that the night was quiet again. The shooting was over.

The only sound was a faint moan from somewhere on the other side of the fence.

"He's got a gun at my throat, Boss," MacDonald warned.

"Drop it, Morgan," Duggan ordered.

Frank considered for a second. Duggan couldn't be able to see him that well. The fire was dying out, the flames being extinguished by the light rain that had begun to fall while Frank was questioning MacDonald. It was entirely possible that Frank could spin around and put a bullet in Duggan before the cattleman could fire. Even if Duggan got off a shot, it would be pure chance if it hit Frank.

But even though a part of Frank wanted to do that, he had told MacDonald that he wanted to stop the killing, and he had meant it. He pulled the barrel of the Peacemaker away from MacDonald's throat and slid the gun back into leather. Then he stood up and turned to face Duggan. Rain pattered quietly against the crown of Frank's hat.

"All right, Duggan," he said.

"What about it, Ed?" Duggan's voice lashed out.

Frank heard MacDonald scrambling to his feet. "I'm all right, Boss," the foreman said. "Morgan holstered his gun."

Duggan grunted. "Better drop it, Morgan."

"I don't think so," Frank said flatly. "I've only got so much backup in me, Duggan. You'd do well to remember that."

Duggan didn't press the issue. Instead he asked, "What are you doing here?"

"I hoped to get here in time to stop you from doing something damned foolish." Frank paused and then added heavily, "I didn't make it."

"We'll see how foolish it is once word gets around about one of those damn greasy-sack cowboys gettin' blown to bits when he tried to cut my fence. After tonight none of those bastards will dare come anywhere near a decent man's fence."

"You think fences are worth killing men over?" Frank's voice shook a little from the depth of his anger.

"You're damned right I do!" Duggan shot back at him. "What's worth defending more than a man's home range?"

Frank couldn't answer that. In a way, he knew that

Duggan was right: A man *did* have an unquestionable right to defend himself, his family, and his property. But those fence-cutters weren't thieves and murderers. They weren't the sort of worthless outlaw trash that Frank had gunned down countless times over the years when he was forced into it. He had never lost a minute's sleep over dealing out death to scum like them.

But the little ranchers and the farmers who found themselves in opposition to Duggan and the other cattle barons were, by and large, decent hard-working men who just wanted something better for themselves and their families. None of them deserved to have a bundle of dynamite blast them to kingdom come.

"Hey, Boss!" The shout came from the other side of the fence. "Some of them are still alive over here! What should we do?"

When Duggan hesitated in answering, Frank said, "Why don't you tell your men to kill the rest of them in cold blood? Murdering some helpless men isn't beneath you, is it, Duggan?"

"Shut the hell up," Duggan growled. "Ed, keep an eye on Morgan while I take a look over there."

"Sure, Boss," MacDonald said. He still had his gun, and now he eared back the hammer so that the metallic ratcheting was loud in the night.

"I'm going with you," Frank declared. He started to follow Duggan toward the fence.

"Boss . . . ?" MacDonald asked.

"Let him come," Duggan snapped over his shoulder. "Just watch him close, and ventilate him if he tries anything."

They made their way to the fence and carefully climbed between the strands of wire, avoiding as much as possible the wicked barbs. Several men were standing around in the rain between the fence and the trees along the creek. About twenty yards along the fence was a gaping hole where the explosion had gone off. Frank looked at it and said, "You blew up your own fence, Duggan. Sort of defeats the purpose, doesn't it?"

"Not hardly," Duggan rasped. "The purpose was to teach those bastards to leave me and mine alone. You reckon they'll do it from now on?"

Frank didn't answer that. He wasn't sure what the reaction would be to tonight's violence . . . but he was willing to bet it wouldn't work out as neatly as Duggan was obviously convinced it would.

Duggan snapped a match into life with his thumbnail and shielded it from the rain with his other hand. He had tucked the Winchester under his arm. The glow from the match fell on the face of a young man who lay in the grass near the fence. He writhed in agony from a bullet-shattered shoulder, but he suffered pretty much in silence. Frank didn't recognize him.

Duggan did, though. "One of Rawlings' bunch, all right," he said. "Name's Bert something-or-other, I think. Get him on his feet. We'll take him back to the ranch, patch him up, and turn him over to the law tomorrow." He looked around. "Any more still alive?"

The answer came from Pitch Carey. "Over here, Boss."

Duggan lit another match and examined another wounded man, this one with a bullet through his thigh and a deep crease on his side. Nearby, two more dark shapes lay in the grass, but they were motionless in death.

"The rest of them made it back into the trees and took off after shooting it out with us for a few minutes," Carey explained.

"Any of our boys hurt?" Duggan wanted to know.

"A few bullet burns." Carey sounded worried as he added, "But we can't find Warren."

"He's back over there on the other side of the fence," Frank said. "I ran into him when I rode up."

Carey started toward him. "You son of a bitch! What did you do to him?"

"Take it easy," Frank told the chunky cowboy. "I had to wallop him, but when he wakes up he'll be fine except for a headache."

Grimly, Duggan said, "I reckon we'd better go have a look at what's left of the fella who cut the wire and set off that dynamite."

Frank's jaw was set tightly as he walked with Duggan and the other men over to the site of the blast. He didn't know if enough of the poor bastard would be left to identify him.

It was bad, all right, about as gruesome as anything Frank had ever seen . . . and he had fought in the war. But only one man had been caught in the explosion, and he had been turned so that the force of it struck him mostly on the right side of his body. His arm and leg on that side had been blown off, along with his clothes, and most of his skin was charred and blackened. Enough of his face remained, though, so that Duggan was able to recognize him.

"It's Vern Gladwell," Duggan said. "Reckon he never knew what hit him."

"That's what you hope, anyway," Frank said.

Duggan turned sharply toward him. "Gladwell wasn't a bad sort. I didn't want this, damn it! I didn't want anybody to wind up dead. But it was their own choice to come over here and try to cut my fence. Nobody made 'em do it."

"Keep telling yourself that, Duggan."

For a second Frank thought that Duggan was going to take a swing at him, but then the cattleman turned away and said to MacDonald, "Go back to the house and get the wagon. We'll put Gladwell and the two wounded men in there."

"I don't know that those fellas will want to ride in the same wagon as Gladwell," MacDonald said.

"Then they can lay out here in the rain all night," Duggan snapped.

Despite Duggan's protests, Frank could tell that he had been shaken by the sight of Gladwell's mutilated body.

"In the morning I want men out here first thing to replace that post and restring the wire," Duggan went on. He faced Frank. "As for you, Morgan, I want you off the Slash D by the time we get there. I'll send your wages wherever you want 'em sent."

"You don't owe me anything," Frank said.

"The hell I don't! When I fire a man, I give him what he's got comin'. You just let me know where to send the money."

Frank didn't bother arguing with him. He turned away and went to look for Stormy.

As bad as the night had been, it could have been worse, he told himself. At least Tyler Beaumont hadn't died.

At least Beaumont hadn't died *here,* Frank amended.

But he didn't know what was going on wherever the young Ranger was.

31

Al Rawlings had split everyone up and also sent messages to those Brown County ranchers who hadn't attended the meeting at his place the night before. The whole thing was planned with military precision, even though Rawlings had never been in the army. The men who fanned out across Brown County on this cool, misty autumn night knew what they were supposed to do and when they were supposed to do it. The fences would be cut at approximately ten o'clock.

Beaumont found himself going with Rawlings and a rancher named Thad Briscoe to cut the fences on Calhoun's Diamond C spread. Beaumont suspected that Rawlings didn't fully trust him, and that was why Rawlings had insisted that Beaumont come with him.

Callie Stratton had wanted to come along, too, but her brother had put his foot down about that. She was back at the ranch, where she wouldn't be in any danger.

Calhoun's range bordered Rawlings's land, so it didn't take them long to reach the spot Rawlings had chosen for them. The fence ran through a stand of trees for about half a mile. "We'll cut it at every post," Rawlings had said before they left. "It's hard working in those trees and brush. It'll take them a week or more to replace that wire."

"What about guards?" Briscoe had asked.

"We have plenty of time to watch for a while before we do anything," Rawlings had explained. "We should be able to tell how often they come by."

That was how it had worked out. The three men left their horses about a quarter of a mile away, tied to some post oak saplings, and approached the fence on foot. They waited in thick brush, watching and listening. A few minutes later, a rider came along on the other side of the fence. He skirted the trees and moved on. Fifteen or twenty minutes later, he came back the other way.

"We'll wait until he's gone by again," Rawlings decided, "and then we'll get that damn fence cut. Tye, you ready?"

Rawlings had given Beaumont the wire-cutters, probably as a test to see if he would actually go through with it. Beaumont nodded and growled, "Yeah, I'm ready."

The question now was whether he could bring himself to go ahead and break the law he was sworn to uphold.

The sentry on horseback passed by and moved on out of sight again, his mount's hoofbeats sounding faintly in the damp air. Briscoe nudged Beaumont in the side. The young Ranger took a deep breath and started to straighten up and move out of the brush's concealment. . . .

A dull boom, sounding almost like distant thunder, rolled through the night. Beaumont wasn't sure, but he thought he felt the earth tremble a little under his feet. It wasn't unheard of for there to be thunderstorms in Texas at this time of year, but it was uncommon. Beaumont hadn't seen any lightning, either.

"What the hell was that?" Briscoe asked in a hoarse whisper.

"I don't know and I don't care," Rawlings replied. "How about it, Tye? You gonna cut that wire?"

Beaumont took a step toward the fence but then stopped. He shifted the wire-cutters from his right hand to his left. Then he turned back toward Rawlings and Briscoe and dropped his right hand to the butt of his gun. Palming it out smoothly, he said, "No, I'm not. You two step out of that brush and drop your guns. You're covered."

"You son of a—" The startled exclamation ripped out of Rawlings. "I knew you were a double-crosser. I *knew* it! How much are the cattle barons paying you?"

"Nobody's paying me but the State of Texas. Now drop your guns and elevate!"

Under the threat of Beaumont's revolver, Rawlings and Briscoe reluctantly complied with the order. As Briscoe unbuckled his gun belt and lowered it to the ground at his feet, he asked, "What do you mean about the State of Texas?"

"I'm a Ranger," Beaumont said tersely. "And as of now, fence-cutting is over in Brown County."

"The hell it is," Rawlings snarled. "It's just getting started, Tye, or whatever your name is."

"Tyler Beaumont," the young Ranger introduced himself. He felt the need to explain. "Look, Rawlings, you've got me wrong. I'm just trying to put a stop to the trouble. I'm not working for the big ranchers or anything like that. In fact, I think what they're doing is wrong. But you can't right that wrong by breaking the law."

"The law doesn't give a damn about anybody who doesn't have money, and a lot of it!" Rawlings said bitterly. "The law's never gonna side with the little fella, and you know it."

"That's where you're wrong," Beaumont told him. "I'll prove it, too. Now back off from those guns."

The two men backed away and Beaumont stepped

forward to retrieve their guns. He kept his Colt trained on them as he bent to pick up the weapons from the ground. A light rain had begun to fall.

He was convinced that the boom they had heard earlier had been an explosion of some sort. Beaumont wasn't sure, but he thought he had heard some gunshots following the blast, too. Something had happened, sure enough, and from the sound of it he thought it had taken place along the fence line of the Slash D.

Beaumont wondered if Frank Morgan had been involved with it, whatever it was.

"Mount up," he told Rawlings and Briscoe. "We're going back to your place, Al, and you're going to call another meeting. I need to tell everyone that there won't be any more fence-cutting."

There was a sneer in Rawlings's voice as he said, "You're a mite late for that, ain't you, Beaumont? Fences are being cut all over the county right now."

"I know it," Beaumont said grimly. "I should have put a stop to it earlier. I thought maybe if I let things play out, Duggan and the others might be willing to bargain."

"But then you couldn't do it." Rawlings laughed humorlessly. "The Texas Ranger couldn't bring himself to cut a fence."

"Shut up and go get on your horse," Beaumont told him.

He kept the two men covered as they walked back to the spot where they had left their horses. They mounted up and rode toward Rawlings's ranch house. The rain began to fall harder.

As they came in sight of the house a half hour later, Beaumont knew something was wrong. Even through the mist he could tell that every lamp in the place must be lit, including in the barn. As they came closer he saw a lot of riders milling around. Callie Stratton stood on the covered porch, her red hair bright in the light from inside the house. She was talking to the men gathered in front of the house. As Beaumont and the others approached, she saw them and cried, "Al! Al, come quick!"

It wasn't until the three newcomers rode up to the group that anyone noticed Beaumont's gun pointed toward Rawlings and Briscoe. They saw as well that the two men were unarmed and knew something was wrong. "What the hell's going on here?" a man shouted.

"We're under arrest, I reckon," Rawlings said scathingly as he reined to a halt. "Tye's really a Texas Ranger!"

"A Ranger!" The startled exclamation came from more than one man.

"Take it easy," Beaumont said sharply. "Nobody's under arrest. I just couldn't let any more fences be cut."

"How about a fence having a hole blown in it?" one of the riders asked.

So that boom *had* been an explosion, Beaumont thought. "What happened?" he asked.

"Vern and the fellas who went to the Slash D ran into a trap," one of the men choked out. "Duggan had dynamite rigged to the fence. It blew Vern to hell when it went off!"

Beaumont felt sick inside at the awful news. He had liked Vern Gladwell a lot. The man was actually one of the more reasonable members of Rawlings's bunch. But now he was dead.

"What about the others?" Beaumont asked tautly.

"Duggan and some of his crew were lyin' in wait. As soon as the bomb went off, they opened up on the other fellas. A couple of our boys were hit bad enough they had to be left behind. Don't know if they're dead or not. The others were able to throw some lead back at the

Slash D and then light a shuck out of there. Got some creases and bullet burns, but nothing too serious."

So one man, Vern Gladwell, was dead for sure and two more might be. The sickness inside Beaumont intensified, but it was joined by a surge of anger. The whole thing never should have gotten this far. Both sides should have been more reasonable, more willing to work things out. He was angry at himself, too, for not finding a better solution.

Well, his cards were on the table now, he told himself. By morning everybody in the county would know that he was a Ranger.

"Look," he said, "I'm going to try to persuade Sheriff Wilmott not to arrest anybody for cutting fences tonight. This needs to be settled in court, not over the barrel of a gun."

"The courts'll just put us in jail for standing up for ourselves!"

Beaumont shook his head. "No, I intend to testify on your behalf—"

"Don't do us any favors, Beaumont," Rawlings said coldly. "Not when you're sittin' there holding a gun on us."

Beaumont hesitated for a second and then holstered his gun. "I said nobody was under arrest, and I meant it. But this is the only time I'll tell you men: The fence-cutting stops tonight!"

"You're only one man, Ranger," one of the riders said ominously.

"There are plenty more where I came from. The governor can send a whole troop of Rangers in here if he needs to."

"Tye's right," Callie said. "We can't fight the Rangers."

"They bleed like anybody else," Rawlings snapped. "Like Chris Kane and Vern Gladwell and everybody else who runs up against those power-hungry range hogs!"

Callie stepped up to him and took hold of his arm. "Come on inside, Al," she urged. "All of you, come in out of the rain. We can't do anything else tonight."

"We can't do anything for Vern at all," Rawlings said bitterly. But he went with his sister, stepping up onto the porch and moving slump-shouldered into the house. The others began to dismount and follow them. A couple of the men gathered up the reins and led the horses toward the barn.

That left Beaumont sitting there alone in the rain. They had all ignored him as they went inside. He wondered what, if anything, they would cook up in there to answer the hideous violence with which Earl Duggan had met them tonight. He wondered as well how Duggan had found out what Rawlings and the others planned to do. That subject hadn't come up, but Beaumont had thought of it. Maybe the men were in such a state of shock over Vern Gladwell's gruesome death that it simply hadn't occurred to them yet.

But sooner or later it would. Beaumont was sure of that. Just like he was sure that no matter what he said, the trouble in Brown County wasn't over yet.

With rain dripping off the brim of his hat, he turned his horse and rode toward the little double cabin on Blanket Creek. He didn't have anywhere else to go.

32

Frank heard the hoofbeats of a horse approaching. Dog lifted his head from where it had been resting on his paws and growled. The rain still fell, but Frank was under the roof of the dogtrot between the two sides of the cabin, so he was relatively dry. He stood up from the stool he had found there and tossed the butt of the quirly he had been smoking out into the rain. Then he picked up the Winchester he had leaned against the wall of the cabin and waited.

A dark, looming figure on horseback came out of the darkness. "Hold it right there," Frank called to him.

Tyler Beaumont's voice came back warily. "Frank? Is that you?"

Frank lowered the rifle and said, "Yeah. Come on in out of the rain."

Now that Beaumont was here, Frank didn't mind opening the door and stepping into the cabin. Earlier, when he had first got here, he'd felt a little like he was trespassing and so had decided to wait in the dogtrot after putting Stormy in the barn. He found a lamp sitting on a table and snapped a match into life with his thumbnail. A moment later the yellow glow from the lamp filled this half of the cabin.

Beaumont came inside, shaking water off his hat. "What are you doing here?" he asked as he hung the hat on a nail. The light rain had gotten his clothes pretty wet, but he wasn't quite soaked.

"Duggan found out you and me have been working together," Frank said. "He told me to get off his range, just like we knew he would if he ever found out."

"And you didn't have anywhere else to go. I know the feeling."

Frank shrugged. "I thought about riding into Brownwood, but I figured we needed to talk."

"About Vern Gladwell, maybe?"

"So you know about that."

Beaumont slumped into a chair, rested his elbows on the table, and put his hands over his face for a moment. When he lifted his head, his expression was haggard and haunted.

"I know about it. So do Rawlings and all the others. I guess the men who made it out of Duggan's trap didn't waste any time spreading the news."

"I didn't know what Duggan planned to do," Frank said.

Beaumont waved a hand. "I know you wouldn't be a party to anything like that, Frank." He clenched the hand into a fist and thumped it down hard on the table. "Why? Why did Duggan do it?"

"He got tired of Rawlings and the others harassing him. He's always fought back, all his life, whenever anybody threatened him or his range. That's all he knows how to do."

"But damn it, things are different now! There's supposed to be law and order. . . ."

"Maybe civilization hasn't got quite as strong a foothold in Texas as some folks think it does," Frank said.

Beaumont just shook his head in despair.

Frank sat down on the other side of the table and started to roll another smoke. After a few minutes

Beaumont asked, "Do you know how Duggan found out about what was going to happen tonight?"

"One of the farmers sold out to him. Don't ask me which one because Duggan never said, and I doubt that he'd tell either one of us."

"It doesn't matter. The damage is already done."

As he thought about Vern Gladwell, Frank could only nod. After a moment he said, "One of Duggan's punchers has been trailing you. He saw the two of us meeting at the cave. That's what tipped off Duggan that I was working with you. They slipped off and left me at the ranch tonight when they went to set their trap. I didn't find out about it in time to stop them."

"What was it, dynamite?"

Frank nodded. "Several sticks tied together, with a friction trigger rigged between them and the barbed wire. I'm not sure Duggan intended to kill anybody. If Gladwell hadn't happened to be standing almost on top of the dynamite when he cut the wire, the blast might not have gotten him."

"But Duggan didn't stop him when he saw what was about to happen, did he?"

"No," Frank allowed. "He sure didn't."

"Some folks would call that murder."

"You'd never get a jury to say that," Frank pointed out.

"No, but a jury would send Chris Kane back to prison, based only on the word of a crazy gunman like Skeet Harlan!"

"No argument there."

Beaumont put his palms flat on the table. "Rawlings wanted to distract Duggan and the other cattle barons from Kane's case, as well as maybe convincing them to stop fighting. But it's just going to make everything worse, isn't it? If that's even possible."

"It's always possible for things to get worse," Frank said. "Maybe it had to come to this all along. The feelings are just too high on both sides for anybody to be able to head off trouble."

Beaumont looked intently at him. "So now what does it come down to? Guns and more killing?"

Frank drew in some smoke from the quirly and blew it out. "That's usually what it comes down to," he said quietly.

"And what do we do? Which side are we on in this fight, Frank?"

The Drifter shook his head. He had no answer for the young Ranger.

The next morning dawned clear, with a deep blue sky overhead and a cool breeze. It was a perfect autumn day for this part of Texas. The beautiful weather didn't do much to cheer up Frank Morgan and Tyler Beaumont as they rode into Brownwood, though.

Beaumont had his star-in-a-circle Ranger badge pinned to his shirt now. There was no point in keeping it hidden any longer. Over a mostly silent breakfast, they had decided to ride into town and see Sheriff Wilmott. The local lawman would know about Vern Gladwell's death already, but he might not be aware of Beaumont's true identity just yet.

Frank saw right away that there was no surprise on the sheriff's weathered face when he and Beaumont came into Wilmott's office. Wilmott just looked up from his desk and grunted. "Heard tell you was a Ranger," he said coldly. "Might have been nice if you'd let a fellow star-packer in on that, mister."

"My orders were to investigate the trouble here and do whatever I could to keep it from getting worse, Sheriff," Beaumont said. "I thought I stood a better chance of accomplishing that by working undercover."

"Well, from the looks of what happened last night,

you were wrong, weren't you? I was over at the undertaking parlor a little while ago looking at what's left of Vern Gladwell. Pitts has got his work cut out for him with that one."

Beaumont grimaced. "I'm sorry about Gladwell. I didn't know what Duggan was planning to do."

Wilmott switched his angry gaze to Frank. "How about you, gunfighter? Were you in on it?"

"No," Frank replied. "In fact, Duggan fired me last night. He found out that Beaumont and I are old friends."

"And the two of you have been workin' together all along?" Wilmott raised his bushy white eyebrows. "A gunslinger and a Ranger?"

"Like I said, Beaumont and I have ridden together before."

The sheriff glared at Beaumont. "Well, Mr. Ranger, what do we do now?"

Beaumont didn't answer the question directly. Instead he asked, "How's Chris Kane this morning?"

"Still gettin' better. He could probably stand trial in a few days."

"His lawyer should be here today," Frank said. "I'm sure he'll request an immediate change of venue."

"Lawyer? What lawyer?"

"The one who's coming down from Dallas to represent him."

Wilmott shook his head. "I ain't heard nothin' about that, and it's none of my affair. I just keep the prisoner locked up until somebody tells me different."

"In the meantime, keep a good guard on Kane to make sure nothing happens to him."

Wilmott shot to his feet. "Don't tell me how to run my jail, Morgan. I never lost a prisoner yet to a lynch mob, or to friends who tried to break him out, and I don't intend to start now." The sheriff leaned forward, resting his fists on the scarred desk. "I don't expect anybody on either side is worried overmuch about Kane anymore, though. Not after what happened last night."

"You're probably right about that," Beaumont said. "What happened out at the Slash D probably pushes all that into the background."

Frank knew what the young Ranger meant. Rawlings and the others had nearly gone to war over what had happened to Chris Kane.

How far would they go to settle the score for Vern Gladwell?

Ace McKelvey was waiting for Annie when she stepped into the building through the rear door. He reached out and took her arm. She gasped, and he knew he had taken hold of her harder than he meant to. He eased his grip and said, "You just got back from the jail?"

"That's right, Ace," she said. "You told me it was all right for me to go over there and see Chris."

The rear door was still open. McKelvey glanced out at the morning sunshine and said, "I don't care what you do at this time of day, as long as you work your shift at night."

"I will, Ace, I promise. You know I wouldn't let you down."

"Yeah," McKelvey said. "I know. How's Kane?"

Annie couldn't help but smile a little. "He's getting stronger every day. I think he's going to be all right."

"Too bad he's going to wind up back in prison."

Annie's face fell at that thought, but then she brightened again. "Maybe he won't go to prison. I heard over at the jail that he's got a lawyer who's going to get him a . . . a change of venture or something."

"Change of venue," McKelvey muttered. "Where'd a range tramp like Kane get the money to hire a lawyer?"

"I don't know, but I was passing by the sheriff's office, and I saw that gunslinger, Mr. Morgan, in there talking to the sheriff. He's the one who said something about the lawyer. And I heard something else, Ace."

"What's that?"

"That fella called Tye . . . he's really a Texas Ranger!"

McKelvey grunted. He had already heard rumors that Tye was a lawman. Now Annie had confirmed it.

"So Morgan and this Ranger were together, eh?"

"That's right. They were talking to the sheriff. Arguing, almost."

McKelvey rubbed his jaw. That wasn't good news. The Rangers had a tendency to move in and take over, and they represented a bigger threat than an old sheriff and a few deputies. But so far there was only one Ranger in Brown County, and he wouldn't be any match for Flint Coburn's gang. Even with Morgan siding him, the odds would still be too high.

But he and his associates had to move quickly now, McKelvey realized. Now that the Ranger was working out in the open, he might send for reinforcements. They had to strike before that could happen.

Luckily, the death of Vern Gladwell might be just what they needed to tip the balance into open warfare at last. All of McKelvey's behind-the-scenes maneuvering had not accomplished what he had set out to do, but it didn't matter now.

The dynamite blast that had claimed Gladwell's life was nothing more than a firecracker compared to the explosion that was about to rock Brown County.

33

Skeet Harlan tensed when he stepped into McKelvey's office late that night and found Flint Coburn already there. Though they were working together, there was an innate wariness and dislike between the two men, the same sort of animosity that was instinctive among men who made their living from the speed of their gun hand and the sureness of their aim.

"What are you doing here, Coburn?" Harlan asked quietly, his right hand hovering near the butt of his revolver.

Coburn had a thin black cigarillo clenched between his teeth. "Ace sent for me," he answered, "just like I imagine he sent for you, Harlan."

"That's right," McKelvey said from behind the desk. "I thought it was time we all got together and hashed out our plans. We don't have much time anymore, not with the Rangers taking an interest in what's going on around here."

"Only one Ranger so far," Harlan pointed out, "and he's no threat. I can handle him."

"So can I," Coburn said with a sharp edge in his voice.

McKelvey lifted both hands, palms out. "Take it easy, boys. It's not a contest. Remember what we're in this for. Brownwood is a plum ripe for the picking."

Harlan and Coburn both nodded in agreement, but they still eyed each other.

McKelvey maintained a solemn expression, but inside he was smiling. Once it was all over, he might not have to worry about disposing of his partners. Given the way they felt about each other, they might just take care of that for him.

The death of Vern Gladwell in the trap that Duggan had set for the fence-cutters was the talk of the county, and everybody seemed to be taking sides on it. That was just what McKelvey wanted. The other two men who had been wounded in the fracas were still alive and had been brought into town by Duggan and his men. Duggan had insisted that they be locked up in jail like Chris Kane, so that was where Doc Yantis had treated their injuries and pronounced that they would live. The fact that they were behind bars was just one more goad for Rawlings and his bunch.

They were ready to be pushed over the brink, McKelvey thought.

"Here's what we're going to do," he said as he placed his hands palms down on the desk. He glanced at the door between the office and the main room of the saloon. It was securely bolted, so nobody could blunder into this meeting. And the saloon was busy enough and noisy enough so that even if anybody stood on the other side of that door with his ear pressed to it, he wouldn't be able to hear what was being said in here.

McKelvey went on. "All the big spreads have started their roundups. They'll be done in a few days and they'll haze all the stock they're selling over to the pens at Zephyr. They'll start shipping out on Monday, but the pens will be full by Sunday. Rawlings and some of his men, backed by some of your gun-throwers, Flint, will hit those pens and stampede the herds. Wipe out as many of the cattle barons and their men as you can.

Once that's done, your men will have their orders to turn on Rawlings' bunch and cut them down, too. Have them make sure especially that Rawlings doesn't survive the fight."

Coburn nodded his understanding of the bloodthirsty orders.

"At the same time, the rest of the small ranchers will ride into town to bust Kane and the other two out of jail and set fire to the town. While that's going on, you and your gang will hit the banks and the other businesses that have plenty of cash on hand. It's possible you may ride out of here with as much as half-a-million dollars."

Hearing it in words like that had an effect on Harlan and Coburn. Half-a-million dollars was so much money, it was difficult for them to comprehend it.

"The law will be too busy defending the jail to put up a fight, and the townsfolk will be fighting the fire," McKelvey continued. "The big ranchers will have their own problems over at Zephyr, so they won't be able to ride to the rescue. We'll loot the whole town before we're through . . . including this saloon, of course."

"Otherwise folks will suspect you had something to do with it if you're left alone," Harlan said.

McKelvey nodded. "That's right. I'm not worried, since I'll get back whatever I lose plus a lot more. I just hope your boys won't shoot the place up too badly, Flint."

"I'll tell them not to," Coburn offered.

Emphatically, McKelvey shook his head. "No. You and Skeet are the only ones who know that I'm part of this affair. I'd like to keep it that way."

"So you can go on living here when it's all over."

"That's right."

"What do you get out of it, McKelvey?" Harlan asked. "The town will be left in a shambles if everything goes according to plan."

McKelvey smiled. "People will have to rebuild. I'll have the money to help them. But when I call in the notes, the whole town will pretty much belong to me."

It was an audacious plan, and Harlan and Coburn didn't even know all of it. He hoped to pick up some of the smaller ranches for a good price, too, including the Rawlings place. Coburn's gunmen would see to it that many of the ranchers were killed in the fighting, which would leave their spreads up for grabs. By the time another year passed, McKelvey thought, not only would he control the town, but he would also be the biggest rancher in the county. And his wealth would grow even more when he sold the right-of-way the railroad needed to complete the line on to Brownwood from Zephyr. It would be a clean sweep, with Ace McKelvey growing rich from several different sources.

After that . . . well, power went with money, and there would be nothing stopping him from climbing even higher on the ladder. Senator, maybe, or possibly even governor.

Not bad for a man who had started out as a tinhorn gambler and rotgut whiskey peddler, now was it?

But whether it was a reality or just a wild dream all came down to what was going to happen this coming Sunday, McKelvey thought. He was confident that the plan would work, but one worry still nagged at his brain.

"Now, what about Frank Morgan?" he asked.

"Don't worry about Morgan," Coburn answered without hesitation. "I've seen how fast he is. That's why I had those two men brace him. It would have been nice if they could have killed him, but since they didn't, I'll deal with him."

"You can beat him if you have to?"

Coburn smiled and flexed the fingers of his right

hand. "I'll beat him whether I have to or not. Just because I *can*."

Skeet Harlan sneered. "You really think you're faster than the Drifter, Coburn?"

"I know I am." Coburn glared at the little deputy. "What's the matter? You want a shot at him, too?"

"That's all right." Harlan added maliciously, "I'll take care of him after he's killed you."

Coburn had been leaning indolently against a corner of the desk. Now he straightened, and his hand hooked into a claw just above the butt of his gun. Harlan tensed as well, ready to draw.

"Both of you stop it," McKelvey said sharply. "We can't afford to fight with each other. We're going to clean up here, as long as we don't ruin it."

With a visible effort, Coburn forced himself to relax. He pointed his smoldering cigarillo at Harlan and said, "One of these days, mister."

"Yeah," Harlan agreed. "One of these days."

"But not before Sunday," McKelvey said. "Remember that."

It wasn't likely any of them would forget. If everything went as planned, the coming Sunday in Brown County would be a red Sabbath indeed.

Frank Morgan and Tyler Beaumont spent the next few days riding around the county, visiting the big ranches where the fence-cutters had struck. There had been a few skirmishes on that damp, moonless night, but no one had been seriously wounded. Not every fence had been damaged, either. In some cases the cattle barons' patrols had run off the fence-cutters before the wire could be snipped.

In the places where fences had been cut, hasty repairs were being done by small crews. The roundup was under way, and the cattle market wouldn't wait. If the herds were late being shipped out from the pens at Zephyr, the delay would cost the cattlemen on the prices they received for their stock.

Few of the big ranchers had kind words for Beaumont, even though everyone now knew he was a Texas Ranger. They couldn't forget that he had ridden with Rawlings and the other greasy-sack cowmen. The fact that Beaumont had been working undercover didn't change things all that much in the minds of the cattle barons. They resented, too, the fact that the Ranger hadn't done anything yet to put a stop to the troubles.

Frank saw all that and knew that as far as Beaumont was concerned, it was a case of damned if he did and damned if he didn't. The youngster had been put in an almost impossible position.

They were still staying at the little ranch on Blanket Creek. There was some lingering tension over what had happened to Victoria on the day she and Beaumont had gotten married, but for the most part Beaumont's resentment had dissipated. He and Frank were able to talk about Victoria without being uncomfortable with each other. It sounded like the two young people were as happy in their marriage as could be expected under the circumstances, and Frank was glad of that.

"I never expected things to stay quiet for this long," Beaumont said on Saturday evening as he and Frank sat in the cabin drinking coffee after supper. "I thought Rawlings would make a move before now."

"He's probably planning something," Frank said. "He's too hotheaded to let things rest for too long."

Beaumont nodded glumly. "Maybe it's time for me to wire Austin and ask for some help up here. This is too big a job for me, Frank."

Frank didn't like to hear his young friend talking like that. Beaumont wasn't usually so pessimistic.

Everything that had happened in the past few months had taken a toll on his spirits.

"Maybe we just need to dig a little deeper," Frank suggested. "I've thought all along that somebody was working behind the scenes to keep all the trouble stirred up around here."

Beaumont looked interested. "Got any idea who it might be?"

"Ace McKelvey," Frank said bluntly.

"The saloon keeper? How would it benefit him to cause trouble between the big ranchers and the smaller ones?"

"I haven't figured that out yet," Frank admitted. "Maybe I should pay him a visit and see what I can find out."

Beaumont nodded slowly. "Might be worth a little time and effort. Want me to come with you?"

Frank pushed his chair back and stood up. Now that he had made up his mind, he didn't see any point in delaying. He had always been that way.

"No, you stay here," he told Beaumont. "McKelvey knows you're a Ranger. He won't be about to let anything slip in front of you."

"He's bound to know that you and I have been working together, too," Beaumont pointed out. "If he's up to no good, he won't trust you."

A faint smile tugged at Frank's wide mouth. "That's true, but I've got that reputation as a gunman. I've never been able to live it down, so I might as well try to get some use out of it."

Beaumont shrugged. "Whatever you say. Just be careful, Frank."

"I intend to be. I don't trust McKelvey any further than he probably trusts me. Funny thing, though . . . sometimes the crookedest hombre is the one who's easiest to fool."

He left Beaumont with that and went to saddle Stormy. He told Dog to stay there and rode off into the evening.

He was only about halfway to Brownwood when he heard the hoofbeats of another horse somewhere nearby. Reining in, Frank waited for the other rider to approach. He knew that a trail from the southwest merged with the main road right about here.

"Evenin'," he called softly as a horse and rider came up on his left, announcing his presence so that the other man wouldn't be spooked.

The stranger reined in and said, "Who's that?" Frank knew right away the other rider wasn't a man at all.

"It's Frank Morgan, Mrs. Stratton," he said. He had recognized Callie's voice.

"Morgan!" she exclaimed. "What are you doing skulking around here, gunfighter?"

He ignored the scornful tone and said, "I'm not skulking, ma'am. I was just on my way into Brownwood and realized there was somebody else on the road." He paused for a second and then commented, "Some folks might think it was more unusual for a lady to be riding around after dark by herself."

"I've never claimed to be a lady," she replied tartly, "and I've got a .45 on my hip and a Winchester in the saddle boot that would make anybody think twice about bothering me."

"Yes, ma'am, I expect they would."

"Don't ma'am me." She clucked her horse into motion again, and Frank fell in alongside her on Stormy. "My name's Callie," she went on.

"And I'm Frank." If she wanted to be friends, he was willing. She might know what her brother was up to these days . . . and even if she didn't, Frank had never minded having a conversation with a strikingly attractive redheaded woman.

Callie got right down to business as they rode along together. "Has Ranger Beaumont sent for reinforcements yet?"

"Not that I know of. Beaumont doesn't let me in on everything he's doing, though."

"He might want to give it some thought. My brother has been talking to that Flint Coburn a lot the past few days. I don't think that's a good sign."

Frank frowned. "I reckon not. Coburn's been in plenty of range wars."

"Isn't that true of you, too, Frank?"

"I never sold my gun to one side or the other like Coburn does," Frank declared. "If he's trying to push your brother into something, you can bet Coburn will get more good out of it than anybody else."

"That's pretty much the way it struck me, too. I don't trust the man." Callie looked over at Frank. "Otherwise I wouldn't be telling you this."

"You want me to have a talk with your brother?"

Callie shook her head. "It wouldn't do any good. Al's too worked up about what happened to Vern Gladwell, and about Kane and those other two men still being in jail. We talked to that lawyer fella, by the way. He's got a motion before the court for a change of venue, but the judge won't rule on it until Monday. From what the lawyer said, you're responsible for him being here, Frank."

Frank grimaced. He had given instructions that his part in the whole deal be kept quiet. The lawyer hadn't been as discreet as he should have been.

"Why would you want to help us like that?" Callie asked.

"I just want to see things settled without any more killing."

"Do you really think that's possible?"

Frank thought about everything that had happened and then shook his head. "No. I'm afraid I don't."

"Neither do I. That's why I'm on my way into town tonight. Al rode in earlier, and he hasn't come back yet. I want to make sure he's not getting drunk enough to start a fight."

"That's a good idea. I'll ride along with you, if you don't mind."

"It's a free country," she said casually.

After they had ridden along in silence for a few minutes, she asked in a more serious tone, "Why do you want to head off trouble, Frank? From what I know of you, you've been around violence all your life. There have been books written about you. They say you've killed a thousand men."

"Books say a heap of things that aren't true," he told her. "I've seen more than my share of bloodshed, though, and smelled powder smoke all across the West. There aren't that many of us left."

"The gunfighters, you mean?"

He nodded. "Our day is past. I can see that. Men like Coburn can't. He's hanging on to the notion that everything can be solved with a gun."

"What would you have folks do, sit around and talk every problem to death?"

Frank laughed. "Lord, no! If it ever gets to the point where folks are afraid to take up the gun when it's truly necessary, this country won't be worth living in. But there's a time and a place for it."

Unfortunately, the time was now and the place was Brown County, he thought. The storm clouds that had loomed for so long were about to break. He felt it in his bones.

They had reached the outskirts of town. At Callie's suggestion, the first place they headed for was the Palace Saloon. That was fine with Frank; he wanted to see Ace McKelvey, anyway. And as Callie said, it was likely they would find Rawlings there.

Sure enough, his horse was tied at the hitch rail in front of the saloon. "I knew he'd be here," Callie said grimly. "Maybe I can talk him into coming home."

They dismounted and tied their horses next to Rawlings's mount. As they stepped inside, Frank saw that the saloon wasn't very busy. That came as no surprise; most of the crews from the big spreads were involved in the fall roundup. They were gathering over at Zephyr, where the railroad ended and the big cattle pens were located. Only a handful of men were inside the Palace.

Unfortunately, one of them was Al Rawlings, and another was Deputy Marshal Skeet Harlan. And from the way they stood facing each other, slightly crouched, hands hovering over their guns, they were about to hook and draw.

34

"Al!" Callie said sharply. "What are you doing?"

"Stay out of this, sis," Rawlings grated without looking around at her. "It's between Harlan and me."

"That's right, Miz Stratton," Harlan said with a leering smile. "Your brother's been boozin' it up and talkin' up a storm tonight about how he's tired of havin' everybody ride roughshod over him. I told him he was comin' down to the jail with me to sleep it off, but he don't want to go."

"Let me take him home," Callie suggested, her voice tight with strain. "There's no need to arrest him."

"I'm not goin' anywhere!" Rawlings declared. "Nobody bosses me around!"

Frank stood slightly to one side. He had already spotted Ace McKelvey standing at the end of the bar, looking worried.

"Better back off, ma'am," Harlan said to Callie. "Wouldn't want you gettin' hit by a stray bullet."

Frank saw the fingers of Harlan's gun hand twitch a little in anticipation. He muttered, "The hell with this," and stepped forward smoothly and swiftly. His Peacemaker came out of leather to rise and fall in a fast chopping motion that ended at the back of Rawlings's head in a dull thud. Rawlings's Stetson absorbed enough of the force of the blow so that it didn't do any real damage, but it packed enough power so that Rawlings's knees unhinged. He went down, stunned, landing on his knees on the sawdust-littered floor.

Harlan's gun was half out of its holster when he froze. Frank's Colt was already leveled. "No need for that, Deputy," Frank said. "Rawlings isn't going to cause any more trouble. Let his sister take him home."

Harlan glared at him. "You're drawin' on an officer of the law, Morgan," he said. "That's reason enough for me to arrest you."

Frank glanced at the gun in his hand as if surprised to see that it was there. "Drawing on you, Deputy?" he said with mocking mildness in his tone. "No, I was just knocking Rawlings down so you wouldn't kill him." He lowered the Peacemaker but didn't holster it. "I wouldn't interfere with an officer of the law."

"Then I'm arrestin' Rawlings!"

McKelvey stepped forward. "It seems to me that there's no need for that now, Deputy. Like Morgan said, Rawlings isn't going to cause any more trouble. Let Callie take him home."

A murmur of agreement came from the few patrons in the saloon, all of them townies.

Harlan didn't look happy about it, but he jerked his head in a nod as he eased his gun back down into its holster. "All right, get him out of here," he said to Callie.

She bent and grasped Rawlings's arm. He was groggy but not out cold, so he was able to stand up and stagger toward the door with Callie helping him.

"What about you?" Harlan snapped at Frank. "Aren't you going, too?"

"No, I came to town for a drink," Frank replied easily. He walked toward the bar. Rusty had a bottle and a glass out by the time he got there.

Harlan started to follow Callie and Rawlings out.

Frank said, "I'd be obliged if you'd have a drink with me, Deputy. Just to show there are no hard feelings."

There were plenty of hard feelings and Frank knew it, but he caught the slight nod that McKelvey gave Harlan. They were in it together, Frank thought, and like a light going on inside his head, he realized that Flint Coburn must be, too. Coburn hadn't shown up out of the blue just because he wanted to help the small ranchers. McKelvey had sent him in to keep tabs on Rawlings's plans and prod them in the way McKelvey wanted them to go. Harlan was Coburn's opposite number. The two of them, under McKelvey's direction, had pushed the two sides closer and closer to open warfare.

It was true that Frank had absolutely no proof of this theory, but it all fit together and his gut told him it was right. He wasn't sure what McKelvey's motive was for causing so much trouble, but when it came to a head, as it had to soon, that would be revealed.

Harlan moved to the bar beside Frank and picked up the drink that Rusty poured for him. He tossed back the whiskey and wiped the back of his hand across his mouth. "There," he said with ill grace. "I've had that drink with you." He turned and stalked out of the saloon. Frank was satisfied. He had given Callie and Rawlings enough time to get away from the Palace.

McKelvey came up beside Frank. "Thanks, Morgan," he said quietly. "I was afraid for a minute there was going to be gunplay in here."

He hadn't been afraid of that at all, Frank thought, but instead of saying that, Frank nodded and said, "I was glad I was able to stop it. There's been enough trouble in Brownwood."

"Indeed. How would you like to step into my office? I'd like to talk privately with you."

For appearance's sake, Frank considered for a second

and then nodded. "Sure." He didn't know what Mc-
Kelvey could have to say to him, but there was only one
way to find out.

"Rusty, give me that bottle," McKelvey said. He took
the whiskey from the bartender and led the way to the
office. Once inside he waved at a leather chair in front
of the desk and got some glasses from a drawer.

As he settled down behind the desk and poured
drinks, McKelvey asked, "How's your young Ranger
friend?"

"Upset because he hasn't been able to defuse the
situation here."

"Has he considered sending for a troop of Rangers?"
McKelvey leaned forward to hand Frank his drink.

Thinking swiftly, Frank said, "He's already done that."

McKelvey looked genuinely surprised. "He has?"

"That's right. They should be here in a few days."
Maybe if McKelvey really was behind the trouble,
that lie would force him into moving before he was
ready. Frank took a sip of the whiskey and put the
glass on the desk.

"Well, that's good to know," McKelvey said, but he
didn't really sound all that happy about it. He lifted
his glass. "Let's drink to the Rangers."

Frank shrugged and picked up his glass again. He
said, "To the Rangers," and swallowed the rest of
the liquor.

He knew almost right away that it had been a
mistake. A terrible wave of dizziness struck him.
He came up out of his chair, reaching for his gun as
he did so, but the reflexes that had never let him
down were dulled now so that they didn't respond
in time. McKelvey grabbed the bottle by the neck
and swung it as he lunged forward over the desk.
The bottle crashed into Frank's head and shattered.
Stars exploded behind his eyes.

He felt it when he hit the floor, but only vaguely. He knew his face was wet but wasn't sure if it was from whiskey or blood or both. He was certain now that he had been right about McKelvey, but that was scant comfort.

The last thing he was aware of was hearing a door open and Skeet Harlan's surprised voice exclaiming, "What the hell!"

"You damned fool!" McKelvey snapped at Harlan as the deputy stepped into the room through the alley door. "Why did you pick a fight with Rawlings? You could have ruined everything!"

"You want him dead, don't you? What does it matter whether he dies tonight or tomorrow?"

"Because he's the ringleader of the small ranchers. Without him, they're less likely to go through with the raid on the cattle pens at Zephyr."

Harlan shrugged. "Well, he's not dead. He's on his way back to his ranch by now, and he can go to Zephyr tomorrow with a hangover. What I want to know is what the hell is Morgan doing here?"

"I saw a chance to get him out of the way. Not only that, but he told me that Beaumont has already sent for more Rangers! They'll be here in a few days."

"They'll be here too late, then, won't they? It's a good thing we planned to wrap this up on Sunday."

McKelvey nodded. "Yes, it'll all be over before the Rangers get here." He prodded Morgan in the ribs with a toe. "Now we need to get rid of this gunslinger."

Harlan slipped a knife from a sheath on his belt and started toward Morgan. "I'll take care of that. One quick slash across the throat—"

"Not here, damn it! Take him out and kill him

somewhere else. Dispose of the body where it won't be found."

Harlan sheathed the knife and regarded Morgan warily. "He's not going to wake up any time soon, is he?"

"I slipped enough dope in his drink to keep him out for an hour or so. Just don't waste any time."

Harlan nodded. He stooped and grasped Morgan under the arms. "Open the door," he said to McKelvey.

Grunting with the effort, the deputy dragged the Drifter's unconscious form out of the office into the alley. McKelvey closed and bolted the door. Harlan strained to pull the bigger man along the alley. He muttered curses under his breath. He hadn't thought this through, he told himself. The first thing he should have done was to go get a horse. He could throw Morgan over the saddle and tie him in place, then lead the horse out of town until he found a suitable spot to kill Morgan.

Huffing and blowing, Harlan gave up on dragging Morgan and left him lying there in the shadows. He hurried along the alley to the street and turned toward the livery stable. He kept his own mount there. At this time of night, the old man who ran the place would be asleep. Harlan could get his own horse and borrow one of the others that were stabled there. Nobody would know the difference.

He moved as quickly as possible, since he was worried about Morgan waking up. No one could have done a faster, more efficient job of getting a couple of horses saddled up, he told himself as he led the animals along the street toward the alley a few minutes later. He tied the reins to one of the posts that held up the awning over the boardwalk and catfooted along the alley to the spot where he had left Morgan.

But the gunfighter wasn't there. Harlan fumbled out a match and struck it. His panicky eyes darted around the alley. Morgan was gone! McKelvey was going to be furious with him for letting the gunfighter get away.

But what could Morgan really do to hurt them now? Harlan asked himself. Events were already in motion. In less than twenty-four hours it would all be over, and he would be a rich man. Let McKelvey stay behind. Harlan was going to take his share of the loot and shake the dust of Brownwood from his boots. The deputy forced himself to calm down. It was worrisome having Morgan on the loose somewhere, but it wasn't going to change things.

The thing was, Morgan shouldn't have woken up yet from the drug that McKelvey had slipped him. What in blazes had happened to him?

The pounding in Frank's head was like charges of blasting powder going off deep inside a mine shaft. He knew that before he knew anything else. Only gradually did he realize that he was lying on his back on a narrow, uncomfortable surface. A bunk of some sort, he told himself, but not a good one.

When he tried to open his eyes, light struck them like a physical blow. He jerked his head in response, and that made the pounding even worse, although that didn't seem possible. He couldn't stop the groan that welled up his throat.

A moment later, footsteps sounded somewhere nearby. When the footsteps stopped, a voice said, "Awake, are you, Morgan?"

Frank finally pried his eyes all the way open and saw that he was in a tiny jail cell. Standing on the other side of the barred door was a man in a black frock coat. After a moment Frank recognized him as Marshal Sean Keever.

"Wh-what . . ."

"What are you doing here?" Keever finished for him. "Jail is where drunks who pass out in alleys usually wind up, Morgan. I've got to tell you, though, I thought better of you. I never expected the famous Drifter to do such a thing."

"You found me. . . ."

"That's right. You were passed out in the alley behind the Palace while I was making my rounds. I brought you here and locked you up. You can sleep it off, and I'll let you out in the morning. You'll have to pay the usual fine for drunk and disorderly."

"Not . . . drunk . . ."

Keever laughed. "That's what they all say." He turned to leave.

Frank let him go. His brain was beginning to work again. He remembered being in McKelvey's office, remembered the drink he had downed just before everything went black. McKelvey had drugged him, of course. Frank had no doubt about that. He was surprised that he was still alive. He would have expected McKelvey to take advantage of the opportunity to kill him.

But Fate had intervened somehow, and now Frank had another chance. He didn't know if Keever was in on the scheme with McKelvey or not. It seemed unlikely that he was, even though his deputy Skeet Harlan was involved up to his eyebrows. Keever was just a dupe, but he had inadvertently saved Frank's life.

Now it was a matter of staying alive, getting out of here, and finding out what McKelvey, Harlan, and Coburn were planning.

That would have to wait a little while, though. Right now Frank was still too weak and groggy to try anything.

He would just have to hope that all hell didn't break loose first.

35

Keever left a short time later, locking up the marshal's office behind him. Frank rested on the bunk and tried to regain his strength. He was the only prisoner in the small city jail. After a while he dozed off, and he didn't wake up until sunlight was streaming in the small, barred window set high in the back wall of the cell.

It was Sunday morning. From the looks of things, a bright, clear, autumn Sunday in Texas.

Keys rattled in the lock of the office door. It swung open and Skeet Harlan stepped inside. Frank stood up, feeling a lot stronger and steadier than he had the night before. Harlan stopped short at the sight of him.

"Morgan! How the hell did you get in there?"

"Your boss locked me up for being drunk," Frank explained. "Haven't you talked to the marshal this morning, Harlan?"

The deputy shook his head as he closed the door. "Keever spends every Saturday night at a whorehouse. His one vice, I reckon you could say. He sleeps until noon on Sunday."

Frank nodded. That must have been where Keever went after leaving the jail.

The wheels of Frank's brain were turning over rapidly. Did Harlan know that he was aware of the connection between Harlan, McKelvey, and Coburn? For the moment the wisest course might be to pretend ignorance. After all, he was at Harlan's mercy, disarmed and locked up behind bars.

Frank managed to chuckle. "I must've really gone on a bender last night. I don't remember a damned thing."

Harlan's face contorted in a snarl and he drew his gun as he came closer to the bars. "The hell you don't," he snapped. "You can't fool me, Morgan. You know too much to live."

Seeing that he had to stall for time, had to keep Harlan talking, Frank changed his strategy and said quickly, "You mean I know about you and McKelvey and Coburn?"

The way Harlan's eyes widened in surprise told Frank that his wild shot had gone home. "Coburn?" Harlan muttered. "How did you know—" He stopped short and then spit out a curse. "You're too smart for your own good, Morgan. You just sealed your death warrant."

"You're going to shoot me right here in the jail?"

"Damn right. If McKelvey had let me cut your throat in his office last night, I wouldn't have this problem now. Damn right I'm gonna smoke you. Then I'll drag you out, put a gun in your hand, and tell everybody that you tried to escape."

"Nobody's going to believe that."

Harlan gave an ugly laugh. "Believe you me, Morgan, after today folks around here will have a lot more to worry about than whether or not you were really trying to escape when I blasted you."

Frank felt himself go cold inside at the tone of Harlan's voice. Still stalling, he asked, "What do you mean by that?"

Harlan hesitated in answering but then shrugged and said, "What does it matter now? In a little while a bunch of cowmen from those little outfits are going to come stormin' into town to bust Kane and their other two friends out of the county jail. Some of Coburn's men will be with them. But while the sheriff's got his hands full defending the jail, Coburn's men will hit the banks and every other business in town. They've got dynamite to blow open the safes, and when they're done they'll leave some of the places on fire behind them. At the same time the rest of Rawlings' bunch, plus the rest of Coburn's gang, will raid the cattle pens over at Zephyr, stampede the herds that are gathered there, and wipe out Duggan and the other big ranchers. When it's over, though, the double cross kicks in, and Rawlings and his friends wind up dead, too. By the time it's all said and done, Brown County will be just about wiped out."

"Except for you and McKelvey and Coburn," Frank guessed. "The three of you plan to grab up everything that's left."

"You got it, Morgan."

"That's why McKelvey's been trying to push the two sides into fighting for weeks now. He wanted a big blowup like this so that everything would be blamed on the trouble over the fence-cutting. It'll just be a range war that got out of hand, and nobody will ever think to point a finger at him."

Harlan sneered. "Pretty smart, ain't it?" He lifted his gun. "That's enough yammerin'. It's time for you to die, Morgan. I just wish I'd had the chance to see how fast you really are."

"You still can," Frank said, seizing any slim chance he might still have. "Let me out of this cell and give me my gun. We'll have it out, just you and me, and may the best man win."

Harlan hesitated, but only for a second before he shook his head. "Don't think it ain't temptin'," he said as he came closer to the cell so that he couldn't miss. "But I'm smarter than that. So long, Morgan."

The front door of the marshal's office slammed open. "Drop it, Harlan!" Callie Stratton called from the entrance as she leveled her Colt at the deputy. Startled, Harlan jerked around toward her.

Frank knew that with the deputy's speed with a gun, Harlan might get a shot off at Callie even if he was hit first. And if Callie hesitated even an instant, Harlan might cut her down. So Frank exploded into action at the same time, lunging against the bars of the cell door and reaching through them. His fingers caught hold of Harlan's shirt collar, and the muscles in his arm and shoulders bunched as he jerked the deputy toward him.

Harlan slammed into the bars. The impact jolted the gun out of his hand. As it thudded to the floor, Frank jerked Harlan against the bars again. This time the crooked deputy's head smashed against the iron and he went limp in Frank's grip. Frank bent and lowered Harlan's senseless figure to the floor. Blood welled from a cut on Harlan's forehead.

Callie rushed into the jail. "Frank, are you all right?"

He flashed a grin up at her. "I'm a lot better than I was thirty seconds ago," he said. "See if you can find the keys to let me out of here."

"Why are you—"

"It's a long story," he said, "but I've got to get out of here and put a stop to what's about to happen."

"You know about what's going to happen?" she asked as she rummaged in the marshal's desk and then came up with a ring of keys.

"I know," Frank said. "I had already figured out some of it, and Harlan told me the rest. Your brother and some of his friends are going to attack the big ranchers at Zephyr, and the rest of them are going to try to break Kane out of jail."

Callie started trying keys on the cell door. "That's

right. That man Coburn promised them some help. He said he had friends who would pitch in. I heard them talking last night after we got back to the ranch. Al wasn't sure at first, but Coburn talked him into it. I've been worried about it ever since. That's why I came into town this morning. I thought I ought to warn the sheriff. I was just passing by here, though, when I looked through the window and saw Harlan about to shoot you."

"Coburn's so-called friends are members of his gang. They're all outlaws and gunmen. They're going to loot the town, and they're also supposed to double-cross the small ranchers and wipe them out, too."

Callie glanced up at him, her eyes wide with horror. "Then it's really a trap!"

"That's right. Coburn, Harlan, and Ace McKelvey have been working together, trying to get everything to this point. And today it all blows up, unless we can stop it!"

One of the keys clicked over in the lock, and Callie jerked the cell door open.

Frank stepped out, grabbed the still-senseless Harlan, and dragged him into the cell. He closed the door and gave it a shake to make sure it had locked.

"Harlan can stay out of trouble in there while I tell Sheriff Wilmott what's going on. Callie, I want you to ride out to Kane's place and tell Beaumont everything I just told you. Tell him to get down to Zephyr and warn Duggan and the others."

She nodded. "We have to head this off, Frank. Otherwise a lot of innocent people are going to be killed."

He found his Peacemaker and gun belt in the marshal's desk, where Keever had put it the night before. "Get going," he said tersely as he buckled on the belt and strapped down the holster. Callie hurried out.

Frank's Stetson hung on a nail on the wall. He took it down and settled it on his head. He hadn't said anything about it to Callie, but he was afraid it might already be too late to keep innocent folks from getting killed.

But he was going to do his damnedest, and he was going to see to it that justice caught up to the plotters who had put all this violence into motion.

He had just taken a step toward the front door of the office when it opened and Marshal Keever stood there, eyes going wide with shock at the sight of Frank Morgan out of the cell. "Good Lord!" the marshal exclaimed.

What a day for Keever to pick to leave the whorehouse early, Frank thought as the marshal grabbed for the gun at his hip.

Keever was no match for Frank's speed. Frank had the Peacemaker drawn and leveled before the marshal's iron was halfway out of the holster. Keever paled and gulped, surely expecting that he was going to die in the next instant, but Frank held off on the trigger and said, "Take it out slow and easy, Marshal, and put it on the floor."

Keever did so, saying, "How did you get out, Morgan?" He glanced past Frank and saw Harlan lying in the cell, out cold. "My God! Is that Skeet? Did you kill him?"

"Your deputy is alive, Marshal, don't worry about that. Slide the gun over here with your foot."

Keever slid the revolver over the floorboards.

"Now," Frank continued, "you're going in the cell with Harlan, and I'm going to try to stop all the trouble he and McKelvey and Coburn have caused."

"What in blazes are you talking about?" Keever demanded, and unless the man was a better actor than Frank gave him credit for being, he was genuinely confused. Frank had suspected that the marshal wasn't in on the scheme, and Keever's reaction seemed to confirm it.

"Ask Harlan when he wakes up." Frank unlocked

the cell door again and motioned Keever in with the barrel of his gun. Grudgingly, the lawman entered his own cell. Frank slammed the door. "I'd explain the whole thing, but there's just not time."

Frank left them there and stepped out onto the street, which wasn't very busy on a Sunday morning like this. He walked quickly toward the county jail several blocks away.

He wasn't sure how he was going to convince Sheriff Wilmott that he was telling the truth about the elaborate scheme McKelvey and his two partners had hatched. Wilmott was an honest man, but he was also simple and direct, not the sort to easily grasp the sort of labyrinthine plotting McKelvey, Harlan, and Coburn had done. Frank would just have to lay out the facts for the sheriff and hope Wilmott believed him.

A deputy with a shotgun tucked under his arm was on duty at the front door of the jail. He straightened as Frank approached. "What do you want, Morgan?" he asked.

"I've got to see Sheriff Wilmott."

"Well, you're out of luck. He ain't here."

"Is he home?"

"Nope. At this time on a Sunday morning, he'll be at church, of course. Where else would a respectable, God-fearin' man be? I'd be there myself if it wasn't my turn to work this mornin'."

"Which church?" Frank asked tersely.

The deputy hesitated. "You ain't gonna go down there and bother the sheriff in the middle of the worship service, are you?"

"No, I'll wait until it's over," Frank lied. "But I want to catch him when he comes out."

"All right," the deputy said grudgingly. "It's the First Baptist, right down the street."

Frank nodded. "Much obliged." He started to turn

away and then paused. "How many deputies are on duty this morning?"

"Just me and another fella. And the jailer's inside."

"You'd better tell the jailer to get on the telephone and call every deputy who's hooked up to the line. You're going to need help before the morning's over."

The deputy's eyes widened in surprise. "Trouble?"

"Bad trouble," Frank confirmed. Then he turned and walked quickly toward the First Baptist Church.

Even with the doors closed, he heard the organ playing and the congregation singing hymns before he got there. He hated to disturb these people at their worship, but there was no time to waste. He opened one of the double doors and stepped inside, taking his hat off out of habit.

A couple of deacons stood there in the vestibule. One of them smiled and motioned Frank toward an empty pew, but Frank just shook his head. He looked over the crowd, searching for Sheriff Wilmott.

The deacon came over and said quietly, "Can I help you, brother?"

"I'm looking for the sheriff."

"Is it important?"

"Very," Frank said.

"I know where Brother Wilmott sits with his family. I'll get him."

Frank waited impatiently while the deacon went along the aisle between the two sections of pews. He paused at one near the front and leaned over, speaking to someone Frank couldn't see. Then Sheriff Wilmott stood up, cast a glare in Frank's direction, and started toward the rear of the church.

Frank was about to speak when Wilmott took his arm and led him outside. "Now what's all this about?" the lawman demanded angrily when he had closed the door of the church. "I don't take kindly to bein' interrupted when I'm visitin' with the Lord."

Frank heard a low rumble in the distance, almost like thunder, but the sky overhead was a clear, beautiful blue. He looked to the east and saw a thin haze of dust rising into the air. It would take a lot of horses to kick up that much dust, he thought.

"Sorry to bother you when you're contemplating Heaven, Sheriff," he said. "But I thought I'd better tell you that Hell's about to come to call."

36

Beaumont heard Dog barking and stepped out of the cabin to see Callie Stratton riding hell-for-leather toward him. Her hat had come off and was hanging on her back by its chin strap. Her red hair streamed behind her from the wind of her swift passage. Beaumont knew right away that something had to be really wrong to cause such urgency on Callie's part. He stepped back into the cabin and grabbed up his Winchester.

By the time he was outside again, Callie was reining her mount to a sliding stop. "Tye," she gasped, still using the name she had first known him by, "there's trouble!"

"Get down and tell me about it," Beaumont said.

She shook her head. "No time." Words began to tumble breathlessly out of her mouth. Beaumont listened intently as she poured out the message Frank Morgan had given her to pass along to him. Beaumont's hands tightened on the rifle as he realized the implications of all she was saying.

"Good Lord!" he exclaimed when she was finished. "I've got to get to Zephyr right away!"

The little settlement where the cattle pens were located was about eight miles away. Beaumont knew the countryside and could reach it in a hurry. But he might still be too late, he thought grimly as he hurried to the barn to saddle his horse.

"I'm going with you," Callie declared as Beaumont rode out of the barn a few minutes later, followed by Dog.

Beaumont didn't want to take the time to argue with her. "Your horse is beat," he said. "If you can't keep up, I'll leave you behind."

She jerked her head in a nod, agreeing to his terms. Side by side they galloped away from the cabin.

Earlier, when Beaumont had been taking care of the morning chores around the place, he had thought it was a spectacularly beautiful day, with blue skies and crisp autumn air.

Now, even though the weather hadn't changed, a pall seemed to have been cast over the day. Beaumont almost felt as if a storm was about to break . . . which, in a way, it was, unless he and Callie could stop it.

Callie kept up, getting everything she could from her gallant horse and surprising Beaumont. They saw the dust in the air and caught the unmistakable smell of a large herd before they came within sight of the pens. As they drew closer, they could even hear the lowing of thousands of cattle. They passed the corrals where the remudas were kept and rode up to the scattering of chuck wagons parked near the full pens that lined the railroad tracks. As they headed toward the Slash D chuck wagon, Ed MacDonald stepped out and raised a hand to stop them.

"Hold it, you two!" the foreman called. "Beaumont, you ain't hardly welcome here. And while I hate to be rude to a lady, you ain't either, Miz Stratton."

"There's no time for that, Ed," Callie said.

"Where's Duggan?" Beaumont asked.

MacDonald was about to argue, but at that moment Earl Duggan came around the chuck wagon and saw the newcomers. "What the hell?" the rugged old rancher grunted. "What do you want?"

"A gang of outlaws is about to attack and try to stampede your herds and wipe you out," Beaumont said.

"Outlaws! You mean sodbusters and nesters and greasy-sack cowpokes, don't you?" With the rough gallantry of his kind, Duggan glanced at Callie and added gruffly, "No offense, ma'am."

"The hell there's not!" she shot back at him. "Yes, my brother and some of his friends are with them, but the men who are really behind it are outlaws like Ranger Beaumont said. They've fooled Al and the others."

Duggan frowned in confusion. "What you're sayin' doesn't make any sense."

"Listen to me," Beaumont said urgently. "This whole range war has been planned so that the men behind it can loot the county."

Some of the other Slash D punchers had come up to listen. Pitch Carey spoke up, saying, "What do you mean, the men behind it?"

"Ace McKelvey, Skeet Harlan, and that gunslinger Coburn. They're all working together."

Several of the men began to scoff at that idea, but Duggan cut them off with a curt gesture. The old cattle baron frowned in thought and said, "That at least sounds a mite interestin'. I wouldn't mind hearin' more, Ranger."

Beaumont opened his mouth to explain, but before he could say anything else, the rattle of gunfire suddenly came through the morning air. The cattle became more frantic, surging back and forth in the pens, putting a strain even on the thick rails that enclosed them.

"Too late for that!" Beaumont said. "Here they come now!"

***

As Frank and Sheriff Wilmott ran into the jail, Frank called to the lawman, "Tell your men to try not to kill the members of Rawlings' bunch! They don't know they're being used!"

"They know they're about to try to break some prisoners out of jail!" Wilmott barked back at him. "They'll have to take their chances." After a moment, though, he added, "But I'll tell the boys to concentrate on Coburn and them other outlaws."

The sheriff snatched a Winchester out of a rack and tossed it to Frank, then followed it with a box of shells. The two deputies and the jailer were also picking up extra ammunition. The jailer, a wiry, silver-haired man named Strickland, said to Wilmott, "I called as many of the fellas as I could get hold of, Sheriff, and told them to get down here as fast as they could."

"Good," Wilmott said as he thumbed shells into a shotgun and snapped it closed. "We're liable to need all the help we can get."

"I'm going out," Frank said. "Most of the gang will head for the banks downtown. Hold the jail, and I'll try to stop the outlaws."

"By yourself?" Wilmott demanded. "One man ain't no match for that gang!"

A thought occurred to Frank. "Let me take Chris Kane with me, if he's strong enough to be up and around and use a gun."

"Kane's a prisoner!"

Strickland said, "I'll go with him and Morgan and keep an eye on him, Sheriff."

Wilmott grimaced and rubbed at his jaw for a second before he said, "I reckon three men against fifteen or twenty is better than one. Go let Kane out and give him a gun!"

Frank and Strickland hurried along the corridor to the cell block. Kane had heard the commotion and was standing at the door of his cell, grasping the bars. "What's going on?" he asked.

"Need some help if you're up to it, Kane," Frank grunted. "Can you move around some and handle a gun?"

Kane stared in confusion at the jailer. "You're letting me out?"

"Yeah," Strickland said with a grin. "You and me and Morgan are gonna go fight a gang of outlaws."

Kane jerked his head in a nod. "All right. I'll do what I can. Don't know how much strength I've got after being laid up, but I'll do my best."

Strickland unlocked the cell door and pressed a six-gun into Kane's hand. "Don't get any ideas about escapin', son," he warned. "You're comin' back here when it's all over. If you live through it."

By now, guns had begun to pop somewhere close by. A rifle cracked from up front in the jail. Frank hoped Wilmott had ordered his men to aim high as much as possible.

He and Strickland and Kane went out the back door of the jail and trotted toward the downtown area a couple of blocks away. As they did, several riders with bandannas masking the lower halves of their faces swept past the jail and pounded on toward them. Frank called out a warning. He and his two companions pivoted. He brought the Winchester to his shoulder. Beside him Strickland crouched and aimed a rifle, while Kane went to one knee and leveled his revolver. All three of them fired at the same time, smoke jetting from the barrels of the weapons.

Three of the onrushing outlaws went out of their saddles, drilled cleanly. Frank and Strickland fired again, and two more men tumbled off their horses. That broke the back of the charge.

But only for the moment. "Hunt some cover!" Frank ordered.

The three men spread out, Frank on one side of the street while Kane and Strickland went to the other side. Kane was moving fast but carrying himself somewhat gingerly. If his partially healed wounds broke open, he might bleed to death. There were more immediate threats, though, like outlaw lead. Here they came again, determined to reach the banks and the other businesses. Frank and his two allies were equally determined to stop them.

For a long moment guns blazed fiercely as Frank and Strickland fired their rifles as fast as they could work the levers and Kane emptied his six-gun. Bullets whined and sang around the defenders as the outlaws on horseback returned the fire.

That much racket drew plenty of attention. The saloons weren't very busy on a Sunday morning, but each of them held a few men. They rushed out to see what was going on. The churches were emptying, too, and although most men no longer carried guns to church, they had rifles and shotguns in the buggies and wagons that had brought them to services. As Frank reloaded the Winchester while he knelt behind a rain barrel, he turned and shouted to the men rushing along the street, "Take cover! Outlaws attacking the town!"

It took only a moment for the citizens of Brownwood to figure out what was going on. Even though "civilization" had come to this part of Texas, the frontier was still in the blood of these men. Even the ones who had not lived through the wilder days had grown up hearing tales of the Alamo and San Jacinto, Cibolo Creek and Palmito Ranch, Adobe Walls and

Palo Duro Canyon. They were ready to fight to defend what was theirs.

The outlaws never had a chance.

The forces of lawlessness swept into Brownwood thinking that these Texans were soft and would be easily distracted and overcome. Instead, the raiders ran right into a storm of lead that scythed through them and sent them flying from their saddles. Wounded men hit the ground, struggled upright, and were riddled as they tried to lift their guns. Frank, Kane, and Strickland led the battle, but within minutes they had a formidable force at their backs.

Down at the jail, Sheriff Wilmott and his handful of deputies were putting up a fierce resistance as well, and the ranchers who had come to free their friends soon realized that their so-called allies, the men Flint Coburn had sent to help them, had deserted them instead. Pulling back, dragging their wounded with them, they regrouped and stared at the big sandstone building with its barred windows. Suddenly, the idea of taking it over didn't seem quite so appealing . . . or even possible.

Nothing was going like it was supposed to go. The carefully laid plans were being shot to hell.

Inside the little town jail, Skeet Harlan had regained consciousness. He listened to the sounds of battle and tried to see out the tiny barred window, ignoring the scared prattling of Marshal Keever. Harlan seethed inside as he sensed that everything was going wrong. He needed to be out there, so he could try to salvage something from this mess. Instead, he was stuck here in this cell with that idiot of a marshal.

The door of the office slammed open and one of the

townsmen ran inside. "Marshal! Marshal Keever!" he cried. "Come quick! There's trouble!"

Then he stopped short and gaped at the sight of Keever and Harlan locked up in their own cell. Harlan flung himself across the cell and grabbed the bars, rattling the door. "The keys!" he shouted at the townie. "Get the keys and let us out of here, man!"

The startled, confused townsman looked around wildly for a moment before his gaze fell on the ring of keys lying on the desk. He snatched them up and ran over to the cells. "Outlaws in town!" he said as he fumbled with the keys and the lock. "They're attackin' the jail and tryin' to get to the banks! You gotta help stop 'em!"

Harlan had no intention of helping to stop the raid. He could tell from all the shooting that it wasn't going as planned. But maybe he could still get something out of it. He shoved the clumsy townie aside, reached through the bars, and unlocked the cell door.

Darting out, he went to the desk and grabbed a spare six-shooter from one of the drawers. He was reaching for a rifle from the wall rack when Keever followed him out of the cell and caught hold of his arm. "What are we going to do?" the marshal yelled, totally spooked.

"I'm gonna get my hands on some money while I still can," Harlan said. He shook off Keever's grip.

The marshal grabbed him again, causing red rage to shoot through Harlan. With a snarl, the deputy palmed out the Colt, pressed the muzzle against Keever's chest, and said, "And you're gonna die." He pulled the trigger.

The gun roared, knocking Keever backward. Keever's coat smoldered from the burning powder that had blasted into it. He made a hideous gurgling sound, and then his boot heels drummed against the floor as he died.

Harlan turned the gun on the gaping townie and fired again, putting a neat black hole in the middle of the man's forehead and a much larger, messier one in the back of his head where the bullet blew out his skull. The luckless man collapsed, already forgotten by the ruthless killer who had just murdered him.

Harlan thumbed fresh shells into the chambers he had expended, stuck the box of ammunition in his pocket, and ran out of the office.

He turned toward the Palace Saloon.

37

Ace McKelvey hurried into his office, his heart pounding with fear and his face coated with beads of sweat. He had just looked down the street and seen Frank Morgan leading the fight against Coburn's men. Morgan! That damned gunslinger was supposed to be dead. Harlan had left here with Morgan the night before, on his way to kill the unconscious Drifter and dispose of his body.

Obviously Harlan had fouled up somehow, because Morgan was not only still alive, but from the looks of things he was about to ruin all of McKelvey's carefully orchestrated plans.

There was only one thing to do. He had quite a bit of money stashed in the safe in his office. He would grab it and get out of here while he still had the chance. Harlan and Coburn wouldn't get their shares, but that was just too damned bad. He had always intended to double-cross them anyway. He would just be doing it a little sooner than he had planned.

Morgan knew that he, McKelvey, was behind the whole thing. And there was no telling who else Morgan might have told by now. McKelvey knew he couldn't stay in Brownwood as he had intended. He had to get away while he still could, but at least he would have enough money to make a fresh start somewhere else. He went to a knee in front of the squat, heavy safe and began twirling the knob on the combination lock.

He had just opened the door and reached inside for the canvas bag stuffed full of greenbacks when the rear door of the office was kicked open. Skeet Harlan stepped in and leveled a Colt at McKelvey.

The saloon keeper froze. His hand hovered above not only the sack of money but also the pistol that lay beside it.

A grin twisted Harlan's ugly face. "Goin' after the loot you've got stashed there, McKelvey? I'm much obliged to you. You've saved me the trouble of making you open the safe."

McKelvey swallowed hard. "I . . . I was just going to come find you, Skeet. It looks like things are going bad out there. We'll take what's in here and get the hell out while we still can."

"What about Coburn?"

"The hell with him!" McKelvey said.

"So you'd double-cross a partner just like that, eh?" Harlan said. "Somehow I figure you were gonna say the hell with me, too, Ace."

McKelvey shook his head emphatically. "No, of course not! You and I have been in on this together from the first. Coburn came into it later. It's you and me, Skeet. We'll go somewhere else and come up with a new plan—"

"I don't think so. That money's going with me. I don't care what you do, McKelvey. The way your fancy plan is falling apart, I don't think I want to be your partner no more."

"All right," McKelvey said desperately. "I'll split the money with you—"

Harlan just shook his head. His finger tightened on the trigger of his gun.

The door of the saloon burst open at that instant, the noise making Harlan's hand jerk just enough as he squeezed the trigger. The bullet ripped into McKelvey's left side and knocked him against the safe as another gunshot roared. McKelvey fought off the pain and grabbed the pistol, twisting around as he slumped against the open door of the safe. He saw the blond whore, Annie, standing there looking down at the blood-stain spreading across the midsection of the housedress she wore. Harlan, spooked by her unexpected entrance, had fired again out of instinct, drilling her.

McKelvey fired, catching Harlan somewhere in the body with the slug. He wasn't sure exactly where he hit the deputy because his eyesight was blurring. He tried to squeeze off another shot, but before he could Harlan's gun blasted twice more, the reports deafening in the close confines of the office. The bullets struck McKelvey in the chest like twin hammer blows, pinning him against the safe door for a moment before he pitched forward on the floor. He saw all his hopes and plans and dreams, all the money and power he would have had, sliding down into a deep, dark, bottomless well.

Then he slid into the darkness after them and saw nothing but death.

Frank, Kane, and Strickland had been forced to fall back a little during the last determined charge by the remaining outlaws, but along with the other defenders who had fired from behind wagons and water troughs, they had mowed down the last of the raiders. As wounded horses kicked in the street and dying outlaws moaned, Frank hurried over to Kane and the jailer and asked, "Are you two all right?"

Kane's shirt was bloody, so that Frank thought his

wounds had opened up again. Kane just grinned, though, and said, "Don't worry, Morgan, it's a fresh crease. I'm okay."

"And I'm not hit at all," Strickland said. "I can thank my lucky stars for that."

"You sure enough can," Frank agreed with a smile. He worked the lever of his Winchester and kicked out the last empty shell.

His head jerked around when a woman screamed. A block away was the Palace Saloon, and Frank thought the cry had come from there. He broke into a run toward the place, tossing aside the empty rifle. Kane and Strickland followed him.

As Frank burst into the Palace, he saw the bartender, Rusty, cradling the limp form of Annie. The whore called Midge followed them, her hands pressed to her mouth in horror. As Rusty placed Annie on one of the tables, he shouted to Frank, "Out the back! It's Skeet Harlan! He killed the boss and shot Annie!"

Frank ran into the office and saw the rear door standing open. He glanced at McKelvey, who was sprawled facedown in a pool of blood, but didn't slow down. Frank could tell that McKelvey was dead, and he couldn't think of anybody who deserved it more.

Unless it was Skeet Harlan. Frank lunged out the door and saw Harlan limping away, a gun in one hand and a heavy canvas bag in the other. "Harlan!" Frank shouted.

The deputy stopped in his tracks and then turned slowly to face Frank. The canvas bag slipped from his fingers and thudded at his feet. "Morgan," he croaked.

Frank saw the blood soaking Harlan's shirt and knew the man was hit. "Drop the gun, Harlan," he said. "It's all over."

Harlan shook his head slowly and grinned a hideous grin. "How about we test our speed like you suggested,

Morgan? I'll leather my iron, you leather yours, and we'll settle it man to man."

"It wouldn't be a fair fight," Frank said. "You're hit. It wouldn't settle anything. Maybe another day."

"Yeah," Harlan said hollowly. "Another day . . ."

He jerked his gun up.

Frank fired, his slug driving deep into Harlan's chest. The deputy went over backward, his Colt booming as his finger involuntarily jerked the trigger. The bullet screamed off harmlessly into the sky. Harlan landed flat on his back, arms and legs flung out to the side. Frank walked up to him, keeping the Peacemaker trained on him just in case.

A grotesque sound came from Harlan's throat. It took Frank a second to realize that the deputy was laughing. "Still say . . . I'm faster . . . I'll see you . . . in Hell, Morgan . . ."

His eyes glazed over and his head fell to the side as life departed from him.

Frank holstered his gun and picked up the canvas bag. He assumed it was full of money but didn't take the time to check. He hurried back into the Palace instead.

When he got there, he found Chris Kane hovering anxiously beside the table where Annie lay. Doc Yantis had arrived while Frank was dealing with Harlan and was examining the young woman's wound. He glanced up at Kane and said, "Don't work yourself up into a state, young fella. It's not as bad as it looks. The bullet went through clean, and I think it missed her vitals. Soon as I get the bleeding stopped, we'll take her over to my office and get her patched up."

"Thanks, Doc," Kane said, his voice thick with emotion.

Strickland said with reluctance in his voice, "I

reckon I'd better get the prisoner back down to the jail. It looks like all the fightin's over."

"I think Kane can be released into your custody for a while longer," Frank told him. "At least until Annie here is out of the woods."

"You don't have to worry about me," Kane vowed. "I'm not going anywhere."

Frank clapped him on the shoulder. "Good work out there. With Harlan dead and everybody knowing what a crook he was, I'd say there's a good chance all the charges against you might just wind up being dismissed, Kane."

The young cowboy nodded and said, "Thanks to you, Mr. Morgan."

Frank waved that off and started toward the door. "I'm heading down to the jail for a minute. I'll tell the sheriff where he can find you if he wants you. I expect he'll still be pretty busy for a while, though."

Wilmott was busy, all right, supervising as his deputies locked up the ranchers who had ridden into town to bust the jail wide open. "You got what you wanted, Morgan," the sheriff snapped when he saw Frank. "None of those hotheads are dead. Some of 'em are shot up a mite, but I reckon they'll live to stand trial."

"It might go a long way toward establishing peace in the county if you saw to it that they don't go to prison, Sheriff," Frank suggested.

"Not go to prison!" Wilmott yelped. "They put bullet holes in my jail!"

"The judge might see his way clear to fining them for disturbing the peace and unlawfully discharging their guns. They never would have done such a thing if they hadn't been pushed into it by McKelvey and Harlan and Coburn."

"Oh, yeah, those bastards. What happened to them?"

"McKelvey and Harlan are both dead." Frank told the sheriff where he could find the bodies. "I don't know about Coburn. I didn't even see him during the fighting."

"I did," Wilmott declared. "He was around right at first, but he took off mighty fast when he saw that things weren't goin' his way. Headed southeast, the last I saw."

"Toward Zephyr," Frank said grimly. This raid had been only one part of a two-pronged attack. He had to find Stormy and light a shuck for the cattle pens at the railhead.

He hoped Beaumont had gotten there in time to warn Duggan and the others.

The riders swept out of the hills southwest of Zephyr, firing and yelling as they came. Some of the cowboys from the big ranch crews leaped into their saddles and raced out to meet the raiders head-on, while others rode around the pens so they would be ready in case any of the cattle broke through the fences and stampeded.

Beaumont found himself riding with Duggan, MacDonald, Carey, and the rest of the Slash D punchers as they started returning the raiders' fire. Callie Stratton came with them, ignoring Beaumont's shouted command for her to stay back. He knew she wanted to find her brother and let him know that he had been duped by McKelvey, Harlan, and Coburn, in hopes that Rawlings would call off the attack.

It was too late for that, Beaumont thought. Nothing was going to stop this fight.

The area near the cattle pens was a madhouse of

riders swirling around each other, smoke and dust clogging the air, spurts of muzzle flame, the whine of bullets, the cries of wounded men. Beaumont knew all the men from Rawlings's bunch, and whenever he saw one of them, he fired to wound and disarm rather than to kill. They didn't have such compunctions where he was concerned, though, and by the time a few minutes of battle had passed, he had several nicks and bullet burns.

Suddenly, Al Rawlings loomed up out of the dust and smoke, drawing a bead on Beaumont from only a few feet away. Before he could fire, Callie appeared beside him and rammed her horse into his. With a shrill whinny, both animals went down, throwing Rawlings and Callie.

Beaumont left the saddle in a dive that landed him on top of Rawlings. He backhanded the gun out of Rawlings's hand and then smashed a punch into his face. While Rawlings was stunned, Beaumont grabbed his shoulders and shook him.

"Rawlings! Listen to me!" Beaumont practically shouted in his face, trying to get through to him. "Rawlings, you were set up! Coburn's an outlaw! He and his gang are going to double-cross you!"

Rawlings blinked fuzzily as he tried to comprehend what the young Ranger was saying.

"It's a trap!" Beaumont went on. "A trap for all of us, for both sides!"

Callie pulled herself over to them, and Beaumont saw that she had been hurt when she was thrown from her horse. He didn't have time to check on how badly she might be injured. She leaned over her brother and said urgently, "It's true, Al! You've been tricked! We've all been tricked!"

"Coburn . . ." Rawlings muttered. "He went to Brownwood with the others. . . ."

"To rob the banks there, not to get Chris Kane out of jail." Beaumont thought he was getting through to Rawlings at last. "Duggan and the Slash D aren't your enemies. Coburn and his bunch are!"

"Lemme up! Lemme up, damn it!" Rawlings surged to his feet along with Beaumont. "Hold your fire!" Rawlings bellowed. "Hold your fire!"

Earl Duggan rode up at that moment and swung down swiftly from his saddle. As he landed on his feet, he raised his gun and lined it on Rawlings. Beaumont stepped between them.

"Stop it, Duggan!" Beaumont said. "It's over. Rawlings knows now he was tricked into fighting you."

"The hell you say!" Duggan exploded. "Coburn and the others couldn't have used him and his bunch if they hadn't already hated us!"

"You fenced us in!" Rawlings shouted over Beaumont's shoulder. "You tried to squeeze us off range that was legally ours!"

Callie pulled herself painfully to her feet. "Will both of you bullheaded bastards just *stop* it! You can hash it all out later. For now, you've got outlaws to deal with!"

With that, she gasped and crumpled as one of her legs went out from under her. Rawlings sprang to her side and kept her from falling all the way. "Callie!"

"I'm all right," she told him. "I just twisted my leg when I got knocked off my horse trying to keep you from killing a Ranger, you big idiot! Now you and Duggan go deal with those owlhoots!"

Beaumont looked back and forth between the leaders of the two factions. "What do you say?"

Duggan lowered his gun at last. "All right," he growled. "Let's go get 'em, Rawlings."

"I'm with you," Rawlings said as he picked up the gun he had dropped.

They plunged back into the fighting, which had swirled past them. The initial charge of the outlaws had carried them all the way to the cattle pens. Men blazed away at each other over the backs of the wildly milling beasts. Some fought from horseback while others were on foot.

Rawlings raced here and there, shouting for his men to stop fighting with the big ranch crews and turn their guns on Coburn's hired killers. The tide of battle shifted as more and more of the men understood what was really going on. But the outcome was still very much up in the air.

Beaumont had helped Callie to one of the chuck wagons. She slumped to the ground next to a wagon wheel and said, "Give me a gun, Tye. I seem to have lost mine."

"I don't have an extra," Beaumont told her as he flashed a grin at her. "Looks like you're out of the fight, Callie."

She reached up and unhooked a skillet that was hanging on the side of the wagon. "Run some of 'em this way," she said as she shook the skillet. "I'll make their heads hurt!"

Beaumont laughed as he thumbed fresh cartridges into his Colt. Blood was dripping in his eyes from a cut on his forehead. He wiped it away with the back of his hand and plunged back into the melee.

He had gone only a few feet when a rider loomed out of the smoke and dust beside him. Beaumont twisted toward the man only to recognize Flint Coburn's lean, hate-filled face. The gun in Coburn's hand exploded, sending a bullet smashing through Beaumont's thigh. Beaumont cried out in pain as the impact of the slug twisted him around. As he fell, Coburn's horse reared above him, and the killer tried to bring his gun down for another shot that would finish Beaumont off.

Frank had hoped to catch up to Coburn before the gunman could reach Zephyr. If any horse in the world could do that, Stormy could. But even the magnificent Appaloosa had his limits, and Coburn had too big a lead. Frank didn't catch sight of Coburn until after he heard the gunshots and saw the clouds of dust and powder smoke hanging over the cattle pens where the battle was taking place.

Surging ahead, Frank spotted Coburn, saw the killer nearly ride down a man on foot. Coburn fired, knocking down the man, and as Frank drew nearer, he felt horror and fury go through him as he recognized Tyler Beaumont. The young Ranger was wounded in the leg and couldn't move. Coburn brought his gun down to fire again.

Frank snapped a shot off first. The bullet burned across the rump of Coburn's horse and sent it leaping wildly in the air. Coburn started to slip out of the saddle and grabbed for the horn. He missed, so all he could do was kick his feet free of the stirrups so he wouldn't be dragged.

Frank swung down from Stormy's back while the Appaloosa was still moving. He covered Coburn as he ran over to Beaumont. "Tyler!" he called.

Beaumont pushed himself into a sitting position. If he was surprised to see Frank turn up just in the nick of time, he didn't show it. "I'm all right!" he called. "Get Coburn!"

That was just what Frank intended to do, but as he swung toward the man again, a cloud of dust rolled between them, making him lose sight of the killer. When the dust cleared, Coburn was gone.

A second later, Frank spotted him ducking around the corner of one of the cattle pens. The shooting was dying away now as the crews from the big ranches and the men from the smaller spreads fought side by side for a change against the outlaws. The air was still full of a terrible racket, though, from the bawling of the cattle and the clashing of their horns. Frank ran after Coburn, stopping at the corner of the pen and glancing around it.

A shot rang out and a bullet chipped splinters from the pole next to Frank's head. A couple of the splinters stung his cheek as he pulled back for a second. Then he triggered a quick shot around the corner and followed it with a sprint that took him toward Coburn's position. A slug sang past Frank's ear. He went down in a rolling dive and came up triggering. The bullets drove Coburn back against the rails of the pen behind him. He hung there for a second, grimacing in pain as blood welled from the holes in his chest.

Then the terror-stricken steers behind him surged against the fence again, and it gave way at last, collapsing under the weight of tons of beef. Coburn was already dying and he knew it, but he screamed anyway as he went down beneath that awful weight. The stampede rushed over him, thousands of hooves chopping and pounding him into the dirt until he didn't even resemble anything human.

Frank leaped over to another pen and pulled himself up on the fence, perching on the top rail and holding on for dear life as it shook underneath him. The stampeding cattle rolled on past him. Already whooping cowboys were dashing up on horseback, trying to contain them.

When the last of the runaway cattle had gone past him, Frank dropped to the ground again and hurried to find Beaumont. Pitch Carey rode up and said, "The Ranger's over there, if you're lookin' for him, Morgan."

"Much obliged," Frank nodded. He hurried over to the Slash D chuck wagon where Carey was pointing.

Beaumont was sitting on the tailgate with Callie Stratton. Rawlings was there, too, along with Duggan and the rest of the Slash D riders. Wing was winding a bandage around Beaumont's wounded leg.

"Frank!" the young Ranger exclaimed. "Did you get Coburn?"

"He's dead," Frank replied with a nod. "That stampede finished him off."

"Serves him right," Duggan growled. "Don't know what he hoped to accomplish."

"What he planned to do was play both sides against each other and then wipe out anybody who was left," Frank explained. "The same thing was going on in Brownwood. The ultimate goal was for Ace McKelvey to take over Brown County, I reckon."

"McKelvey!"

Frank nodded. "I'm thinking he was the mastermind behind the whole thing. But Coburn was in on it with him, and so was Skeet Harlan."

Ed MacDonald said, "I can believe it of Harlan. He was always a vicious little polecat."

Duggan said to Rawlings, "And you were a damned fool to let them use you that way."

"Me a damned fool?" Rawlings shot back. "What about you? You caused as much trouble as I did. Hell, you blew up Vern Gladwell, as fine a man as I ever knew!"

Duggan frowned. "I'm sorry about that."

"It'll take more than sorry. There'll always be bad blood between you and me, Duggan. There'll always be trouble between you range hogs and the fellas who just want to make an honest living and have their own spreads."

"No, there won't," Beaumont said flatly. "It's over. You fellas will work this out, or the Rangers will work it out for you."

"Well . . ." Duggan rubbed his grizzled jaw. "I don't reckon it'd hurt anything to put up some gates in those fences and let you drive across our range when you need to. As long as you keep your cows on your range the rest of the time."

"I wouldn't want my cows eatin' your grass," Rawlings snapped. "It'd probably gaunt 'em right up."

Duggan snorted. "I've got better grass than you'll ever have on that greasy-sack outfit of yours."

"Oh, shut up," Callie said. "Both of you. I'm tired of the fighting. There's been a lot of wrong and a lot of hurt on both sides, but like Tye says, it's over. You've got to learn to get along now, or else."

"Or else what?" her brother challenged stubbornly.

Callie lifted a hand and waved it at the carnage around them. "Or else you'll have a lot of killing to do all over again. And I don't think anybody wants that."

For a moment no one said anything, but then Rawlings nodded. "No, I don't want that. There's been enough killing." He looked at Duggan and declared, "We'll work it out. But I won't shake your hand."

"Don't want you to," Duggan growled. But he returned Rawlings's nod.

Frank and Beaumont looked at each other, and weary smiles creased their gun-smoke-grimed faces.

On this violent Sunday, the fence-cutting war had finally come to a close.

38

Frank Morgan and Callie Stratton walked along the street in Brownwood, moving slowly because Callie's injured leg was still sore and she had to use a cane. A week had passed since the battles at Brownwood and Zephyr, and things were pretty much back to normal. A lot had happened in that week: The charges against Chris Kane had been dismissed, Rawlings and his friends had been levied fines and suspended jail sentences for their part in the trouble, and a new town marshal had been appointed to replace Sean Keever, who had been found dead in his office along with one of the townsmen. Nobody was quite sure what had happened, but Frank was convinced that Skeet Harlan had murdered the two men. There had been a couple of loud, angry meetings in the town hall between the big ranchers and the owners of the smaller outfits, but no gunplay had been involved. They were making real progress, Frank thought.

He and Callie had attended services at the First Baptist Church this morning, and now they were on their way to the livery stable, where Frank would pick up Stormy and Dog. "Have you heard anything from Ranger Beaumont?" Callie asked as they walked along the street.

"He's doing fine," Frank replied. "He's back in Weatherford with his wife. I reckon he'll be a mite gimpy for a while, but he's got a good woman to take care of him." *A mighty good woman,* he added to himself. "He'll be Rangering again before you know it."

They passed the Palace Saloon. Rusty had taken it over. Nobody knew where McKelvey had come from or whether he had any heirs, so Rusty would run the place for the time being, and maybe permanently.

Annie wouldn't be working there any longer, though. Chris Kane had taken her out to his ranch where she could recuperate from her wound with him looking after her. Frank had a feeling that was where she would stay from now on.

"What about you, Frank?" Callie asked. "What will you do now?"

"I'm not sure. Some folks call me the Drifter, you know, and there's a reason for that. I guess I'm just too fiddle-footed to stay in one place for too long."

"You could stay here," Callie said softly. "You've made friends here, and . . . you'd be welcome."

He paused and looked at her, reading the meaning of her words in her green eyes. And while the prospect was tempting, he knew he couldn't do it.

She knew it, too. With a wistful sigh and a smile, she said, "Ah, well, it was worth a try."

They walked on to the livery, where Stormy was saddled and waiting. Dog sat patiently beside the big Appaloosa. Callie petted the shaggy cur for a moment and then turned to Frank.

"Take care of yourself."

"I will," he promised. He took the hand that she held out to him, leaned forward, and brushed a kiss across her cheek.

Then, with a smile, he turned to the horse, put his foot in the stirrup, stepped up, and swung his leg over Stormy's back. As he settled down in the saddle and lifted the reins, he said, "I'll be back one of these days."

"Don't expect me to wait for you," Callie told him crisply. "A no-account gunfighter like you . . . you may never get back."

"Well," Frank admitted, "maybe not."

With that, he turned the Appaloosa and heeled the big horse into a trot. Dog fell in behind him. Hipping around in the saddle, Frank lifted a hand in farewell.

Callie leaned on her cane with one hand and returned the wave with the other. "Don't expect me to wait for you, gunfighter," she whispered.

But she knew in her heart that she would do it anyway.

AFTERWORD:

NOTES FROM THE OLD WEST

In the small town where I grew up, there were two movie theaters. The Pavilion was one of those old-timey movie palaces, built in the heyday of the Mary Pickford and Charlie Chaplin silent era of the 1920s. By the 1950s, when I was a kid, the Pavilion was a little worn around the edges, but it was still the premiere theater in town. They played all those big Technicolor biblical Cecil B. DeMille epics and corny MGM musicals. In CincmaScopc, of coursc.

On the other side of town was the Gem, a somewhat shabby and rundown grind house with sticky floors and torn seats. Admission was a quarter. The Gem booked low-budget B pictures (remember the Bowery Boys?), war movies, horror flicks, and westerns. I liked the westerns best. I could usually be found every Saturday at the Gem, along with my best friend, Newton Trout, watching Westerns from 10 A.M. until my father came looking for me around suppertime. (Sometimes Newton's dad was dispatched to come fetch us.) One time, my dad came to get me right in the middle of *Abilene Trail*, which featured the now-forgotten Whip Wilson. My father became so engrossed in the action, he sat down and watched the rest of it with us. We didn't get home until after dark, and my mother's meatloaf was a pan of gray ashes by the time we did. Though my father and I were both in the doghouse the next day, this remains one of my fondest childhood memories.

There was Wild Bill Elliot, Gene Autry, and Roy Rogers, and Tim Holt, and a little later, Rod Cameron and Audie Murphy. Of these newcomers, I never missed an Audie Murphy Western, because Audie was sort of an anti-hero. Sure, he stood for law and order and was an honest man, but sometimes he had to go around the law to uphold it. If he didn't play fair, it was only because he felt hamstrung by the laws of the land. Whatever it took to get the bad guys, Audie did it. There were no finer points of law, no splitting of legal hairs. It was instant justice, devoid of long-winded lawyers, bored or biased jurors, or black-robed, often corrupt judges.

Steal a man's horse and you were the guest of honor at a necktie party.

Molest a good woman was a bullet in the heart or a rope around the gullet. Or at the very least, getting the crap beat out of you. Rob a bank and face a hail of bullets or the hangman's noose.

Saved a lot of time and money, did frontier justice.

That's all gone now, I'm sad to say. Now you hear, "Oh, but he had a bad childhood" or "His mother didn't give him enough love" or "The homecoming queen wouldn't give him a second look, and he has an inferiority complex." Or cultural rage, as the politically correct bright boys refer to it. How many times have you heard some self-important defense attorney moan, "The poor kids were only venting their hostilities toward an uncaring society"?

Mule fritters, I say. Nowadays, you can't even call a punk a punk anymore. But don't get me started.

It was "howdy, ma'am" time, too. The good guys,

antihero or not, were always respectful to the ladies. They might shoot a bad guy five seconds after tipping their hat to a woman, but the code of the West demanded you be respectful to a lady.

Lots of things have changed since the heyday of the Wild West, haven't they? Some for the good, some for the bad.

I didn't have any idea at the time that I would someday write about the Old West. I just knew that I was captivated by the Old West.

When I first got the itch to write, back in the early 1970s, I didn't write westerns. I started by writing horror and action adventure novels. After more than two dozen novels, I began thinking about developing a western character. From those initial musings came the novel *The Last Mountain Man: Smoke Fensen.* That was followed by *Preacher: The First Mountain Man.* A few years later, I began developing the Last Gunfighter series. Frank Morgan is a legend in his own time, the fastest gun west of the Mississippi . . . a title and a reputation he never wanted but can't get rid of.

The Gunfighter series is set in the waning days of the Wild West. Frank Morgan is out of time and place, but still, he is pursued by men who want to earn a reputation as the man who killed the legendary gunfighter. All Frank wants to do is live in peace. But he knows in his heart that dream will always be just that: a dream, fog and smoke and mirrors, something elusive that will never really come to fruition. He will be forced to wander the West, alone, until one day his luck runs out.

For me, and for thousands—probably millions—of other people (although many will never publicly admit it), the old Wild West will always be a magic, mysterious place: a place we love to visit through the pages of books; characters we would like to know . . . from a safe distance; events we would love to take part in, again, from a safe distance. For the old West was not a place for the faint of heart. It was a hard, tough, physically demanding time. There were no police to call if one faced adversity. One faced trouble alone, and handled it alone. It was rugged individualism: something that appeals to many of us.

I am certain that is something that appeals to most readers of westerns.

I still do on-site research (whenever possible) before starting a western novel. I have wandered over much of the West, prowling what is left of ghost towns. Stand in the midst of ruins of these old towns, use a little bit of imagination, and one can conjure up life as it used to be in the Wild West. The rowdy Saturday nights, the tinkling of a piano in a saloon, the laughter of cowboys and miners letting off steam after a week of hard work. Use a little more imagination and one can envision two men standing in the street, facing one another, seconds before the hook and draw of a gunfight. A moment later, one is dead and the other rides away.

The old, wild, untamed West.

There are still some ghost towns to visit, but they are rapidly vanishing as time and the elements take their toll. If you want to see them, make plans to do so as soon as possible, for in a few years, they will all be gone.

And so will we.

Stand in what is left of the Big Thicket country of east Texas and try to imagine how in the world the pioneers managed to get through that wild tangle. I have wondered that many times and marveled at the courage of the men and women who slowly pushed westward, facing dangers that we can only imagine.

Let me touch briefly on a subject that is very close to me: firearms. There are some so-called historians who are now claiming that firearms played only a very insignificant part in the settlers' lives. They claim that only a few were armed. What utter, stupid nonsense! What do these so-called historians think the pioneers did for food? Do they think the early settlers rode down to the nearest supermarket and bought their meat? Or maybe they think the settlers chased down deer or buffalo on foot and beat the animals to death with a club. I have a news flash for you so-called historians: the settlers used guns to shoot their game.They used guns to defend hearth and home against Indians on the warpath. They used guns to protect themselves from outlaws. Guns are a part of Americana. And always will be.

The mountains of the West and the remains of the ghost towns that dot those areas are some of my favorite subjects to write about. I have done extensive research on the various mountain ranges of the West and go back whenever time permits. I sometimes stand surrounded by the towering mountains and wonder how in the world the pioneers ever made it through. As hard as I try and as often as I try, I simply cannot imagine the hardships those men and women endured over the hard months of their incredible journey. None of us can. It is said that on the Oregon Trail alone, there are a least two bodies in lonely unmarked graves for every mile of that journey. Some students of the West say the number of dead is at least twice that. And nobody knows the exact number of wagons that impatiently started out alone and simply vanished on the way, along with their occupants, never to be seen or heard from again.

Just vanished.

The one-hundred-and-fifty-year-old ruts of the wagon wheels can still be seen in various places along the Oregon Trail. But if you plan to visit those places, do so quickly, for they are slowly disappearing. And when they are gone, they will be lost forever, except in the words of western writers.

As long as I can peck away at a keyboard and find a company to publish my work, I will not let the old West die. That I promise you.

As the Drifter in the Last Gunfighter series, Frank Morgan has struck a responsive chord among the readers of frontier fiction. Perhaps it's because he is a human man, with all of the human frailties. He is not a superhero. He likes horses and dogs and treats them well. He has feelings and isn't afraid to show them or admit that he has them. He longs for a permanent home, a place to hang his hat and sit on the porch in the late afternoon and watch the day slowly fade into night . . . and a woman to share those simple pleasures with him. But Frank also knows he can never relax his vigil and probably will never have that long-wished-for hearth and home. That is why he is called the Drifter. Frank Morgan knows there are men who will risk their lives to face him in a hook and draw, slap leather, pull that big iron, in the hopes of killing the West's most famous gunfighter, so they can claim the title of the man who killed Frank Morgan, the Drifter. Frank would gladly, willingly, give them that title, but not at the expense of his own life.

So Frank Morgan must constantly drift, staying on the lonely trails, those out-of-the-way paths through the timber, the mountains, the deserts that are sometimes called the hoot-owl trail. His companions are the sighing winds, the howling of wolves, the yapping of coyotes, and a few very precious memories. And his six-gun. Always, his six-gun.

Frank is also pursued by something else: progress. The towns are connected by telegraph wires. Frank is recognized wherever he goes and can be tracked by telegraphers. There is no escape for him. Reporters for various newspapers are always on his trail, wanting to interview Frank Morgan, as are authors wanting to do more books about the legendary gunfighter. Photographers want to take his picture, if possible with the body of a man Frank has just killed. Frank is disgusted by the whole thing and wants no part of it. There is no real rest for the Drifter. Frank travels on, always on the move. He tries to stay off the more heavily traveled roads, sticking to lesser known trails, sometimes making his own route of travel across the mountains or deserts.

Someday perhaps Frank will find some peace. Maybe. But if he does, that is many books from now.

The West will live on as long as there are writers willing to write about it, and publishers willing to publish it. Writing about the West is wide open, just like the old Wild West. Characters abound, as plentiful as the wide-open spaces, as colorful as a sunset on the Painted Desert, as restless as the ever-sighing winds. All one has to do is use a bit of imagination. Take a stroll through the cemetery at Tombstone, Arizona; read the inscriptions. Then walk the main street of that once infamous town around midnight and you might catch a glimpse of the ghosts that still wander the town. They really do. Just ask anyone who lives there. But don't be afraid of the apparitions; they won't hurt you. They're just out for a quiet stroll.

The West lives on. And as long as I am alive, it always will.

BOOK YOUR PLACE ON OUR WEBSITE AND MAKE THE READING CONNECTION!

We've created a customized website just for our very special readers, where you can get the inside scoop on everything that's going on with Zebra, Pinnacle and Kensington books.

When you come online, you'll have the exciting opportunity to:

- View covers of upcoming books
- Read sample chapters
- Learn about our future publishing schedule (listed by publication month *and author*)
- Find out when your favorite authors will be visiting a city near you
- Search for and order backlist books from our online catalog
- Check out author bios and background information
- Send e-mail to your favorite authors
- Meet the Kensington staff online
- Join us in weekly chats with authors, readers and other guests
- Get writing guidelines
- AND MUCH MORE!

**Visit our website at
http://www.kensingtonbooks.com**